"You are mine," he ground out. "You know you are."

She stared up at him in silence, barely daring to breathe.

He was panting, his onyx eyes flashing like heat lightning. She did not know what he intended, she only knew he was far stronger than she. His hard chest against her, she could feel his rushing pulse.

"You know you are mine," he whispered again. "Say it."

Was he asking for permission to deflower her? she thought in alarm. She meant to ease him back to reason with a tactful reminder that she was soon to marry another man—a man who would probably kill her if she came to her wedding night not a virgin—but when she opened her mouth, only one word slipped out. "Yes."

By Gaelen Foley
Published by Fawcett Gold Medal Books:

THE PIRATE PRINCE
PRINCESS

PRINCESS

Gaelen Foley

FAWCETT GOLD MEDAL • NEW YORK

A Fawcett Gold Medal Book
Published by The Ballantine Publishing Group
Copyright © 1999 by Gaelen Foley

Excerpt from *Prince Charming* by Gaelen Foley copyright © 2000 by Gaelen Foley

www.randomhouse.com/BB/

Library of Congress Catalog Card Number: 99-90447

ISBN 0-449-00246-2

Manufactured in the United States of America

First Edition: July 1999

10 9 8 7 6 5 4 3 2 1

This book is dedicated to my lifelong and most loyal friends,
my sisters,
Shana, Elizabeth, and Janeen.

Special thanks to my mom, whose insight, based on her years of work with victims of family violence, contributed greatly to my understanding of the scars such tragedy leaves, and the hope for healing that its brave survivors inspire in us all.

She is a pearl
whose price hath launched above
a thousand ships,
And turned crowned kings
to merchants.
                        —SHAKESPEARE

He after honor hunts; I after love.
                        —SHAKESPEARE

CHAPTER
⊰ ONE ⊱

May 1805

The sound of her rapid, shallow panting filled the narrow space between the box-hedge walls of the garden maze. The hedges towered over her, closing in on her, and the pounding of her pulse was so loud in her head she knew they would hear. She inched down the narrow lane, her bare toes creeping silently over the cool, lush grass, her chest heaving. Constantly she looked over her shoulder. Her whole body was shaking, her hand bleeding, maybe broken from punching Philippe in his smug, sneering face with the sharp edge of her huge diamond ring. But at least she had managed to throw herself out of his iron grasp and had torn into the maze, where she thought she could evade them. She dared not call out for help because only the three men would hear.

No one else was outside on such a night, when the breeze spattered rain from a sky deepest indigo smeared with gold clouds. The cicadas roared in waves, while the wind, as it rose and fell, brought fragments of a tinkling minuet spilling out over the vast gardens and the royal park from the ball in progress—her engagement party. Her fiancé had been unable to attend.

She jerked her face wildly to the left, hearing movement on the other side of the dense hedge.

He was right there. The acid taste of the wine she'd drunk rose in the back of her throat.

1

She could see the shape of him, tall, bedecked in his finery. She could see the shape of the pistol in his hand and knew her pale silk gown was sure to be visible through the branches. She crouched down and moved silently away.

"Don't be afraid, Your Highness," came Henri's mellifluous voice from several rows away. "We're not going to hurt you. Come out now. There's nothing you can do."

They had split up so they could surround her. She choked back a sob, clawing to keep hold of her fragile control as she tried to decide which way to go. She had run around in this maze since she was a little girl, but she was so frightened she had lost all sense of direction.

She heard the lulling splash of the fountain in the tiny center courtyard of the maze and used the sound to try to orient herself. Clenching her fist so tightly her nails dug into her palm, she huddled against the bush, edging inch by inch down the lane. At the end, she pressed her back flat against the scratchy bushes, too scared to turn the corner. She waited, shaking, praying, trying to gather her nerve, her stomach in knots.

She didn't know what they wanted.

She had been propositioned many times by the gilded, predatory courtiers of the palace, but no one had ever attempted to haul her away before. No one had ever used guns.

God, please.

She would have cried, but she was too terrified. The breeze rose again. She smelled cut grass, jasmine, man.

They're coming.

"Your Highness, you have nothing to fear. We are your friends."

She bolted, her long, black hair streaming out behind her. Thunder rumbled, the scent of a summer storm on the wind. At the end of the lane, she stopped, again too petrified to turn the corner, lest she find Philippe or the blond one, Henri, standing there waiting to catch her. She kept thinking how her ex-governess always said something like this would happen to her if she didn't mend her wild ways, stop acting so bold.

She vowed she would never be bold again. Never flirt. Never trust.

Her chest lifted and fell, lifted and fell.

They were coming. She knew she could not remain where she was for more than a few seconds longer.

I am trapped. There is no way out of this.

And then there came another voice, barely audible, a ghostly whisper.

"Princesa."

The single word seemed to rise from the earth, or to slip out of the very air.

She nearly sobbed aloud to hear it, wanting with all her heart to believe it was not her panicked brain playing tricks on her. Only one person called her by that name, the Spanish version of her proper Italian title, Principessa.

If ever she'd had need of him, it was now.

Beautiful, blackhearted Santiago.

He alone could have saved her from this nightmarish game, but he was far away on the king's business, intelligence-gathering and protecting the ambassador in Moscow, where the new alliance against Napoleon was being formed.

Darius Santiago was an insolent, arrogant heathen, of course, but he did not know the meaning of fear and she quite believed he could do anything. She had not seen him in nearly a year, but he was always lingering near the outskirts of her heart, with his arrogant smirk and his coal-black eyes, as though watching her from across the miles by some occult vision.

"I grow weary of this chase, *ma belle,*" Henri warned. She saw movement through the rows, made out tousled blond curls. She saw the Frenchman stop and cock his head, listening.

Wide-eyed, both hands pressed to her mouth to silence her ragged panting, Serafina began backing away. At a tug on her hair, she almost screamed, whirling to find that one of her long black curls had merely snagged on the grasping bushes.

"Princesa."

She knew she heard it that time! But how could it be? She froze, her gaze darting wildly.

Could he know somehow that she was in danger? Could the bond between them still be so strong?

And then she realized she felt him there, felt his strange, silent power all around her in the night like the imminent storm.

"Make your way to the center courtyard," the dark, airy murmur instructed her.

"Oh, my God," she whispered, closing her eyes, almost sick with relief. He had come.

Of course he had come.

Even though he did not want her, even though he would never love her, she was of the royal blood and he was honor-bound to protect her.

Darius Santiago was the king's most trusted man, a master spy and assassin. His loyalty to her father was absolute. If ever there was dark work to be done protecting the kingdom and the royal family of the small Italian island kingdom Ascencion, Darius was there to shoulder it without complaint. His presence here now made her realize there was even more to Philippe's attempt to abduct her than she had guessed.

She lowered both hands from her mouth to her sides. Her chest still heaved with each breath, but she lifted her chin, awaiting Darius's instructions.

"Go to the courtyard, Your Highness. Hurry."

"Where are you?" she breathed, trembling. "Help me."

"I am near, but I cannot get to you."

"Please help me," she choked, stifling a sob.

"Shh," he whispered. "Go to the inner courtyard."

"I'm lost, Darius, I forget." Blinded now by the tears she had been staving off since Philippe had first seized her, she stared through the dense green lace of the hedge trying to see him.

"Stay calm, be brave," he softly instructed. "Two right turns. You're very close. I'll meet you there."

"A-all right," she choked out.

"Go now." His whisper faded away.

For a moment, Serafina could not seem to move. Then she pierced the cold fog of fear, forcing herself. She set out for the tiny, brick-laid courtyard, legs shaking beneath her, her scraped knee still burning from before, when she had slipped on the grass. The mist-hued gown of gossamer silk she had been so delighted to wear now had a tear at the knee. Each movement was torturous with her effort to be silent, slowed by her tremors of fear, but she painstakingly followed the lullaby of the fountain splashing in its carved stone basin.

With every inch gained, her mind chanted his name as if she could conjure him, *Darius, Darius, Darius.* She came to the first corner.

Steeled herself. Peeked around.

Safe.

She moved on, gathering confidence. Images flashed through her mind of Darius watching over her all through her childhood, calming her with a look, her stern, beloved knight who would always protect her. But when she had finally grown up, nothing had gone according to plan.

Darius, don't let them get me.

Ahead she saw she'd have to slip past a break in the left wall of the lane where it intersected another path. She prayed her pursuers weren't down there to see her pass. At the break in the hedge, she hesitated, her courage faltering.

A bead of perspiration ran down her cheek.

Let them put that in the newspapers, she thought madly, brushing it away with the back of her hand. *Shocking news— the Princess Royal sweats!*

She shut her eyes briefly and said a prayer, then darted past, stealing a fleeting glance down the lane as she went. Some twenty feet away, Philippe's thuggish driver lay sprawled on his face, unmoving. A length of wire glinted in the moonlight. He had been garroted, she realized, sickened. Darius had passed this way.

She marched on with stiff, jerky strides while cold horror spiraled down to her belly. The cicadas' song stretched to one flat, vibrating note she thought would snap her nerves. When she reached the end of the lane, she grimaced, fighting a silent, mighty battle for the courage to look around the corner. She forced herself.

Clear!

The entrance to the courtyard was in sight at the far end of the corridor. She was almost there. All she had to do was pass yet another gap in the bushes halfway down the lane.

She turned the corner and ran for it.

Her breath raked over her teeth, her bare feet bore her swiftly over the silken grass. The break was coming, while straight ahead lay the entrance to the courtyard. The sky flung a handful of rain on the breeze into her face. Clouds covered the gold half-moon.

"Get back here, you little bitch!" a deep voice roared.

She shrieked and looked over her shoulder as Philippe tore around the corner behind her.

As she passed the gap, running full force, Henri exploded out of the intersecting path. He caught her in both arms and she screamed. Philippe was bearing down fast, and then Darius was there, death gliding out of the shadows, attacking with the leap of the wolf.

Henri shouted, lost his hold on her trying to ward off Darius. She tore free, tackled her way clear of him, heard ripping silk as she pulled, wrenching forward. She sprinted toward the courtyard, sobbing now. She stubbed her toe on the bricks, stumbling into the small enclosure. She passed the leering, stone grotesque of the Pan fountain, with its mossy mouth trickling water, and flung herself into the shadowed corner.

She crouched down, praying Philippe would choose to stay and help his friend fight Darius rather than coming straightaway after her, but the prayer was no sooner through her mind than the Frenchman loomed in the entrance between the neatly trimmed hedges.

Panting hard, he saw her at once, and his sneer turned his handsome face ugly. He strode to her and hauled her up from her crouched position. She cried out. He hurled her about face and put a knife to her throat just as Darius came running up to the entrance.

She sobbed his name.

Philippe wrenched her. "Shut up!"

Darius drew himself up short, breathing hard as he took in the scene before him. His fiery onyx eyes pierced the night with hellfire intensity. Heat lightning flashed across the sky with a brilliancy that illuminated his dark, exotic beauty for an instant—then darkness.

Serafina fixed her stare and all her faith on him as she clung with both hands to the steely arm around her throat.

"Stand aside, Santiago," Philippe warned. "You come any closer, she dies."

"Don't be an ass, Saint-Laurent. We both know he doesn't want her harmed." His tone was coolly scornful, his stance relaxed, but danger emanated from him as he sauntered into the courtyard, his body sleek and lean, gold moonlight glancing off his broad shoulders. Impeccably attired in black, he moved with predatory grace.

He had a high brow under a glossy, raven forelock. Inky, brooding eyes reflected all the tumult and fire of his passionate, secretive nature. The austere angles of his high-boned cheeks and haughty, aquiline nose warred with the sensuality of his rich, sulky mouth. A small scar like a crescent moon marred the sculpted sweetness of his lips with a bitter twist.

Serafina stared, mesmerized, but Darius did not even look at her, as if she were of no consequence. Instead, he spiked Philippe with a sharp glance, a half-smile on his lips.

"I thought you were a professional, Saint-Laurent," he said, his soft, lulling voice tinged with a Spanish accent. "Is this how you conduct business? Putting knives to young girls' throats?" He gestured toward them with idle elegance. "I often wonder how you people stomach it," he remarked. "Serving a man who is without honor."

"I didn't come here to philosophize with you, Santiago," Philippe ground out, as tense and heated as Darius was cool. "I'm going now, and she's coming with me."

"If you believe I shall let you pass," he said gently, "you are deceiving yourself."

"I'll cut her!" Philippe warned.

Darius gave him a chilling smile. "Your master wouldn't like that."

The silence sharpened to a razor's edge as the two men stared at each other, both trained to kill, each waiting for the other to strike, until Serafina couldn't bear it any longer.

"Please," she choked out, "let me go."

At her plea, Darius's coal-black eyes flicked to hers. For one disastrous instant, she read the truth there—the fury, the desperation behind his cool control. The fleeting look vanished at once and his scarred lips curved again in that mocking half-smile, but it was too late.

Philippe had seen it, too. "What's this?" he asked with a taunting laugh. "Have I stumbled upon a weakness? Is it possible the great Santiago has an Achilles' heel?"

Darius's finely chiseled face hardened as he cast the facade aside. His long-lashed eyes narrowed on Philippe, glittering in the dark.

"Ah, of course," Philippe went on, heedless of the danger, "I recall someone telling me you were her bodyguard when she was just a wee thing."

Darius's voice softened to a terrifying murmur. "Lower your weapon."

"Get out of my path."

"Release the princess. Surrender is your sole option. Your men are dead, and you know full well I want you alive."

"Hmm, he grows angry," Philippe mused aloud. "He must be rather attached to you, my dear."

The words pained her more than he could ever know.

"You are making things worse for yourself, Saint-Laurent. I'll remember how you annoyed me when you and I have a talk later about your associates and your orders."

"Ah, but my orders don't exist, Santiago. I don't exist. I cannot go back empty-handed, so you see, you'll get nothing from me," Philippe snarled.

Darius started toward them with slow, wary strides.

"Stay back!"

He paused. "Move away from the princess," he said very softly, his stare unwavering, relentless.

Serafina was saying a fragment of a prayer over and over again in her mind. Against her body, she could feel Philippe's heart pounding in his chest. He tightened his hold on her neck. She felt his increasing desperation as he cast about for some means of escape. She glanced at the knife poised so near her throat, then shut her eyes, praying more desperately.

"Tell me, Santiago . . . between colleagues," Philippe barked suddenly. "Now that your little charge is so, shall we say, grown up, haven't you ever wondered? I mean, look at her. Some say she is the most beautiful woman alive—in the top three, at least. Certainly my patron agrees. Helen of Troy, he says. Men fight wars to possess such beauty. Shall we have a look?"

Her eyes flew open wide as Philippe laid hold of her dress where Henri had already torn it. She gasped with shocked horror as he ripped it open down her back with one lightning-like movement.

"There, there, *ma belle,*" Philippe crooned, "don't fret."

She sobbed once, cringing where she stood. She lowered her head, powerless to stop him as he pushed the ripped ends of her dress down to her waist, baring her upper body.

This could not be happening, she thought. Not in her beautiful garden, the very heart of her safe, pretty, insulated world. Cheeks aflame, she bit her lower lip, fighting tears of rage. She tried to pull her waist-length hair forward to cover her breasts, but Philippe protested.

"*Non, non, chérie.* Let us see what beauty God hath wrought." With his left hand, he brushed her hair softly back again behind her shoulders.

"You bastard," Darius whispered.

She could not bear to meet his eyes.

Hands at her sides, she stood there shaking with humiliation and rage, exposed before the only man she had ever wanted. The only one who did not want her.

Not so very long ago, she had loved Darius Santiago with a painful, adolescent ardor. She had tried to show him three years ago, the night of her debut ball, that she had grown up for him at last, was no longer a child; she had tried to show him that none of his women could love him as she did. But he had fled her and left the island, hurrying off on some new mission. Now he was witness to her humiliation, forced to view her body, the gift she had tried to give him—now, when it meant nothing.

Just then the night sky flung down another swift cloudburst of cold rain. She flinched, then shuddered when the first drops struck her bare skin.

She could feel a volcanic force of pure rage building from where Darius stood, but somehow the only thing she could focus on was her pride, her last defense. She held fast to it as if it were a tangible weapon. She lifted her head high against the crushing shame. Tears in her eyes, she stared straight ahead at nothing.

Philippe laughed at her. "Haughty thing. Yes, you know you are stunning, don't you?" he murmured, running one finger from the curve of her shoulder down her arm. She fought not to shudder with revulsion. "Skin like silk. Come and touch her, Santiago. She is exquisite. I don't blame you—any man would have a weakness for such a creature. We can share her if you like."

At this, her stricken gaze flew to Darius, but then a cold shaft of horror spiked down her spine, for he was feasting his eyes on her bare breasts, his gaze devouring her nakedness.

"Darius?" she asked in a pleading whisper.

Philippe's fingers flicked in eager agitation over the knife's hilt, but his smooth, sure voice held a note of triumph. "Come and taste her. No one needs to know. Really, after all you've done for your king, isn't she the least you deserve?"

Finally, Darius looked up from his intimate perusal of her body. She caught the flash of white teeth in his cold, wicked smile. He began sauntering slowly toward them, and directed his question to Philippe. "What do you suggest?"

Her very mind choked. Images exploded in her memory of the last time she had seen Darius, six months ago. As usual he had ignored her from the moment he set foot in the palace, but that day, she had opened the door to the music room in the middle of the afternoon to find him ravishing one of his many lovers against the wall. His loose white shirt had been hanging from his shoulders, brown chest bared, his black breeches clinging upon his lean hips as the woman with her skirts hitched up fumbled to undress him. When Serafina had opened the door, he had looked over and held her shocked gaze for a second.

She still remembered the smoldering look in his eyes as she stood in the doorway, mouth agape, eyes wide. She remembered the mocking smile of seduction he had sent her before she slammed the door and fled. It was quite the same as the one on his scarred lips now.

"I'll hold her for you," Philippe said.

"Oh, she wouldn't fight me," he murmured. "Would you, angel?"

Her cheeks turned crimson. She lowered her head, heart pounding madly. Trembling violently, she could not bear to look at him as he stalked toward them.

She swore to herself this was part of a ruse. She was the Princess Royal! Darius would never—never.

But he was unlike any man she knew, this Spaniard with his terrible beauty. She could neither predict nor manage him as she did the others. She only knew that he feared nothing and that, for all his loyalty to her father, he obeyed no law but his own.

One slow, relentless stride after another, he came to stand perhaps three inches away from her, so close his chest nearly brushed her breasts. She could feel him breathing against her.

She was trapped between the two tall, ruthless men, her breath jagged, her exposed skin racing with shivers, hot and cold. He was going to touch her at any moment, she knew. Cheeks blazing, she wanted to die for shame of the perverse desire he wove into her fear. Usually she was quick-witted, but at the moment she was mute, staring brokenly at a silver button on his coat right at her eye level.

She could not think of a single thing to say to try to save herself, could not find her voice to invoke her father's name, nor her fiancé's—in this moment, she could not even picture Anatole's face. Terror wiped her mind blank, and Darius filled her senses—fierce, elemental.

His nearness, the sheer male force of him, overwhelmed her. Her nostrils were filled with the clean, musky scent of him, mingled with the smell of horses and leather, the exotic spice of the cheroots he was always smoking, and the coppery taint of blood. She could feel the heat radiating from his powerful body, feel the thrumming tension coiled in his hard, sinewy form.

Then it all happened at once. He seized Philippe by the throat and knocked her out of his grasp. Philippe's blade flashed, stabbing at him. He ducked back, grasping Philippe's right wrist while Serafina went stumbling, landing on her hands and knees near the edge of the courtyard. Pulling the remnants of her bodice up over her shoulders with shaking hands, she immediately scrambled about face to see if Darius was hurt. The fountain partly blocked her view. There was a clatter of metal.

Philippe cursed as his weapon went skittering across the bricks. He lunged after it. Darius kicked it away and laid hold of him. Flailing wildly, Philippe tore free and bolted.

Darius was upon him. He grabbed Philippe by the back of the collar and hurled him around, throwing him down onto the flagstone, blocking the exit.

She looked up in dread when she heard the whisper of metal, and saw Darius's ebony-handled dagger, the slim elegance of the blade kissed by moonlight.

Oh, God.

When Philippe threw up both hands to ward off the first blow, Darius's dagger slashed across both his open palms.

Serafina turned her face away, but she heard every dragging second of their fight, every gasp and choke and low curse as Darius savaged him.

The cicadas screamed. She longed to run. When Darius swore in some unknown language, she opened her eyes and saw him lift his dagger in both hands for the final cut, saw his beautiful face alight with savagery.

Don't.

She squeezed her eyes shut tight as the knife plunged straight down like a bird of prey. Philippe's scream was short, followed by a silence.

Then she heard only the breeze blowing through the junipers. She became aware of the sound of a man's fierce panting. She felt like she was going to throw up.

It dawned on her with sudden hysteria that she had to run. She had to escape from here, get away from him at once before he came to sate the lust she'd read in his stare. He was the deadliest man in the kingdom and he was out of control, reduced by rage to the law of his boyhood—the law of the streets.

Never taking her eyes off him, she shoved to her feet in one jerky motion as Darius raked a hand through his hair, pushing his forelock out of his eyes, a black, demonic shape against the lesser dark of night. A second later, he wrenched his knife out of Philippe's breast.

She watched him, wild-eyed, clutching the silk remnants of her bodice together as she inched sideways along the perimeter of the courtyard. She ignored the prickly branches raking the tender skin of her back. He was blocking the only exit, but she would claw her way through the thick hedge if she had to.

Darius rose from Philippe's lifeless body. He took a handkerchief from the pocket of his impeccable coat, the cotton pearl-white in the dark. Wiping the blood off his hands, he paused and suddenly turned, giving the body a vicious kick in the ribs.

Serafina let out a small scream, taken off guard by his swift, tempestuous movement.

Darius looked over at her, staring harshly at her for a second, as if he were only just remembering she was there.

Then he stood very still, panting, a tall, silent figure looming in the darkness.

"What are you doing?" His voice was unnervingly quiet.

Trapped in his steady, piercing gaze, she froze.

"Jesus," he muttered, closing his eyes for a second.

She said nothing, gathering her torn dress tighter against her in both sweating palms as she calculated the odds of successfully running past him.

He heaved a sigh, shook his head to himself, then went and splashed his face under the cold bubbling fountain. A moment later, he walked toward her, slipping off his black jacket.

She shrank back against the bushes from him.

He held out the coat, offering it to her.

She didn't dare move even to take it, didn't dare take her eyes off him.

He had killed three men all in a night's work, he was known to do indecent things to women in the middle of the day, he had stared at her breasts, and then there was the other matter, more troubling still, that eight years ago she had been marked with this man's blood.

It had happened in the city square on her twelfth birthday, when someone tried to shoot the king. She had been standing there smiling at her birthday festivities, holding her papa's hand, when the would-be assassin attacked. And Santiago, this beautiful madman, she thought, dove into the path of the bullet, his hot, scarlet blood splashing her cheek and her new white frock.

Since that day, deep down in a primal, illogical place inside of her that responded to things like the warmth of fire and the smell of cooking food, deep down in her blood and bones where she was not princess, not political pawn, but simply woman, she knew she belonged to this man.

And the most terrifying thing of all was that she sensed he knew it, too.

His intense, fiery gaze softened slightly under his long lashes.

She couldn't stop shaking.

Again, he offered the coat.

"Take it, Princesa," he said softly.

Without warning, her eyes brimmed at his gentle tone.

His long lashes flicked downward, as if he had no idea what to do with her.

"I'll help you," he said reluctantly, holding out the coat so she would only have to slip her arms inside the sleeves.

Hesitantly, she let him put it on her like a child.

"I thought . . ." she began. She bit down on her lower lip, unable to finish.

"I know what you thought." His voice was low, fierce. "I would never hurt you."

Their stares locked, clashed, both wary.

She was the first to drop her gaze, astounded by her own unfamiliar meekness. Her ex-governess would never have believed it. "Didn't—didn't you need him alive?"

"Well, he's dead now, isn't he?" he said in weary disgust. "I'll manage." One fist propped on his hip, for a moment he rubbed his forehead.

"Thank you," she whispered shakily.

He shrugged and walked away, returning to the fountain.

Finally, now that she saw the danger truly was past, all the strength drained from her. Tears overtook her, blinding her.

She sank down where she was, collapsing slowly in a heap on the bricks. Wrapping his jacket tighter around her, she sat, braced her elbows on her bent knees, and held her head in both hands, fighting tears for all she was worth.

I will not cry in front of him, she thought fiercely, but a moment or two later, she succumbed. She couldn't help it.

When she sobbed aloud, he looked over in surprise. Frowning, he came back to her, standing tall above her. She could not summon any sense of pride, she just cried, sniffled furiously, and brushed a tear off her cheek with the back of her hand, unable to look up beyond his shiny black boots with their cruel, silver spurs.

He crouched down, searching her eyes. "Hey, Princess. What's this? You trying to ruin my night?"

She stared at him in amazement. *Ruin* his night?

She jumped when he reached out toward her, but he merely offered her a neatly folded handkerchief, producing it out of nowhere with a bit of Gypsy sleight of hand.

After a moment's hesitation, she accepted it, remembering as she dried her eyes how she used to think he was magic when she was a little girl, for he could pull a gold coin out of her ear and make it vanish again.

He studied her, the arrogant smirk on his lips at odds with the troubled look in his eyes. "What's the matter? You scared of me now, like everyone else?"

Her answer was a single, shaking sob that came all the way up from her lungs.

The smirk faded. "Hey, come on, little Cricket. This is me," he said more gently. He looked almost shaken. "You know me. You've always known me. Since you were this big, yes?" He held up thumb and forefinger about an inch apart.

She glanced at his hand, then met his eyes uncertainly.

It was a half-truth. All her life he had been there, in the shadows, but no one really knew Darius Santiago. He would not allow it. Indeed, he saved his most scathing mockery for those who tried to love him, as she had learned.

Twenty years ago, just before she was born, her parents had taken Darius off the streets, a feral boy-thief who, by an act of valor, had saved her mother's life. In thanks, Papa had made him a royal ward, raised him as his own son—insofar as Darius's magnificent pride would permit him to accept what he viewed as charity. From the time she was old enough to realize that she was something of a disappointment to her parents, a firstborn daughter rather than the hoped-for son and royal heir, she had found an ally and protector in her fellow outsider, the half-Gypsy boy whose only friends, it seemed, were the horses of the royal stable.

He lowered his long, thick lashes, and his voice was softer. "Well, it's all right if you're scared of me now. I don't blame you. Sometimes I even scare myself."

"You killed them," she whispered. "It was horrible."

"That's my job, and yes, sometimes it is horrible," he replied. "I am sorry you saw it. You should have closed your eyes, Your Highness."

"I did. I could still hear."

He bristled. "The man insulted your honor. He got what he deserved." He rose and walked away.

Holding her head in one hand, her elbow braced on her knee, Serafina watched him stalk off across the courtyard, his broad back and narrow waist snugly fitted in his black waistcoat, his enormous arms draped in full, white sleeves.

Now I have offended him. He was an acutely sensitive being, she well knew.

"Come, Your Highness," he said, remote. "It's going to be a long night. The French have a few more spies planted in the palace. I don't know who they are yet and I've got to catch them. Until I do, we've got to get you out of here immediately."

She heaved a sigh and climbed to her feet, her legs still shaky from her ordeal.

Darius waited for her by the fountain but he still would not look at her, closed within himself. Hands on his hips, he lifted his finely sculpted face and assessed the brooding night sky.

The watery moonlight slid down his high-boned cheeks, kissed his bittersweet, beautiful mouth with its golden glow.

When she joined him, he turned from her to lead the way. "First we'll have to go see your father. He'll assign someone to take you into hiding—"

"Darius, wait." She laid a hand on the broad curve of his arm. "I didn't mean—"

"Time is of the essence, Your Highness." He pulled away.

As he stepped beyond her reach, her hand slid off his arm. Glancing off his shoulder blade, her fingertips trailed through an invisible patch of warm, slick wetness on his black waistcoat.

She froze. Slowly, she turned her palm upward.

"Darius," she breathed, staring down at her bloodied hand.

"What?"

"You're bleeding."

She heard his low, cynical laugh as he struck a sulfur match on the stone grotesque of Pan, lighting a cheroot.

"Who gives a damn, Serafina?" he said bitterly under his breath. "Who gives a damn?"

With careless grace, he flicked the still-burning match into the fountain and walked away as its bright flame winked out.

CHAPTER
⇥ TWO ⇤

Only one thing remained for a man of honor whose life had become a living hell: a glorious death. At the moment, Darius Santiago longed for it.

She was afraid of him, yes, with good reason, he thought bitterly. She was the only pure thing he had ever known, gentle and innocent as daylight, and now she had seen him kill like an animal—kill, and relish the killing.

He had taken such pains to shelter her from the darkness of himself—and now this.

As he walked away from her, Darius simmered with self-directed fury, shaken and unnerved yet again by the maddening, heavenly creature. He could not wait to be rid of her and on his way again so he could resume pretending she didn't exist.

To see her was pain.

Often, far away on his missions, he imagined that if he could just see her, be near her, smell her, he would bask in an ecstasy as on some narcotic drug, but, of course, it was not so. That was merely the illusion that had sustained him for the past year or so, on his downward spiral. Now he saw the truth. Every moment in her presence was torture because she was everything he needed, and he could not have her.

He could not have her. That was all he knew. But soon he would find release.

Urgency thrummed inside his veins. He had to get out of here, away from her. As soon as possible, he'd be on his

way. He had walked away from her three years ago, on that
starry April night when she had slipped her arms around his
neck, kissed his cheek, and whispered that she loved him—
absurd!—and he would walk away again tonight, just as soon
as he'd seen her to safety. Even now, he was walking away,
fleeing what he most desperately craved.

He had taken only three or four steps away from her, however, when she caught up to him and firmly took his hand.

"Oh, come along," she said, with exasperation edging her
soft, slightly scratchy voice.

Taken aback, he lifted a brow, too mystified to protest as she
tugged him by the hand, pulling him behind her like an errant
child.

She marched across the courtyard, ever so like the fairy
queen in a snit, he thought. The opulent riot of her long, loose
spiral-curls flounced down her back with every vexed step.

"I will never understand you, Santiago," she huffed. "Don't
you even care that you are wounded?"

He was always Santiago when she was scolding.

"Doesn't hurt," he lied, his careless bravado honed to a
razor's edge. Secretly, however, he was pleased that the cut
had bought him a little of her charity. Perhaps it would also
take her mind off what she had been through and what she had
witnessed.

"Why didn't you tell me at once that he cut you?" The scowl
she threw him over her elegant shoulder showed off the clean,
patrician lines of her delicate profile and the absurd length of
her black-velvet lashes. "Why must it always be a guessing
game with you? How could you stand there bleeding and let
me go on bawling like baby? Oh, never mind. Is it bad?"

"No need to call the embalmer yet. Well," he amended,
"maybe for him."

She stopped short as she came to the dead body blocking
the exit. She peered down at her dainty bare toes, inches from
the pool of blood. He ignored the blood, more interested in the
silver rings adorning her toes.

Little Gypsy, he thought in secret delight.

A few of her stray, sooty curls fell forward, softly framing her pale, heart-shaped face as she lowered her head. Then she glanced up at him in distress.

He growled at her obvious need for assistance. "Allow me," he muttered, loath to touch her.

Her creamy cheeks heated with a summer-rose blush when he bent down slightly, slipped his uninjured right arm around her hips, and lifted her against his chest. Inwardly, he groaned to feel her flat belly and lush breasts pressed to his feverish body.

She was the king's only daughter and he'd really had no need to know that her rich, berry lips matched her nipples exactly.

Serafina wrapped her arms around his neck, looking down at the dead man in morbid fascination as Darius stepped over the corpse. She was very light, he thought as he held her. Tall and proud, but delicately boned. He set her down quickly on her feet in the grass on the other side.

She pulled his jacket tighter around her, folded her slender arms under her spectacular bosom, and regarded him keenly. "Are you hurt anywhere else, or is it just the shoulder?"

She waited, gazing up at him expectantly, but somehow he forgot to answer, promptly caught up in her otherworldly violet eyes. Ah, but those eyes were his weakness. Lucid and sweet, they were the color of June twilights, fields of hyacinths in heaven, or the lavender of sunset on snow. Eyes that haunted his dreams. He realized he was staring and shook himself free of her spell, disgusted with his own susceptibility.

"It's not serious," he said at last, hoping he was right. He felt the warm trickle of blood inside his shirt, but he didn't have time to be wounded. He had a job to do. *Thank God for that.*

She lifted one brow, giving his skeptical look right back to him.

"It's nothing," he reiterated crisply.

"I'll be the judge of that," she said, then firmly took his hand again.

He glanced warily at her as she led him down the maze's narrow lane like an impatient governess with an impossible charge. She seemed very determined about something. He supposed he should probably worry.

At the intersection of the lanes, once more the princess stared at the dead Frenchman as if she could not comprehend how his blond, curly head had come to be skewed at such an impossible angle.

Darius decided he didn't much like her interest in his handiwork, nor did he appreciate her wary, sideward glance that flicked to his arms, as if to say, *You did that with your bare hands?*

He gave her a quelling look, pulled his hand out of hers, and walked on, striding down the breezy corridor between the hedges. Serafina caught up, skipping now and then to keep up with his longer paces.

"What did they want, anyway? I thought they were my friends."

"Sorry, they weren't," he said, flicking the ashes off his cheroot and trying desperately to regain his sharp, efficient control.

"Napoleon sent them?"

"Fouché, to be exact—Napoleon's minister of police. Officially speaking, the emperor knows nothing of this."

"They didn't want to kill me, surely?" she exclaimed.

"No."

"To stop my marriage, then?"

Her stunning looks and lighthearted manner made it easy to forget how intelligent she was, he thought, an oversight men made to their folly. With a smile, she could twist any male around her finger, even the mighty Prince Anatole Tyurinov, it seemed, considering the fact that she had managed to wrest some concessions from the Russian about freeing half his serfs over a period of two years.

"Yes," he answered, "to stop your marriage. If the French had you in their possession, your father would have no choice but to hand over control of Ascencion's navy. They've been polite about it till now, but your fiancé's introduction into the equation made these despicable, underhanded tactics unavoidable on their part."

She stifled a sound of impatience as she looked away, scowling prettily again. "But now that Napoleon has command of Spain's ships, why does he still want my father's navy?"

"Nothing is ever enough for Bonaparte, you know that," he answered with an exhalation of smoke. "Besides, he still hasn't amassed the forces necessary to take England. He's going to need all the vessels he can get his hands on. Frankly, he'll never carry it off," he remarked.

"I hope not."

The wind rose, carrying to them the smell of the sea as it raked through the towering hedges. She skipped a step to keep up, brushed a long, blowing lock of her hair away from her mouth, and glanced up at him rather anxiously.

"I suppose Napoleon thought he could legitimize kidnapping me by forcing me to marry his little namby-pamby, Eugène?"

"According to my sources, yes, that was the notion."

She gave a delicate snort.

He suppressed a smile. The Jewel of Ascencion was admittedly hard to impress.

Eugène Beauharnais, Napoleon's twenty-four-year-old stepson, was perhaps the only contender for Serafina's hand of whom Darius did not heartily disapprove. The young aristocrat was honorable, loyal, and even-tempered—and any man who dared think of marrying this girl, he knew, would need the patience of Job. Unfortunately, Eugène was on the wrong side of the war. Even still, Darius almost would have preferred him instead of the husband the king had found her to ward off Napoleon's threatened invasion—the vainglorious golden giant Prince Anatole Tyurinov.

Desirous of a royal bride to overawe his friends and rouse envy in his enemies, the glorious Anatole, as Darius had come mockingly to think of him, had visited the kingdom several months ago to inspect Serafina's famous beauty. Darius had been on duty in Moscow during their fortnight's courtship. The match had been quickly arranged.

Too bloody quickly, he thought rather bitterly. He had not even completed his background check on the prospective bridegroom for the king, but the bargain was sealed.

In exchange for her hand, the thirty-three-year-old Russian war hero had pledged to take his army of a hundred thousand troops and bring a rain of fire on Paris itself if Napoleon made any move against the tiny, neutral Ascencion.

The peace had been preserved by the stalemate, the wedding date set for the first of June, less than a month away, but Darius had already made up his mind that it would never take place.

He stole a covert glance at the breathtaking young woman by his side.

He did not doubt that Serafina had beguiled Tyurinov—she did not often use her beauty for the mighty weapon it was, but when she did, a man didn't have a chance. But he wondered, not for the first time, what her feelings were in return. Between his blue-blooded pedigree, martial victories, and golden good looks, women tended to go insane over the glorious Anatole. Perhaps Serafina had found him worthy of her. Perhaps she had fallen in love.

The thought coiled his stomach in knots. He decided he didn't really want to know.

Just then, a low rumble of thunder rolled across the sky.

Serafina and he glanced at each other. He was about to suggest that they run, but he was too late. The summer downpour the sky had promised all evening began, steadily pelting them with soft, fat raindrops.

They both just stood there looking at each other and getting wet.

"Ah, well," he said at last with a weary sigh. He threw his

ruined cheroot into the grass, and lowered his head as the rain soaked his sleeves and his hair.

Serafina tilted her face back to catch the rain. She turned her hands palms upward, cupping them.

He glanced at her standing there in his jacket, which reached almost to her knees. She was bedraggled and barefoot like a waif, basking in the rain like a flower, and out of nowhere, slowly she began to laugh.

At the rich, careless sound of her laughter, he fought a smile, but when she looked over to meet his gaze, laughing at he knew not what, he lost the battle and found himself laughing quietly, too.

She lifted her hands over her head, wrists together, palms open, and twirled around once in a circle, her head thrown back to the rain, her long curls spinning out around her, raindrops on her hair like diamonds.

"Darius!" she exclaimed. "You saved me!"

She danced over to him with a single fairylike motion, laid one warm hand on his belly to brace herself, and, lifting up onto her toes, kissed the hard, wet line of his jaw, rain streaming in rivulets down her face.

With that, she flitted away and ran off like a woodland nymph, trailing silvery laughter through the rain.

Dazed, he could only stand there for a minute, staring after her. Vaguely, he pressed his hand to his stomach where she had touched him. He watched her catching raindrops on her tongue, and for a moment, he ached.

A thunderbolt struck nearer then, like a cannon's shot, like Zeus's wrath.

Darius shook his head as if to clear it, raked a hand through his rain-slick hair, and squinted against the rain, wondering who the king would get to take her into hiding and guard her.

Luckily, he himself would be too busy catching spies.

Serafina waited ahead for him, stamping in a grassy puddle. He caught up to her and they left the maze side by side, drenched by the rain as they ran through the octagonal parterres and down the promenade lined by tall columns of bushes sculpted into spirals.

The rain was sizzling on the cobbled path when they arrived at the little waterworks building not far from the maze. Tucked under mounds of lilacs the exact color of her eyes, the sleepy little service building was a small square of red brick.

Both of them soaked to the skin and breathless from running, he held the door for her. Her panting laughter echoed in its single room, empty but for some garden implements and the valves and gauges and metal contraptions which controlled the many fountains on the grounds.

Bending gracefully to the side, Serafina wrung out her long hair with both hands while he groped his way through the pitch-dark, trying to find the small wooden door which led to the passage connecting the waterworks to the palace.

"Wait for me. I can't see you."

He stopped, holding out his hand to her. She ran into it in the dark.

"Are you grabbing me?" she asked in playful indignation.

"You'd like that, wouldn't you?" he muttered.

"Exceedingly!"

"Flirt." He shook his head half in wonder at her swift recovery after her ordeal. Then again, she was much tougher than she normally let on. Like him, she merely played a part, but he had always known the real Serafina. "Young lady, you are definitely due for a lecture."

"Oh, how I miss your lectures, Darius!"

He bumped into something and muttered an oath.

"The blind leading the blind," she said, giggling and clinging loosely to his arm.

"What am I to do, take you in through the front entrance? Do you want to meet the Russian diplomats looking like a drowned rat?"

"I never look like a drowned rat. I'm Helen of Troy, remember?"

Taken aback by the cynicism undercutting her blithe tone, he merely said, "Trust me."

"Lord, are you going to find it or not? I haven't got all night."

"Eureka," he replied.

He opened the little door. It creaked in the dark.

She peered warily into the doorway. "It's black as a tomb down there."

"Never fear, I know the way."

By his early twenties, he had worked his way up to the post of captain of the Royal Guard, heading palace security, but he'd known of the secret passages within the building since he was a lad. Underfoot while the palace was under construction, he'd explored every inch of it, almost as if he had known that once it was completed and filled with lords and courtiers and such, there would be no real place here for a young half-Gypsy thief, no matter how much he adored the godlike man and gentle lady who had taken him in when he'd had nothing and no one.

Even as a boy, it had been important to show King Lazar and Queen Allegra that their generosity was not misplaced. He had been fairly sure they wouldn't send him away, for they treated him like a member of their own family, but he wasn't taking any chances. He had applied himself to learning to read, getting an education, silently studying the people around him, and mastering every weapon he could find. He had been given the chance to become something higher and better than he was, and he channeled his anger into striving for excellence. As a ward of the king, he could have had countless advantages, but he had insisted on lifting himself up by his own merit, for he never wanted his benefactors to think for one second that he served them out of any other motive than gratitude, honor, loyalty, and love.

Carefully, he led their daughter down the spiraling metal stairs to the passage below.

Because the corridor was perfectly lightless, he let her keep holding his arm, but in the dark, with her so close and with the warmth and the scent of her enveloping him, it was strange how vivid his imagination grew.

Visions came to him of maneuvering her against the smooth stuccoed wall and kissing her, tasting her mouth, parting his jacket, and cupping her beautiful breasts in his hands, caressing her until she forgot the other man's touch on her silken skin, until he had obliterated it with his own.

Shaken by the intensity of the impulse, he squared his shoulders, lifted his chin, and picked up the pace, his spurs striking the flagstones with each swift stride.

He could have any woman he wanted.

Any but this *one.*

"So, Darius, how did you manage to be in the right place at the exact moment I needed you?" she asked, giving his arm another fond tug. "Gypsy magic?"

She was the only person who could mention the more disgraceful half of his heritage without insulting him.

"Hardly. It was no coincidence. I tried to come ashore in secret but Saint-Laurent must have caught wind of my arrival. I presume he felt forced to make his move whether he was ready or not."

"I see." She was silent for a moment, then her tone was hesitant. "Darius, I know you must report to Papa, but I don't want you to tell him what Philippe . . . did. It would only hurt him."

Her request startled him—he didn't think she could see that far beyond herself—but his own ready compliance surprised him even more. Lazar would want to know the full extent of the French insult to his daughter, but she was right. What purpose would it serve? It would only inflame the proud King Lazar di Fiore to agitate Napoleon worse.

"Yes, Your Highness," he murmured with the disquieting thought that he was adding up all sorts of secrets from the king these days.

"First we'll have to go to my apartments so I can change this dress. If Papa sees how torn it is . . ."

"I understand."

"Thank you," she whispered. And after a moment she added, "I am so very glad you are home, Darius. I worry for you so when you are gone."

He felt her hands slide down his arm, gently clasping his hand in both of hers. He swallowed hard. In the darkness, he opened his hand and linked his fingers through hers, pulling her gently around the corner.

Soon they ascended the lightless, narrow stairs. They turned on the landing, but as they started up the second flight, he began to feel disturbingly light-headed. He ignored the faint, sick dizziness at first, but midway up the stairs he leaned against the wall suddenly, overcome by a wave of nausea which he knew could only be the result of blood loss. His shoulder hurt like hell.

"Darius? What is it?"

"I'm all right." Stars burst before his eyes on the blackness.

"Sit down. I'll go for the surgeon."

"No, it's nothing, I don't—want that—bumbling idiot. I'll just—" He lost track of what he was saying in a wave of dizziness. His breath turned to shallow panting. He sagged against the wall.

"Stay here. I'll go find a candle and have a look at that wound—"

"No! I don't need anything," he growled.

"Sit down, at least." She held on to his arm, steadying him needlessly as he sank down onto the step.

How humiliating, he thought.

"Oh, I wish I could see you. It's so dark in here," she said, fussing over him. "Tell me exactly what happened."

He merely laughed at her, lowering his head toward his knees to fight the nausea.

"Were you stabbed, or is it an incise wound?" she asked in a patient tone.

"Bastard gave me a good slice over the shoulder," he mumbled, chastened, for the girl sounded genuinely concerned.

"The front?"

"Front and back, I think."

"Any tingling in your fingers? Numbness?"

"I don't know," he sighed, closing his eyes as he leaned against the wall. "I'm just so damned tired." He hadn't meant to say it. Not so earnestly, so quietly.

In the dark, her soft hand came to rest on his cheek, caressing him. "I know you are, poor creature. You never stop, do you? You never give yourself time to heal."

Her touch was heaven. He rested against her hand for a moment, then pulled away abruptly, appalled that she should say such a thing, appalled he had admitted to such weakness.

"I'm fine. Just not as young as I used to be," he muttered. With one hand, he loosened his cravat. It helped marginally. He took a deep breath and steeled himself. "All right. Sorry. Let's go."

"Sorry?" she echoed.

He forced himself to stand.

The way she took his elbow now annoyed him. He shook her off. "For God's sake, I'm not an invalid. It's just a little scratch."

"All right, Darius. It's all right," she said soothingly, backing off, but still near.

He growled at her placating tone.

By the time they came out into the dimly lit servant hall on the third floor of the royal block, he was feeling steadier and had regained his arrogance. He swept a hand before her, presenting the way with sardonic gallantry. "After you, Your Highness."

Her skeptical glance flicked over him, her violet eyes a little too shrewd for his comfort, then she turned and walked ahead. As they went down the hall, she stared at the brooms and brushes neatly arranged on the walls, the shelves of crisp linens. Cynically, he realized she had probably never seen the palace before from the servants' side.

Little did she know her servants were his main source of

information, he mused, for no matter where his missions took him, he followed her every move from afar. Lately, he knew, she had been more outrageous than ever—the suitors, the parties, the tantrums, the shopping. She always turned reckless when she was nervous or afraid, and it was not difficult to surmise the source of all her latest brushes with scandal—the swift approach of her wedding day.

As if I'd ever really let that vainglorious brute get his hands on her, he thought, bristling with carefully contained ferocity. He wished he could have told her right then, to put her mind at ease, but he could not jeopardize the mission. When it was over, she would know the gift he had given her.

A short way down the corridor, they came to an innocent-looking panel on the wall between two cases of utility shelving. Darius paused in front of it, ran his hand down the seam, pressed firmly, and stood back as it popped open.

He glanced over at Serafina as the panel whispered back into the wall, opening into her darkened bedchamber.

He watched her violet eyes widen. Then her gaze slid downward, and she paled slightly.

He waited for her to throw a maidenly fit of outrage to realize he had this secret access to her inner sanctum, but she kept her jaw stubbornly clamped.

"Saint-Laurent's associates are still at large," he said by way of explanation. "I'm not letting you out of my sight. Your Highness," he added meaningfully—her humble servant.

She stared straight ahead as a blush flooded her creamy cheeks. "You need not explain, Darius. I have complete trust in your honor."

She sounded so determined, he wondered whom she was trying to convince. Nevertheless, her words pleased him.

"Who else knows of this panel?"

"No one, my lady."

The architect was dead, the king had probably forgotten, and Darius had not seen fit to tell his successor to the post of captain of the Royal Guard about this particular door. It was nothing against Orsini personally. Darius simply trusted no one where the princess was concerned. He had never even considered violating her privacy—not seriously, anyway—but most men didn't have his self-control.

Maintaining his show of cool amusement while his shoulder throbbed, he gestured. "After you."

She lifted her chin, slipped around the chair that sat in the way, and swept regally into her chamber. He followed, stepping over the threshold onto what most of the men he knew would deem holy ground. He turned back to slide the panel shut, then drifted into her magic bower.

Rain pelted the wide windowpanes. Thriving plants lined the sills and the floor all around the windows. Her bed was an enchantment, canopied clouds of gauzy white mosquito netting and pink satin sheets. A white Persian cat slept curled amid the plump pillows.

Serafina glided across the room, where she opened a door. Light slanted into the dark bedroom, then she disappeared into the adjoining room. He lingered, taking in the scene.

An ornate birdcage was near the bed, the tiny door standing open. He noticed the teal parakeet studying him from its post on a curtain rod above the window, then her little pet monkey leaped out of nowhere, giving him a start. It screeched at him, the intruder, and began cavorting around the rails of her bed.

Ungrateful creature, he thought, sternly regarding the talapoin monkey hissing at him.

Darius had given the animal to Serafina as a gift for her fifteenth birthday. He had told her it looked like her. He disregarded the monkey and narrowed his eyes, his gaze picking out the items on her bedside table several feet away, silly female frippery. A hairbrush. A novel.

Just then, her lithe silhouette appeared in the doorway. She was toweling her long hair.

"Darius."

He looked over and smiled, caught at his spying.

He sauntered toward her, noting that she had discarded his big, shapeless jacket in favor of a dressing gown, the sash tied in a bow around her slim waist. She tossed a towel to him and went to collect the little monkey, speaking sweet, babyish nonsense to it. It scampered up onto her shoulder and promptly perched atop her head, the tiny black hands holding on to her forehead.

Serafina turned to him, striking a pose like a fashion illustration. "Do you like my hat?"

"Charming," he said dryly.

"Oh, thank you." She walked over to the monkey's cage and gently pried the animal off her head, wincing as it grasped at her curls. Then she gave it a kiss on the head and tumbled it into its cage. She smiled at him, brushing past him on her way into the other room.

"Come," she said.

He slowly dried his face and ran the towel over his hair, eyeing the slim, elegant curves of her figure as he followed her. Sauntering coolly into the adjoining room, Darius almost stepped on a pile of torn wet silk in the middle of the floor.

His eyes glazed over, staring down at the remnants of her dress. She must have simply peeled the thing off. His gaze swung to her as he realized that very likely nothing lay beneath her blue satin dressing gown but fair skin, still damp with rain.

God, give me strength.

As if her sole aim were to torment him, she now bent down gracefully before the hearth, where a low fire burned. His practiced eye appraised the smooth curves of her backside, and his mind brimmed with splendid, sinful notions.

Ah, but she trusted him far too much.

She borrowed a flame from the hearth and lit an expensive beeswax candle from it. This she carried from one wall sconce to another, brightening the little sitting room with the cheerful blaze of a dozen lights, careless as ever of the cost.

"Sit," she ordered him, nodding to the laziest-looking armchair he'd ever seen.

"No, thank you."

She looked over at him in surprise. "No? You nearly passed out on the stairs, Darius. Sit, please."

"My clothes are wet and there's blood all over my shoulder," he said crisply, stung by the inglorious reminder.

"Do you think I care about the chair more than I care about you?" She laughed. "What a clod you are, Santiago. Sit down, for heaven's sake, before you fall down."

With a long-suffering sigh, as if he were not wholly grateful for the invitation, he threw the towel she'd given him over the back of the chair so he wouldn't get blood on the fine, pale yellow brocade.

"Try not to take forever," he drawled as he dropped into the chair. "I have a policy against waiting for females to dress."

She gave him a knowing smile, then turned to root through the odds and ends on the mantel. He blew his forelock out of his eyes, folded his left ankle idly over his right knee, and sat there toying with the silver spur on the edge of his riding boot.

He watched her for a moment or two, enjoying the way the light from the wall sconces played over the satin's glossy surface, following her curves. Then his gaze wandered around the room done up in shades of peach and cream and gilt.

So, this is her world. Oddly, the comfortable chaos of her life's day-to-day clutter did not irk his meticulous military sense of order. Against the broad-striped wallpaper hung portraits of her cat, her white mare, her family, and a few prettily arranged display cases, some exhibiting ornate bits of lace he guessed she had made, others with pressed flowers she'd collected. In the corner her archery equipment lay in a heap, while on the nearby low table a microscope inlaid with mother-of-pearl edged out the tea service.

Ah, yes, the great lady naturalist, he thought in an odd mix of fondness and mockery. On the floor near the table was a fat textbook creased open to a page showing drawings of the stages in the life of a butterfly. He frowned, squinting down at the book when he noticed it was in Latin.

"Darius."

He looked over inquiringly as she pulled a long, white ribbon out of a porcelain box on the mantel. He was startled to notice that beside the box was a small framed portrait of himself.

It was a copy of the life-sized one the queen had insisted upon commissioning after he'd been shot saving the king's life. He was in full-dress uniform—white jacket, gold medals, red sash—and one very serious, piercing stare.

The eyes of an ancient in a young man's face, he thought, oddly saddened by the picture.

His life would be over, it seemed, before it had even begun. Yet he felt a strange, fierce ache in his chest to see that she kept this memento of him in full view, where she would pass it every day.

"Darius," she said again, breaking into his thoughts.

"Yes, Your Highness?" he asked absently.

She didn't even glance at him. "Take off your shirt."

He paused, not sure he'd heard her correctly. His stare swung to her back and her sweet derriere wrapped in blue satin. She merely continued tying the white ribbon around her flamboyant mane of unruly curls, mink-black against her pale skin.

His tone was carefully amused. "Excuse me?"

"Take off your waistcoat and shirt, please."

"Ahh, Your Highness," he said lightly. "Believe me, I'm flattered, but I'm not in the mood."

She jerked her lovely face over her shoulder to scowl at him. "I'm not propositioning you, Santiago. For heaven's sake! Don't just sit there bleeding like a dolt. Undress. Now."

For about two seconds, he considered obeying, then he merely watched her march across the room to another door, relieved to see at least she had the decency to blush. Most of the women he knew lacked that charming ability, or lost it, at any rate, by the time he was through with them.

She disappeared into the next compartment carrying a

candlestick. He leaned forward in curiosity, peeking in. *Aha,* her dressing room. There were gowns on pegs, rows of the shoes the chit never could keep on her feet.

When she came back into the sitting room, she had some hand towels draped over her arm, a sewing basket in one hand, and a bottle in the other of what appeared to be whiskey. She set everything on the floor near his chair, then dragged the ottoman over and sat down on it across from him.

"Is there a problem, Santiago?" she asked, folding her graceful hands in her lap.

He stared at her.

"This will not do. You still have on all your clothes."

Isn't that my line? he thought, regarding her suspiciously.

Lifting both brows, she gave him a bland smile of waning patience. "Why do you prefer to suffer?"

"Because then I always know what to expect," he replied with his most arrogant smirk.

She ignored it. "Why won't you let me help you?"

He eyed the sewing basket, then glanced at her. "With all due respect, Your Highness, I'd rather not serve as the royal pincushion."

"I know what to do," she said. "I help at the pensioners' hospital once a week."

Dubiously, he arched one brow. He knew the saintly queen commanded her daughter to spend at least one day a week living for aught other than herself and her pleasures, but surely these visits to the pension house only involved giving out radiant smiles and bestowing a few words of meaningless cheer to the wretched.

"If I need stitches," he told her, his heart pounding suddenly, "I'll do it myself."

"You said the cut runs over your shoulder to your back. Use your head. How do you intend to reach a wound that's on your back?"

"I'll see the surgeon."

She gave a smile of sugared treachery and reached up to tap

his chin fondly with one fingertip. "Don't tell lies, Santiago. I know you won't see him. Don't you trust me?"

Was she deliberately being obtuse or tormenting him just for fun? he wondered, inching back in his chair away from her. Maybe an aged pensioner of seventy could endure the touch of those silken hands without ravishing her, but he wasn't half that old yet.

She shrugged to herself, then went on about her business, rising to go pour water into the unused teapot, then putting it over the low fire to boil. Returning to him, she knelt down on the floor and opened the sewing basket.

"Will white suffice for your stitches, Colonel, or would you prefer something more dashing?" she asked, trailing one graceful fingertip over the various hanks of thread. "Scarlet? Gold filigree, perhaps?"

"I really haven't time to play doctor with you."

"Don't make me pull rank on you," she advised him, the sewing needle between her lips as she pulled out a neat loop of white thread and unwound some of it. "If you refuse, I shall have to make it an order. Strip, sir."

He didn't move. He couldn't, suddenly. His heart was pounding and he couldn't find his voice.

Done threading the needle, she set it carefully aside. She laid both hands on her thighs, gazing up at him.

He stared down at her, feeling increasingly cornered, unable even to spit out the words to explain his protest. What was he to say, *Don't touch me*? He wasn't that skilled a liar. Truly, over the past few years there had been moments, desperate moments near the edge of his solitary endurance, when he wanted this girl so much he quite despised her. He could not be fire for her, so he had chosen to be ice.

Now she was gazing at him as only she ever did, as if she saw things in him no one else could see, those unforgettable violet eyes looking too deeply into him, her gaze like a flash of lightning, illumining landscapes within him he preferred to keep dark.

Save me. The thought trailed through his mind, he knew not why. He could only sit there, captivated, immobilized, half-terrified. Someone wanted to help him and he didn't know how to react. Not just anyone.

Serafina.

The only living thing he'd ever trusted.

The only one he couldn't have.

Staring at her, he couldn't force out a single word.

Yet somehow she seemed to understand him.

"Very well," she said softly, searching his face. "You just sit. I'll do it."

He couldn't find the wherewithal to stop her or to move. He knew she shouldn't be touching him. She knew it, too, of course, but when had she ever done as she was told? And when had he ever disobeyed a royal command?

She slid his untied cravat from his shoulders first, then came closer, kneeling between his legs. Wary as a wild animal, he watched her every move as she unbuttoned his simple black waistcoat. He was only minimally helpful as she pushed it down carefully off his wounded shoulder, then freed him from it. His shirt remained, sodden, ripped, bloody. A lot of blood.

"Poor thing," she murmured. When she reached out and began gathering the wet cotton of his shirt in both hands so she could slip it off over his head, he pulled back, staring at her, heart racing.

"What's the matter, Darius?"

He swallowed, dry-mouthed. The way she said his name could make him drunk.

Between his legs, she stood, bracing her hands on his knees. He watched her rise and felt his loins pulse, felt his whole being in thrall to her, as if he were an uninitiated boy being slowly seduced by a goddess.

Hands on her hips, she frowned at him in puzzlement. Then a strange, tender smile of understanding curved her lips.

"Shy?" she asked softly.

He stared at her, unable to speak, his soul in his eyes. He did not know all of a sudden what was happening to him.

Slowly, he nodded.

She reached out and caressed his cheek, then gently brushed his forelock out of his eyes. "I won't hurt you, Darius. Don't be shy. After all"—her gaze slid away from his—"you saw mine."

Mischievously, her eyes flicked back to his.

Her impudent remark shocked him out of the trance. He stared at her in awe.

"You bad little girl," he breathed, suddenly afire for her.

Her smile flashed.

Jesus, what was he doing? His very hands burned with the need to touch her, run his palms from her slim waist down her elegantly curved thighs, part that dressing gown and smell her rain-scented skin. He curled his fingers tightly over the edges of the chair's arms, fighting it for all he was worth.

If anyone ever found out about this, he thought feverishly, if the king ever found out about this . . .

Then he realized he would be dead in a few weeks anyway, considering the suicide mission ahead of him once he'd finished routing the spies, so what did it matter?

It was too late to get out of this now and he should at least let her dress the wound.

Maybe she knew what she was doing, which he doubted, but he could talk her through it, and it would save him a trip to the bumbling surgeon's.

But as he hesitated, strangely, he thought of all the men he'd slammed up against walls over the past few years, warning them away from her, enforcing the ironclad rule that Serafina di Fiore was off limits. The rule applied to him, too

Especially to him.

Hell, he thought, bristling, he wasn't the one who had started this tonight.

It wasn't as if anything was going to happen, after all. He would not let it. Tonight his black temper had slipped the leash, true, but he still ruled over his passions with an iron fist. Not for nothing was he descended on his father's side from Torquemada of the Spanish Inquisition. Besides, it would be over soon and then she would be somebody else's problem.

His heart raced faster as she read his wary surrender in his eyes, an answering flicker of anticipation in her own that told him perhaps she wanted to touch him as badly as he wanted her to do so.

"Well?" she asked coolly.

They stared at each other in equal challenge, both riveted, both panting slightly. The moments ticked by, the mantel clock booming in the silence, the rain drumming, wind-driven, against the glass.

Finally, he shrugged in nonchalance, as if nothing mattered a whit to him—if she seduced him or if he bled to death—but he doubted she was fooled.

"Take it off," she whispered.

He lifted his shirt off over his head and held it bunched in one white-knuckled fist.

The first thing her gaze fixed upon was not his wound, but the tiny silver medal hanging on a long, sturdy chain around his neck.

Ohh, hell, he thought suddenly, his heart sinking.

Now he was in for it. He had forgotten the damned thing was there.

He held very still—trapped, unmasked, revealed to her.

With a look of disbelief, Serafina sank down on her knees between his open thighs and captured the medal reverently in her palm, her knuckles brushing the skin between the swells of his chest. She stared at it, then lifted the violet innocence of her gaze to his, her lips parted slightly in wonder and question.

It was the medal of the Virgin she had given him after he'd been shot like a dog right before her eyes on her twelfth birthday.

To this day, she hated her birthday.

She could never accept that the shooting wasn't her fault.

She had stayed at his bedside constantly. All the while he wandered in the nightmare dreamscapes of fever, he had been vaguely aware of her talking to him, whispering prayers, her soft, froggy little voice his lifeline.

They told him later that when they had tried to make her come away from his bedside, she had gone berserk, kicking and punching, biting and scratching, rather than leave his side.

He had never forgotten that. He had never expected that anyone would ever be that loyal to him. She had put the medal on him herself once he was out of the woods. It would protect him, she had said. And then she'd said that other amusing thing—what was it?

He stared into her eyes, remembering that impish, little-girl whisper close to his ear.

You are the bravest knight in all the world, Darius, and when I grow up, I'm going to marry you.

CHAPTER
⚜ THREE ⚜

"You still have it," she said faintly, wide-eyed as she stared down at the tiny silver medal, still warm in her palm with his body's heat.

"Still have it," he replied, sounding a trifle hoarse.

Wonderstruck, Serafina searched his soulful, onyx eyes. She held her breath, not daring to overstep her bounds again by foolishly reading into this discovery some significance that was not there, but surely, surely it meant something that Darius still wore this trinket she had given him so long ago. It was all she could do not to laugh aloud and hug him.

An indescribable glow of joy, painfully sweet, sparked in her chest and spread, flowing upward, beaming from her suddenly misty eyes. "Told you it would work."

He gave her an embarrassed, little-boy smile and lowered his gaze.

For a moment, she studied him lovingly by the warm light of the sconces. His sun-bronzed face was more angular than she'd noticed before, and pale from losing blood. His eyes were sharper, more wary than ever, with faint dark circles beneath them, more tiny, careworn lines at their corners. Gorgeous as always, she thought, but he didn't look altogether well. He was too lean, too intense, with a restless, hunted look.

"You haven't been eating," she chided softly.

He shrugged as he mumbled a denial.

Sometimes, she knew, he even starved himself, making austere fasts as part of his self-punishing regimes in his quest for knightly perfection. Constantly he strived, piling glory upon glory as if, deep down, he did not believe he would ever really be good enough. Privately, it broke her heart.

She thought again of the rage he had unleashed on Philippe and wondered about the firestorm inside him just beneath his armor of cool invulnerability, all his suffering concealed by his magnificent pride.

Well, he had made up his mind to let her help him in this way, at least, she thought in determination. It was a start.

She let the medal fall once more against his gleaming chest and rose from her knees, bending to kiss his forehead lightly.

"I'll be right back," she whispered, then went to fetch the now-boiling water.

She poured it into two basins, the steam rising to warm her face. She carried the two basins over near the chair where he waited, then she washed her hands thoroughly, wincing at her cut, swollen ring finger.

Briefly she tried to remove the monstrous jewel from her finger, but the gold band was skewed all out of shape. There was no time to muddle with it. She turned to her patient.

"Now, then. Let's have a look." Barefoot, she padded around to his left side to tally the latest damage his courage and selfless loyalty had cost him.

His smooth, sun-browned skin twitched at the first touch of her hands as if she'd tickled him. She caressed him firmly to still the involuntary response, trying at the same time to conceal her own reaction to the beauty of his finely honed, powerful body.

His skin was warm and smooth as velvet. His muscles were like tempered steel and she would have liked, she thought, any valid excuse to stroke him and explore him at her leisure. His hard, sculpted chest entranced her. The curve of his throat beguiled her. She could not resist the temptation of running one hand slowly, carefully over the rock-hard musculature of his arm as she approached his wounded shoulder.

Darius sat obediently, head down. She felt him slowly relax, saw his long-lashed eyes drift closed as she began to work on him.

As she wiped the blood away from his left shoulder, she reached over and touched the star-shaped scar just below his right shoulder blade. There, the would-be assassin's bullet had struck him eight years ago, on her birthday. He should have died of that wound, the doctors said. The priest had given him last rites and Papa had wept, which was unheard-of. She herself had gone a little mad. She didn't like to think about it, but what she'd seen him go through had inspired her interest in medicine as a hobby.

She wrung out the cloth in the water basin, then examined the knife wound more closely.

It was deep. She probed. It bled.

"Tincture of amaranth will help slow the bleeding, but I'd feel better if we stitched you, just to be safe," she said thoughtfully after a moment. "You'll need about nine stitches, I think. Would you like a drink before I begin?"

"I don't drink spirits."

She rolled her eyes. "I know that. I'm not suggesting you get foxed, I just thought you might want something for the pain."

"No," he said sternly.

"Suit yourself, you wretched paragon," she muttered, dousing one of the clean, dry cloths with the whiskey.

She pressed the cloth to the cut, staring at his face because surely now, with alcohol dousing the wound, he would show some reaction. But he merely swallowed down the pain, then turned to her, eyes narrowed, the insolent look firmly in place. She shook her head at him in grudging admiration.

Next she applied some of the pungent tincture from the little vial onto one of the clean hand towels. She held it to the gash for a few minutes.

Darius and she sat in silence. She smiled when she glanced at his face, for he looked like he was falling asleep sitting up.

I'm so damned tired, he'd said. It was the only time in her memory that he'd admitted to any kind of weakness. Frowning slightly, she decided that between his loss of weight, his indifference to his own injury, and the way he'd torn Philippe apart, she was quite worried about him.

Checking the wound a few minutes later, she saw the amaranth had indeed slowed the bleeding. The royal surgeon did not hold with the old herbals and folk medicines, but Serafina had seen them work. When it came time to take up her needle, however, her mouth went dry.

She could do this, she told herself. She had to. His wound required it. She would do it just the way the textbooks said, just the way the royal surgeon had showed her. She had assisted a dozen times in her eagerness to learn and had even performed the procedure once herself with the doctor looking over her shoulder. Besides, she thought, trying to encourage herself, she was excellent at lace and embroidery.

With her left hand she pressed the edges of his incised flesh gently together, then brought up the needle, wincing with hesitation when the moment came to pierce him.

"Hold still, now," she coached him, stalling. "This won't hurt a bit."

He let out an impatient sigh. "Whenever you're ready, Your Highness. I thought you knew what you were doing."

She shot a scowl at the back of his glossy black head, but his remark gave her the impetus to do what she must. She pricked the bronze velvet of his skin.

"Ow," he muttered as she pushed the needle through.

"Aha, so you are human, after all."

"Watch what you're doing, please."

"Thankless rogue," she mumbled.

Her hands perspired but were steady as she closed the gash with each careful stitch, fully absorbed in her task as his blood stained her hands. She lost herself in concentration, until at last she tied off the thread and snipped it triumphantly with her sewing scissors. Reaching for the cloth, she wiped away the slight amount of bleeding that had occurred during the procedure.

"There you are. How does it feel?" she asked as she washed her hands in the second basin, then dried them.

"Better."

"Hmm, now you're humoring me. Try not to move it too much for a few days."

"Right," he said cynically.

"You are impossible," she murmured. She stepped near him again, examining her work.

It was somehow automatic to run her hand through his hair now that the crisis was past, second nature to bend down and kiss him lightly on the temple.

"You were very brave," she murmured playfully.

Only when Darius tilted his head back and looked at her for a long moment did it occur to her that perhaps she was being too forward with him again. Instantly she blushed, scolding herself. She was not a child anymore who could climb all over him like he was her own pet wolf.

She looked away. "Never fear, Santiago," she said with forced lightness, "I shall not hurl myself at you again." She picked up her scissors and began sharply ripping a clean linen sheet into strips to use as bandages for him. "Ow!"

"What is it?"

"I hurt my hand when I smashed Philippe a facer," she muttered.

"What?" Darius began to laugh skeptically.

"You think I'm joking? I got him with my ring. See?" She stepped nearer and held out her injured left hand to show him.

He took her outstretched hand and examined it, his black forelock veiling his eyes.

The gold filigree of the setting had bent with the force of the blow. The acorn-sized diamond of her engagement ring was squashed off to the side. The gold band had buckled slightly on an angle, cutting into the tender flesh between her fingers.

"I punched him. That's how I was able to get away from them. I ran into the maze. I thought I could hide there. It always worked when I was trying to evade my governess."

He lifted his head and stared up at her in frank amazement. "Well done, Serafina."

Usually the compliments of men made her yawn, but the simple acknowledgement from him made her blush bright red.

He gently drew her closer. "Come here. You sit right down, girl," he murmured. "You should have looked after yourself first."

She stammered a self-conscious protest, but she obeyed when he directed her with a nod to the ottoman across from him. Muscles rippling all down his chiseled belly, Darius reached over and lifted the second basin of now-tepid water from the low table nearby. He set the basin on her lap, his fingertips brushing her knee. She steadied the basin with her right hand as he picked up the soap and let it float in the water.

"Let's get this off you."

"It's stuck."

"We'll see about that," he growled. Taking her left hand gently between both of his, he dunked her hand in the basin all the way up to her wrist. He held it under the water for a moment.

Both staring down at their joined hands, neither of them spoke.

Next, he took the small oval of soap, smoothing it back and forth across her palm with his thumb until tiny bubbles appeared. He massaged the bubbles gently all over her hand, up the tapered length of each finger and her thumb. She could have groaned aloud with the pleasure of his touch, tingling all the way up her arm. Her heartbeat quickened with each caress of skin on wet, slick skin.

When he had coated her hand in the pearly sheen of the suds, he took the gold band of the ring between his thumb and forefinger, squeezing it hard, but with precision. She kept her head down, biting her lip against the pain, but she watched the powerful muscles leap all the way up his arm with his careful exertion. Then he changed his grip, holding the gold band with all four fingers and thumb, and began working it off of her finger.

"Am I hurting you?" he murmured.

She shook her head, her voice captured in her throat.

The ring was still bent too much to fit over her swollen middle knuckle.

"A little more," he said.

Again, he soaped her hand, sliding his wet forefinger slowly into the V between each of her fingers. She watched the play of muscle across his hard chest, gazed longingly at the small, tawny circles of his nipples, and the silver medal shining against his gold, gleaming skin.

So beautiful, she thought with a soul-deep ache, for he would never be hers. Her longing for him filled her with self-directed anger and misery. Would she never get over this man? Had she no pride? She had tried to hate him but could not.

She stared sorrowfully at his downswept lashes and high cheekbones and the intent look on his finely sculpted face as he squeezed the gold band back into a rough circle and tried to pull it off her. Again, it didn't work.

"I think there is no getting rid of it," she whispered.

Under his forelock, he looked up, meeting her gaze with a directness that nearly knocked the breath from her. His voice was soft but ferocious. "I will free you from it. Trust me."

She stared at him, taken aback.

He lowered his head again. Carefully he eased the ring over her knuckle at last and removed it from her finger. When he looked up and met her gaze, the fiery intensity glowed in his eyes, this time with dark satisfaction.

"You did it," she breathed.

"Leave it off."

"A-all right," she stammered, wide-eyed.

He rinsed the suds from her skin very tenderly. Placing the broken ring in her hand, he curled her fingers around it in his own. The curved scar on his lip tilted as he gave her his rarest, truest smile. He had a smile like molasses, dark and rich and bittersweet, and it melted her completely.

"Get dressed, Princesa, then we'll go see your father," he

murmured, but before he let her go, he lifted her hand to his lips.

She stared in amazement as he closed his eyes, bent his head, and pressed to her injured knuckle a single, ardent kiss.

Serafina had gone into the dressing room to put on a fresh gown while Darius slipped his damp, bloodied shirt back on and went out into the hallway, where he ordered a footman to fetch his aide, Lieutenant Alec Giroux. He instructed the servant to have Alec meet him at his suite in the royal block as soon as possible.

Shirt flowing open down his chest, Darius paced in the sitting room while Serafina dressed in the adjoining compartment.

Those moments with her had fired his resolve with new passion.

Now all he had to do was meet with the king, catch the spies, and be on his way to Milan.

Seven weeks ago, when one of his most trusted contacts informed him of the French spies who had infiltrated the palace, Darius had left Moscow at once. He had been forced to cut short his meticulous background investigation of Anatole Tyurinov, but he had already learned more than he needed to know, and there had been no time to lose.

On the voyage back from Russia to Ascencion, he had spent the weeks at sea refining his plans and making peace with his fate.

He knew what he had to do. The king's hands were tied in this matter, but his own were not.

Serafina would not be the virgin sacrifice to buy them protection from the tyrant Napoleon.

The brute Tyurinov would never get his hands on her.

At the same time, Darius could not allow Napoleon to invade with his superior forces and take Lazar's throne from him. He had to protect his benefactor, the kingdom, and Serafina all at once. It was an impossible situation, but he had one final bit of Gypsy magic up his sleeve. He need only go to the heart of the problem.

To Milan.

He paused in his pacing, eyes ablaze. No one could be allowed to guess what he intended, not Serafina, not even the king. It would only put them in danger.

On May 26, mere days before Serafina's wedding, Napoleon was scheduled to appear in Milan to receive the Iron Crown of Lombardy.

Darius would be there, too.

He was an able diplomat and a good spy, but when it came to the assassin's art, he had a gift.

With one true shot of his rifle, he could disable the French war machine and remove the need for Serafina's marriage to the Russian.

Napoleon Bonaparte must die.

He had no illusions about surviving the mission. Others had tried to assassinate the emperor and all had gone to the gallows or stood before the firing squad.

It didn't much matter to him. The deed would immortalize him, and a glorious death was better than this life where he could not reach for the one thing that might have saved him— the promise in Serafina's eyes of a dream beyond anything he had ever experienced.

He only knew he would not fail. One bullet, and he could make the world a safer place for everyone.

One bullet, and Serafina would be free.

"Here I am!" she called gaily, stirring him out of his dark thoughts.

He turned as she emerged from the dressing room with a dazzling smile, a vision in violet silk. His heart clenched.

"Shoes," he ordered.

She flashed him a mock pout and turned back to get some slippers, then came out again and twirled for him. "How do I look?"

Fighting a smile, he eyed her up, from her slippered toes to her luxurious midnight tresses still loosely tied back with the white ribbon in a bow.

If she was not worth dying for, he did not know what was.

"You'll do," he said.

He picked up his waistcoat and cravat, draped them over his arm, and escorted Her Highness out into the hall.

CHAPTER
⊰ FOUR ⊱

His spurred bootheels struck loud with each step, resounding down the marble corridor, while her skirts made an airy rustle as she strode beside him. Darius felt her watching him, and looked down at her with a dry, inquiring expression.

"Why do you always look so serious?"

He heaved a growling sigh and attempted to ignore her, but Serafina would not have it.

"So, Colonel. About these spies. What happens next?"

He glanced over his shoulder, then spoke in a low tone. "Your father and I will select a small band of highly trained men to protect you. They'll remove you from the palace and keep you guarded until I've apprehended the remaining members of Saint-Laurent's organization."

"Where will they take me?" she asked, wide-eyed.

"Safe house."

"What's that?" she exclaimed.

He reached over and pinched her cheek, amused by her alarm. "Oh, just a pleasant little country house with some ingenious fortifications. You'll be perfectly safe. Think of it as a holiday," he suggested. "Rusticating."

"Rusticating." She wrinkled her refined nose. "Can my friends come?"

"No. You'll have to manage without your entourage for a while," he said rather sarcastically. "You will also have a very limited staff. And no animals."

She frowned. "I don't think I like this."

"It's not optional."

"I shall be bored out of my skull." Suddenly she whirled to him. "Will you be going, Darius?"

He shuddered. "Er, no."

She stared at him with that intelligent gaze belying her frivolous, darling-of-the-court manner. "You should, Darius. You could use a holiday."

"I have spies to catch, my lady."

"Hmm," she said, eyeing him askance.

When they reached his suite, he found Alec waiting outside the door.

"Good Lord, Colonel, what happened to you?" the fair-haired junior officer cried, seeing his bloodstained shirt.

"Oh, the usual," he drawled.

He instructed Alec to send a few men of the Royal Guard out to the maze to dispose of the bodies, then ordered him to seek an audience for them immediately with the king. Alec gave him a smart, martial bow in reply, but Darius smirked to see his assistant steal a lovelorn glance at the Jewel of Ascencion.

She gave a haughty sniff and turned away, nose in the air. The lieutenant scurried away.

"He's harmless." Darius chuckled, unlocking the door.

"Tell him he can keep his eyes to himself, thank you," she said primly.

He laughed under his breath. As if she did not love it that every man who saw her was her slave.

"Stay here. I'll be right back. Shout if anyone approaches you."

He opened the door slowly and entered his suite, weapon drawn. He was always a target, so there was the chance that his rooms had already been broken into. He took a careful moment to listen and smell the air, stealing silently from room to room until he was sure the suite was clear. Returning to the entrance, he led the princess inside and shut the door behind her.

He had no business bringing her into his rooms, but propriety or no, he thought stubbornly, he wasn't letting her out of his sight. His Majesty would expect no less of him. Besides, it would only be for a moment, just long enough for him to dig some fresh clothes out of his traveling trunks, unloaded scarcely an hour ago from the ship, and to put them on.

It was dark in his suite. Knowing his window was probably being watched, he didn't bother to light a glim. He dragged one of his sea chests out into the middle of the floor and opened it while Serafina went exploring his private domain with her light, dancing step over the creaking floor, humming to herself.

Well, she certainly made herself at home, he thought sardonically. For someone who was the target of an abduction plot, she didn't seem overly concerned.

Because she feels safe with me, trailed the thought through his mind. He ignored his own aching reaction to the realization, pulling out a starchy lawn shirt and fresh cravat.

Quickly he donned them, then opened another trunk to scrounge up a fresh waistcoat and jacket—black, of course. It amused him to play up his sinister role as the king's cold-blooded assassin, for it kept the courtiers somewhat at bay. Whether it was jealousy or simple prejudice against his Gypsy blood, he only knew they despised and mistrusted him. They called him a calculating adventurer and warned one another that any day now he would turn on the king. Whenever he came home, they baited him, trying to see how far they could push him, for they knew he would uphold the king's new law against dueling, and he refused to fight under Lazar's roof.

Buttoning his waistcoat in the dark, he strolled into the next room to find Serafina bathed in moonlight by his large four-poster bed, staring down at his guitar. The instrument lay in its black leather case, which she had opened. When she touched the strings, the fine Spanish guitar breathed a mournful sound.

"What are you doing?" he asked very quietly.

She yanked her hand back. "Nothing."

He stalked over to her and shut the case, narrowing his eyes at her. "Come on." He pivoted and walked silently out of the bedroom. She followed. Just as he reached for his jacket, draped over a chair, there came a light scratch at the door.

In two strides, he was by Serafina's side. Effortlessly he maneuvered her against the wall behind the door and motioned for her to be silent. She nodded, her eyes wide, glistening in the dark like violet quartz.

Soundlessly approaching the door, he laid his hand on the knob. The scratching sounded again.

He unsheathed his dagger.

Heart pounding with dread, Serafina waited, fully tensed, but when Darius opened the door, she found a different kind of danger had come to pounce on her champion now.

"Darling!" said a worldly, tinkling voice.

Instantly Serafina's eyes narrowed to angry slashes.

Darius murmured a cool, uncomfortable little laugh. "Jules. What a surprise."

In the wedge of light slanting across the floor, she saw their shadows as Lady Julia Calazzi threw herself into Darius's arms and began kissing him for all she was worth.

Serafina spied, peeking with one eye through the crack in the door. With one hand, the voluptuous brunette in the wine-red dress was tearing at the clothes Darius had just put on. With the other, Julia held the back of his head, driving him deeper into the ruthless kiss she was giving him.

Ugh, I can't watch this. Serafina turned away in disgust. She folded her arms over her chest and glared into the dark room. It was bad enough to have to hear it.

"Oo, Santiago, I am starved for you," the woman moaned between kisses. "Let me in."

Serafina peered through the crack in the door again to observe Darius's reaction.

Well, she thought, she had to give him credit. He tried. Of course, he had to know she was spying on him, so perhaps he was minding his manners. He was surprisingly polite as he pried Julia back, but the notorious seductress seemed to think he was only playing hard to get. Plucking at his clothes, she laughed at his protests.

"We can do it in the hall if you want, darling, but I'd prefer your bed. Then you can tie me up again," she added in a wicked whisper.

Serafina's brows shot up.

Darius cleared his throat violently. "Er, now's not a good time," he started gingerly.

"Why not, darling?"

"Just got in. I have to see the king."

"Let him wait. I need you first. So badly. So very badly," she panted, grasping his waist and pressing him with her body, but when Julia pushed Darius against the doorframe right on his bad shoulder, Serafina's temper snapped.

Looks like it's my turn to rescue him! she thought, ignoring the inner protest that Darius would be cross if she interfered. She didn't care. La Divine Julia couldn't have him tonight, and that was that.

"Did you miss me, darling? I missed you. You know I'm mad for you," Julia panted, running her jeweled fingers through his hair.

"Husband out of town again?" he asked, beginning to sound irritated.

"He's dead, darling, haven't you heard? I am finally free of the old goat!"

"Ah. I see you are heartbroken. My condolences."

Julia laughed. "You delicious scoundrel! How like you to condole me for the loss of a man you cuckolded! Rest assured, I'll land on my feet. I always do. Now let me in! We'll toast his good riddance."

"Julia, really, I'm in the middle of something—"

She slipped her arms around him again, kissing his neck as he protested. "Oh, you're so busy, I know, darling. Tell me all about it," she murmured, laughing.

Serafina edged farther into the room while Darius blocked the woman at the doorway and smoothly ran through half a dozen excuses, flattery and all, to no avail. He never noticed as Serafina made her way silently toward his bedchamber.

When she was there, she stood out of sight, muffling wicked laughter.

"Darius," she called in her scratchiest, sleepiest, most pampered voice, "come back to bed, my love. I *need* you!"

In the doorway, Julia's wheedling and Darius's charming refusals both abruptly stopped.

At last, Julia gasped as though she had had the wind knocked out of her. "You *bastard*! Who is she?"

"I—"

He said nothing more. The great lover was quite at a loss, it seemed.

Serafina bit her tongue lightly just to keep from laughing aloud. Oh, revenge was a wonderful thing, she thought, remembering that day she had walked in on the pair in the music room. She had been crushed for a week afterward.

"Have your fun, you ungrateful cur. Use her well!" Julia snarled in a whisper. "And when none of your pretty toys proves willing or able to indulge your perversions, you can come crawling back to me."

Hmm, perversions? Serafina wondered.

"But I promise you this—I will find out who she is and I will *destroy* her!"

"Don't you think perhaps you're overreacting, my dear?" he asked blandly. "I never made you any promises."

Serafina heard the slap.

For a moment, she only stood there, stunned, wide-eyed in the dark.

Julia had slapped Darius.

Slapped her brave, noble, wounded knight.

Infuriated, she whirled out of her hiding place and marched toward the door in a wrath of vengeance, but Darius was just closing it. She tried to slip around him, but he grabbed her by the waist.

"Oh, no, you don't, little wildcat."

She strained for the doorknob. "Let me go! I'm going after her! How dare she hit you? She hurt your shoulder! I saw her—"

"That, Your Highness, was totally uncalled for," he growled, holding her fast. "You have just officially made my life hell. You had no business interfering in my—"

"Perversions?"

She heard him suck in his breath swiftly.

"Do you really tie her up? Why?"

"Serafina!"

"Is it fun? Oh, I've shocked you." She laughed with glee.

He released her waist and straightened up to his full height. In the dark, she could just make out the shape of him as he growled a sigh, righted his clothes with a crisp jerk to cravat and jacket, then raked a hand through his hair.

"Your father will be waiting, Your Highness."

She chuckled at his chagrin.

"You're very pleased with yourself, aren't you?" he muttered as he took a handkerchief out of his pocket. He wiped the crimson rouge from Julia's lips off his face.

"Yes. Here, you missed." Serafina took the cloth from him, held his chin, and wiped the last smudge of Julia's rouge off his face, by the corner of his mouth. "As for you, Colonel, I am shocked that you are wooing married ladies." She gave him back his handkerchief. "For your information, Julia Calazzi is a malicious schemer," she told him sternly, folding her arms over her chest. "Really, you should show some taste."

He threw his forelock out of his eyes with an arrogant toss of his head. "Nice body, though, and she's always willing to try new things."

Her eyes widened. "Do not say such things to me!" she huffed, blushing.

"You started it," he muttered. "Anyway, it just so happens that Julia has, shall we say, intimate knowledge of every man in this court. She can be very useful."

"Oh, so you give her your favors in exchange for information. How mutually cold-blooded! I thought perhaps you were in love with her," she said, studying her fingernails.

He scoffed.

"Obviously she is in love with you," she pointed out.

"Women like Julia don't fall in love."

She shook her head. "Don't be too sure. I'd be careful with her if I were you. I've seen how she treats her enemies."

"Well, congratulations. You're the one she wants to destroy now," he said sardonically.

"I'm shaking," she purred at him.

He reached for her wrist, pulling her none too gently toward the door. "Come on, you hellion. What were you going to do to her anyway, smash her a facer?"

"Maybe," she shot back, flouncing a few steps ahead of him as they set out down the hall, but it was right then she decided, with all the stubbornness she possessed, that if she was in need of a protector for the next few weeks, then, by goodness, she was the Princess Royal and she should have the very best.

Only the great Santiago would do.

She was sure she could persuade Papa of the wisdom of this decision.

Fairly sure.

Yes, she thought fiercely, Papa could get some other man to do his dirty work for a change. Darius was tired, wounded, and worn out. He would never look after himself properly unless he was forced to. With a wound like that, he had no business running about trying to catch spies. Somebody had to take care of him or he was going to self-destruct. Her mind was made up. Even if she had to twist Papa around her finger, Darius was coming with her.

Somehow she sensed it might well be a matter of survival for both of them.

Julia Calazzi was still shaking by the time she slipped around the corner, down the dimly lit marble hall from Santiago's suite. Leaning her head back against the wall, she closed her eyes and strove for calm. Her heart pounded with hellish fury.

She knew that scratchy, luxurious voice.

Now that she had realized, belatedly, who was in the room with him, Julia was torn between relief and an even greater alarm. Calling Darius back to bed was just the sort of joke the little witch would enjoy, just to grate on her. But Julia knew full well that Santiago would never lay a hand on the king's precious baby girl.

There must be some mischief afoot, she decided. Offhand, she could think of any number of possible disasters brewing in the palace that could have brought Santiago rushing home. Philippe Saint-Laurent? Orsini? She knew of them all.

Well, she thought, it comforted her to realize he was probably merely on duty, protecting Her Highness, as always. Yet this thought, too, brought a faint sneer to her face. Why had no one ever protected *her*?

Over the past several years, Julia Calazzi had staked her claim on the king's right-hand man, the elusive, the beautiful, blackhearted Santiago. The whole court believed that if anyone could ever snare him, she, La Divine Julia, would be the one.

She did not care that her friends pursued him for the occasional dalliance, for truly, a night in his arms was a harlot's dream. Their knowing what a fantastic lover he was only enhanced her victory. Though most had enjoyed him, all acknowledged that she was the only one equipped with the wits and treachery to match him, trick for trick.

Only, over time, as she had grown close to him—insofar as anyone could be close to Darius Santiago—Julia had come to realize what no one else saw, a situation which boded very ill for her planned conquest. He was smitten—poor, tragic, laughable fool—with that spoiled, silver-spoon beauty, the king's daughter.

God, she despised the Princess Royal. Why did everyone act as though that barefooted little heathen was God's gift to the world?

Still angry, Julia winced at the prick of her nails digging into her palm. She opened her fist and looked down at her hand, still red from the slap she had dealt him.

That had been unwise, she mused, flexing and clenching her jeweled hand in thought. She could hardly afford to alienate him—literally, could not afford it. Her face hardened as she recalled for the thousandth time the tedious burden of her financial situation.

Her husband had died leaving her nothing but debts from his witless investments, but Julia vowed to herself that as soon as she could cast her snare around Santiago's neck, her worries would be over.

That Darius was rich was little known because he did not believe in ostentatious display. Not only did he have the ear of the king and countless international personages, but his political maneuverings and his own ship-and-trade firm had served in building his massive fortune. Even lesser known was that, with his father's death, he had become *Count* Darius Santiago, with vast holdings and vineyards in Andalusia.

Not even the king knew of this. The one thing Julia had been unable to learn was why Darius refused to claim his title.

She only knew that when he was her husband, she would force him to. Otherwise, well, what would people say? she thought. La Divine Julia, marrying a commoner?

At a sound down the hall, she peeked around the corner and saw the door to his room open. He came out. She ducked back, spying on him as he glanced one way down the hall, then the other, his movements graceful and silent as a wild panther's. Julia crept forward again and watched.

Staring at him from halfway down the hall, she could feel his riveting magnetism. His jet-black hair gleamed in the dim glow of the wall sconces. Her gaze ran hungrily over him.

God, she missed him in her bed. As a lover, he had the hands of a guitarist and the soul of a poet. She had once known every inch of his hard, gorgeous body, but his attitude toward her had changed perceptibly after Her Royal Perfection had walked in on them making love that day in the music room. Since then, his gallantry toward her had seemed rather forced, Julia thought with a touch of anxiety. Sometimes he even seemed to be avoiding her.

Down the hall, Darius opened the door wider and led Serafina out of his room.

Instantly, the tug of desire in the pit of Julia's stomach turned to a knot of animosity. She clenched her jaw to hear them joking together, and to see how Serafina's radiant beauty caught fire when she gazed at him, her fresh cheeks flushed and pink, though the girl was haughty and cool with every other male.

Julia clenched her fist tightly again, noting the way his dark, velvety eyes followed the young girl's every move.

Nauseating.

They took undisguised joy in one another, and her blood boiled to witness it. Bitterly, she marveled that they had come out of his bedroom at all.

But no, no! Miss Perfect-on-her-Pedestal was as pure as the driven snow.

Anatole would see to that, she thought wryly.

The stunning pair moved off down the intersecting hall, both raven-haired and beautiful of form, like matched horses. Silently, Julia watched them go. When they were out of sight, she turned away, folding her arms tightly over her chest.

So long as Princess Perfect was near, she knew she could not compete for Darius's attention, not really. Hell, she could be in bed with him only to realize he was thinking of that girl. It had happened before. She had no choice but to bide her time until Anatole returned to take Serafina away.

Unconsciously, Julia's rouged lips curved into a cold smile when she thought of the Russian prince. How amusing! The famous war hero had traveled all the way from Russia to woo the princess, and had stayed until the betrothal and alliance were drawn up, but Julia had quickly found that the bridegroom was as vulnerable to temptation as any man.

Shoving away from the wall to prowl silently down the hall, Julia recalled with smug pleasure the minor vengeance she had taken on Serafina, just for spite. Likewise on the battlefield, Anatole, the great, golden brute, had been every inch the conqueror in bed.

When Darius and Serafina came to the king's privy council chamber, he opened the door for her. She brushed by Darius into the oak-paneled room and found that her father had not yet arrived to meet them.

She swayed nonchalantly toward one of the two leather-bound chairs before the massive desk and plopped down into it, swinging her legs over one side, lightly kicking her feet. Darius shut the door and strolled toward her, hands in his coat pockets.

"Your Highness?"

She examined the tips of her tresses for split ends, mentally rehearsing her strategy to make Papa assign Darius to her. "Would you quit calling me that? Did it ever occur to you that I might hate being the princess?" she asked idly. "What is it?"

"I just wanted to say . . ."

She looked over in surprise at his struggling tone.

He stared at her, mute, his inky eyes full of unreadable emotion.

"Yes?" she asked gently.

He shrugged slightly and lowered his head. "Thanks for the stitches."

Slowly, she smiled at him. "You're welcome, Santiago."

"Don't be afraid about those spies, you hear? I'll take care of everything," he said with a good-boy earnestness that touched the very core of her heart.

"And who will take care of you?"

He tapped his chest.

"Of course. Yourself," she said stiffly, lowering her gaze.

"No, I wear the medal here, remember?" he asked softly. "The Virgin."

She looked up again, startled. He offered her an almost bashful half-smile, and for a long moment she merely stared at him, contemplating what was perhaps the single greatest mystery about him: *How can a man be so ruthless, and at the same time, somehow, so . . . pure?*

He was very still, then he walked toward her with slow, measured paces.

There was a look in his dark eyes that made her heart begin to pound with a wild thrill. She watched him round the back of her chair. When he stood behind her, he reached down and gently tugged one end of the bow she'd tied around her hair. The white ribbon came undone and he pulled it free.

"I'm stealing this," he whispered.

Tilting her head back against the chair, she smiled in languorous pleasure. "Take whatever you want from me."

"You shouldn't give a man such invitations," he told her with a dark smile.

"Not just any man," she said.

He avoided her gaze as he considered this in silence, combing his fingers lightly through her hair.

"Mm," she breathed, closing her eyes, heart racing as he slid his fingers slowly through her curls. He had never touched her this way before. Her head reeled.

"I like your hair down," he murmured at length, sifting it through his hands.

"Then I shall always wear it so," she sighed.

He said nothing, arranging her hair in front of her shoulders however he willed, playing with it, smoothing it against her skin. Slowly, he pressed a length of it along her neck. Inch by inch, he ironed a curl flat with his fingertips down across her chest, stopping at her neckline. When he released it, it popped back up into place, but his fingers remained where they were.

Eyes closed, she drifted, basking in the pleasure of his touch. She could feel him staring at her breasts, for their crests swelled to aching hardness with his hands so near them, so warm on her skin. For a moment, perversely, a part of her was glad of what Philippe had done, forcing Darius to look at her. It was right that Darius should be the first man to see her body— not Anatole. She held her breath as he tenderly explored her chest and shoulders with soft, gliding caresses, tracing her collarbones and the little notch between them.

Her whole body went heavy with sweet lethargy. He ran his fingertips gently up the curve of her throat with an expert touch, then behind her ears, playing with her hair again.

"Such beautiful hair," he whispered. "I am memorizing every naughty little curl."

"I say, Darius, are you flirting with me?" she asked, her voice dreamy and drugged.

"Why, no, child," he murmured. "That would be against the rules."

Just then, through the door and down the long hall, they both could hear her father coming, sweeping closer like a cheerful storm, bellowing orders to a lackey.

She flicked her eyes open and looked up in wonder and tor- ment, meeting Darius's tempestuous gaze. Wrapping the white ribbon around his hand, then slipping it into his pocket, he paced across the dim room. There, he turned to her, leaning against the bookcase in an idle pose of nonchalant elegance, hands in pockets.

He watched her intensely. "It was good to see you again."

"You make it sound as if this is goodbye."

"It is," he whispered, his eyes soulful, luminous in the shadows.

"Oh? And where might you be going?" Linking her fingers, she waited archly for his reply.

He didn't give one.

"Of course. Top secret, as usual." She feigned a yawn. "You know, you really are the most charming hypocrite, Santiago."

His broad shoulders stiffened. His onyx eyes narrowed at her. "Why do you call me that?"

"You think you are getting rid of me. That's the only reason you touched me."

He absorbed her accusation, but he did not deny it, nor did he apologize for the startling liberty he had taken. Hands in pockets, he merely stared at her for a moment, then lowered his head.

Fool, she thought, adoring him. It was that rascal boy-thief in him, she supposed. He thought nothing would be given to him freely, only what he could steal.

"Forget it," he muttered. "It was a mistake. Just . . . remember me. And be happy. That's all I ask."

"How, Darius?" she asked with a joyless laugh. "Tell me how to be happy and I assure you, I will try. Better yet, show me. You will have adequate chance to do so when we are rusticating."

He looked up in shock.

She gave him a serene smile.

Safest to give him a little warning or else he might not forgive her for pulling rank on him, she calculated. It was all very well for his pretty mouth to tell lie after lie, but if ever anyone lied to him, he could easily turn dangerous.

Instantly he pushed away from the bookcase. "What are you scheming?" he whispered, glancing at the door, then back at her, his eyes ablaze.

"I'm going to repay your loyalty whether you like it or not," she told him stoutly. "You need a rest, Darius. Your wound is deep."

"Absolutely not, and that is final!"

"It is not final," she said with a laugh of protest. "It will be fun."

They both glanced at the door, for they could hear the king as he called a question to the palace steward, still a way off down the hall. They heard the old man's unctuous voice, delaying His Majesty.

They ignored it.

"Not possible! I've got huge responsibilities riding on me, Serafina—"

"Aye, the weight of the world, poor sweet."

"I will not have you interfering in my affairs!"

"Somebody's got to take care of you, if you won't take care of yourself. It's my fault you were hurt, anyway. I feel responsible."

"Nonsense, I was only doing my job."

"Well, maybe it's my job to take care of you."

He gave her a baffled look, then glanced at the door again. "I can't go with you. You have no comprehension what is at stake!" he whispered angrily.

"I know perfectly well what's at stake," she said indignantly. "I'm the one who is to pay the price, aren't I? But I have a little time of freedom left, and I shall spend it as I choose, with whom I choose." She folded her arms over her chest and leveled a pout at him. "I'm the Princess Royal and you can't tell me what to do."

"Serafina," he clipped out.

She watched with interest as he came striding toward her.

"You will not interfere. Do you understand me? I am needed elsewhere. There is a crisis—"

"There is always a crisis," she said in boredom. "Someone else can handle it this time. Must you always hoard the glory? Give another man a chance."

"I don't hoard the glory!" he scoffed, stopping midstride with a lofty look of righteous affront. "I merely want the job done right!"

"It will be, my dear," she soothed. "You refuse to take care of yourself, so obviously I'm going to have to take care of you. Do you so hate the idea of spending time with me?" She sighed, not really wanting to know the answer to that. "It's for your own good."

His eyes narrowed. "This is because of Julia, isn't it? This is about jealousy. You don't own me," he said savagely. "You have *no* claim on me."

She stared at him, then lowered her head, saying nothing. He could kick and buck and behave in however ugly a manner he liked. She was not backing down.

He must have realized he had hurt her, however, because he came to stand in front of her, near the desk. "Don't do this to me," he said heavily. "Can't you see it is impossible?"

"I don't see why you object."

"You and I?" he whispered fiercely, bending down to glare at her. "Locked up together in the middle of nowhere? Do you have any idea what could—" He faltered, swallowing hard.

"What could happen?" she finished for him. "Why, anything, I suppose. Maybe we'll finally be friends again. Or, maybe we'll kill each other, I don't know. Then again, maybe, if I'm lucky, you'll get the urge to tie me up." She slanted him a wicked smile full of mirth.

Staring at her in shock, he loomed over her, giving her his darkest, severest, most intimidating look, but with Papa on his way, it didn't much scare her.

"You will not do this," he vowed.

"Oh, yes, I will."

He stared at her as if no one had ever defied him before. Of course, even she had to admit that it was only her rank and her ability to manage Papa that gave her the advantage.

"It's for your own good," she said with finality.

Darius cursed under his breath in exasperation, pivoted, and strode away from her. "The answer is no, and that is final. No mischief. I am warning you."

"My Papa's coming, Santiago. Don't make me blackmail you," she said sweetly. "I believe you have my hair ribbon in your pocket?"

His eyes widened, then narrowed to blazing slits. "You treacherous *brat*."

"You taught me everything I know." She gave him an angelic smile, twirling a curl around and around her finger.

CHAPTER
❧ FIVE ❧

She can't do this to me, he thought desperately. Only, he knew full well she could. If he protested too much to the king, it would look like he was being unreasonable, even suspicious.

"I'm warning you," he whispered to her, knowing it was futile. He knew from long experience that when she took an idea into her head, there was no stopping her.

At that moment, the door banged back and there stood Darius's boyhood benefactor, His Majesty, King Lazar di Fiore, a bold and seasoned warrior with black hair shot through with silver at the temples. His powerfully built frame filled the doorway, and his pirate grin broke out across his rugged, weathered face at the sight of Darius.

"Greenling!" he boomed with a hearty laugh.

The room got smaller as the king strode in, filling it with his forceful, charismatic presence. Darius offered a quick, informal bow, but Lazar clapped him in a bear hug, affectionately thumping him square on his wounded shoulder.

Darius grimaced.

"Papa, you silly oaf, be careful! He's hurt."

Lazar released him and turned with an inquiring look to his firstborn. "Oh, there you are. Where the devil have you been? You'd better get back to the ballroom or your mother's going to strangle you. She's been looking for you for two hours. You know, Cricket, it really is considered bad form to leave a ball thrown in your own honor, no matter how tedious the thing is." Then he turned back to Darius. "Hurt, she says?"

He smirked arrogantly. "A scratch."

Lazar grinned in approval of his bravado. "Pure steel, this one, my girl. Make no mistake!"

She rolled her eyes. One slim knee crossed over the other, her slippered toe bobbed rhythmically. Pretty as a picture, he thought, but well he knew in her haughty mood she was a force to be reckoned with, damned little Queen of Sheba. Oh, she was biding her time, watching him coolly, matter-of-factly, her slender arms folded under her sumptuous bosom, that luscious pout still fixed on her lips.

Lazar turned to him. "What brings you back early? I thought you'd be escorting Tyurinov's party from Moscow."

Serafina cast Darius a wary look. He cleared his throat.

"Sir," he said delicately, "perhaps you'd better sit down."

Lazar lifted his chin as his dark, penetrating eyes narrowed. "Oh, hell. What now?" He walked wearily around to his desk, pausing to look out the wide bow window with a sigh.

While he stood for a moment peering out at the darkened landscape, his back to them, Darius and Serafina glared at each other.

Stop fighting me! she mouthed at him.

He narrowed his eyes and shook his head in warning threat.

They both snapped back forward again with innocent looks when the king turned around, pulled out the chair, sat, and rubbed his eyes for a moment with the heels of his hands. "All right. Hit me."

"French spies have infiltrated the palace and tried to abduct Her Highness tonight, about an hour and a half ago."

Lazar stared at him incredulously, then his weathered face darkened with storm. He turned to his daughter. "Are you all right?" he asked fiercely.

"I'm fine," she replied, then her gaze slid sideward to Darius. "Thanks to Santiago."

"What happened?" Lazar asked in a murderous tone.

Darius recounted a sanitized version of the night's events. At every second, he was wholly aware of the elegant young woman beside him, her pose stiff, chin high, her proud gaze down.

When Darius was through with the report, Lazar looked at Serafina. She didn't move, but she swallowed hard. Without a word, her father rose, walked around his desk, and bent down to give her a huge hug.

Darius stood there, uncomfortable with the display of affection. "Sir, Her Highness should be taken to the D'Este Villa and guarded. In the meantime, I will eradicate the remaining members of Saint-Laurent's ring—"

"In a moment, lad," the king murmured. "First let me see to my daughter."

Serafina suddenly hugged him back and began crying again.

Darius turned away, stifling a sigh. Oh, she was her daddy's girl, all right. He would never get used to her instant, spontaneous expressions of whatever she happened to be feeling. He wanted to be disgusted with her and with her softhearted father, who would unfailingly set the pressures of the world aside for his brood, but Darius found he was most disgusted with himself.

Simple, human touch, he thought. Of course. That's what she had needed when she was crying before in the little courtyard. He had known it, but he had been unable to give it to her, afraid to risk it. Afraid that if he held her, he would kiss her, and if he kissed her, he would touch her and please her until she invited him inside her. Then he could never hold back. He would take her, give her every inch of himself. Gladly, he would drown himself in her and let the consequences be damned.

Oh, he must *not* be assigned to guard her, he thought feverishly, for she didn't try to disguise her desire for him any more than she hid her tears.

Take whatever you want from me. What a thing to say!

Shaken, he took a few steps away, leaving father and daughter in privacy. He heard Lazar talking softly to her but he couldn't make out all the words, nor did he want to.

He could scarcely remember now what lies and excuses he had spouted at her, but there was no way to tell her the pathetic truth about why he had refused her too-tempting suggestion. Even his urgency to go snuff out Napoleon was just his own excuse to himself, he admitted, for he could safely afford up to a week's delay.

The real reason was because he knew exactly what would happen. She would pet him and dote on him and lull him with her softness, her gentleness, her caring and tenderness, until he lowered his guard and opened himself to her, and when she really knew him—when she looked inside of him through the eyes of a woman, not a child, and saw that he was nothing— she would stop idolizing him and, oh, God, if that happened, it were better if he'd never been born.

"Are you sure you're all right?" he heard Lazar ask her gently at last.

Behind him, he heard her sniffle.

"Yes. I'm better now, Papa. Honestly. Just hearing him describe it again . . . I'm sorry."

Darius kept pacing at a respectful distance, but when he heard his name mentioned, he paused.

"Papa, Darius was so brave. You should have seen him. If he hadn't been there . . . But he was, just as he always is! And he had this enormous cut and he didn't even mention it! He just wanted to make sure I was unharmed. He is the best, bravest, noblest person *ever*."

He couldn't breathe for a moment. Her words went clean through him like a silver blade, forcing the air out of his lungs. Heart pounding, he stole a glance at the royal pair.

"I know he is, my dear."

Serafina was staring up at the king earnestly. Darius knew all too well the effect of those eyes. "Please, Papa, I know you must send men to guard me, but please let Darius come with me. I'll be frightened out of my wits every second unless he's there."

Half turned away, his head lowered, Darius held his breath, waiting for the king's reply.

"Of course, kitten," Lazar said gently, giving her a kiss on the forehead. "I wouldn't dream of trusting you to anyone else."

And there it was.

Darius was very still, elated, agonized, humbled.

How could he protest after such a heartfelt plea? He could not. Once more, she conquered with softness, and he feared her because her single weapon was the only one he could not use or wield or even comprehend. Against it, he had no defense, no past experience to draw upon. He couldn't fight it. He could only run and keep running, even when he wanted with all his heart to be caught and forced to surrender.

A few minutes later, he had his orders.

He put up a show of protest strictly out of pride. "Sir, anyone can guard her. Once she's removed from the palace, the danger to her is very small. Who are you going to get to catch the spies?"

"I don't know. Orsini, maybe."

"Orsini." Darius rolled his eyes. "Fat pig. He'll fumble it."

"He's not that bad. I can't use you," the king said reasonably, visibly amused at his assessment. "They know you're here, obviously. They'll be expecting you. I've got to put someone on them they'll never suspect. Besides, you got rid of Saint-Laurent, who was the most dangerous of them, from what you've said."

"And if they send more men?"

"Exactly my point," Lazar agreed. "If they try to follow her, you're the man I want in command to fight them off."

"They won't live long enough to follow her if you let me go after them. Orsini!" he scoffed.

"You don't seem to understand." Lazar clapped him on the arm and gave him a fatherly look. He glanced toward Serafina, then lowered his voice. "Am I to send Orsini with her? Do you take my meaning?"

Darius abruptly shut his mouth, realizing.

"One day, you'll have children, Dare, and when you do, for your sanity's sake, pray you never have beautiful daughters," Lazar said. "You are the only man in the kingdom that I know I can trust with her."

Darius absorbed this and felt a bit sick.

"Yes, sir," he mumbled, crestfallen, feeling the noose tighten. Well, he thought in defeat, he would merely have to ignore her the whole time. Treat her coldly. Shut her out.

Hell, he was an expert at that by now.

He noticed Serafina watching him, then the king leaned toward him. "And when we find these French bastards," he added, "you and I will personally tear their bloody throats out. They go after my daughter, they've crossed the line." He looked away so she could not see his face, his eyes blazing with fury. "By God, I shall go mad with rage. My *daughter*."

"Sir, remember, now, it's just politics. It's not personal," Darius warned, as if he himself had not slashed Philippe Saint-Laurent to ribbons for the same reason less than an hour ago. "Anyway, she's her father's daughter, a real fighter, and she's all right. She kept a cool head. She handled herself in a manner most worthy of her line."

"Aye. That's my girl." Lazar nodded and glanced at Serafina, his lips pursed in a thin line. "You watch out for her."

"With my life, sir."

The king gave a single, hard nod. Their brief consultation concluded, Darius took leave of them to make all the necessary preparations, starting with finding and briefing Orsini, the current head of security. Before he left the room, he bowed to the princess in the expected courtesy.

"Thank you," she said meaningfully with a deep gaze into his eyes. She seemed careful not to gloat.

"Your servant, my lady," he said coolly, but unseen by the king, he made certain to give her the hardest, meanest look he could contrive.

* * *

"*Look at him.* You are so lucky," Els sighed as she stared hungrily at Darius. Her real name was Elisabetta but nobody called her that. She was a tall, leggy redhead of twenty-two with green eyes and no morals, but Serafina adored her flair for the outrageous. "He radiates pure *sex*," Els added in a scandalous whisper.

Scarcely an hour had passed and already the unmarked coach waited under the porte cochere to whisk Serafina away into hiding. She stood under the Roman arches in the warmly lit side foyer saying goodbye to her two best friends, while Darius stood a short distance away conversing quietly with her mother and father.

He had given her stern orders not to tell anyone what had happened in the maze, nor where they were going, but she wished she could have unburdened her heart to her friends about her ordeal tonight.

"I can't believe your parents trust him. He is so barbaric," Cara said, watching Darius in mingled terror and fascination. At nineteen, Cara, a petite, blue-eyed blond, was the youngest and most staid of the inseparable trio.

After what had happened tonight, Serafina was hugely relieved that her attempt to matchmake between Cara and Philippe Saint-Laurent had failed.

Philippe had shown an interest in Cara, but after allowing the Frenchman to escort her on a turn through the garden, the petite blond had reported back to Serafina and Els that she found Philippe too forward, arrogant, and smooth-talking.

Presently, Cara turned to Serafina with a worried gaze. "Do you mean to say your mother isn't even sending a chaperon?"

Serafina tore her stare from Darius. "Well, the hour's so late. Mama said in the morning she's going to find someone for me, but my father told her not to worry about it."

"Not to worry?" Cara cried, her blue eyes widening.

"They trust Darius. He used to be my guard—it just makes sense. Besides, if they implied they doubted his almighty honor, he would be mortally insulted."

"I know Their Majesties trust him, but darling," Cara said in distress, "what will people say?"

"Oh, who cares what people say about anything?" the feisty Els remarked, absently fixing her sleeve. "People are stupid."

Serafina ignored her. "No one is going to know. Mama will say I am going to visit my elderly Aunt Isabelle, who is too old and frail to travel down to town for the wedding."

"But surely your mother could send one of her ladies-in-waiting," Cara suggested.

"Darius won't have it. He says no one can be trusted until the enemies in our midst are unmasked. Besides, he said those women would only be a distraction to his men."

"To his men! Ha. To him, he means—because he's slept with them all!" Els whispered wickedly, her green eyes sparkling.

"He has not!" Serafina retorted. "It's just more unnecessary people to protect. Look, it's almost time to go," she said more softly. "Are you sure we are all smoothed out, then? I don't want to go away with bad feelings still between us—"

"Of course we are!" both girls chimed, and they both hugged her.

She hugged them back, glad to make peace after their quarrel in the ballroom hours ago. She was still shaken by the realization that perhaps they were no more true friends to her than the rest of her coterie, who valued her chiefly, she knew, because proximity to royalty boosted their own status. She had asked the girls to come to Moscow with her to bolster her courage for the first few months in her new home, but at once they had given her excuses.

"We're both so sorry. We just can't do it," Cara explained earnestly. "I can't leave my family."

"It's my health," Els said hastily. "I always get sick in the cold. I would die under all that snow—unless I had a man like your Anatole to keep me warm," she teased.

"You're welcome to him," Serafina replied dryly. "Well, never mind. It was just an idea. No hard feelings."

"Are you sure?" Els asked prettily.

"I'm sure."

"I don't see what fault anyway you find with that golden god you are marrying," Els told her. "He's perfect. Besides, he's rich, famous . . ."

"He'll be away at war most of the time," Cara offered helpfully.

"She's right," Els said, then paused. "But if you really don't fancy him . . . I think you may have found your solution."

"What do you mean?" Serafina asked.

"After you are married, take him," she said carefully, glancing at Darius, "for your lover."

Serafina turned pale.

Els laughed. "Why not?" she whispered. "It's the obvious solution. You must have a lover, of course. All truly elegant women have lovers."

Serafina recovered her composure abruptly. "I'm afraid Russia is not like Italy, darling. The men there are too uncivilized for modern marriages."

She had been warned by Anatole himself.

"Simple. Then you'll just have to sneak."

Serafina burst out in shocked, appalled laughter. "You are so wicked! Oh, Els! How shall I live without you?" She gave her a big hug.

"Serafina!" her mother called suddenly.

"Coming!" she answered. She looked back at them in distress. "Don't forget to stop by and visit Kwee-Kwee, and give Bianca some catnip. Write to me!"

"Where will you be if we need you?" Cara asked earnestly.

Serafina almost blurted it out, unused to hiding anything from her friends, but she saw a disturbing flicker of something in Cara's blue eyes that reminded her of Darius's warning. "Some country hovel. I don't really know where."

Inwardly, Serafina frowned to herself. Surely she had imagined that fleeting, hard look in her fair-haired friend's expression, she thought, for even now Cara was giving her another worried frown of concern. "If you can't have any chaperons, at least I ought to come with you. I can be ready in a few minutes—"

Serafina squeezed her hand. "Thank you, I wish you could, but Darius is being strict about this. He says it's too dangerous."

"Serafina!" the queen called again, starting toward them.

"Uh-oh, let's get out of here," Els murmured guiltily, knowing full well that the queen disapproved of her ever since she had seduced the crown prince a few months ago.

Charming Rafe had bragged of it high and low, but after the queen caught wind of it, he'd been like a dog with his tail between his legs. Serafina had had to argue for all she was worth for Els to be allowed to stay at Belfort and remain in her company.

Cara, on the other hand, beamed at the queen and went sailing over to her. Serafina often thought that Cara would have been the perfect daughter for Mama instead of herself, for they were a hopeless pair of goody-goodies.

Els gave Serafina a quick kiss on the cheek. "Be safe," she whispered, then vanished.

When Serafina joined the other two, Cara took leave of her with a hug. "Godspeed, dearest," she said, then hurried off.

Serafina was left standing with her mother.

If someone as self-centered, pleasure-loving, and lazy as herself held anything sacred, Serafina reflected, it was her mother. Outwardly, to her friends, she might mock the queen's charitable crusades, but inwardly, Serafina respected her mother to the point of awe.

Queen Allegra di Fiore had a presence that commanded with compassion. At thirty-eight, she was unshakable, and, as Serafina had learned at an early age, quite impossible to lie to. She never had to raise her voice; there was more discipline in one disappointed look from her than in the shrill scolding of twenty haggard governesses, and it worked on the lords of Parliament as effectively as it did on her children.

She was beautiful, with ivory, freckled skin and gold-streaked auburn hair, little grays here and there that she merely laughed at. She moved softly in spite of her large, pregnant belly, and she embodied everything Serafina knew she herself would never be—wisdom and power and grace. She was like a mighty angel, and Papa often said she was the best thing that had happened to Ascencion in seven hundred years.

No, she reflected, she was more like her father. Wily, stormy, stubborn, and proud. Even the strange color of her eyes came from her father's side of the family. The violet hue appeared in the royal line only once every few generations, she'd been told.

Her mother gave her a gentle, encouraging smile and slipped her arm around her. "Come. You're not frightened, are you?"

"No, Mama."

Arm in arm, they walked toward the two tall, dark men.

Mama stopped to embrace her as Darius finished up with the king.

Serafina only half-listened to the queen's soft assurances that Darius would take good care of her and that she must do exactly as he said, for her safety depended on it. Head on her mother's soft shoulder, she stared at nothing, wondering if it was a mistake to have foisted herself off on him.

He had given her the cruelest look. What if she couldn't make him forgive her for pulling rank on him? Of all the men in the kingdom who fell at her feet, why was it that the only one who held her interest was the one who wanted nothing to do with her?

Well, she thought, he was stuck with her now.

In the past hour, her protector had proved frightfully efficient. Already he had sent outriders ahead to secure the safe house property that would be their shared country home for the next week or so until the spies were caught. He had stopped by her apartments and put the fear of God into her poor maid, Pia, with one terrifying, tranquil smile, asking her with Lucifer's own courtesy to please pack her things quickly.

Giving her mother a final kiss on each freckled cheek, Serafina stole another peek at Darius from the corner of her eye. The candlelight burnished the ends of his glossy black hair with gold and warmed his skin to a rich amber. His dark, mysterious eyes held a sharp look of sober watchfulness.

He glanced at her as she left her mother and approached to say goodbye to Papa. Her towering sire held her in a warm embrace, then looked down at her with his warm, crooked grin.

"Behave yourself," he said, giving her cheek a pinch. "I mean it."

She bobbed prettily on her toes, smiling at him. She adored the man. "Yes, Papa."

Darius glanced at her. "Ready?"

She nodded. Her heart began to pound. She clutched her reticule demurely in both suddenly sweating hands.

Darius kissed her mother on the cheek and murmured to her not to worry about a thing, then shook hands firmly with the king.

"Keep us informed. I'll await your courier," Lazar murmured.

Darius nodded as he opened the thick wooden door and held it for her. Immediately the hall filled with the hiss of the pouring rain. Darius did not look at her as she brushed past him.

The thunder and lightning had stopped, but rain coursed in little waterfalls from the eaves of the porte cochere. It was a warm night.

As Serafina stood waiting under the iron chandelier, she glanced up at the moths swarming around the sturdy candles, risking their wings over the fire. Then, through the screen of rain, she stared out at the dark landscape, seeing in every pooled shadow Henri with his broken neck, or Darius wrenching his knife out of Philippe's breast.

She could not believe she was the object of so much conflict and international commotion.

She shrugged deeper into her smartly tailored, pearl-gray traveling gown and studied her elaborate military escort. The coach was flanked by armed men on horses, Darius's hand-picked squad of about thirty men.

Her parents stood in the doorway while Darius jogged ahead, going lightly down the steps to the coach, where he opened the door for her, his head ducked slightly against the downpour. As she hurried toward him, he glanced into the roomy interior of the coach as if checking it for monsters, then he offered his hand and assisted her inside.

She settled into the velvet squabs, struck by the fanciful notion that she could almost pretend they were newlyweds and he was taking her away from her family as her husband.

The thought pained her.

She leaned toward the coach window and blew her parents a kiss, pausing to watch them standing together, arm in arm, with the light of their love almost visible around them.

I will never know how that feels, she thought in strange detachment.

Meanwhile, Darius walked up and down the line of men, checking on everyone one last time. His black Andalusian stallion had been tethered to the back of the carriage. He tugged on the horse's lead rope to make sure it was securely tied, gave the restless animal a brisk pat on the neck, then strode back up to the side of the coach. He accepted two rifles from a subordinate and sprang up into the roomy coach with her.

He turned his back on her to secure the rifles in the rack above his seat, but he sat down at last on the velvet seat opposite her, tugging his impeccable black jacket neatly into place. He leaned over, slammed the coach door, and flipped its three locks into position.

He stared at her for a second with an intent look, his eyes slightly narrowed, as if he were scanning a mental checklist.

He sliced her parents a crisp wave out the window, then banged on the coach to signal the driver to move.

They were off.

Serafina stared at him, wide-eyed in the dark, her heart in her throat as it finally sank in that she truly had gotten her way. For the next few days, perhaps even a week, she had Darius Santiago, her idol, her demon, all to herself. She wasn't sure if she was ecstatic or terrified.

Neither of them spoke as the jostling vehicle gathered speed.

The cavalcade clattered through the gates and pulled out onto the puddled road. Open fields soon gave way to sparse woods, and still they said nothing. Their silence seemed to magnify the rolling, creaking noises of the coach, with the rain drumming on the roof. The ground rose; their destination lay in the cool, forested highlands of Ascencion.

Though Serafina tried to fix her attention on the landscape rolling by, the weather made it too black to see much. From time to time she peered anxiously into the man-shaped pool of shadow across from her. She could feel Darius watching her. Unspoken questions hung on the air, filling the claustrophobic space of the coach.

Fear whispered through her as he held his silence until she couldn't bear it anymore.

"How does your shoulder feel?" she attempted meekly.

In answer, he merely pinned a chilling, luminous stare on her, half his dramatic face contoured in shadow, half in the rain's lurid glow.

She shrank back slightly against the squabs. "Don't be mean. It was Papa's decision. I only told the truth."

He said nothing.

"Darius," she pleaded softly, "you're scaring me."

"You should be scared. Christ, don't you know that by now? Don't you see what I am?"

"No, what are you?"

He shook his head in disgust. The road wended. She looked

away, staring out the window for all she was worth. They passed a farm in a vale. The road continued to climb.

She heard him move, heard the click of the little door to the compartment under his seat, then she could feel him come nearer. He put a pillow on one end of her seat. He held a blanket in his hand.

"Lie down."

"I'm not tired—"

"Yes, you are. It's three in the morning. That's past even your bedtime."

"You don't know my bedtime."

"One-thirty."

She stared at his black silhouette for a long moment, taken aback. "How do you know that?"

"Gypsy magic. Understand something, my dear," he said blandly. "You wanted this arrangement. You got your way, and now you're going to have to live with it. You will sleep when I say sleep, wake when I say wake, eat when I say eat, breathe when I say breathe. For the next week or so, Your Highness, you are mine, and I will not tolerate any nonsense out of you. Cry if you don't like it. See what it gets you." He threw the light blanket at her. "Now lie down and don't make another sound."

She was outraged. On the other hand, she knew when argument was futile.

Bristling, she decided there was no point in being uncomfortable. She spread out the blanket over her and lay down on her side, resting her head on the pillow. She unfastened the top button of her high-necked traveling gown, and as an afterthought reached down and slipped off her doeskin boots. They dropped, first one, then the other, onto the carriage floor.

Darius was very still, then he moved toward her and tucked the blanket under her stockinged feet.

She stared at him as he settled back into his seat, braced his elbow on the edge of the window, and rested his cheek in his hand. There was a silence of several minutes.

"Darius?"

He sighed without looking at her. "Yes, Serafina?"

She hesitated. "I'm worried about you, Darius."

"Serafina." He cast her a weary look. "Don't make a project of me."

"I can see you are unhappy. Am I to turn a blind eye to your sorrow, after all you've done for my family and for me? Am I not to care for you at all?"

"That's exactly right," he said sharply. "You are not to care for me and I am not to care for you, and that's the end of it."

She stared at him. "We can't even be friends?"

"Friends," he scoffed. "What does that mean? No, we cannot be *friends*."

"Oh," she said softly, wounded. Then, after a moment, "Why?"

"Why," he merely echoed. There was a very long silence, filled with the pounding of the rain on the coach's roof. Then he spoke again, and his voice was very quiet. "It's too dangerous."

"Too dangerous for the great Santiago?" She lifted her head from the pillow but he refused to meet her stare, gazing out the carriage window at the night.

"Go to sleep, Your Highness," he said very quietly.

She knit her brow and laid her head back down on the pillow, watching him in silence.

Darius went on staring out into the darkness, his finely chiseled face expressionless, the blue reflection of raindrops on the glass sliding down his face like silent tears.

At last, she fell asleep, and only then he looked at her.

For a long time, he just stared while she slept, her luxuriant sable curls flowing around her, one pale, graceful hand hanging from the seat, bobbing slightly with the rocking of the coach. He forced his gaze away, raking a hand through his hair with a slow, carefully controlled sigh.

He yearned for a smoke.

For hours, he stared at the black nothing of the landscape, gazing at Serafina now and then, wondering what the hell he was going to do.

He'd had himself mentally prepared for death in a state of empty calm, no easy trick for someone whose survival instincts were so savagely powerful. All he had wanted was to stay numb until his job was done, but that trick was impossible when he was anywhere near her. She made him feel . . . so much. All he had wanted was peace, but she roused a storm in him, like the winds stirring the sea into a fury. Pain flooded and crashed inside his emptiness: He had ignored it too long, and now he feared there was more of it inside of him than any man could bear.

I have to get out of here.

Ah, but where could he go that these furies would not chase him? He had journeyed often to distant lands—deserts, mountains, seas. It was himself he could not escape.

He could only pray that that sweaty ox Orsini would catch the spies in time for him to make his rendezvous in Milan on schedule. How he was supposed to conduct himself with the Princess Royal in the meantime, Darius had no idea. He was not sure how he felt about her at the moment, only that it was not the simple matter of calm, responsible duty he ought to feel.

He trusted her.

He didn't trust her.

He craved her.

He feared her.

Obviously she had some kind of designs on him, as her insistence on his coming here with her showed. Perhaps she was thinking of a fling before her wedding, he thought a trifle bitterly. Another rich girl's adventure with the boy from the streets.

He lowered his head. The thought that she might want something like that from him hurt, but as he gazed at her, sleeping there like an angel, he couldn't believe it of her.

When they finally arrived at the villa, Darius gathered her into his arms and carried her inside. He stepped over the threshold and went up the stairs, his cut shoulder aching slightly under her slim weight. He found the best bedroom and laid her on the bed. She didn't wake.

He pulled the light cover over her and stared down at her pale, lovely face in the dark, stroking her hair softly for a moment. His heart clenched. *Why me? Why the hell are you fixed on me when the whole world is in love with you?*

He shook his head to himself, at a loss.

She stirred a little, turning her delicate, heart-shaped face, then stilled, one hand loosely curled near her cheek on the pillow.

He leaned down and kissed her smooth forehead, then left without making a sound.

CHAPTER
⚜ SIX ⚜

Serafina's eyes fluttered open to a pale pink room suffused with golden light.

She lay quite still, hovering between waking and sleep in that moment where there was no future and no past, and all was bliss. A fresh, summery mountain breeze blew in through the open window, stirring a few strands of her hair to tickle her cheek. She merely lay there, soaking in the wonderful light and the feeling of soul-deep calm.

She heard her maid's voice outside and realized the coach must have arrived bearing those household staff members Darius deemed trustworthy, along with the supply wagons carrying the rest of her luggage and the soldiers' provisions for their extended stay.

Darius.

She gave a slow, luxurious stretch and folded her arms under her head, smiling up at the ceiling like a satisfied lover, a bride waking after her wedding night.

Vaguely she recalled him carrying her into the villa and placing her gently on this bed. She was still garbed in her traveling gown.

Too bad he didn't undress me, she thought wryly. On second thought, if the greatest lover in the kingdom ever decided to take her clothes off her, she had blasted well better be awake to enjoy it.

Don't even joke about it, she chided herself, a shadow

falling across her sunny mood as she thought of her husband-to-be.

Anatole had already warned her about his rules and expectations, and she knew he would be on the lookout for any interest she showed in another man, however innocent. It seemed that the fact she had refused all marriage proposals for the three years since her debut had led him to conclude she was a vain coquette who enjoyed the limelight and thrived on male flattery.

He had dared to say to her that she needed taming. Oh, he had been very frank about his conclusions, rudely questioning her morals, nearly hinting that he doubted her chastity.

Papa would have put him through a wall if he had heard Anatole speaking to her that way, she thought. Her brother, Prince Rafael, would have called him out. What Darius would have done to him, she didn't dare imagine.

Fortunately, she had been alone with him, a chaperon walking several yards behind. She had swallowed the blazing retorts she could have given him, striving at least to make a show of obedience. Her country needed his armies, she had told herself over and over. Bearing the general's arrogance was a small price to pay to protect Papa. How could Anatole know, after all, that the real reason she had been holding out for so long was that she had been waiting in vain for her Spanish knight to come to his senses?

Obviously, *she* was the one who needed to come to her senses, she thought with a scowl.

Restlessly, she got up from the bed and pushed these thoughts away, pleased with her own resiliency after last night's ordeals. Perhaps it was the mountain air, but she could not remember the last time she had slept so peacefully.

She glanced about at her surroundings. The villa was not a grand place, she gathered, if this room was any indication. The plaster on the walls was wavy, a spider had built a palatial web in the corner, and everything was dusty. Beneath her stockinged feet, the floorboards creaked noisily as she walked toward the vanity, fearing to see what sort of tangle her hair was in without its hundred strokes the night before.

She paused to gaze down at the colorful but faded tapestry rug arranged on the floor spanning the foot of the bed. It depicted a fantasy of eternal spring, a celebration of life, with youths and maidens dancing around a maypole, and the world in flower around them.

Loosening her dress with an absent expression, she was gazing down wistfully at the pastoral idyll when suddenly a low-toned Spanish voice broke into her thoughts.

Glancing, wide-eyed, toward the window, she tiptoed over and edged one corner of the sheer white curtain aside, peeking down at Darius. She clenched a handful of the gauzy curtain, feeling giddy.

Beautiful, beautiful, beautiful, she thought with a sinking, inward little sigh.

The color of his complexion was glorious, golden-bronze in the morning light, while his jet-black hair was slicked back, still slightly damp from his morning ablutions, she presumed. She indulged herself in a leisurely study of the lean, elegant length of him from this safe distance.

His muscled build was sleek, elegant, and superbly athletic, not bulky and herculean like Anatole's. His arms were powerful in pristine white shirtsleeves, his waist flat in the snug black waistcoat. Her eye followed the sinuous curve of his back, then slid downward appreciatively to the charming curves of his backside.

The palace ladies were right, she decided with a private smile. Every inch of him was quite perfect.

He stood with his assistant on the steps leading down from the porch. As Alec scribbled down every word he uttered, Darius squinted against the sun and watched his squad at their tasks with a critical eye. In his right hand he held his sword, point in the dust. He was twirling it idly with a flick of his nimble, thief's fingers, while in his left he held a cup of coffee.

Presently he took a sip, then lifted his sword and propped it jauntily over his shoulder, scanning the men present, she supposed, for someone worthy of practicing against him. Though he was an acknowledged master of the dagger, the sword, guns, cannons, cavalry, and even some oriental weapons with names she couldn't pronounce, daily training was fundamental to his spartan credo.

Well, she thought, as his physician, she did not intend to allow him any swordplay for at least three days until his gash had had a decent interval to begin healing.

She spun away lightly from the window and hurried to freshen up and dress, eager to go to him.

Located about twenty miles from the royal palace and the capital city of Belfort, the D'Este Villa had been built in the Baroque period, fallen into ruin, then was restored thirty years ago in the violent period of upheaval during the king's youth in exile, when Genoa had ruled Ascencion with an iron fist.

Behind its fortified wall, the five-hundred-acre property was designed for self-sufficiency. There was a garrison with a barracks and a small magazine and a stable that housed fifty horses. Chicken coops, sheds for goats and sheep, and a stocked pond kept the kitchen supplied.

After laying the sleeping princess in her bed, Darius had spent the night getting rained on and carrying out a hundred necessary tasks overseeing the process of turning the country villa once more into an army camp. He made sure the horses were stabled, the armaments and powder kegs properly stored in the magazine. He'd held a brief meeting with his squadron, assigning men to their posts in the four quadrants of the property, dispensing other orders.

Overnight, one of the two wagons carrying his men's provisions arrived, reporting that the other had become stuck in the mud miles down the road. He sent a contingent out to dislodge it, and when it arrived, he found it was also carrying the four savage guard dogs he had ordered. The wild barking of the animals gave him a headache, born partly from hunger. He marveled that the noise didn't bring Serafina out to look around, but hers was the slumber of the innocents.

Finally, he had inspected the wall, walking the entire perimeter to make sure all areas were in good repair. By the time the rain stopped and the sun rose amid the morning's fog, he'd turned the initial chaos into a well-oiled military machine.

Now he was exhausted, but he still had to organize his headquarters in the villa's little library. He had maps of the local terrain to review as well as correspondence to catch up on and the books of his own small ship-and-trade firm to balance, and the ongoing headache from his worthless inherited holdings in Spain to be answered.

His shoulder hurt. He was half-starved but breakfast wasn't ready yet, so he stood on the wooden porch, smoked a final cheroot, and took satisfaction in watching the order he had created, each man under his command doing exactly what he should be doing, exactly when he should be doing it.

It was a sight he would have liked to have thrown in his father's face.

He went into the musty little library that was to be his office and found his aide unrolling the maps for his review, efficiently weighing the scrolled edges with paperweights.

The boy was a godsend.

Alec glanced dubiously at his haggard commanding officer. "Breakfast will be ready in a few minutes, sir. Shall I have the servant bring it in here?"

Darius growled wordlessly.

"Coffee?"

He nodded and dropped wearily into the wooden chair behind the desk. He stared down at the maps, bleary-eyed, then put his wire-rimmed reading spectacles on to read over his paperwork, while the younger man hastened out of the room to fetch coffee. Alec had scarcely closed the door, however, when Darius heard a warm, scratchy voice in the hall.

"Good morning, Lieutenant! Where is the Colonel, please?"

An instant cascade of thrills rushed through his weary body, bringing a surge of new life. He whipped off his spectacles just as Serafina burst triumphantly into the room.

Alec peered in worriedly behind her. "Her Highness—uh—sir—"

Darius let out a sigh. "Never mind, Alec," he said. "That will be all."

Alec glanced curiously from Serafina to him. Darius regarded the princess as she blithely shepherded Alec out of the library, closed the door behind him, then turned and leaned against the closed door, both hands behind her. She grinned at him.

"May I help you?" he asked dryly.

She let out an irrepressible laugh as if he'd said something marvelously witty, then ran across the room to him, skipped around the desk, and threw her arms around him, planting a kiss on his cheek with a loud smack.

"Good morning, Darius!" She squeezed him about the neck.

"Good, you're awake." He pulled aside but not entirely away, scowling. "We must review security procedures."

"Nonsense, we must have breakfast." She loosened her hold around his neck but kept her arms draped around him as she smiled prettily at him. "Come and eat with me. Breakfast is almost ready."

His mouth watered. "I have work to do."

"Don't work, play with me. You're on holiday!"

"On the contrary, Your Highness, I'm in hell."

She knitted her brows at him. "That's not a very nice thing to say." She released his neck and rose. She hopped up and sat on the desk, right on the maps. Planting both hands behind her, she leaned back across the desk, using her body to block him from his paperwork. "Tell you what. I'll help you with your work, then you can finish all the sooner and play with me."

He looked up at her and found her smiling innocently at him. She crossed her ankles and swung her slippered feet.

I really don't have a prayer with this girl, he thought.

"How is your shoulder feeling today?"

"Fine, Your Highness."

"No, no, no, don't call me that." She wagged a finger at him. "I'm not the princess here."

"Oh? Who might you be?"

"I'm not sure yet. No one in particular. I'll let you know when I find out."

He abruptly yawned. He covered his mouth, eyes watering. "Pardon me."

Suddenly she gave him an appalled look. "You haven't been to bed yet, have you? Darius!" she cried. "Go. This instant!"

He regarded her dully.

When he made no move to obey, she sprang off the desk and came around to his side, pulling on his hand. "Come on."

He didn't budge.

"I'm putting you to bed!"

He let out a furious growl and yanked his hand away to rake it through his hair. "Don't say such things to me." He rested his elbows on his desk and glowered at her as he rubbed his throbbing temples.

"Why not? You put me to bed last night, didn't you?"

He shot her a haughty look, then sat back, sullen, in his chair.

"Oh, Darius, my fierce one," she said with her sweet, soothing laugh. She touched his face, trying to make him look at her, but he jerked his chin away, scowling.

She lowered her hand, gazing at him while he stewed. Studying him intently, she rested one juicy hip against his desk, her slim arms folded under her breasts. "You're very handsome when you scowl."

He gave her a dirty look.

Laughing softly, she reached out and gently smoothed his hair out of his eyes. "You need to learn to relax—"

He grabbed her wrist and forced her hand away. "Stop touching me, for God's sake! Why are you always touching me? What are you trying to do to me?"

She stared at him with a look of surprise that swiftly turned to hurt. "I only meant to be friendly."

"Well, don't!" He looked away, heart pounding. He shoved his fingers through his hair in agitation, then got up roughly from the chair, crossing the library toward the door. He opened the door and held it for her, though she hadn't moved from the desk. His soldierly stare bored straight ahead. "If you please, Your Highness, we have security procedures to review."

He felt her gaze on him turning cold.

She crossed the room and brushed past him at the door, her tone as flat as his. "Very well. Carry on, Colonel."

He walked her through the house, showing her how to slip away without a trace, teaching her how to hide.

He was the expert on that, she supposed. He introduced her to all the villa's exits and the hiding places built into the floors and walls, issuing commands and detailing procedures of exactly what she was to do in case of emergency.

Her mood was so glum after his violent rejection of her attempt to be affectionate that Serafina barely paid attention as she followed the stern and exacting Colonel Santiago through the villa. On their impromptu tour, she was more interested in the house than in Darius's tedious lecture on security procedures.

She saw a morning room with lace curtains and a lemon tree in a clay pot in the corner, the topmost branches of which reached all the way up to the dentals of the white crown molding. They went through a long, rectangular drawing room. Here, as throughout the house, the rugs and furniture were all slightly threadbare, and everything was dusty with disuse. Yet, to her, the villa's shabby gentility was a welcome contrast to the palace, with its soaring spaces of pristine white marble.

She paused to glance out the mullioned windows and found that the parlor overlooked a charming flagstone patio. Through the old, bowed glass, she saw that the back garden had been allowed to grow into a wild thicket. An old grape arbor stood in the center of the garden with a rough-hewn table underneath the tangled vines. Impatiently, Darius summoned her to the next room and continued his lecture. She only half listened.

Across the hall from the drawing room lay a stately dining room, dominated by an old mahogany table with seating for twelve and huge mirrors on each of the four walls to maximize light from the cobwebbed chandelier.

Gazing at the room, she glanced over and found Darius staring at her. He looked away.

She lowered her lashes. "I like this place, Darius," she ventured quietly. "It feels like a home, doesn't it?"

"How should I know?" he asked blankly, then he left the room.

With waning patience, she followed him upstairs. To her surprise, he showed her that there was even a hiding place in the pink bedroom. Darius pulled back the pastoral-fantasy tapestry rug to reveal a floor compartment big enough for a person to hide in.

"You get in here if I tell you to. No arguments. If the French discover our location, they may try and steal you again."

"Darius, really," she said in boredom. "Captain Orsini will find them in time."

"Orsini couldn't find his arse in his britches," he muttered as he closed the wooden door and pulled the rug back into place.

She chuckled.

"Now I have one more thing to show you." He stood and offered a hand, helping her up. "I chose this villa as your safe house because it lies over the secret royal tunnels. If we are attacked, I will of course defend you with my life, as will every man here—"

She winced. "Don't say things like that."

"We will defend you with our lives," he continued, "but if we fail—in particular, if I should fall to the enemy—you will have to evacuate the property alone. Come with me and I'll show you what you are to do."

But she had gone pale, staring at him.

He glanced at her, tilting his head. "Have I scared you?"

How could he talk about the possibility of his own death without the slightest fear or the slightest sign of interest?

Her fright seemed to amuse him. "Oh, little Cricket, don't fret," he said, giving her a mocking but indulgent smile. "You are perfectly safe here. The chances of their finding us are very slim," he went on. "This villa is remote. We're well manned. I merely like to be prepared for the worst. Come. This way."

Wrapping her arms around herself, she followed him outside, down the few stone steps from the entrance, down onto the unevenly cobbled drive, where weeds sprouted up between the stones.

Lifting her gaze to the cloudless azure sky, she took a deep breath of the cool mountain air. It was a fine day after the night's storm. Every emerald leaf beamed with captured droplets.

He walked on ahead, but she turned back, shaded her eyes, and gazed up at the sun-blasted, tumbledown villa.

The red tile roof was bowed, a few shutters were missing, and here and there the pastel-yellow paint was peeling, but its large stones were sturdy, and its form was one of elegant, Palladian symmetry. On the sides of the house, the once-sculpted topiaries were overgrown into green, misshapen hulks. The flower beds had run amok with tall white daisies and bright gold black-eyed Susans. Closer to the ground, clouds of scarlet geraniums shook in the dry highland breeze.

She was charmed. *A little tender loving care is all you need,* she thought, then her protector's voice broke into her reverie.

"Serafina, do stop dawdling."

Her patience with him was wearing thin. If he had called her by her title, she would have given him a scathing set-down for his insolent tone. However, he had used her name, so she forgave him and hurried after him. Together they walked across the compound to the path leading into the property's woods.

* * *

As they walked, Darius noticed his men's furtive glances at the goddess.

Don't any of you even look at her. He sent the soldiers back to work with a menacing glare, bristling with a surge of the same bizarre possessiveness he always felt around her.

"Hurry up," he muttered, slowing his longer paces and waiting for her to catch up.

Neither of them spoke as they entered the path, but he was acutely aware of her as she strode gracefully through the dappled woods by his side. He listened to the soft rustle of leaves and pine needles under their feet, then looked over his shoulder and briefly scanned the woods to make sure no one was following.

He stole another covert, sideward glance at her lovely, pale face, but he only succeeded in getting caught up in her beauty each time he looked at her. He was beguiled by her classical profile, the sweep of her long, feathery lashes.

"This way," he murmured, brushing her hand to get her attention. *Hands like silk, how soft they had felt on his skin, stroking him, healing him.* He gritted his teeth. "Go to the left where the path forks, then look for the white poplar. Remember it. It marks where you must turn off the path," he instructed her.

She took a long look up at the towering tree.

He glanced at her, homed in on her snowy throat where her soft, fluttering pulse beat. His gaze floated downward over the silken expanse of her chest, modestly revealed by a square-collared, girlish dress. He looked straight at the lush swells of her breasts, and saw that her nipples were erect, pressing against the soft, light blue muslin.

He dropped his gaze, his mouth gone dry. "Come, Princesa."

He led her toward the stand of firs, mentally cursing himself but helpless before the fact that, truly, she had the most beautiful breasts he'd ever seen, two ripe, generous handfuls, peaches from the Garden of Eden.

Exactly, he thought. Forbidden fruit.

It was just as well he was going to die soon, because he didn't much care to linger in a world where such breasts could exist but he could never kiss them, fondle them.

It would be so easy.

"These three big pines—the tallest ones—form a triangle," he explained in a martial tone. He swept a few needle-laden branches out of her way and indicated for her to walk into the center of the tiny grove.

She brushed past him into the small open space within the wall of pines, where she folded her hands demurely behind her and watched him with an expression of virginal hunger.

That look nearly snapped his control. He let the branches fall. "It's a trapdoor," he said. "See if you can find it. Open it."

Obediently, she fluffed out her skirts and swept down to her knees, then began feeling around through the thatched grass and pine needles.

Hands on hips, Darius watched her brush the pine needles away from the iron latch. The way she bent over her work merely enhanced the sweet fullness of her cleavage, then suddenly she gave a little cry of pain. He looked up quickly from her chest to her face just as she popped her finger into her mouth.

"What happened?"

"A pinecone bit me," she said with her pout.

Dryly, half-wanting to throttle her, he lifted one brow at her. A second later, he became caught up in the prospect of her finger poised between her full lips. On her knees on the soft green forest carpet, sucking her finger, she was somehow the most innocently erotic thing he'd ever seen. He stared at her, mesmerized.

She removed her finger from her mouth. It came out glistening wet. She shot him a look of defiance and wiped her finger on her dress. "It doesn't hurt," she said in a parody of him. She seized the handle in both lily-white hands that had never done a day's work, and strained against the rusted trapdoor. "It's stuck!"

He fought the urge to help her. "You must be able to do this yourself."

"I can't!"

"You can," he said quietly. "What if I can't always come to your rescue? You must be able to survive on your own."

"Fine words from you," she muttered, but she kept trying. "My brother is mapping these tunnels for Papa. I bet you didn't know that, in your omniscience."

He shook his head.

"The maps are going to be Rafael's present for Papa's fiftieth birthday. My mother is making a big surprise party for him. You'll probably be there, won't you? I won't. I'll miss it, of course. I'll be in Moscow. With my husband."

No, you won't, he thought, but he bit his tongue, gazing at her as one soft, sooty curl came free of the bow and fell against her rosy cheek. *You are so pretty.*

When the door suddenly creaked free, she plopped back onto her derriere with the force of her pull, but she glowed with a blush of self-satisfaction and sat there grinning at him.

He made a mental note to oil the hinges so they wouldn't squeak. If there was an emergency, she would have to make as little noise as possible.

"Hurry," he sternly prompted. "They're coming. They're armed. And if they catch you, your family loses everything."

Her grin dissolved. She quickly rose and ventured down the steps to the underground tunnel. His heart clenched at the way she moved like a frightened kitten down there in the dark. Gingerly, she lifted the cobwebbed torch from its holder.

"Light it. The flint should be there."

She searched

"You'll have to find the flint, shut the trapdoor, and only then light the torch," he directed. "They mustn't see the light or they'll find you."

"I've got it."

Once she had located the flint, she struggled to pull the trapdoor shut over her.

Darius waited above for many minutes, pacing like a man with his wife in labor, while she worked below to practice lighting her torch with the flint.

"I can't do it!" came her furious voice, muffled through the earth.

He leaned down near the seam of the door so she could hear him. "Keep trying. You can do it, Serafina."

"I can't do anything!" she wailed. "I'm just a—a useless hothouse flower!"

He smiled as he sat down on the closed trapdoor to wait. "Aren't you the girl who smashed Philippe Saint-Laurent a facer? Stop being a baby. I'm not letting you up until the torch is lit."

He heard more grumbling from below. "Disgusting, drippy, icky cave. Probably infested with bats. Something's wrong with this flint. . . ."

He chuckled to himself.

Finally, she completed the drill. He opened the trapdoor for her and watched her come back up the steps. Pleased with herself, she preened a bit. He hid his amusement and closed the trapdoor, covering it again with the thatch.

They strolled back to the house, then their companionable silence turned awkward as they arrived once more at his make-shift office in the library. He stole a glance at her and realized in regret that it was wisest to part company with her now. He crossed the office to his desk, where he sat down and began sorting through the maps. He could feel her staring at him.

He ignored her.

"Darius?"

"Yes, Your Highness?"

He heard her hesitation. "What are you going to do now?"

"Work."

"Aren't you going to eat breakfast?"

"I'll get to it."

"Is there anything I can do to help?"

"No, thank you."

Silence.

He stole a wary glance at her from under his forelock and saw the waver of vulnerability on her soft, plump lips.

"What is it?" he asked coolly, refusing to succumb to the tug at his heart.

"What am I to do now?" she asked in a small voice.

He shrugged. "I am here to protect you, not entertain you, Your Highness."

She spoke in a tone of strained patience. "I know that."

"Well, then?"

She held him in a beseeching gaze, then dropped her head. "Don't you ever get lonely, Darius?" she asked, barely audibly.

"Everyone's lonely, Serafina." He examined the topography scale on the map of the local area, then her cold words struck at him.

"Go on, shut me out. I never would have guessed it, but I see now you're just like everyone else."

"Beg pardon?" He looked up, rather taken aback.

He found her chin high, her cheeks flushed with anger, her fists bunched at her sides.

"Everyone looks at me but nobody sees me, Darius. You used to, but you don't anymore. Now you won't even look at me. Maybe I should open my gown. That seemed to get your attention. I could be standing here naked before you and you wouldn't care—"

"For God's sake, Serafina!" He threw down the pen and visored his face in both hands, elbows propped on the desk, his thumbs pressing his throbbing temples.

She was silent for a moment. "Why don't you want to be with me? What did I do to wrong you so terribly?"

"Nothing." He didn't move. He could feel her staring at him.

"There must be a reason. How do you think it feels when the one person you depend on and care for most walks out of your life?"

"I know exactly how it feels," he bit back, and immediately wished he had not said it.

He had been nine years old the last time he had seen his mother. Of course, by the time she finally left for good, he had already hardened himself to her frequent disappearances, so he scarcely cared, or told himself so.

"You hurt me, Darius."

He did not know why his heart was pounding. Carefully, coolly, he shrugged. "It's your own fault. You should have used better judgment. You should have kept your feelings to yourself. You gave me no choice but to leave."

"You had a choice," she said softly in a voice full of meaning.

He leveled a wary stare at her from under his forelock. "Ah, so, we're finally going to have this conversation, are we?"

"Are we?" she echoed sorrowfully. "I'm sure you can come up with some excuse to dodge away this very moment, if you try."

He let out an exasperated sigh and covered his eyes with one hand. "Leave it alone, Serafina. Just leave it alone."

"Do you think not talking about it will make it cease to exist? I thought you were a brave man, Santiago. Wasn't it you always telling me when I was a little girl that I must be truthful, honest? You should take your own advice."

"Why are you doing this to me?" he asked heavily.

"Because I am sick of your hiding and your silence and your pretending there is nothing between us. I will not allow you to ignore me a moment longer! Furthermore, I am worried about you. At the very least, I deserve answers. Why did you run from me?"

"What was I supposed to do?" he retorted. "Don't you see the position I am in—or is it that you can't bear for one man not to fall at your feet?"

She gasped.

"You ask the impossible," he said. "Do you think I don't know what you want? Do you think *I* feel nothing? But sometimes, Princess, what we want doesn't matter. Sometimes what we want is wrong."

She stared at him while his chest heaved with the force of his anger.

"Wrong?" she asked softly. "Surely you don't mean that."

He looked away. "You know damned well a match between us would have been absurd."

"Well, God forbid we should ever appear absurd." She wandered to the window and looked out. "I waited for you, you know. I suppose I'd have waited forever, but you never came, then this crisis with Napoleon arose, and I had to assume the duty of my birth."

His glance flicked to her profile. "Then . . . you marry him strictly out of duty?" he asked in a careful tone, holding his breath.

From across the room, she gave him a tortured look. "Go to hell, Santiago."

"What?"

"How dare you ask me to reveal my heart to you when you refuse to show your own? You cruel man."

"You want answers?" he cried, flushing with an exquisite pang of guilt. "Fine, then! I'll tell you why I never asked you to marry me—because it would have been the joke of the century! You were born a royal princess, and I'm the bastard son of an impoverished Spanish count and a Gypsy dancer! We'd both have been ruined!"

"What do I care? At least we'd have been together!" she shouted, her violet eyes afire.

"You would ruin yourself to be with me?" he asked, incredulous. "Are you mad?"

"I don't care what anyone says or thinks! I hate everyone, anyway!" she burst out. "Do you think I enjoy my life as an ornament, living in a fishbowl, on display? I am surrounded by people who neither know me nor care to! I wanted to be with you!"

"You say that, but you don't know what it's like, being on

the outside," he said harshly. "You don't know what it's like, never belonging anywhere."

She gave him an anguished wince. "You belong with *me.*"

He strove to soften his tone. "Look at us, Serafina. We are from different worlds. I would not wish my world on my worst enemy, let alone drag you into it. Haven't I always sought only to protect you? I care for you too much to ruin your life. I cannot do what you ask. I don't have it in me."

"To love someone?"

"I don't know how," he said.

She lowered her head. One hand on her hip, she pinched the bridge of her refined nose for a moment, then lowered her hand and looked up. "These are all fine excuses, Darius, but I hope someday you will let *somebody* love you, even if it isn't me. I don't know what you are afraid of, but I never would have hurt you. Not for the world."

He didn't know what to say. God, he had to get out of here. There was a long, awkward pause.

Serafina folded her arms over her chest and scrutinized him. "Perhaps that's what I'll do to amuse myself today. Find you a suitable wife."

"No woman will ever tie me down," he muttered.

With a glance world-weary beyond her years, she arched a brow at him. "But you tie them down, I hear."

He scowled at her.

She gave a short, joyless laugh and turned away, walking toward the door.

"Where are you going?" he demanded.

"To entertain myself, as ordered," she answered, not turning around. "You see? I don't always need to get my way. Enjoy your solitary suffering, Colonel. It becomes you. Have a nice day brooding. I wouldn't dream of intruding on your self-absorption."

He narrowed his eyes at her slender back.

"I will have to check your stitches later, however," she

added. "I know you like to suffer, but I must draw the line somewhere. One of us has to be sensible."

"You, sensible?" he baited her, almost as if a part of him wished to delay her exit.

She cast him a sweet, treacherous smile over her shoulder. "Oh, but do keep in mind that as soon as my mother sends those chaperons, you're not going to be allowed anywhere near me."

With that, she walked out, leaving the door wide open behind her.

At once, the breeze from the open front door was fresh but made all his neatly stacked papers flutter chaotically.

"Damn it," he mumbled, trying to hold them all down, but it was useless. They flew like feathers from a shredded pillow, scattering over the floor.

Exasperated, he gave up trying to catch them and watched the sway of her hips instead with slow, burning hunger. She strode down the hall to the foyer straight ahead.

He couldn't stop himself from watching her go out the front door, watching the breeze mold her skirts around her long legs as she stepped outside and lifted her face to the sunshine, light twining like golden ribbons through her blowing sable curls.

She turned back with a dazzling smile.

"Darius, it's a wonderful day!" she called in her warm, scratchy voice.

Longingly, he stared, knowing she could not see him down the hall. It was only her futile, bullheaded faith that kept her peering into the shadows, waiting for him to emerge.

God, how he craved that light, that carefree wholesomeness.

Violet eyes brilliant in the sun, she might have been the goddess of love standing there; he almost believed she could open her hand and bestow the abundance of nature. She was strong and proud and pure, everything he wanted, needed.

Couldn't have.

No, he would go to his grave never having been loved, never having been known by anyone.

Violently, he threw down the pen and rose from his desk. He crossed the room, slammed the door, and stood in his dim cage, trembling.

CHAPTER
❧ SEVEN ❧

Serafina spent the afternoon gathering medicinal plants for her collection of herbs. At least it was something to do.

Using a footstool for a desk, she sat surrounded by tall grasses in the middle of a field, her wide-brimmed straw bonnet shading her face and shoulders from the beating afternoon sun. Around her, butterflies teetered from flower to flower, and daisies waved in the breeze. She thumbed through her massive botany tome, trying to put Darius Santiago out of her mind.

Why was he like this? Why did he say things deliberately to drive her away? All she wanted was to help him. She had so much to give, and no one to give to.

Restlessly, she got up, fixed the lid on the basket in which she had stored her plant specimens, and walked off, barefoot, toward the woods. She had found a small stream under the woods' shady boughs, and needed to collect more of the wood violets which grew on the muddy banks.

Though she did not like being alone, admittedly, the afternoon out here under heaven's blue dome had been one of the most peaceful days she had spent, of late. Her pace in the social whirlwind had been frantic since her engagement a few months ago, for she knew Anatole might never let her come back to visit Ascencion again.

There was no way around it: Her husband-to-be was a bully and his price for his protection was her complete obedience. She could not escape the gnawing fear that, over time, the strain of living in submission to him would slowly crush her spirit.

She thrust these thoughts aside and plucked a daisy as she walked, her feet cushioned by the dry, tall grasses.

She liked to be barefoot whenever possible. Having her feet firmly planted on the ground made her feel more connected to the earth and all living things.

She wished Darius would have come out to share the day with her.

Am I still in love with him? Am I that hopeless?

She glanced in distress at the blue sky from under the brim of her hat. She saw a hawk circling, fixed to fall on some poor field mouse. It made her think of Napoleon's imperial eagle, and the vision flashed through her mind of this lovely field, charred and strewn with the bodies of soldiers, the azure sky blotted out with the black smoke of gunpowder.

She squeezed her eyes shut, routing the image.

There would be no war, not when she had the power to stop it. She was *not* Helen of Troy, who had betrayed her people for the sake of her lover and her own reckless heart.

There could be no war, even if the only man she would ever love was in hell, as she knew he was. She had seen the mad, fractured suffering in his onyx eyes. Though she did not understand its source, she felt his pain as her own.

Perhaps it was just as well she did not have the skill to reach him, she thought bitterly.

Bound to her duty, she could not save Darius, nor could Darius save her. But in that moment, she was agonized, torn between loyalties. For, in truth, she would have given anything to taste the nectar of true love just once in her life.

Just for a day.

All afternoon, Darius worked on his report to Czar Alexander and the Russian government. The document was an integral part of his larger plan. The lengthy report comprised his official testimony on the facts about Prince Anatole Tyurinov's political ambitions, which Darius had unearthed during his covert inquiry into the young general's background, as well as his legal and financial affairs.

Darius had honestly never meant to sabotage the betrothal.

True, there was a secret, savage part of him that seemed to feel that if *he* could not have Serafina, no one could, but he had held it in check and conducted his investigation fairly and with an open mind. *He* had no royal crown, nor armies with which to protect Ascencion, after all, nor did he even want a wife. The Russian match appeared best for Ascencion, and what was best for Ascencion was best for Lazar, to whom Darius owed everything.

He had never expected to learn that Tyurinov was angling to replace his twenty-five-year-old cousin, Czar Alexander, as the supreme ruler of Russia.

Several years ago, Czar Paul, Alexander's father—a known madman—had been murdered by a handful of men in the government, who then presented the throne to the gentle, scholarly Alexander. The common speculation was that Alexander had had a hand in the plot, but these rumors were swept under the carpet in Russia's collective relief merely to be rid of the evil Czar Paul.

Tyurinov had been quietly resurrecting the rumors of Alexander's involvement in the murder, painting Czar Paul as a martyr, the strong-handed ruler Russia needed, and Alexander as a patricide. Tyurinov had a huge army in the palm of his hand, of course, and by his manipulations, he had won the support of many of the older nobles, who deplored Alexander's liberal new policies and French-influenced manners.

With his charisma, his victories, his authentic royal blood, and his famous hatred for the godless Napoleon—whereas Alexander's stance toward the Corsican wavered—Tyurinov was well loved by the vast Russian populace. With a woman like Serafina by the man's side, Darius could well imagine that Tyurinov would quickly have the entire Russian court at his feet. The right wife was essential in the political arena.

Darius had been compiling his list of the Russian nobles whom Tyurinov had won over to his treasonous cause when Lazar sent him word that, due to increased pressure from the French, and seeing that his daughter found Tyurinov agreeable during their visit, he had already given the match his blessing.

Darius couldn't believe it. He had been incensed. How could the king make such an important decision without waiting to hear from him first? Darius had not even sent him his report yet. Though the wedding date had already been set, Lazar wrote that he wished Darius to continue the background investigation, and if possible, to bring it to a swift and happy close.

Though it seemed pointless, Darius pursued the thread of Tyurinov's political ambitions, only to discover, to his shocked horror, the truth about the death of Princess Margaret, Tyurinov's first wife.

At that point, Darius did some careful thinking.

Prone to hotheadedness especially where his little girl was concerned, the king, Darius calculated, would be outraged—partly in fury at himself for being taken in by Tyurinov's charm. Without forethought, Lazar would call off the marriage at once. But to deny Tyurinov his chosen bride based on the accusation of murder—without evidence—would have caused a mammoth scandal. One with possibly grave political consequences for Ascencion. After all, Russia was always in need of Mediterranean ports. Such an insult to the cousin of the czar could easily have provided the Russians with a handy excuse to try to take Ascencion by force, exactly as the French wanted to do.

So Darius had searched frantically for evidence that would hold up against one of the most powerful men in the civilized world. To free Serafina from the disastrous match, he needed proof so damning that even Tyurinov's closest friends would abandon him.

His search was cut short, however, when he received the tip from one of his most trusted colleagues that the notorious

French spy Philippe Saint-Laurent was running an operation out of the palace at Belfort, with orders to abduct the princess before she could be married.

This new threat had forced Darius to leave Moscow immediately. His departure meant he had to abandon hope of finding evidence against Tyurinov. The prince had covered his tracks too well. More drastic measures would need to be taken.

And so Darius had begun honing his aim with a rifle.

The girl was more damned trouble than she was worth, he thought grouchily as he set his quill pen down, pulled off his wire-rimmed reading spectacles, and stretched his neck this way and that. He flexed his cramped right hand, absently inspecting the black ink smudges on the heel of his palm. His gaze traveled over the pages he had spent the past several hours drafting, strewn over the desk.

Why was his life so complicated? he wondered. In his quest for the evidence, he had spun convoluted webs of lies. He had invented various new identities for himself, manipulated countless people, bribed a few, had even seduced one of Tyurinov's ex-mistresses for information. He had broken laws, burgled Russian government offices.

Spending so many months studying the golden, glorious Anatole, he had come to hate the man. Everything Tyurinov stood for was a lie. Darius knew he, too, was a liar and not worth much, but at least he did not pretend to be a hero to the world, and the wicked things he did, he did to protect the people who had been kind to him. Tyurinov had no honor.

Indeed, he mused, as he chewed thoughtfully on the arm of his spectacles, Tyurinov would have scoffed at his antiquated code, for the only law the prince obeyed was self-interest.

The worst part of it in Darius's view was that Tyurinov did not even love Serafina. If the man had truly cared for her, that might have made a difference, but her beauty had made her merely a trophy to Tyurinov, an object to be attained in order to glorify himself and announce yet again his greatness to the world.

And how did Serafina feel about the glorious Anatole? Darius wondered for the thousandth time, trying to scoff at his own insecurity over the question. But truly, had she been taken in by the prince's well-documented charm?

She was a smart girl, and Darius had taught her as a child to be wary of anyone who was overly friendly, but she was a young woman now, ripe for love.

The thought made his groin tighten with a tingling warmth.

Turning his face restlessly toward the one window, he saw the sky was ablaze with gathering sunset, the gold and pink streaked with violet.

Soon it all would fade to black. There would never be another chance.

Go to her.

His gaze moved over the treeline in silent distress.

As soon as the chaperon comes, you're not going to be allowed anywhere near me.

At those remembered words, he suddenly slid a fresh sheet of paper toward him, dipped the quill in the inkwell, and wrote swiftly, his heart pounding.

Sir,
    It is inadvisable to send more staff at this time. Her Highness is well and our location is secure.

                                                    Your servant,
                                                    D.S.

Quickly, before he could change his mind, as though his very life depended on it, he folded the page and sealed it with wax.

It was the most selfish thing he had ever done, the most deceitful, and the most necessary.

He pushed back from the desk, strode out of his office to the foyer, and barked for Alec.

The young lieutenant came running. "Sir?"

"Deliver this message to His Majesty."

"Yes, sir."

"Find out what you can about Orsini's progress. Come back tomorrow using one of the alternate routes we've outlined."

Alec saluted. "Yes, Colonel."

Darius turned to go, then hesitated. He glanced over his shoulder at his aide. "Er, Alec?"

"Yes, sir?"

"Where is Her Highness?" he ventured.

If Alec found his question amusing, wisely, he did not show it. "I'm not certain, sir. I'll find out."

"Good. I'll be in my room." Darius lifted a pear from the freshly arranged fruit bowl on the console table in the hall and took a large bite as he jogged up the stairs.

Above, he went into his small, drab, spartan room and crossed to the sturdy, oaken armoire. He opened the door with a click and reached in to pull out a long, slender case with a handle. He carried it to the bed, then opened the case and stared down at the sleek, expensive rifle he'd had made for the express purpose of blowing Napoleon's head off.

It was the most beautiful gun he'd ever owned, artfully crafted for precision.

He ran his fingertips down the smooth, mahogany barrel. The smooth-bore flintlock was Dutch-designed. It had a range of one hundred fifty yards, with a special folding telescope attachment for enhanced aim.

He closed the case. He would practice later.

Putting the black leather case back into the armoire, he went to the side table to freshen up. The water revived him after hours of desk work. He splashed his face, brushed his teeth, slapped on some cologne, combed his hair, and mocked himself for these attentions to vanity, knowing he was going to see Serafina.

He glanced in the mirror at the man there, retying his simple cravat. Warily, he met the stare of the half-breed stranger with the mean, fiery eyes and the hideous scar on his mouth, an everlasting reminder that he had never been wanted anywhere.

Yet Serafina seemed to require him.

Why me? he thought for the thousandth time.

"Don't question it," he dryly advised his reflection. He left his room, locked it, and went in search of the royal protectee.

Striding down the second floor's balustraded landing, which overlooked the entrance hall, he bellowed once more for Alec.

"Haven't found her yet, sir!" The lieutenant appeared at the bottom of the stairs.

"What?" Darius peered over the rail, frowning down at him.

"No one has seen her in hours. The men thought she was with you!"

"She's not with me!" His stomach suddenly plummeted in dread. "You mean to say they haven't seen her?"

"Yes, sir! No one has."

"Goddamn it, why the hell have I got two dozen men here guarding her? Do I have to do everything myself? Did you check her rooms?"

"Yes, sir. She's not in there."

"Well, she's got to be somewhere! I'm going to throttle her," he muttered under his breath as he searched the house himself, just to be sure, then marched out to the stable.

He prayed she had merely wandered off, perhaps exploring the secret tunnels he had shown her earlier. He doubted this, for she had been afraid of the bats, but it was better than thinking the French had somehow managed to snatch her already.

One of the men found her maid. Darius cornered the woman. Pia stammered that Her Highness had spoken earlier of collecting plant samples.

"How dare she leave without my permission?" he demanded, as though the poor woman had an answer.

Standing around him and the maid, his men stepped back, paling to see their usually unflappable colonel angry—and he *was* angry, angrier than he had cause to be, but her disappearance struck some inexplicable nerve in the core of him. She had no right leaving him without saying anything. What if he couldn't find her? Panic clutched at his chest, throbbed in his wounded shoulder which she had stitched.

Five hundred bloody acres, he thought as he swung up onto his stallion's back. She could be anywhere. He drove his heels into Jihad's midnight flanks and galloped out to the fields to find her.

Cradled in the field's tall grasses, Serafina had dozed off as she watched cloud shapes in the sky.

In her light, restful sleep, she fancied she heard rolling thunder over the hills, then she felt a vibration in the earth beneath her body, like the pounding of mighty hooves. Her awareness of him took shape as it had last night in the maze. The thunder formed into his voice, angrily calling her name.

She realized she wasn't dreaming and sat up suddenly with a gasp.

The sun was setting! She had lost all track of time. As she scanned the surrounding fields, he burst into view, sweeping up over the crest of the next hill astride his Andalusian stallion. He had not yet seen her, shouting her name as he glanced in both directions.

She could just make out the furious rictus of his face as he drove the horse at a ruthless gallop, cutting across the far end of the field. The horse's tail streamed out like black smoke behind them, and the setting sun glinted on the man's weapons.

She stood, heart pounding, not sure if she should call out to him or not. She realized he was looking for her, but the sight of the hellish pair frightened her. If he turned the horse toward her, they would trample her.

"Serafina!"

She heard, then, something more than anger in his deep voice—fear, pain drove the rolling thunder. *Set me as a seal on your heart, as a seal on your arm; for stern as death is love . . .* The words came to her out of nowhere as she stood staring at man and horse, awestruck by their terrible beauty. It was a quote from the Song of Songs she had read once and never forgotten. *Relentless as the netherworld is devotion; its flames are a blazing fire. Deep waters cannot quench love, nor floods sweep it away.*

He saw her.

Serafina did not move. She was not sure she could have if she tried, frozen by his enraged stare.

He is coming for me now.

Darius looked away as he reeled the horse around. Jihad reared in the turn. She heard his deep, harsh command, spoken in that same unknown language in which he had cursed Philippe, then the horse leaped forward and they charged her.

She stared, unable to move, transfixed by their terrible beauty. Defenseless, mesmerized by heady terror, she watched Darius Santiago and his hell-horse bearing down on her like one of the riders of the Apocalypse. *Was this how Philippe felt in those last seconds?*

As they neared, she could see in his face just how furious he was.

"Serafina!"

No fear. He would not hurt her. She must believe this.

Steadily, she watched him approaching like a black storm, but she held her ground, for her heart whispered the truth to her. It was the wound inside him, driving his rage. Only she could help him.

Calm him. Soothe him.

A few feet from her, Darius pulled the stamping, snorting black to a rearing halt. She watched as daisies were trampled beneath the sharp, mighty hooves.

As he reeled the horse in a circle, trying to quiet him, he blasted her with a fiery glare over his shoulder, his black hair tousled, his chiseled face flushed with anger. "So there you are."

She said nothing, gazing at him in gentleness.

"What the hell did you think you were doing, running off without saying anything to anyone? I have been looking for you for half an hour!"

"I am safe," she said softly.

"How was I supposed to know that?" he demanded. "You should have taken men with you!"

"Darius, calm down."

"Don't tell me to calm down!"

She shrugged, turned, and walked away.

"Where do you think you're going?" he asked incredulously.

She picked a daisy and did not answer. Counting its petals with a show of nonchalance, she ambled toward the woods, quaking inwardly.

He spurred his horse and followed. "I asked you a question."

"I cannot talk with you when you're in this state." She walked on, but heard that he had stopped.

"It's your fault I'm in this state!"

She stepped into the twilit woods, listening for him, wondering whether or not he would follow. He didn't.

Warily, she glanced over her shoulder at him. He had dismounted and was standing by his horse, head down, apparently striving to get his emotions under control.

When he looked up, his dramatic face in profile to her as he gazed out over the field, the fiery glow of sunset lit his face, turned his amber skin rose-gold, and caught threads of maroon and blue-black in his silky hair.

Beautiful.

He blew out his breath and raked a hand through his hair.

Staring at him from the bosky wood, she touched her belly vaguely, low, where a strange flutter of warmth had begun to pulse.

All of a sudden, an extraordinarily naughty idea occurred to her.

No, she didn't dare!

But of course she did.

Her heart suddenly raced as she watched Darius wearily turn to the horse and run the stirrups up on the saddle, knotting the reins to leave Jihad to graze. She could tell by his slow, heavy motions that he wasn't angry anymore.

Biting her lip to hold back a nervous, giddy laugh, Serafina turned toward the woods again with a new sense of excitement, eager to thwart him and vex him for being so mean. Her gaze darted about the surrounding rocks and trees, coming to rest at a stand of young saplings nearby. Feeling reckless, she fled soundlessly into the saplings' midst.

Chagrined, impatient, and begrudgingly contrite, Darius trudged toward the woods, head down, as he peeled off his black riding gloves and lightly slapped them against his palm, considering whether or not to grovel.

How could he lose his temper like that? he thought in self-loathing. Mostly, he was relieved that she had faced him without fear. He did not think he could ever bear again to see that terror of him in her eyes, as when he'd looked up from slaughtering Philippe Saint-Laurent and found her staring at him in horror.

She was tougher than anyone gave her credit for, he had to admit. She looked fragile, but his rare hothouse flower had the resilience of a wild daisy.

He stepped from open field into shadowy wood. "Your Highness?"

Not seeing her or hearing her, he strode about fifteen feet down the wide path, where he came to a small, grassy clearing. He stopped, and his shoulders slumped.

Once more, she was nowhere in sight. He heaved a sigh.

"Your Highness?"

No answer.

"I see. This old game." He turned, looking around. "It wasn't amusing when you were five. Come out. Now."

She didn't.

"That's an order!"

He heard a nymph's silvery laughter and a few snapping twigs. He whirled in the direction of the sound and immediately gave chase, grinning in spite of himself as he shoved his way through the branches of a cluster of saplings.

He came out into a place where the trees were thinner. Walking slowly, he glanced one way and the other, but he saw no errant princesses.

"Very well, perhaps I deserve this, but Serafina, you know full well I am responsible for you. I will not tolerate you running off by yourself. What if I had needed you for something? What if something had happened—"

Something small and round pelted him in the back of the head.

"Ow!" He spun about face as the acorn she had thrown at him bounced to the leafy forest floor.

He scowled into the thicket that lay in the direction from which the missile had come, rubbing the back of his head. "You are beginning to irritate me, Your Highness. I'm in no mood. You can see it's getting dark. Supper will be ready soon."

He could feel her stifled laughter all around him. Her merriment permeated the glade like the babbling of the brook, which was not too far away, judging by the sound.

In spite of himself, Darius was charmed. He smiled ruefully. "Ah, Cricket," he murmured. "My whimsy, mischief garden girl."

By his feet, he found evidence of her passing—a daisy she had dropped.

He crouched down and picked it up gently, recalling the countless times she had tried to make peace with him since that April night three years ago. It had been the hardest thing he had ever done, resisting her that night. Only slightly less heartbreaking were the times she had come to him afterward, making blushing, awkward apologies. He had lived by the rule that it was imperative never to weaken toward her. It was best for her to forget him.

For that reason, he had met all her friendly overtures, all her attempts to include him in her activities with her friends, with an aloof, stony silence.

He closed his eyes, nestling his cheek against the flower's petals.

So gentle.

A wave of loneliness and loss washed through him. How like her, forcing him to play with her when he had refused, given the choice. Hide and seek, her favorite game. Was it not he, in truth, who was hiding? Always hiding.

He opened his eyes again and was still, for he could feel her watching him.

"Why do you go on forgiving me?" he asked softly, not knowing whether she could hear him, not sure if he could bear to hear the answer.

He checked the wave of emotion and rose, the flower trailing from his hand. He walked to the center of the glade and looked around.

"Very well," he declared to the woods at large. "You have every right to be cross at me. I was rude to you this morning. I ordered you to entertain yourself, and when you complied, I ended up screaming at you. I'm sorry. Will you come out now?"

He heard a small, feminine snort from behind a cluster of wild vines.

He smiled craftily to himself and crept nearer, but she must have seen him coming, for when he thrust his arms into the twisting branches and parted them with a triumphant cry, he found she had already eluded him.

"Hmm." He walked back toward the center of the grove and looked around. "Perhaps you will accept my apology when I say I have taken steps already to make it up to you."

He listened, certain he had her full attention. Where was the chit?

"There will be no chaperons come to plague you," he announced.

He heard branches move and looked over to see a pair of violet eyes peering out at him from between the green leaves.

He let out a hearty shout and sprang toward her. She shrieked and bounded off like a doe, crashing through the woods. He chased, feeling his heartbeat thrumming in his veins.

He laughed as she bared her ankles and knees, climbing over a large log barring the path ahead of him. She shrieked again in mock terror when she saw him, yanked her skirts over the log, and kept running down the path, laughing, her curls flying, daisies falling behind her as the wreath of flowers on her head came undone. Daisies tangled in her long, black hair.

Darius leaped the mossy log as she disappeared around the bend in the path, but he could still see her pale dress through the trees, draping her slender body, fleeting and graceful. Heart pounding, he got her in sight again as he rounded the bend, and then, in a burst of speed, he sprinted up behind her and tackled her. She twisted in his arms, trying to squirm free even as she was falling with him. That was how she ended up lying on her back under him, their faces inches apart.

Breathing hard, he grinned at her. "Got you."

She gave him a defiant pout, but her eyes were sparkling under their thick, velvet lashes.

Resting on his elbows, he plucked the last daisy from her hair and brushed it down her nose. When she wrinkled her nose and turned her face away, he tickled her neck with it.

She laughed, still slightly out of breath. "Stop that, you rotten beast."

"Am I heavy?"

"A ton!"

"Good." He tickled her under the chin with the flower.

She smacked his hand away, giving him a harmless scowl. Playfully, he scowled back at her, then she smiled, as if she could not help herself. Such a smile. It took his breath away.

Pure innocence. Pure sweetness shining from her violet eyes. Not for the glorious Anatole, not for some blue-blooded prince, but for him—the nothing. The worthless, Gypsy bastard. His playfulness faded.

"What is it?" she whispered uncertainly as the crickets sang around them and the breeze sighed through the boughs far, far above.

"You." His voice was captured in his throat. As if he were a boy, his hand trembled as he cupped her face. He felt clumsy, inept. Her creamy cheek was like satin, and his touch was reverent.

She searched his eyes, looking startled.

"You are so beautiful," he choked out.

"Ohh, Darius," she whispered with a melting smile, even as her body softened under him. She slipped her arms around his neck and hugged him close. "Thank you."

He savored her innocent embrace in silence. He was in heaven, wrapped in her loveliness. He could feel her ripe, firm, perfect breasts pressed to his chest, and he ached to touch them. He could feel her flat belly, her womanly hips cradling his pelvis.

When she drew back and gazed up at him, her eyes promised him that everything she had to give was his for the taking, his alone. Whatever her reasons, however misguided, she chose him, and, God, how he wanted her. His whole body was trembling against her.

He swallowed hard. "Serafina, I have not been honest with you."

"Shh," she whispered, placing her fingertip over his lips. "I know, I know."

"I can't run anymore. I'm so sick of pretending—"

"Shh," she breathed. "You don't have to explain. You're with me now."

He stared at her.

Lifting her hand, very gently she traced the crescent-shaped scar on his mouth with her fingertip. He flinched but did not pull away, watching her face, unsure if he felt redemption or despair.

Without warning, she curled upward and kissed the curved scar softly, lingeringly.

He slid his arms beneath her and held her to him, tangling

his fingers in her curly hair. She whispered his name, kissed his cheek and neck. She caressed his arms, carefully avoiding his hurt shoulder.

Striving for sanity, he closed his eyes, but the smell of her skin was too tempting. He lost the battle, dipped his head, and pressed a kiss to her throat.

He heard her whispered groan. She lay back on the forest floor and tilted her head back, offering herself. He stroked her hair as he covered her throat in kisses.

He did not know how long they went on like that, holding and touching, exchanging soft kisses like two innocent children, rapt with discovery. Certainly it was not the way he conducted his usual seductions.

This was nothing like that. His soul was on fire. With her, he was as raw and heated and uncertain as the virgin in his arms.

Dusk deepened in the woods. Their movements released the earthy scents of the dried leaves and the soft, velvety moss that was their bed. Night birds sang lonely melodies of love.

He became intensely aware of her hands sliding over his body, exploring his back, his sides, his hips. Somehow she had untied his cravat without his noticing. She caressed his neck, hooking her finger through the silver chain bearing the medal she had given him. Kissing the crook of her neck, he felt her hips lift beneath him in fiery instinct.

Lust slammed through his body. He gave her left leg a nudging caress with his right knee. She yielded, opening her thighs, allowing him to lie between her legs. He was rock-hard, certain that one touch of her hand could make him explode.

His pulse was wild, and he could feel her heartbeat pounding in her body. She ran her fingers through his hair. He dragged his eyes open and looked at her, panting slightly.

She was breathless, her lips slightly parted. Her violet eyes were glazed with wonder as she discovered her desire, feverish with need that mirrored his own. She tilted her head back, staring at him hotly, as if he were already sheathed deeply inside her.

He slid his fingers through her hair, cradling her head in his hand. He wet his lips, swallowed hard, hesitating, afraid of he knew not what.

So afraid.

"Serafina," he said in a trembling whisper.

"Yes. Darius, yes." She slipped her arms around his neck and pulled him down to her.

The future, the world beyond the forest dissolved along with his resistance. Years of resistance, futile from the start. He belonged to this girl, body and soul, and he knew it.

With relief so exquisite he could have wept, he smoothly lowered his head and kissed her lips.

CHAPTER
⊰ EIGHT ⊱

She kissed him back ardently, her whole soul in it. She could barely believe it was happening. She was kissing Darius Santiago—her idol, her demon, her knight.

He cupped her face as he kissed her lips softly again and again, dizzying her. He tasted of mint and warmth and male. He was so gentle, each kiss a soft caress of his warm, sculpted mouth on hers. She could feel his rushing pulse under her palm as she stroked his neck. She gloried in the weight and strength of his muscled body atop her. Sifting her fingers through his silky black hair, she returned his kisses eagerly.

He began kissing her more insistently, stroking the corner of her lips with the pad of his thumb. He seemed to grow impatient.

She tried to pull back. "I don't know what you want—"

"Open your mouth," he murmured, his low voice roughened by desire.

"What, are you sure?" she began, but when she parted her lips to speak, he filled her mouth with a kiss a thousand times beyond her dreams.

Astonished, she sank back helplessly in his arms. He clenched her hair in his hands and stroked her tongue deeply, richly with his own, hungrily. It was a kiss that merged them, a wild, mystical, and mutually claiming kiss that tasted of eternity.

She could feel the impact of the boundary they had crossed, resounding out into the universe, altering everything.

When she tilted her head and began kissing him back in this soul-deep way, tentatively at first, he gave a soft, heady groan.

"Oh, God, I adore you," he whispered.

She stopped, absorbing his words with amazement. She captured his angular face between her hands and searched his eyes. "Do you mean that?"

He returned her gaze without facade or pretense.

"I would die for you," he said.

She stared at him, pained with sweetest anguish, then pulled him gently toward her and intensified the kiss. For a long moment, they were completely caught up in kissing, then she felt his hand inch lower, toward the neckline of her dress, as if he burned to touch her breasts but did not dare. His fingertips skimmed horizontally along her modest neckline. She thought of all the times she had caught him staring and smiled to herself against his mouth, covering his hand with her own.

"Is this what you want?" she murmured, moving his hand lower, molding it over her breast.

He drew in his breath, partly a moan. She closed her eyes and lay back again in drifting pleasure as his warm hands caressed and explored her, gently kneading her flesh. She opened her eyes heavily when she felt the small tug at the buttons on the front of her dress. He gave her a challenging look from under his glossy forelock, as if daring her to stop him. She smiled sightly, watching him. "Mmm." She shivered when he slid his hands inside her bodice, gently pulling it down.

He moved back and stared at her breasts, then lifted his stare to hers. He seemed too moved to speak.

The knowledge that she pleased him sent a pang of joy down through the core of her body.

Slowly, he knelt over her, kissing her forehead tenderly while he grazed his fingertips lightly down the valley between her breasts. He caressed her midriff, then brushed her nipples lightly with his knuckles, watching her face for her reaction, glancing down at their instant plumping. He leaned down and brushed his face against her breasts.

"Oh, Serafina." He shuddered with longing against her. "You are so soft."

He cupped her breasts in both hands, burying his face between them. He turned his face to kiss the inner curve of one, then the other. She felt her nipples swell and harden beneath the gentle kneading of his hands until they ached with fullness. His eyes closed, he rooted against her softness. Heart racing, she leaned, arching her back slightly, offering herself instinctively. He opened his mouth and accepted her taut, swollen nipple for a first, tentative suck.

She gasped and her eyes shot open wide at the hot, wet tug of his mouth. She stared at the black branches far overhead with the indigo sky beyond them. She had never felt such pleasure.

Spurred on by her response, he wrapped his hand around her breast and suckled upon her, his mouth hot and wild. Her eyes drifted closed again. She moaned softly, holding him.

Hungrily, he moved to the other breast, sucking hard.

Suddenly he paused, as though surprised.

She barely had time to wonder why when he groaned aloud and gripped her breast harder, sucking her nipple with fierce, uncontrollable passion. He was inflamed, his hands all over her, stroking her legs, between her legs. He moved up over her and took her mouth with deep, forceful kisses. She was overwhelmed by his passion.

"I tasted you. I tasted your milk," he whispered fiercely. She did not know if that was possible, but she had no time to wonder, for without warning, he swooped down over her and claimed her mouth.

Driving her lips apart with his kiss, he forced the lingering sweetness of her body's milk from his tongue onto hers. She cried out with surprise when he pinned her wrists to the forest floor and stared brashly into her eyes.

"You are mine," he ground out. "You know you are."

She stared up at him in silence, barely daring to breathe.

He was panting, his onyx eyes flashing like heat lightning.

She did not know what he intended, she only knew he was far stronger than she. His hard chest against her, she could feel his rushing pulse.

"You know you are mine," he whispered again. "Say it."

Was he asking for permission to deflower her? she thought in alarm. She meant to ease him back to reason with a tactful reminder that she was soon to marry another man—a man who would probably kill her if she came to her wedding night not a virgin—but when she opened her mouth, only one word slipped out. "Yes."

He stared at her.

She was not sure what she had just done. She could not read him, wasn't sure if her admission had satisfied him.

He touched her face, stroked her hair, then suddenly bent down and scooped her into a fierce hug. "Angel. I frightened you."

"No, Darius," she told him bravely.

He held her for a long moment. "We should go. They're looking for us."

Neither of them made any move to get up.

"I shouldn't have let this happen," he said.

She gazed at him. "It's too late now."

"I am afraid you will regret it." He avoided her eyes. "You know it can't last."

She touched his cheek, turning his face to meet her stare. "I'll never regret it, Darius. Will you?"

He looked at her for a moment, then slowly shook his head. "No. It's just that I can't promise you anything beyond our time here." He covered her hand with his own. "If you get close to me now, it will hurt when it's time for us to go."

She sighed and laid her head on his shoulder. "Any amount of time with you is worth the pain to me," she murmured.

"My fearless Princesa. You continually amaze me," he said with a soft, sad chuckle as his arms tightened around her.

She looked at him thoughtfully.

"Did you really get rid of my chaperons?"

"Oh, yes, indeed,"

"How?" She braced herself on his chest and gazed down at him. Her hair swung down like a silken veil around him.

"Told Belfort it was too dangerous to send any more staff right now."

"You lied to my father?" she exclaimed. "You?"

He knit his brow. "I would hardly say I lied. A carriage could easily be followed."

She laughed in delight. "You lied to Papa so that we could be together!"

"So what if I did?" he retorted.

"Nothing. I always knew you liked me best. Now you have fought the dragons for me." At his scowl, she gave him a fond squeeze. "You know how I hate having some old dragon-lady looking over my shoulder every second."

'I know. I would, too."

"I owe you one for this, Santiago."

"Really?" he drawled. His jet-black hair tousled, his mouth beestung with kissing, he eyed her breasts.

Her eyes widened. "Darius, really." Quickly, she scrambled off him with a heated blush and began buttoning her dress.

Chuckling at her alarm, he pinched her cheek and swept to his feet. As she hurriedly righted her clothes, he turned back to her and offered his hand. She grasped it and jumped up with a smile of undisguised adoration.

They left the woods hand in hand, walking in silence.

Darius captured Jihad in the field while Serafina gathered up her botany tome and her basket of plants. She put her brown kid ankle boots back on without fastening them. Darius insisted that they both could ride the horse, so she soon found herself seated sidesaddle across his lap while he rode astride.

She balanced her basket on her lap as she leaned securely against Darius, savoring the steadying feel of his arm around her waist. Her head resting on his chest, she stared up at him while he guided the horse homeward through the thickening dark.

The horse carried them back through the fields at a stately walk. By the time the lights of the yellow villa came in sight, the gray-pearl dusk had turned into a clear, starry night. When they rode back into the compound, one of the men spotted their movement in the darkness.

"There's the colonel!"

Half a dozen soldiers came running toward them.

"Colonel!"

"Have you found her?"

"It's all right," Darius called as they came presently under the sphere of light from the nearest wrought-iron lantern. "I have found the princess, as you can see."

Serafina blushed, looking about her, as eyebrows were raised when the soldiers saw the royal protectee seated in their colonel's lap.

Darius carried on in his curt, businesslike way as if there were nothing one jot unusual about it. "You," he said sternly to a young private, "go tell the kitchens Her Highness will dine in half an hour." He gave a few more miscellaneous commands, then ordered the others back to their posts.

She observed his impact on his men with one part admiration, one part amusement. His style of giving orders was certainly different from her father's. The king's orders were notoriously sketchy and swift, for he expected or at least hoped that the men around him would use their own brains. Darius was not so optimistic. He expected his orders to be carried out meticulously, unquestioningly, the same manner in which they were given by him.

When the men had scattered to their duties, Darius clucked to Jihad and the horse walked on.

"They will gossip," she murmured tautly.

"My men are loyal." He flinched a little to speak the word, then said nothing more, brooding. She knew he was thinking of her father.

She thought of Anatole and did not feel the slightest twinge of guilt. However, it would not do for rumors to get back to the Russian diplomats. "What if they spread tales when we return to Belfort?"

"Who says we are ever going back?" he murmured. "Maybe I'll kidnap you myself."

"Would you, please?" she asked wistfully.

He laughed softly, sadly, then shifted both reins into one hand and caressed her shoulder, pulling her closer as they neared the stable. "There, there, little pet. Never worry about my men."

"You sound very sure."

"I am sure. Let nothing frighten you." Fondly he nuzzled her hair. "If there is any unpleasantness, I shall attend to it. Trust me. Hungry?"

"You are changing the subject."

He gave her a devastating smile as he reined in before the wide, open stable doors. "I'll see you at dinner, angel. Wear something pretty for me. Preferably low-cut, if you please."

"You are impossible," she whispered, smiling in spite of herself.

His dark eyes danced. "I pride myself on it."

Half an hour later, she sat gazing across the dinner table at Darius, thinking with a contented sigh that he was the hand-somest man on the earth, and the bravest, and the cleverest, and the best.

Fresh-scrubbed and dashing in his officer's uniform, he was seduction incarnate. The shiny gold buttons on his smartly cut scarlet coat were undone, revealing the white satin waistcoat beneath. His white cravat was immaculate as always. He wore black broadcloth breeches, gleaming black boots, and his silver dress sword.

Dim candlelight from the chandelier sculpted his high cheek-bones in shadow and kissed his sun-bronzed skin with a soft glow. His lips looked soft and plump, and the dramatic angles of his face had softened, for his mood was sensual and relaxed.

She savored his presence, making sure he ate plenty, and thanking all the pagan gods like the ones sporting in the lush Baroque fresco on the ceiling above her that she had no chaperon.

Sipping her wine, she glanced up again uneasily at the marvelous painting overhead, which depicted the lovers Mars and Venus caught in the golden net fashioned by the jealous husband Vulcan.

She opted not to point it out to Darius. He hadn't noticed it, staring only at her face and at the plunging neckline of the lilac silk she had worn sheerly to indulge him.

"I adore you, Santiago," she declared, resting her cheek dreamily in her hand.

He looked up, finished chewing, took a drink of red wine, and crooked a finger at her, wiping his mouth with his linen napkin.

She straightened up in her seat. "What is this—you are summoning me like the sultan?" she exclaimed indignantly.

"I only want to give you a treat, Princesa." He plucked a strawberry from the centerpiece, dipped it in his wine, then held it out to her with a flash of wickedness in his dark eyes. "Don't you want it? Come and get it," he said softly.

"Ooh, a treat for me?" Laughing, she rose from her seat and leaned toward him across the table, reaching for it.

"No, no, you have to come and take it if you want it," he chided with a devilish smile, coaxing her toward him until she climbed up onto the table and, laughing all the while, crawled slowly toward him on hands and knees across the table, sliding laden silver platters out of the way to clear her path.

"Here comes my dessert," he taunted.

She giggled. "My, what a large appetite you have!"

"A little closer," he murmured, holding the strawberry tantalizingly just out of reach of her mouth. She tried to get it and he pulled it away.

"Scoundrel, I want it," she pouted.

"Come and get it. Hurry. It's dripping," he whispered, eyeing the drop of wine that had collected at the strawberry's tip. "Catch it, Serafina."

She did. She caught the drop of wine on her tongue, licking the underside of the ripe, red strawberry slowly while he held it for her.

"Very good," he murmured. "Would you like to bite it?"

She opened her mouth.

He pulled the strawberry back, a gleam in his dark eyes as he looked from it to her. "Ah-ah, you may not have it. Not until I say." He laid the strawberry against her mouth, caressing her lips with the tip of it, back and forth, until she parted them slightly, staring at him.

She closed her eyes and tasted it with the tip of her tongue, then parted her lips wider and took it halfway into her mouth.

"No biting." he chided gently.

Eyes closed, she made a sound of impatience, sucking it.

"I don't think I have ever been so jealous of a piece of fruit before in my life," he mused as he pulled the strawberry back just a bit, leaving part of it still in her mouth.

She started laughing again. "Is this what they mean by forbidden fruit?"

"You're dying to eat it, aren't you?" he whispered.

She nodded slightly, her heart racing with the thrill.

"Serafina, I must confess," he said, "I am having the most ungentlemanly thoughts."

She opened her eyes with a teasing gaze and licked her lips richly. "I couldn't tell."

"Brat," he said, as he conceded the strawberry. "You win."

"As usual." She claimed her prize, nibbling the strawberry out of his fingers.

Just as she lightly bit his finger, the door opened. The headwaiter's eyes shot open in shock to find the Princess Royal on her hands and knees on the dining table, eating a strawberry out of her protector's hand.

She froze, nearly choking as she swallowed her mouthful of strawberry.

There was dead silence.

Not knowing what else to do, she burst out laughing. "Oops!" Wide-eyed, she pushed up into a kneeling position and sat back on her haunches, wiping her mouth with the back of her hand. Meanwhile, Darius pinned the hapless fellow in a stare only a fool would challenge.

The servant paled as if he had just unwittingly walked into a wolf's lair.

"Dismissed," Darius said in deadly tranquility.

The man fled.

"You got us in trouble now!" she whispered as she crept back to her seat.

He sat back in his chair and idly lifted his wine, but the expression in his eyes was shuttered, as if he were making a mental note to take care of something unpleasant.

After dinner, Darius loosened his cravat and wandered outside to smoke.

Serafina went in search of his guitar. She removed it from its black leather case and carried it outside, presenting it to him in shy, wordless request. She knew he hated to play for anyone.

He regarded her skeptically for a moment, shoved his cheroot between his lips, and accepted the instrument. Moving with his customary loose grace, he sat down on the stoop and tuned the strings, head bowed.

Serafina brushed past him, trailing her hand over his good shoulder as she passed. She left the porch and walked out onto the cool, lush grass, to stand gazing up at the half-moon and the million stars.

Around her on the ground, the cicadas' song was a vibrating resonance. Fireflies pierced the darkness, drifting, vanishing. Above her, now and then, bats flew by, winging their wild paths between clusters of pines. The breeze blew and stilled, however the whim struck it.

She felt strange and light, as if she could float up away into the stars from sheer happiness. The first soft, intimate notes rose behind her from his guitar. She knew better than to turn and watch him play.

His guitar spoke for him. It always had, and tonight the simple melody was sweet and pensive, sometimes shimmering softly like the flight of a hummingbird before a flower, at other times lifting into airy, flowing weightlessness with a rhythm that made her feel as if she were riding a horse made of the galloping wind.

On some absurd caprice, she lifted her arms at her sides and began to turn in circles, her head flung back, watching the stars, a kind of artless, childlike dancing. He saw what she was doing and decided to have some fun with her, playing faster and faster. He launched into one of the deliciously dizzying flamenco tunes she had always found very wicked indeed, and she twirled like a gypsy, as if he controlled her very body with his music. By the time he ended the song, she collapsed on the grass, giddy with laughter, her head reeling.

She could feel him gazing at her, but the world spun too much for her to look at him. She groaned, a trifle nauseous for a moment from spinning just after eating, then laughed at her own foolishness.

"What an imp you are," he murmured. He finished smoking his cheroot, which he had set aside, and gradually the world steadied again for her.

"Where did you learn to play?" she asked.

"From an old man who raised bulls on the next farm over from my father's alcazar."

"What was his name?"

"Don Podro. He had been a great matador. When I was a small boy, I went there often to see the bulls," he said. "I wanted to be a matador," he added a moment later, laughing sadly.

She rolled onto her side on the grass and propped her head under her hand, looking at him in delight. "Did you? Why?"

"Ah, they are so grand. Standing there proudly, never flinching as they stare down two thousand pounds of fury charging at them. Do you realize the control it takes, the courage? You should see a bullfight one day, if you ever can. Of course, loving animals as you do, you would probably hate it."

She was charmed. "Why didn't you become a bullfighter, Darius?"

He shrugged, looking away with another soft, almost shy laugh. "Why kill animals when there are so many wicked men in the world? Quiet, now. I have a song for you."

She rolled onto her back again and stared up at the stars while he began a different melody, mournful and strange. She had never heard anything like it before. It might have been a medieval troubadour's ballad of love in vain, or an ancient Moorish lament. It was slow and intricate, with occasional trills on the highest string over the low strings' dirgelike minor chord, keeping time. The song was both dignified and exotic, full of carefully restrained passion, as if it had been carved from some profound heartbreak, and as she lay on the grass, so near the man she had loved all her life, it seduced her completely.

She closed her eyes, her arms sprawled on the grass above her head. She lost all track of time, swept up in the dark, mysterious music that seemed to embody him, pouring forth invisibly from his very soul.

It ended, she wasn't sure when, she only knew something inside of her ached when the silence returned.

When she finally dragged open her eyes, Darius was standing above her, a black silhouette against the trillion stars. She didn't move, but her breath caught in her chest, for she could feel his desire, his gaze taking in every inch of her body, spread out before him like an offering to her dark god.

"Princesa," he whispered, offering his hand to help her up.

She made no move to take it, only staring into his eyes with unmasked need. *Make love to me,* she thought. *Finish it.* She closed her eyes briefly, aching for him deep in the core of her body, her bosom lifting and falling quickly with sudden breathlessness.

"Hey. Princess."

She opened her eyes, wretched with longing.

"On your feet, soldier," he whispered with a smile.

Suddenly she was profoundly depressed.

"Come with me." He waited, hand outstretched.

"Where?"

"You know where, Serafina."

She held her breath, searching his mysterious eyes, as her weariness fell away. Moving like a girl in a dream, she took his proffered hand and climbed slowly to her feet.

Neither spoke, nor broke the stare as they walked toward the house.

This is a grave mistake, she thought, heart pounding, as he opened the door for her.

Yet in she went.

He watched her in hungry approval, his eyes afire. He followed her into the darkened, narrow hall. The door banged behind them. They were barely over the threshold when he thrust her firmly against the wall and began kissing her. She moaned, quivering to feel the hard length of his body pinning her against the cool wall. He ran his hands down her sides, holding her by her hips.

He had secrets to teach her tonight, she knew, and his mouth tasted of wine.

Darius Santiago, her demon, her love, was going to give her what she had longed for forever, but on the brink of having her wish granted, she was afraid.

If she went upstairs with him now, how would she keep her sanity when he stood by and watched her marry Anatole, with naught in his black eyes but the gleam of an intimate memory, the arrogance of yet another conquest? She couldn't bear it.

Ah, but his hands were warm, and his mouth was sweet.

When at last he ended the kiss, his breathing was deep and hot. He lifted her chin with his fingertips and looked into her eyes. "I don't want you to be afraid of anything tonight," he whispered. "I won't take your innocence. I swear this on my honor. I won't do anything you don't want me to."

He released her and stepped back, waiting for her.

But she didn't follow. Leaning against the wall, she covered her face in both hands.

"Princesa?"

She dropped her hands heavily to her sides and looked up at him in pure misery. Understanding slowly flooded his dark eyes as he narrowed them, stricken.

"Oh, this is wrong," he whispered. "I'm sorry. I thought—I don't know what I thought."

Abruptly he pulled away from her, raked one trembling hand through his hair, then pivoted and took a stiff, soldierly stride away from her.

She stopped him with a hand on his arm.

He turned back to her, his chin high, his proud profile etched in shadows and pain. He stared at her with a burning, tortured look.

She reached out, grasped a handful of his shirt, and pulled. Then he was in her arms, driving her back against the door, kissing her madly, his lips like fire. She clung to him, touching him everywhere. Stroking her face, he parted her lips with his fingertip and ducked his head to devour her, filling her mouth with his ravishing kiss. She fed from it, swept away by the intensity of his desperate passion.

Her surrender was total as he lifted her in his arms and carried her up the staircase and down the hall to her bedroom.

CHAPTER
◄ NINE ►

Darius set her on her feet but never stopped kissing her as he produced a set of keys, his hand shaking as he fumbled to unlock the door. He turned the knob, shoved the door open, and swept her inside.

He shut it behind him and pulled her down onto the floor.

She heard the keys drop, their fall softened by the dusty Persian rug, then his nimble, thief's fingers smoothed up her back, plucking her buttons free. They were on their knees in each other's arms, unable to wait a second longer, even to make it to the bed. He kissed her all the while, stroking his tongue coaxingly, dizzyingly over hers.

He slid her sleeve down over her right shoulder and bent his head, kissing her shoulder, her neck, her chest, while his fingers tangled almost roughly in her hair. She closed her eyes, cradling him in her arms as her wild pulse raced. She threaded her fingers through his silky hair while he kissed her throat, sucked her flesh, and bit her lightly. She moaned when he took her earlobe between his teeth, kissed her ear, nibbled it hungrily, filling her head with the sound of his hot, predatory panting.

Then he laid her down.

He was atop her, kissing her mouth again, kissing her senseless as she basked in the glory of his muscular body covering hers. The closeness was so sweet she could have wept.

After a few moments, he straddled her body and straightened up onto his knees.

"Why are you stopping?" she asked anxiously, curling upward to clutch at his shirt.

"I'm not stopping." He smiled darkly in the slanting moon-light. It haloed his ebony hair and limned his broad shoulders in blue. "Lie back."

She obeyed, watching his every move. He stared down at her body as he petted her arms and chest.

"Show yourself to me, beauty," he whispered.

She obeyed. Slowly, she slipped her left sleeve down over her shoulder, freed her arm from it, then freed her right arm. Shyly, she pushed the bodice of her violet silk down to her midriff and stared up at him, her eyes pleading for gentleness.

He gazed into her eyes, then took off his coat, his cravat and waistcoat, then slipped his shirt off over his head. He bent down and held her gently, showing her the ecstasy of warm, bare skin on skin. He kissed her lips for a long moment with exquisite tenderness, his scarred mouth chaste and warm over hers.

He kissed her cheeks, her brow, her eyelids while she basked in the bliss of his body against hers. After a final kiss on her lips, he straightened up gracefully again, straddling her body as before.

Transfixed, she gazed up at his dark, exotic beauty and thought him like a magnificent rebel angel who had slipped into her dreams by sorcery to seduce her. Reaching down, his hands traced her collarbones lightly, skimmed her sides, her waist. His fingers glided up and down the valley between her breasts with a velvety caress.

"Tell me I am the first to touch you," he whispered.

"Of course you are. I have waited for you all this time," she said dreamily. "I knew you would come back to me."

He gave her a sulky smile from under his forelock. "How could you know? It was never my intention."

She smiled with drifting pleasure. "I knew."

He leaned down and kissed her. "Tell me I am the first to kiss you. Really kiss you."

"You know that you are. I am yours completely."

He whispered her name as he caressed her hair, then he claimed her mouth. Arms wrapped around each other, they drowned together in endless kisses full of a love that would brook no more denial. She yielded as he parted her lips and plunged his tongue deep into her mouth, and then she did the same to him, back and forth until they were both shaking with desire.

He stopped, panting, and looked over his shoulder in a quick survey of the room. Then he scooped her up in his arms again and stood, carrying her over to her bed, where he laid her down.

"That's better," he purred. Lying beside her, he lowered his head and kissed her nipple wetly, then sucked hungrily upon her.

She cried out with wrenching pleasure, corkscrews of fire twisting through her body from the hot, wet, insistent tug of his mouth. Panting, he quickly captured the left breast and did the same. He could not seem to make up his mind which one he wanted, or if he wanted both at once.

He made her frantic with passion. Mindful of his wound, she caressed his silky skin, his strong back and powerful arms, his smooth sides. She could not stop touching him, caressing his powerful arms and back, running her fingers through his glossy black hair as he devoured her breast with his reckless, fiery, suckling kiss.

She heard high, breathless groans of abandon in the room and realized distantly that they were coming from her lips. Darius didn't seem to notice. Feverishly, he kissed his way back up her neck, and when he took her mouth again, he was rough, hot, needy, his heavy, muscled body trembling above her.

Dragging a slow, deliberate caress down her belly, he began touching her hips and legs through her silken gown. He cupped his hand around her thigh and softly coaxed her legs apart, then rested his hand between her parted thighs. She drew in her breath and closed her eyes as the heat of his hand permeated the silk of her dress.

"Scared?" he whispered, letting her get accustomed to his touch.

"N-no."

He smiled tenderly. "Good."

At first he merely petted her very gently down there with his open hand, watching her face. She shivered. He bent his head to kiss her breast again and reached low, almost to her ankle. Smoothly he ran his hand up along the inside of her calf and up her thigh.

She bit down sharply on her lower lip in anticipation as he slid her dress higher.

"Is this all right?" he murmured.

"Yes, yes," she gasped, her pulse racing under his lips when he bent his head to kiss her throat. She began trembling with excitement, and then his fingers caressed her wet, pulsating flesh, gently stroking her secret place.

She groaned aloud.

"So ready for me," he breathed. "But I want you soaked, dripping. Withhold nothing from me, Serafina. Give me all of your pleasure, every drop." He kissed her lips chastely while, under her skirts, he stroked her.

He kissed the corner of her lips, teasing her, maddening her as he flicked her lips with the tip of his tongue until she opened her mouth and turned her face to meet his kiss fully.

She sank into the mattress in sheer ecstasy, her hands clutching the coverlet.

Her head thrown back, she moaned loudly as he found the precise way she longed to be touched.

"Shh," he whispered, smiling a little against her mouth. "No one must hear us."

"I can't help it, it feels so good," she said, her voice a scratchy, wanton purr.

"Ah, but we're just getting started." She curled her hands

around his shoulders as he slowly penetrated her with two fingers.

When she groaned aloud again, he gently covered her mouth with his left hand while with his right he continued to pleasure her. "Shh, angel. Quiet, or we're going to get caught."

Eyes closed, she kissed the fingers of the hand he'd pressed to her mouth. She licked between them, melting his attempt to silence her. Panting with lust, he pressed the tip of his middle finger into her mouth. She kissed and sucked it hungrily, her whole body beginning to undulate.

"Yes," he whispered, rock-hard against her thigh. "Very good, Serafina."

With his every, gently thrusting caress between her legs, in and out, her hips lifted to meet his deep caresses. She moved with his hand, becoming wild and barbaric, demanding an ever-faster rhythm.

He lowered his head and began licking her nipple in delicate circles as his clever, coaxing fingers worked a slow, sensuous magic. He made her wanton. She couldn't help it. She spread her legs wider for him, arching helplessly against his slick, perfect touch. He took her breast in his mouth and suckled her. She could feel her wetness ooze lusciously between her thighs, and knew only Darius could have made her body respond this way.

She clung to him, her arms around his neck, as he slowly penetrated her with one finger, then two, then she was mindless. She was wholly under his control now, and she reveled in it. His hand was wet and hot with her juices. Her every muscle was poised for the splendid cataclysm that was still an unknown mystery to her. Her eyes were closed in intense, breathless concentration on the totality of her sensation, but she could feel him watching her.

"God, you are so beautiful," he whispered.

She moaned his name. Wrapping her arms more tightly around his neck, she returned his kiss fiercely, taking his mouth, stroking his tongue with her own as he had done to her, thirsty for him. The taste of him was pure and clean and sheer male. A soft moan escaped her at the sweetness of him.

She still could not believe she was kissing Darius Santiago. It was without question the greatest event of her life.

Suddenly he moved atop her, lying between her legs. He braced himself on his arms over her.

"Touch me," he commanded, panting, his voice roughened with want.

She was eager to obey, caressing his hard belly and chest, but he grasped her wrist and, with a sultry little smile, showed her that wasn't exactly what he meant.

As she molded her hand over the bulging outline of his manhood in his trousers, her lashes swept up to lock her gaze with his, her lips parted with daring, wanton joy. His face was harsh with raw need. Then he closed his eyes as she caressed him through his clothes, stroking the throbbing rod that spanned a width almost as wide as her palm and so long it nearly emerged from the waist of his trousers.

The little, deep groans that escaped him fed her want. She marveled when his hips thrust slightly against her touch. His desire made her bolder still.

"I want to see it," she whispered.

He laughed breathlessly, arching his head back over her. "My naughty angel. I don't think that would be wise—"

But she was already carefully unfastening his trousers.

Eyes flickering with black flame, he made no attempt to stop her. She slid her hands inside his falls. He drew in his breath, and she watched ecstasy steal over his finely chiseled face, his eyes drifting closed, his lips parting.

Then he hung his head, the forelock falling into his eyes again.

With both hands, she explored him in wonder, eager to please, and too curious to be timid. No wonder he was so virile, she thought. His sex was like a cylinder of steel swathed in finest satin. She recalled some gossip among the palace ladies, who all agreed he was tremendously well endowed.

It angered her that they should know that. No doubt any one of them would have had a better notion what to do at a moment like this, she thought in frustration. The man of her dreams was in her arms and she had only the sketchiest theoretical knowledge of how to satisfy him.

"Darius?"

He glanced down at her.

She gave him a look of frustration, embarrassed by her ignorance. "I'm sorry," she began.

Understanding flashed in his dark eyes. "Don't apologize, angel. I love your innocence." With a tender little smile, he leaned down and kissed her, while lower, he wrapped his hand over hers on his smooth shaft, teaching her his pleasure.

"Mm, that's very good, Serafina," he breathed as he removed his hand.

He ran his fingers through her hair as she squeezed and stroked firmly, kissing his chest now and then, flicking her tongue over the tiny circles of his nipples. He moaned softly, his hands wandering down to cup her breasts, squeezing her nipples lightly between his thumbs and forefingers. At the pleasure he gave her, she quickened her caresses upon him.

The faster, rougher pace seemed to arouse him exceedingly. He hung his head, slid against her touch, his muscles working in pure poetry. After a few minutes, he gripped her shoulders suddenly.

"No more. You'll make me come in my britches like a schoolboy," he panted, dragging his heavy-lidded eyes open to hold her in a decadent stare.

"What does that mean?" she asked, wide-eyed as she leaned up on one elbow.

A lazy half-smile curved his scarred lips. "Keep that up and you'll find out."

"Maybe I will." Watching his face, she squeezed harder, testing his response.

He gasped low, then bit his lip, eyes closed. "You're ruthless, Serafina. And very, very talented."

"Thank you." Gripping him in both hands, she applied herself to intensifying the look of passion in his face, smiling to herself with a drifting sense of wonderful debauchery. She wanted him drunk and helpless with pleasure, as she was.

He clenched her shoulder, moving against her hands, his compact hips thrusting with her.

"*Unh,* God, I have no control with you," he moaned. "Serafina, this is torture. This has already gone further than I intended. We have to stop."

"Shh," she whispered, quieting him as she lovingly stroked him.

"I want to be wet with you," he said with sudden urgency. His hands were shaking as he pushed his trousers farther down his hips and lay between her legs.

"Oh, my!" she gasped, shocked by the pleasure of his member throbbing hotly against her, then she blushed bright red when he ran his fingers deep between her legs and slicked his towering hardness with her pearly fluid. Glancing down to watch, she quivered at the sight of his hand wrapped around himself, smoothing her wetness up and down over his manhood.

He lay atop her again, and she shivered under him as his silken length glided upright against her teeming flesh.

He groaned. She arched again. He pressed.

Her heart was pounding.

"God, I want you."

"Yes," she said.

"I cannot bear this," he breathed. "I need to be inside you."

"Please," she groaned.

"Don't say yes. Ah, God, Serafina. This is torment."

She wanted to help him. In a trance of pure erotic instinct, she reached down and caressed him, holding his member, throbbing and rigid and wet, against her passage.

"No, no!" he whispered. Pulling back, he stopped her in breathless desperation, looking shocked, wild. "We can't do that. We can't. I won't."

"Why not?"

"No, Serafina. No!"

"Come back," she purred with a wanton smile. "We'll just pretend."

He looked down at her like he wanted to devour her.

She lay back, gripped him in her palm, and slowly began moving against him, hips lifting to ride up and down the bottom curve of his shaft. She squeezed him rhythmically in her hand all the while, pleasuring him and herself by rubbing his hard flesh just where she wanted him, letting her body guide her.

"You're amazing," he breathed.

Moments passed. They were frantic together. Her body was a fire wrapped around him, consuming him; she gasped for air like a hungry flame, but after a few minutes more, she stopped and stared up at him in sudden, unbearable frustration, not knowing what it was she wanted.

"What is it, angel?"

She nearly pouted. "Please, Darius, make it stop."

"Oh, my poor baby," he whispered, smiling down at her in fond amusement. "Yes, I think it's time." He moved back, then lay down beside her.

She stared at him in distress as he gathered her into his arms. "You must help me. I am going mad."

He laughed very softly and ran his smooth, sure hand down her hip as he kissed her ear. "You'll recover. I promise."

She moaned loudly, her fingers raking the coverlet, her whole body undulating when he laid his hand over her woman's flesh, pulsing so deeply it ached. He stroked her gently.

"What will happen, Darius?"

"You'll see. You'll like it, trust me." He kissed her fevered brow.

She put her arms around him and held on for dear life, heart racing, her whole body rigid.

"Ah, Serafina, you are everything beautiful and good to me," he murmured in a husky voice as he dipped his fingers smoothly in and out, thrusting deftly, his thumb swirling in fantastic circles over her center.

She moaned helplessly, writhing with his touch.

"That's right, angel, let it go. Let it all go, give it to me," he whispered.

She clutched him tightly, gasped suddenly in a strangled cry, as explosions of shattering pleasure burst in a series through her body, radiating from her feminine core.

Darius's breath was harsh at her ear.

Light seemed to rush through her limbs, racing along her nerve endings, flooding her body with sensations that went on and on, blinding colors behind her eyelids in the dark. She felt like she was dying and then, just as suddenly, she went limp in his arms, gasping with the aftershocks of pleasure, but before she could quite comprehend what had hit her, Darius leaned toward her, kissing her in hot demand.

When he took her hand and wrapped it around him, this time she understood what he needed. His hand guided hers in rough, urgent insistence, then he sank slowly from his side and lay on his back, completely under her command. Her power over this magnificent, deadly male awed her in that moment. She felt his hardness swell and pulse as he thrust through her grip again and again, his muscled body rippling under her touch. Gripping her shoulder so tightly she thought there'd be bruises, he pulled her down for a frenzied kiss, then he only held her near as he panted, eyes closed, a look of tantalizing pain on his chiseled face.

"Don't stop," he gasped out helplessly.

She stroked him, wholly focused on pleasuring him, when suddenly he gave a low, anguished cry of release, she a barbaric gasp of triumph, and his hips lifted—he was like steel in her hand, discharging the hot, shooting glory of his seed, raining it on his hard, flat belly.

She stared, amazed. He groaned. His body went perfectly rigid, then slowly eased slack as all the tension flowed from him.

He lay on the bed, spent, panting, his expression one of exhausted bliss.

She watched him in fascination.

He cast a forearm over his brow and, still panting slightly, swept his lashes open and gazed at her from under his arm. He laughed a little when he saw her, or perhaps he was laughing at himself, but his onyx eyes were shining with silver stars.

Well, I must have done it right, she thought.

His hand idly caressed her knee. "Where am I?" he murmured dazedly after a moment.

"Rusticating," she whispered with sparkles in her eyes.

CHAPTER
❧ TEN ❧

A short while later, they bathed together by candlelight, Darius behind her, Serafina sitting between his legs, leaning back against his chest in luxurious indolence. Lazily, he soaped her arm while she rubbed her foot idly over his under the tepid water. They barely spoke, communicating through the silent language of touch as they washed each other.

After their bath, Serafina sent for an elaborate midnight snack of cold sliced meats, cheese, bread, and wine. By that time, all the servants in the household had figured out what was going on, so they abandoned any pretense otherwise. Lounging in her bed, both of them in their robes, they ate, picnic-style, and fed each other bites of their simple feast.

She coaxed him into speaking of his travels in distant lands. She listened, taking the tray away when he was done eating. Idly smoking a cheroot as he leaned against the headboard, one knee bent, he told of his stint training troops for Ali Pasha in the lonely, windswept mountains of Janina.

She picked up her silver-handled hairbrush and returned to sit, cross-legged, on the bed near him. She began brushing her hair as she listened, fascinated by the complexity, intelligence, intensity, and wry mischief of the hidden man who was revealed when the great Santiago cast off his arrogance. At length, his voice trailed away midsentence, and he just gazed at her, looking mystified.

"What is it?"

"I feel more at ease with you than I ever have with anyone in my life."

She smiled at him, her heart soaring. "And this surprises you?"

He pensively flicked his cheroot over the ashtray. "No. But you're different than I thought you'd be."

"What do you mean?"

"I can't explain it."

"Better? Worse?"

"Stronger," he said. "Yet softer." Then he crushed out his cheroot, set the ashtray on the floor beside the bed, and moved toward her, taking the hairbrush out of her hand. "Turn."

Delighted, she obeyed. Gently, slowly, he began brushing her hair.

He is the sweetest, tenderest man, she thought as her eyes drifted closed in relaxation. He was ever so careful not to pull her hair, patiently sorting through any tangles he came across.

"May I ask you something, Serafina?"

"Anything. Whatever you like."

He considered in careful silence. She smiled to herself as she sensed him struggling with his shyness.

"Yes?" she prodded him.

"I can't seem to figure out . . . what you see in me."

She turned around and looked at him in blank amazement. "Can't you?"

He stared at her as though he couldn't speak, his eyes full of emotion and vulnerability. Her astonishment softened to tenderness. She touched his cheek. "Yes, you need to hear it, don't you, my love?"

He lowered his head, as though ashamed.

She stroked his cheek. "It's all right, Darius. I'd be glad to tell you, but it may take a while." She smiled a little. "There are a lot of reasons."

She turned forward again, and tentatively, he resumed brushing her hair. He said nothing, but his attention was acute. She could feel it. She closed her eyes, feeling strangely protective toward him.

"I love it that you choose to stay blind to the faults of the people you care about. You are so incredibly loyal and selfless and giving," she said slowly. "You have a very fine sense of honor and justice. You've got a brilliant, if devious, mind. Indeed, it's lucky for the world you're a good man, because you could have been a master criminal instead of the brave, wonderful hero you are." She sighed, wrapping her arms around her bent knees. "Of course, you are gorgeous and a very good kisser, but we won't talk about that," she said archly. "Ah, and you can be very funny! How I relish seeing you deflate some of those pompous asses of the court with your cool, cruel wit! But if any poor underdog is ever outnumbered, you will always go to his rescue."

He was silent, running the brush in long strokes through her hair, all the way down her back.

"It's sweet to see the way you take some of those hopeless cadets from the military academy under your wing and try to stouten their courage—mustn't forget courage, one of your most famous qualities. You are an example to so many of those young men, but it never goes to your head," she mused. "I love it that you walk away from fights with stupid, loudmouthed men who could not possibly survive you. I think it's charming that you have a wise saying for everything. Oh, and one of my favorite things about you is that, come what may, you always, *always* have a plan. I love it that you are always kind to shy people— Darius?" she asked suddenly, noticing his stillness.

She turned to him and found him head down, shoulders stiff.

"Sweetheart?" She lifted his chin with two fingertips.

His eyes were tempestuous with emotion, his gaze stark and perfectly wretched.

"Darling, what is it? Have I said something wrong?"

It appeared he could not speak.

She waited, petting his forelock out of his eyes.

"No one ever said anything like that to me before," he said in a choked whisper.

"I could go on," she said with a tender smile.

"Please don't. I couldn't bear it."

"Darius. Darling, listen." She caught his face gently between her hands. "How can you not know these things? Is that why you push yourself so hard? Can you doubt your own worth? Is that why you must work ten times harder than any other man, and take all the dangers on yourself, and even starve yourself, to achieve some kind of ideal perfection? Yes, I know about that, too, so don't try to deny it."

He gave her a look of hopelessness.

"Darling, you have nothing to prove. Why do you have to be perfect?"

"I'm not perfect." He tried to pull away, but she didn't let him, and he didn't fight her. He just sat there and shut his eyes for a moment, his jaw set at a stubborn angle. "I'm not even close," he whispered.

Pained by his confession, she leaned forward and pressed a kiss to his forehead. "You're wrong, Darius. Hear me: *You are good enough.* You are perfect just as you are—"

He jerked his face away impatiently.

"You are," she said emphatically. "All your striving, just let it go for now, my dear. Give yourself some healing time, yes? Do it for me?"

He slid her a wary look. "For you?"

She ventured a faintly teasing smile. "I don't have to pull rank on you, do I?"

His wariness gave way to a bittersweet smile. Slowly, he shook his head at her.

I love you, she thought, holding his gaze with a smile on her lips and tears in her eyes. She lifted her hand and brushed his forelock out of his eyes. "Sleepy?"

He nodded.

"Come." She blew out the candle and arranged herself under the light cover, holding out her arms to him. He came to her.

Darius lay on his stomach beside her, his face turned to her, his right arm sprawled across her midriff, his fingers resting in the crook of her left elbow.

They were silent.

He stared at her in the dark. She caressed his heavy arm.

"What are you thinking about?" she asked.

"Today."

"What about today?"

"I am happy," he said, as if testing the word, strange to form, on his tongue.

She smiled at him.

"This . . . warmth," he whispered. "I have never known anything like this in my life. There could be no better gift than to be with you this way. Thank you for this day. Thank you for the things you said." He moved toward her and kissed her mouth lingeringly, then laid his head on her chest and went to sleep, one hand tangled in her hair, as if to make sure she wasn't going anywhere during the night.

Eyes closed, she nestled her face against his hair, loving him, suffused with a tender sense of protectiveness toward him. She closed her eyes in bliss.

Mine, she thought. Arms around him, she drifted off to sleep.

He awoke in the pearl-gray light of dawn and knew that overnight his whole world had changed. The scent of her skin filled his nostrils, the softness of her body pillowed his head. She was still sleeping, one slender arm still draped around his neck.

Darius lifted his heavy head from her chest and gazed down at her, utterly lost in her. He stared at her bare skin, pearlescent in the half-light, her elegant white shoulders. Her robe lay in a pool of blue satin on the floor beside the bed, for he had found it had been impossible to sleep the whole night through without touching her again, waking her with kisses and caresses, catching her cries of climax on his tongue.

Her sooty curls fanned out on the pillow in luxuriant disarray. Her plump, berry lips were slightly parted, her breathing steady and slow. The warm, white sheets that smelled of sex were tangled around her hips like the garb of a classical goddess.

Closing his eyes, he savored the memory of her surrender, then pressed a gentle kiss to her skin and rested his head on her midriff. It was the most peaceful moment of his life.

In far-off regions of the house, he could hear the servants at work. He could smell breakfast cooking, could hear his men changing shifts below as the weary night guard shuffled into the barracks and the day men took their places. His impulse was to rise and follow his usual regimen: wash up, get dressed, check in with his squadron, exercise his horse, practice until breakfast, eat, and oversee the day. But last night he had made a decision to explore another kind of life ... while he still had time.

Hope, he mused, was a dangerous thing. Even now it was whispering to him that if he could shoot Napoleon and escape from Milan, he would be incontestably worthy of Serafina then.

He'd be a hero to the world. All Europe would hail him. He could look Lazar in the eye and ask him for his daughter's hand.

Hope would have him ignore the fact that the chances of survival were nil.

Heedless of the impossibility of it all, his heart soared with the dreams which for years he had been pretending did not exist. He owned an excellent property overlooking the sea on the outskirts of the city of Belfort. He'd build her a house there on the crest of the hill, a villa of casual elegance just to suit her, with red-tiled roofs, breezy, arcaded walks, fountains, enormous gardens, a domed menagerie for her animals. He'd buy her dresses and let her give parties, even if it meant seeing all those artificial people he despised, just so he could watch her shine. And if he ever felt ready to share her, he'd give her a child. . . .

Agonized, he lifted his head again and gazed down at her, this soft, fragile, yet feisty, maddeningly willful, irresistibly charming, and generous, most necessary creature.

How had he lived without her this long?

Wistfully, his gaze followed the intricate coils of one sable curl, twining over her shoulder and down across her slowly rising and falling chest, spiraling soft black silk on her white-blossom skin. She had the longest lashes he had ever seen. Tiny, very light blue veins graced her eyelids, and her delicate skin was as soft and white as the petals of a camellia.

Her beauty depressed him under the circumstances.

Morosely, he rolled onto his side next to her, planted his elbow on the pillow, and watched her sleep in an unbearable mix of adoration and despair, but then his heart lifted when he caught the flicker of a smile on her lips as she slept.

Little imp, what was she dreaming? he wondered in soft delight.

The smile faded, only to burst out a moment later with a sudden giggle that woke her.

When she realized she had waked herself with laughing, Serafina laughed harder, and when her violet eyes opened, she didn't seem to find it the slightest bit strange that she should awake to find the king's top assassin gazing, lovelorn, down at her.

"You must tell me," he drawled.

Her just-waking voice was pebbly, scratchier than ever. "I was having the funniest dream! It was about you! Wait—first kiss me!" She threw her arms around his neck and gave him a kiss on the lips, stretching her slim, supple body slightly against him. Then she hugged him warmly. "Mm, Darius, you feel so good to me."

He scooped her into his embrace and rolled onto his back, pulling her atop him. Her wanton ringlets swung down around him in sable cascades. He loved the way her light weight felt

atop him, her lush breasts pressed to his chest, her thighs straddling his hips. He ran both hands from her shoulders down the
curve of her back to her bare backside, cupping both soft, firm
cheeks in his hands.

"You were saying?" he asked politely as his rod roared to
fiery life, rock-hard and ready.

"Feeling frisky again, Colonel?" she purred, her violet eyes
laughing at him.

He reined in his want by an act of will, folding his arms
under his head. "I want to know what you were dreaming
about me that was so frightfully funny."

With a cheerful grin, she pushed herself up to kneel astride
his waist. She yawned and stretched wide, fully natural with
her nakedness before him. He watched the lift of her breasts
and the slimness of her flat waist, just as she no doubt intended
him to.

She threw her hair back over her shoulders to give him an
unfettered view of her exquisite self, then coiled her mane into
a long, silky black rope, and held it piled on top of her head. A
few stray ringlets fell free, softly framing the delicate sculpture
of her face.

"I was dreaming about the time you were first assigned to
the Household Guard, protecting me and my brother. Remember those days, Darius? You must have been, what, about
eighteen?"

He winced. "You're making me feel old, child."

"You are old."

He scowled. She laughed and leaned down to kiss him.
"Ohh, I'm just teasing you." He hoped so, for at thirty-four, he
was fourteen years her senior.

"How scared I was of you," she blithely continued. "So stiff
and serious! So dignified!"

"Well, naturally. I was outraged that a mighty warrior like
myself should be assigned for a royal nursemaid," he said.

She laughed. "I was dreaming of the first day you showed
up at the nursery. I was never so scared in my life!"

"Of me?"

"Ugh!" she exclaimed, fluffing out her hair so that it spilled around her upper body again. "Those fiery black eyes—that scowl! You marched in when I was in the middle of a temper tantrum."

"I remember. You'd flung yourself onto the floor. Whenever your nurse tried to lead you away, you'd make your entire body go limp—"

"Like a noodle," she chimed in.

"So that if anyone wanted to move you, you had to be dragged."

"Nobody dared drag me," she archly pointed out. "What a spoiled little monster I was."

"Not spoiled," he said softly. "Just headstrong. And unhappy. Besides, whatever it was you were protesting, you had smacked your head on the floor when you threw yourself down. That's why you were crying."

"Everyone was cajoling me, 'Oh, please, Principessa, what do you want? Name your price, anything, just stop screaming!' I'm thinking, *I want my Mama, but she's got more important things to do, like saving the world. I want my Papa, but he's always busy.* If I want to see either of them, it has to be at the appointed time and I must be on my best behavior. I hate my nurses. There's nobody nice in the whole world!"

Darius shook his head, watching her with a half-smile.

"I'm kicking and thrashing down on the hard floor. My baby brother—whom I despise—is caterwauling somewhere nearby. Ten frazzled adults are pleading with me, and then I see these shiny black boots with silver spurs. Up and up I crane my neck, feeling icy doom upon me."

He laughed. Her eyes sparkled, starred with black lashes.

"Do you recall what you said to me, O fierce one?"

"That I would box your ears?"

She shook her head. "Worse. You called me a baby and told me I was making a fool of myself. I hated your guts," she declared, then smiled. "For about ten minutes. You got rid of my governesses with one of your scowls. 'Back off!' you said, with your voice like a whip. I said to myself, 'Well, at least he has a brain.' You made me do everything I didn't want to do, such as eating my food rather than painting the nursery walls with it, but do you know what? Whenever you were around, I always felt calmer. Strange," she purred with a suddenly mischievous look.

She leaned down and slipped her arms around his neck. "For when I'm with you now, calm is the last thing I feel. No . . ." She caressed his bare chest. "I must confess to a most feverish state of excitement." She gave him another soft kiss full on the lips.

His hands molded the curve of her lower back, and his temporarily slackened arousal responded at once. He was solid in seconds, his blood hot for her. He caressed her thighs astride his hips, wondering if she was game for more love play or if he ought to give the girl a decent break. She made a soft sound of pleasure at his caresses.

Entranced by her innocence, he slipped a hand around her nape and kissed her, wondering how much longer he could go on like this. The need to lay her down and bury himself inside of her was almost more than he could bear.

She ended the kiss with another happy little sigh and laid her head on his chest, stroking his biceps. He kissed the top of her head and moved his arms around her, linking his fingers over her silky-smooth back.

"How about your childhood, Darius?" she asked at length. "What was that like?"

His long, leisurely caress froze midway down her back. His whole body tensed. She couldn't have found a better way to quash his amorous mood.

She pushed up from his chest and looked at him with calm, penetrating intelligence, as though she had long since deduced it had been horrible.

Horrible.

When he found his voice, it came out a trifle hoarsely. "Let's not spoil the day." He forced a false, painful grimace of a smile.

She blinked slowly, her eyes still sleepy, and searched his face with a troubled look of compassion. She nodded and gave his cheek a soothing caress with her knuckles. "It's all right, Darius. It's all right."

Her gaze fell to the scar on his lips and he thought in sudden panic, *No. Don't ask me.*

She drew breath to speak. He didn't give her the chance.

"So, what do you want to do today?" he asked smoothly. With a playful growl, he spilled her off him and swept to his feet, his knees shaking slightly as he jumped out of bed and began dressing.

When two or three minutes passed and she still had not answered, he turned around. His forced smile died to find her looking at him. Still in bed, she lay on her side, her head braced on one hand. He cast about for anything to say.

"What would it take to make you trust me?" she asked softly.

He stared at her, heart pounding. At last he shook his head. "I'm sorry. I can't help it."

She nodded, searching his eyes with a gentle gaze. "Good enough." She sat up and held out her arms to him. "Come here. Let me check your stitches before you put on your shirt."

He finished buttoning his trousers and walked back to her, sitting on the edge of the bed, his shoulder to her. She examined her work. He was tense the whole time, barely hearing her as she told him the stitches looked good and that he was healing nicely.

Sitting behind him, she startled him when she embraced him and snuggled against his cheek. He tensed, bracing himself for a fight, knowing with every atom of his being that any second now she was going to demand again that he spill his guts.

She was just thinking over the words to ease into it. He knew it. He had been through it a hundred times. *How did you get this scar?* Every damned woman he met wanted to vivisect him.

"Darius," she murmured.

"Yes?" he said tautly, an armory of defenses at his fingertips. *Damn it, I trusted you.*

"Let's fly kites."

"What?" He turned around and stared at her.

"You remember those Chinese kites you gave me one year for Christmas? I still have them!" she said brightly. "I brought them." She kissed his cheek. "Come on, it'll be fun."

She went on chattering happily, but he was no longer listening, staring suspiciously at her. Something very strange was going on.

A short while later, they were traipsing out into fields crowded with butterflies and wildflowers under the wide, blue sky.

Darius wasn't sure exactly what he had gotten himself into.

The yellow ribbons on Serafina's wide-brimmed straw bonnet billowed out behind her, getting in his face, tickling, teasing him as he followed her. He hefted their picnic basket in his right hand, a folded blanket under his left arm, with a strange feeling in his brain that he had stepped into a dreamworld.

On a secluded hilltop acres away from the main compound, yet within the confines of the villa's wall, they came to a large, glittering pond in the middle of a green pasture.

"Oh, Darius, it's lovely!" she exclaimed.

"I found it looking for you yesterday." Squinting against the sun, he scanned the area for any possible threat, then reminded himself it was broad daylight and he had twenty men posted on the walls. *Relax, for God's sake,* he told himself, then he gave Serafina a lazy grin. "Let's go."

They crossed the field.

The grasses were up to their knees, and wildflowers abounded, little stars of yellow, white, and purple. Insects chirped, and here and there grasshoppers arced across their path. They found a shady spot under a huge elm tree. Darius spread out the blanket, snapping it open with soldierly efficiency. They left the picnic basket behind and went to fly the kites.

The kites were beautiful to see against the azure sky, the swirl of colors from their festooned tails plunging and soaring.

He forgot about everything, for more beautiful still was Serafina's delight. He indulged her when she clapped her hands for him to make the kite race along the surface of the water like an eagle scanning for fish. Of course, he grew cocky at the game, trying to make it zoom nearer and nearer the water until he finally sank the kite in the pond.

Serafina laughed her head off as he stared at his broken toy in dismay. The kite floated, parti-colored, on the water's surface like a drowned jester.

He pulled the string and it moved sluggishly toward the reedy shore.

She pointed, laughing to the point of tears. "Go get it, Santiago."

He growled without menace and rolled up his sleeves. He kicked off his boots and rolled his black trousers up to his shins. She was still giggling as he squared his shoulders and marched, resolute, to the pond.

Serafina helped him carry the kite out of the water, and while Darius went about laying it out on the grass to dry, she returned to their blanket in the shade and unpacked their picnic, her bare feet tucked under her. It was simple fare much the same as what they'd had last night, sliced meats and cheeses, grapes, a marvelous loaf of bread, and wine, but somehow she felt she had never dined so richly.

In a few minutes, Darius joined her, barefoot in the grass, black waistcoat hanging unbuttoned over his loose white shirt.

"Hello, handsome," she said with a coquettish smile.

He gave her a rueful look. She watched him kneel down on the blanket. He reached into the leather satchel he'd brought and produced his battered copy of his favorite book, *Don Quixote.*

He offered her the book. "Read to me. Any page. Doesn't matter."

She took the book from him, shifted off her knees, and sat on the blanket. He lay back propped on his elbows and looked around as though he couldn't decide how to arrange himself comfortably. She smiled at him when he caught her eye. She patted her lap in invitation.

He arched a brow. "Tempting."

"The best seat in the house."

He came toward her on hands and knees and lay down on his back, resting his head on her lap, his long legs sprawled out over the blanket, one knee bent. Settling against her, he let out a tremendous sigh of contentment. "You're comfortable."

She smiled to herself and opened the book.

He ate the cheese and grapes while she drank wine and read aloud to him, combing her hand through his damp hair, sifting his forelock through her fingers, absently unfastening the top few buttons of his shirt to caress his chest and play with the medal of the Virgin.

All the while, he twirled one of her tresses around and around his finger, his face nestled against her body. When the slight tug on her hair stopped, she glanced down and found him dozing, eyes closed.

She lowered the book and stared down at him, feeling her whole chest compress with emotion at the beauty of him, trusting her so sweetly, he—the spy, the assassin—who trusted no one. On this magical afternoon, she felt as though she had captured a unicorn. Yes, she thought fancifully, a unicorn stallion with great liquid brown eyes.

The thought that she must soon let him go free again was enough to make her want to cry. She shoved the thoughts violently away. The future did not exist here. There was only him, and now.

Plucking a blade of grass, she tickled his sun-bronzed cheek with it.

"There's an ant on you," she whispered.

"Mm, no," he mumbled, eyes closed. "It's just you being a nuisance."

She smiled and threw the grass away, then set the book down, dog-eared. She began stroking his chest and flat belly through his shirt, staring earnestly at his face as she fought with her uncertainties.

His eyes swept open. "What's the matter, butterfly?"

"Oh, Darius." Cradling his head in both arms, she leaned down and reverently kissed his brow. She stayed like that for several minutes, holding him, eyes closed. "You are so sweet. I want—I want to keep you all to myself."

His laugh was as soft as a sigh. "All right."

"I wish we never had to leave. Darius, why do we never get what we wish?"

He cupped her cheek. "That's just the way life is. Don't be sad. You are too pretty ever to be sad."

"I can't stop thinking about it."

"Give me a kiss," he whispered as he curled his hand around her nape.

She did.

He was right. His kiss made her fears vanish. She sighed as she melted into his embrace and drank the kisses thirstily from his sculpted lips. He gathered her into his arms, pulled her down onto the blanket with him, and made her forget.

For three days, they were constant companions.

As if from a distance, Darius observed the king's most trusted man courting disaster and didn't care. He tasted rest it seemed for the first time in his life, a soul-deep sweetness that lingered, an end to the exhaustion of constant watchfulness, and an easing from him of the iron grip that was his decades-old, acute wariness for his own survival.

Serafina cuddled him like he was one of her animals. Though

he played it fairly cool, he thrived on every minute of her attention, moved by the sweet joy she took in fussing over him.

Merely hearing her call his name in the house did profound things to him.

He would not have thought it possible, but she became even more beautiful as her happiness blossomed, and it awed him, almost beyond his grasp, to imagine that he, the Gypsy bastard, the nothing, was the cause. He could only watch her like a half-wild animal, marveling at the way she tamed him. Dimly he sensed that somehow this woman was the answer to every need he'd ever suffered, even those which had gone unmet for so many years he'd given up on them.

She absorbed every particle of his attention. He saw a man who was like a child for her, soaking up her laughter and her smiles, her artless caresses, and he wrapped her love around him like a blanket on a cold winter's night. He fed upon her innocent kisses that turned so frequently to feverish desire, and yet the sense that theirs was a chaste and sacred bond never left him.

They ignored the future and neither dared speak aloud what he knew both of them foolishly daydreamed—that it was forever. That this ancient villa with its fading yellow paint was their house.

That he was her husband.

That she was his wife.

He knew it was absurd. He didn't care. He knew it would hurt terribly later. Didn't care. They were playing like children at a reality that could never be, but for now it was easy to forget that a war-torn world existed beyond the estate's protective wall.

He didn't get any work done, aside from penning some correspondence to his estate manager in Spain. He wrote the man his instructions from their bed, using the smooth curve of Serafina's naked back for a desk. For days, he didn't practice or train, didn't even want to look at the elegant rifle he would soon bring to Milan.

Caught up in learning for the first time how to live, he didn't want to think about death.

His whole existence turned upon her kiss. His dignity, he decided, was a small price to pay for the joy he had found. She was the delight of his life. In the mornings, they languished and played in bed together well past breakfast. In the afternoons, they watched clouds, painted outdoors with watercolors, collected botanical specimens from the woods and fields. They waded in the little lake, they had picnics, and somehow, in spite of unbearable temptation and frustration, they refrained from making love.

On the fourth night, as they lay in bed, their bodies entwined, they stared for innumerable moments into each other's eyes, doing nothing but caressing and touching.

But soon he felt her skin heating with the blush of arousal, his innocent seductress. She slipped her arms around his neck and gave him a hungry kiss. His muscles trembled with his awareness of how unbearably easy it would be to slip inside her, take what was his, and quench the endless ache.

This he vowed he would not do. He vowed it with the last shred of honor he had left. He would not leave her ruined and possibly with child when he went off to die. It was bad enough that she would mourn him.

She whispered his name, running her hand down his stomach. He shivered.

Slowly, he lay back on the cool sheets, pulling her atop him. He tasted her mouth deeply while his hands roamed up and down her back, caressed her arms, kneaded her backside, her silken thighs enfolding his hips. When she moaned softly with desire, he rolled her onto her back again, on the edge of desperation.

The curtains billowed over the open window, carrying to them the fragrances of the night. They petted and played, spending themselves lavishly, recklessly, while the precious moments continued ticking away, sand steadily draining from the hourglass.

Something's wrong.

Darius awoke suddenly in the middle of the night, with crisp, instant alertness.

The room was dark. Beside him, Serafina slumbered peacefully. He held very still, listening.

All he heard was the stridulating song of insects and Serafina's restful breathing, but his heart was pounding and the hairs on his nape stood on end.

He sat up, swung his legs over the side of the bed, and reached silently for his breeches and a shirt, then pulled on his boots. He walked quietly to the door and listened, hearing nothing.

With a dark glance back at Serafina, he opened the door and went out. Moving soundlessly down the hall, he descended the wooden stairs, avoiding the steps that creaked. On the first floor, he rounded the newel post and glanced into the first room he passed, the dining room. Here, as in every room on the first floor, he had stationed a man at the window.

"All clear, private?"

"Yes, sir. All's quiet," said the soldier.

"What's the hour?"

"Three, sir."

Darius gave a firm nod. "Hold your post."

He checked in with the others without incident, but the instinctual sense of warning did not diminish. His sixth sense, honed so early in life, had saved his neck too many times for him ever to ignore its sometimes illogical proddings. Still uneasy, he went into the small, spartan room he had abandoned days ago, and opened the armoire, where he took out a black leather case which housed his usual arsenal of weapons.

Lifting his ebony-handled dagger from its velvet bed, he felt better the instant his favorite weapon was in his hand. He tucked a pistol into the waistband of his breeches for good measure.

Restlessly, he paced through the house and went out to the back porch, where he found Tomas, the sergeant of the squad, smoking a cheroot.

"Something wrong, Colonel?" the sergeant asked, offering him his cheroot.

"I don't know," he murmured as he bent down, accepting it. "I have a bad feeling."

Tomas shrugged, stifling a yawn. "Everything's quiet so far tonight."

"Maybe too quiet." He took a deep drag, and sauntered to the edge of the porch, gazing out at the woods. The air was cool and balmy, the half-moon riding high.

"Have you seen anything unusual?"

"No, sir. The sentries have the dogs out with them. I'm sure we'll hear those monsters barking if anyone's out there."

"Let's hope so." He exhaled a stream of smoke, took a second drag, and gave it back to Tomas, then wandered inside. Restlessly, he paced through the house, glanced out the windows here and there, but what he could make out of the night-clad landscape was still.

At length, he made his way to the kitchen for a drink of water. He took a metal ewer from the cupboard and went to the hand pump, pumping until the cool mountain springwater gushed with a tinny ring into the ewer. He thought he heard something, maybe horses' hooves.

He swiveled his head to look over his shoulder, brows knit. He heard men's voices in shouted conversation coming from out in front of the house, but the water's noise splashing into the metal pitcher obscured the words.

Idiots. They'll wake Serafina, he thought in annoyance.

He went to the window and stared, seeing one of the black government coaches parked in front of the house, the horses still blowing. He could see the royal insignia emblazoned on the door. Then he squinted in puzzlement to see Captain Orsini in the driver's seat.

What the devil is that sweaty ox doing here? He's supposed to be catching spies, Darius thought. He watched Tomas walk toward Orsini, and finally the water quit running and he could hear.

"Well, I've got clearance and those are my orders!" Orsini was saying. "They want me to bring her back now. I don't know why. You think they tell me anything?"

"Let's see your documentation. There's no way His Majesty could give an order like that without Santiago not already knowing about it," the sergeant protested.

Orsini never got the chance to reply.

It all happened in perhaps ten seconds.

Darius's eyes widened as the coach door burst open and two black-masked men with crossbows jumped out. In smooth symmetry, they took two steps apart and dropped to their knees, firing in deadly silence on the men posted at the door. Like clockwork, six more masked men sprang out of the carriage and rushed the house.

Darius was already bolting for the hallway. *"To arms!"*

He paused on his way out of the kitchen when the knife rack hanging on the wall caught his eye.

He lifted a carving knife from its place on the rack. He whirled around the corner into the foyer just as the front door crashed open. The masked men leaped over the dead front-door guards and poured into the house in neat, lethal pairs.

Darius hurled the carving knife into the chest of the first man over the threshold, then lifted his pistol, bracing his aim with his fist, and shot the second in the face.

"Serafina!" he roared as he swept out his dagger. *"Lock your door!"*

They were upon him.

CHAPTER
❧ ELEVEN ❧

One of the masked French agents lifted a large gun and aimed at his chest.

Darius whirled back behind the base of the stairs just as the bullet slammed into the library door. He flattened himself against the corner, heart pounding.

When the Frenchman stepped into view, Darius brought up his elbow and drove it straight into his chin. The masked head whipped back and the Frenchman fell flat on his back. Darius stepped over him and punched him in the face to make sure he stayed unconscious, then, dagger in hand, he glided silently back out to the foyer, a battleground now where twenty men grappled. The French had thrown stinkpots to create a smoke-screen. Eyes watering, Darius squinted against the foul, choking smoke.

Serafina.

He had to get to her. He could barely see, and the melee blocked his path to the foot of the stairs. Wildly swinging lantern light bounced off the smoke. Flintlocks flared with the report of shots fired amid the din of frantic, angry shouts. The front door was hanging open and he could see the bodies of the guards stationed there lying across the threshold, arrows sticking out of their chests.

Just then, he saw two of the enemy agents break away and rush the stairs.

Beyond thought, Darius raced after them, pushing ferociously through the fight. They were running up the steps, but he was right behind them. He seized the first of the two agents several steps shy of the upper hall. The man turned on him suddenly, slicing at him with a smallsword. Darius dodged the blow and wrenched the man's arm. He used the force of the other man's swing to send him sailing with a shout over the rail into the fray below.

Turning forward again, he saw that the second one, at the top of the stairs, had turned and was ready for him, sword drawn.

Another came running up the steps behind Darius, hemming him in.

He cursed mentally, looking at one Frenchman, then the other with a wordless snarl. He bristled as the one lower on the steps closed in, holding him at bay.

All of a sudden, a wedge of light spread over the landing as the bedroom door opened above. *No.* Serafina took a half-step out into the hall, her anxious, lovely face illumined by the taper she held aloft.

"Stop it!" she screamed at all of them.

"Get back!" Darius roared.

The Frenchman on the landing turned and stared for a split second at the goddess in the white peignoir, her sable curls flowing wildly about her shoulders.

Darius seized the moment and spun, kicking the man on the lower step square in the face. As the Frenchman crashed backward down the steps, Darius lunged upward, driving his dagger in between the ribs of the man on the landing. Darius dropped him, leaped over the body, and grabbed Serafina about the waist, sweeping her into her bedroom.

"Lock it and stay put!" he commanded. "That was not in the drill!" he growled, then pulled the door shut in her face.

He whirled around, blocking the door as he waited to hear both locks slide home, but no more black-masked agents appeared.

The enemy had been vanquished.

Panting and covered in sweat, his muscles trembling

slightly, Darius leaned his head back against her door, his chest heaving.

Back and forth she paced in the pink bedroom, arms around herself, her night rail flowing out around her. Just then, a soft knock at the door broke into her dread.

"Angel?"

She tore back the locks with shaking fingers and threw open the door. "Are you hurt?" she cried.

"I'm fine," Darius said soothingly as she took his forearm and pulled him into the room.

Frantically, her gaze scanned the tall, powerful length of his body. "Are you sure you're all right?"

"Yes." He took her gently by the shoulders.

"Blood!" She grabbed his wrist, examining a smear on his sleeve.

"Not mine," he said. "Calm down. Look at me."

Heart pounding, she jerked her head back and met his even stare.

"Shh, you see? I'm all right," he whispered.

She stared up at him, then flung her arms around his neck and held him with all her strength, squeezing her eyes shut.

"You had no business coming out of this room, angel."

"I'm sorry. I had to see if you were all right." She was willing to apologize for anything, she was so relieved he was unscathed.

He smoothed a lock of her hair behind her ear. "Get dressed, beauty. I'll be back."

She followed him to the door uncertainly.

One hand on the doorknob, he turned back and touched her face, tilting her chin upward with two fingertips. He leaned down and brushed her mouth with a nuzzling kiss. She laid her hand on his chest, caressing the V of his hot, damp skin where his shirt lay open. Her fingertips came across the warm, tiny medal she had given him so long ago.

Catching it in her palm as her mouth lingered against his,

she sent up a prayer of thanks to the Blessed Mother for protecting him yet again.

"I'll be back," Darius whispered, ending the kiss.

"You saved me again," she told him with a starstruck gaze.

He cupped her cheek and gave her a tender smile in the dark. "Because you are my princess and I am your knight." He gave her a wink and silently slipped out the door.

She sighed, holding a hand to her heart. She stepped into the doorway after him and watched him walk away, soaking in the beauty of his loose, wary grace as he stalked down the hall, but then her gaze wandered to the scene below.

Several lanterns had been lit, and by their glow she could see the squadron's medics already getting to work. Her throat burning with the smoke-roughened air, she walked to the top of the stairs and stared at the chaotic scene below.

Wounded men lay strewn about the foyer, while the nimble medics knelt here and there beside them, gave aid, cleaned wounds, wrapped bandages, and efficiently moved on to the next patient. One man was borne away on a stretcher. A few were dead.

Darius had done this. Savage, wild Darius. This was the work of his hands, the same hands that were so gentle on her body and that could pluck such beautiful music from his guitar. Her magnificent unicorn stallion had gone on the rampage to protect her, wild and lathered as a deadly warhorse with slashing hooves and fiery eyes.

Shaken, she quickly closed her bedroom door and dressed. Grabbing the sewing basket containing her medical equipment, she left her room to see if she could be of help.

"Where is he?" Darius asked in a low, deadly tone.

"This way, sir! I'll show you!"

Darius followed the young private around the house to the back garden, where he found Orsini closed in by a ring of infuriated soldiers. The captain of the Royal Guard was on all fours, his broad, meaty face sweating. Every time he tried to get to his feet, they shoved him violently back down again. The men looked like they wanted to lynch him on the spot.

"You're in for it now," one of the men said as Darius stalked into their midst.

Orsini cursed and attempted to crawl to the far edge of the ring of jeering soldiers and servants when he saw Darius. Darius stood shoulder to shoulder with his men for a moment, staring down at Orsini.

"You pig," he spat, then strode toward him, seized him by the collar, and threw him on his face in the turf. He grabbed Orsini's right arm and wrenched it up behind his back. "Do you know what we do to traitors on this island?" he snarled.

"They made me do it! They had a gun to my head!"

He wrenched Orsini's brawny arm higher. "I see you are not going to cooperate. That suits me fine."

"I'm not a traitor! I took a few bribes—I never meant for anything like this to happen! They forced me!"

"Listen carefully. You lie to me once, I'll break your arm. Lie again, and I'll cut it off."

"No, no! I know you're crazy enough to do it," he blubbered.

"You're damned right I am. I want names. Shall I bring out the dogs?" he asked, producing his dagger. "They've scented blood tonight, Orsini. They're hungry." He waved his dagger slowly back and forth before Orsini's eyes. "Hold out his finger," he said to the men.

A spate of nervous laughter rippled among the men, but Darius's stare did not waver, for his threat of torture served a dual purpose. The demonstration would not only gain him whatever information Orsini was hiding; it would also serve as an implicit warning to his men and the servants that he would enforce their silence on the matter of his affair with the princess by whatever means necessary. Two of the men seized Orsini and forcibly stretched out his arm, prying his fingers open from their fist, while another brought two of the snarling, snapping guard dogs on chains.

"Here, puppy, puppy," Darius called softly with a smile, taking Orsini's finger in one hand, his dagger in the other.

Orsini blubbered.

"Oh, come, it's just a finger. You've got nine more. I'm going to give you one more chance, then I'm going to start throwing these beauties some treats. What do you say?"

"I don't know anything!" he screamed out.

With that, Darius cut Orsini's finger to the bone. He shrieked, the men laughed in astonishment, and Darius merely stared, smiling a slight, satanic smile at him.

It was all the persuasion Orsini needed.

Bleeding everywhere and sobbing with thanks that Darius had left the finger attached, Orsini give him the names of the three spies remaining in the palace under deep cover. Satisfied, Darius rose from his crouched position and jerked a nod to his men.

"Lock him up for court-martial."

Orsini kept all his fingers. Nevertheless, he would hang.

The young soldier stared at Serafina in awe, as if he had forgotten all about the nasty wound above his ear where the bullet had grazed him. She held the linen wrap of his head bandage in place, while the medic affixed the end with a few drops of wax from a candle.

"Don't lie flat. Keep yourself propped up," the surgeon ordered before moving on to the next man.

Serafina remained with the patient a moment longer. "Thank you for protecting me," she said softly.

"Y-yes, Your Highness!" he said, his eyes like saucers.

She gave the boy a compassionate look and squeezed his hand, then rose and followed the surgeon to his next patient. When another medic appeared, she stepped back, deferring to his superior skill.

She wasn't needed. She was probably only getting in the way, she thought, but no one dared say so. Not knowing what else to do, she stood there watching the two skilled doctors work on the man's wounded leg. The medic was wrapping another layer of bandaging to stanch the flow of blood when suddenly she heard Darius.

"Serafina!"

She looked over to find him striding toward her, his onyx eyes ablaze, his exotic face dark with anger under the glossy raven forelock.

"What are you doing down here? I told you to stay put!" He seized her by the wrist and pulled her out of the dining room and into the hall. "Why do you want to involve yourself in this? What a nightmare," he muttered.

She did not bother to argue but followed him, uncomfortably aware of male eyes on her as she climbed the staircase. Darius noticed, too. His black scowl over her head made them lower their stares.

"Did you learn who the spies are?" she asked as he hurried her back into her bedroom and pulled the door shut behind him.

"Yes."

"Who are they?"

"Nobody you know. Listen, if I ride for Belfort at once, I can take them unaware."

Her blood ran cold in her veins and she paled. "You're leaving tonight? Now?"

He glanced away. She saw tension in his taut jaw.

"Darius, it's the middle of the night!" Her voice rose in pitch. "You aren't even waiting till the morning?"

"The danger is past now for you," he said with careful restraint. "The medics and the wounded will stay here with a crew to clean up, but within the hour, Alec and Sergeant Tomas will take a contingent and escort you back to the palace. You should be home by midmorning."

She gripped his forearm, trying to force him to look at her. "I will see you there, won't I?"

He turned to her, saying nothing. They stared at each other

for a long moment, then Darius swallowed hard and looked away. "We both knew this moment would come."

She drew in her breath sharply and stepped away from him, pressing her fingers to her lips as she strove to steady herself.

"Serafina."

"So, this is how our idyll ends. In blood and death. Of course," she said bitterly, her back to him. "It is my fate, is it not? Helen of Troy. God, I wish I had never been born."

When she felt his strong, warm hands alight on her shoulders, she turned, throwing herself against him. He caught her up in his arms and kissed her, parting her lips roughly, consuming her as he clenched her body against his.

Caressing his face with trembling hands, she drank of him in wild desperation, running her fingers through his silky black hair, clutching handfuls of it as if she could keep him with her forever. He tried to end the kiss. She wouldn't let him.

She kissed him deeply, her whole soul in it, knowing it was the last time she would ever hold him. Gathering him closer and closer to her, she felt herself falling apart as she tried to memorize the texture of his hair, the taste of his mouth, the satin smoothness and warm, smoky smell of his skin.

At last, he caught her face between both his hands and pulled back, staring into her eyes with fierce tenderness and agony, the ancient depths of his onyx eyes profound with feeling.

She reached for him again, catching his hands, pulling at him. "I can't lose you. I'll see you at Belfort, yes? Say yes. Come to my room—use the secret door you showed me—"

He silenced her, laying a finger over her lips.

"Be strong for me," he choked out.

She vowed to herself that she would. She closed her eyes, fighting for control, as he rested his forehead against hers.

"If you ever need anything," she whispered, shaking, "anything at all, if you are ever in trouble, come to me. I will always help you, I will always . . . love you, Darius."

He clutched her to him, grasping two handfuls of her hair as he buried his face in the crook of her neck. "Princesa," he breathed unsteadily.

He pressed one final kiss against her neck below her ear, then he pulled out of her arms and she sobbed, for he was gone.

The tears in his eyes were born of the whipping wind, he told himself, for Darius rode as though the devil himself were chasing him, pushing the mighty black stallion to the limit at a grueling pace. He tried to focus his mind on the rhythm of horse's hooves striking the dirt road, but in his chest was an emptiness, his heart torn from him. He wanted to scream, to stop the horse, take his sword, and beat it against a tree until he'd drained some of his pain and rage, but he did not, fighting for self-control with all his strength.

By God, I won't let them catch me, he thought, over and over again. *I'll blow that Corsican bastard's head off and I'll come back to her. I will.*

He didn't believe his own promise, but this litany gave him enough of a thread by which to keep himself tied together, until at last he galloped through the gates of Belfort just as the sun was peeping over the eastern hills. At the stable yard, he flung himself down from his lathered, blowing stallion, entrusting the animal to a groom with a few curt instructions.

He knew exactly where to find the first of the three spies. He stalked into the stable, down the main aisle. At the far end of the barn, he could see the courtiers gathered for the king's daily morning gallop. Some were drinking coffee, some taking swigs from elegant hunt flasks.

The smug-looking dandy he wanted was smoking and idly tapping his riding crop against his leg. The man finished his cheroot just then, threw it into the dust, and stepped on it with one polished bootheel. When he looked up, his glance happened upon Darius stalking ruthlessly toward him.

Fear flashed across the man's countenance.

"Greenling, what are you doing here?" boomed a voice down the stable aisle behind him.

The king had arrived but Darius ignored him, never taking his eyes off his prey. The Frenchman's gaze swept the stable area in that split second, scanning for escape.

Darius broke into a run. The Frenchman bolted.

"What the devil?" some of the courtiers said as Darius pushed through their midst, chasing as the Frenchman made a dash around the side of the stable.

Darius caught the man swiftly, tackling him. The king came striding up behind them.

"What the devil's going on?"

"I demand an explanation," the Frenchman protested.

"Oh, I think you understand, *monsieur,*" Darius said softly, wrenching his right arm up behind him and shoving his face into the dewy turf.

"Santiago?" the king said expectantly.

"Sir, the princess is secure. Right now, there is more cleaning up to do," he murmured, just as several of the courtiers joined them and began asking questions.

Darius and Lazar exchanged a look.

"Go on, I'll take it from here," the king said with a nod.

Next, Darius strode into the palace. The palace steward greeted him with the usual courtesies, but Darius pulled the tidy little man aside.

"I need to know where Viscount D'Abrande's rooms are."

"Ah, let me think. All His Highness's cronies are housed on the third floor of the south wing. The viscount's rooms are on the left side of the hall, I believe, about midway down—but you won't find him there this morning, sir. Ahem." The palace steward cleared his throat. "Prince Rafael and company, I'm afraid, are sprawled about in the billiard room. Another drinking bout," he whispered.

Darius smiled tranquilly. "Perfect. Thank you, Falconi."

Within ten minutes, he seized the young viscount, dragging him out of the billiard room.

While some of the young lords protested on their false friend's behalf, they were all too groggy and sore-headed to put up much of a fight against a man they all feared even with the courage of liquor.

Dragging the struggling young viscount toward the door, Darius paused by the pool table where Prince Rafael, Lazar's son, was sleeping peacefully. He slapped the prince lightly a few times in the face to wake him.

"What, what?" Sandy brown hair mussed, clothes rumpled, the tanned, sinewy nineteen-year-old struggled up onto his elbows on the green velvet of the billiard table. Rafe dragged his bloodshot, gold-green eyes open and offered Darius a dazed grin, setting off the cleft in his chin that made the girls of Ascencion sigh. "Hey-ho, Santiago."

"Have a little decorum, would you?" Darius said tersely.

"Sure," the youth agreed cheerfully, turning on his side on the table. "In an hour or so, maybe." The heir apparent folded his hands under his cheek and went back to sleep.

The kingdom's doomed, Darius thought grouchily as he hauled the struggling viscount into custody.

Finally, Darius marched toward the royal block, holding his anger carefully in check. He stopped at a suite down the hall from Serafina's apartments. He blasted the door open with a savage kick and strode into the girls' suite.

"Who's there?" demanded a voice.

Darius paused in the girls' sitting room, looking over as a feminine outline appeared in the open doorway to one bedroom.

"Santiago?" the redhead called Els demanded. "What is the meaning of this?"

"Close the door, you little hussy, it's not you I'm after," he growled as he crossed the sitting room and forced Cara's bedroom door open.

"What are you doing?" Els shouted. "Cara?"

"Stay back!" he ordered her.

When he slammed Cara's bedroom door open, he found himself looking down the barrel of a pistol, alpine blue eyes coldly meeting his. He began laughing softly.

"Get out of my way," the girl ordered.

"Put down the gun."

"Cara!" Els burst out in amazement.

"Your friend has been aiding the enemy, Els," Darius said smoothly, never taking his eyes off the girl. "She's not as pure as she'd have you all think. Every move Serafina or the queen makes, she's been passing it all on to the French. Philippe Saint-Laurent seduced her for that express purpose."

Cara took a step toward him. "Don't come any closer! I'll shoot you, you devil! I hate you! You killed my Philippe! I found out that you did!"

"Put the gun down, Cara. If you cooperate, perhaps I can get your sentence commuted from hanging to life imprisonment, or perhaps even banishment."

"*Hanging?* What is going on?" Els cried. "I don't believe this! Where is Cricket? Obviously, there has been some mistake. Cara, just do as he says. We'll sort it all out—"

"Shut up, you slut," the blond snapped.

Darius lunged at her, driving the gun upward. It went off, shattering a crystalline sconce on the far wall. Cara threw the gun at him and leaped onto the bed, trying to run across it and escape, but Darius caught her, flinging her onto the tangled coverlet on the bed. She kicked at him, her night rail flying about her knees. He pulled her onto her feet.

"You Gypsy whoreson! Leave me alone! I'll kill you!"

Cara continued hissing useless threats and epithets at him as he pulled her right arm up behind her back and drove her toward the door.

Els was in tears, blocking his path. "Don't do this, Santiago! She could not possibly be a spy! Look at her! She's a little angel!"

"I'm not a spy! I'm a good girl!" Cara became hysterical. "Els, don't let him take me away! This is a lie! I would never betray Cricket or the queen!"

Angrily, Darius jerked her slight frame in his arms. "Enough."

"Let her go, please, Santiago, there must be some mistake," Els begged him, plucking at his sleeve.

"There is no mistake," he said more gently. "Els, listen. Serafina doesn't know yet. She'll be back in a few hours. She's going to need you."

"I understand." Els stepped out of the way, shaking her head in disbelieving reproach at the blond.

In the hall, Darius warded off Cara's kicks and punches, growled at her attempt to bite him, and coldly laughed when she offered to go down on her knees for him in exchange for one chance to escape.

The sun had just peeked over the horizon.

Her arms wrapped around her, Serafina slumped against the interior wall of the coach, staring out the window, her body rocking with the vehicle's motion. Fifteen soldiers on horseback flanked the coach.

When she closed her eyes, she saw only Darius. She forced herself to get some rest, lulled by the rocking and creaking of the coach. She knew she would need her strength to face Anatole.

At about ten in the morning, the coach arrived at Belfort, pulling into the lavishly landscaped drive. Serafina suddenly perked up, seeing the sleek, powerful figure of a man dressed in black on the front steps, smoking a cheroot. When the man flipped his black hair out of his eyes, her whole being lit up from within.

He's waiting for me!

She saw Darius gesture to a servant, who went quickly to the front door. A moment later, her father came marching out and stood with Darius at the top of the steps. Then Serafina squinted in puzzlement, recognizing Els's flamboyant red mane as her best friend joined the two men, her pale green skirts rippling in the breeze. The coach had barely stopped when Serafina bounded out, not waiting for the footman. Her heart beating fast, she ran to the trio as they came toward her.

"There's my girl!" said her father warmly, giving her his crooked smile. She launched into his arms, feeling an instant, tremendous surge of relief and safety as she always did in his presence.

Head pressed to her father's bulky shoulder, however, she stared only at Darius, beaming at him with pure love.

But the chiseled perfection of his face was as cold as a statue's. She thought she saw a fleeting trace of something in his eyes, but he met her gaze without expression, then turned away. Stunned, she stared at him, slow to comprehend, refusing to let the fact sink in.

It was over.

Really, truly over.

No, no, he is just being his old, aloof self because Papa is standing right here. He doesn't want Papa to guess how we have known each other. . . .

But the excuse withered even as it trailed through her mind. In vain, she willed Darius to look at her, but he held himself remote. Then she felt the horrifying truth sinking down slowly, ever more deeply into her bones, revealing the final disillusionment. He had been her one great love, while to him she had been just another affair. He had warned her from the start.

She closed her eyes—aghast, sickened.

As her father released her with a smile, she stood there rather dazed, completely at a loss. Surely she and Darius were not standing here pretending there was nothing between them. No, it was an awful dream; her real life existed at the yellow villa, in the pink bedroom— Her breath snagged suddenly on something like a sob. She cut the sound short.

Her father looked curiously at her. Els murmured hello and Serafina looked over at her, still reeling from the blow. Had he just been amusing himself with her, passing the time? Had his love been real at all? When she saw the red rim around her friend's emerald eyes, her attention left her own catastrophe for a moment. Els was not one for crying.

She touched her arm. "What's wrong, Elsie?"

Els, Papa, and Darius all looked at one another.

Her father took a deep breath as if to speak, then exhaled swiftly, shaking his head. "You tell her, Dare. I can't."

Darius turned rigidly to her with a level, soldierly expression, avoiding her eyes. "We have a situation, Your Highness."

"A situation? What kind of situation?" Suddenly she gasped. "Is it Mama—the baby?"

"Nothing like that," he said tautly. He hesitated. "Your Highness, would you care to step inside and sit down—"

"Tell me now!"

"As you wish," he said, then he began to explain.

She couldn't believe it. She could not believe Cara had done it, nor that Darius had lied to her upon learning from Captain Orsini that her friend was implicated as a spy.

The whole day, she wasn't allowed to see Cara. With parasols to shade them from the sun, Els and she took a long walk on the beach, trailing their bare beet in the sand and trying to make sense of it all. Followed by a retinue of servants and chaperons at a respectful distance, they stopped now and then to gaze at the white sails of Ascencion's fleet in the bay.

Serafina had never seen Els in so serious and sad a mood. Fortunately, the redhead's distress over Cara's downfall helped distract Serafina from her realizations about Darius. As a couple of hours passed, she was even able to convince herself that he had been just as upset this morning about losing her as she was over losing him. Indeed, maybe he *had* been so stiff and cold because Papa had been standing there.

She knew he had tried to be gentle, breaking the news to her about Cara this morning. He had probably wanted more than anything to take her into his arms and comfort her, but he had been unable to. After all, no one had forced him to stand out there waiting for her carriage to arrive.

Hope clung like a thorn in her flesh. Her one consolation was that maybe, just maybe, he would come to her tonight. That, she told herself, would be the decisive factor.

The day dragged by and she didn't see him again.

Late into the night, she lay awake, willing him to appear, trying to conjure him, her demon love, but the secret door never opened, and quietly she cried herself to sleep.

It was two A.M. Darius was sitting idly in his suite, just sitting hour after hour, smoking, thinking, and staring at the wall. Holding his dagger by its ebony handle, he would hurl it at the wall, where it would stick in the plaster with a shuddering thud. He would stare at it awhile, get up, wrench it out of the plaster, sit down. Repeat. Ignoring his hunger. Organizing and reorganizing his plans in his head. Asking himself questions he'd already answered a hundred times, and willing himself to see some other solution he might have missed.

He didn't want to die, but too bad, he thought. He crushed out another cheroot in the already full ashtray and sat for a long time, slouching in his chair, watching the shadow of the dagger meld into the other shadows.

The blackness was closing in on him. It took all his strength not to go to Serafina. He would not give in to it. A clean break was best for her, no matter how much she needed him in this moment, nor how frightened he was and how alone.

He sat back, silently tortured, weighed down in the chair by his exhaustion.

For a long time, he listened to the song of crickets beyond his windows, breathed the cool night air perfumed by lilacs, almost dozing in the chair until the silence was broken by the creak of the door.

He looked over in surprise and saw it was not the servant he'd sent to the cellars for some wine, but Teresa, one of his former lovers. He looked away as his mood turned blacker.

He wished the dagger was in his hand, for it would have delighted him to send it plunging into the door next to her head. She locked the door behind her and crept toward him. He rested his chin on his fist, waiting.

She came to stand before his chair and offered him a hesitant smile. Despite his hostile stare, cautiously she came closer, as he knew she would. He tensed as she lowered herself to her knees between his sprawled thighs.

Without expression, Darius watched her slowly begin to touch him, watched her fingers savor the satin of his waistcoat and, bolder after a few minutes, undo his cravat. He wondered why he was so numb. What was wrong with him that always drove people to act this way with him?

She reached between his legs, subtle as ever.

"No," he mumbled, but he didn't push her hand away.

She caressed him upward, his belly, his chest.

"No?" she asked with a knowing look, banked lust under her heavy-lidded eyes.

"Leave me alone," he said in a strangled whisper, but she just untied the neck strings of his shirt, boldly raking his bare chest with her nails. At last he felt his skin catch fire in the wake of her clawing touch that hurt in a way she could not know.

Her hot hands massaged the tired muscles of his thighs through the sturdy cloth of his black trousers, curled around his calves. He heard her breathing coming faster, deeper.

He still refused to speak to her or make any move toward her, hating her. She pressed herself against him, wrapping her soft arms around him, brushing his clenched jaw with her cheek, kneading his neck in her trembling hands. He was so weary. He felt like he was being raped for the hundredth time, too weary to struggle anymore. He just wanted her to go away. He smiled bitterly at her angry groan when she pressed her lips to his and he declined to kiss her back. Why should he?

She left his lips to tease his earlobe between her teeth.

"Please, Santiago, let me," she whispered into his ear, an exasperating tickle. "I'll do whatever you want. You know I'm good, let me, *ooh*, Santiago . . ."

The whine of a bitch in heat. She sickened him. His own lust sickened him. Hands on her shoulders, he didn't know if he was forcing her down or holding her off. They stared at each other.

God, he loathed her, but he rather liked her red mouth.

Something in his eyes must have made her think she'd won.

"Mmm," she said, settling closer between his open thighs. But when she reached for the buttons on his falls, he began to panic.

It had never mattered before that he didn't want these women. What mattered was that they wanted him. Somebody, anybody, wanted him, even if it was only for this.

Not this time.

His hold on the woman's shoulders tightened. "Teresa," he said harshly.

She looked up at him, her eyes bright with the fever of desire, her tongue skimming lightly over her lips. He stared intensely at her.

"I don't want you," he said. "Go."

Taken aback, her eyes widened, then she gave him a worldly smile. "You don't?" she asked, caressing his hardness through his clothes. "What game are you playing, gorgeous?"

He stopped her, grasping her wrist and slowly twisting. "No game. Get out."

She pulled her hand free of his grasp, staring at him in confusion and the start of fear. "What's wrong with you?"

"Get out!" He suddenly stood up and pushed her, deeply angry all in a flash. She fell back, catching herself on her hands as she stared up at him in astonishment.

"I said get out," he said savagely, restraining the urge to kick her.

In seconds, she was gone, slamming the door behind her.

Sitting back down in his chair, he waited for the pounding of his heart to slow to a normal rhythm. He raked a hand through his hair, got up, and went to the door, locking it. Then he turned slowly and leaned his back against it. He realized he was shaking. He wrapped his arms around himself and hung his head.

CHAPTER
⊰ TWELVE ⊱

The next morning, Serafina stood on the stepping stool before the full-length mirror, gazing in apathy at her reflection while the seamstresses put the final touches on her bridal gown. Her mother had overseen all the wedding preparations and now beamed with pride, gazing at her.

"You look perfect," the queen announced.

Serafina forced a wan, answering smile. Her mother, she supposed, attributed her bleak mood to the shock of Cara's betrayal.

This morning, she had learned that Cara had been interrogated for hours last night and had finally signed a confession to the charges of treason. Taking pity on her, the queen had asked that Cara's sentence be commuted. Now Cara was to be banished, but the men would hang.

Hating herself for her own hopeless naïveté, Serafina was beginning to see the wisdom in Darius's philosophy of trusting no one.

"Would Your Majesty care to see our progress on the child's christening gown?" the head couturiere asked the queen while her assistants worked on Serafina's magnificent train.

"I would!" Mama said brightly.

The couturiere led the way into the adjoining room. The moment the queen left the fitting room, her ladies-in-waiting all began gossiping in hushed voices.

Serafina rolled her eyes and ignored them, then scowled

down at the young seamstress who had accidentally pricked her calf with her needle. "Ouch!"

"So sorry, Your Highness!" the girl cried, turning pale.

"Hrmph," she said, then returned her attention to the murmured conversation going on behind her.

". . . can't believe he threw you out of his room!"

"Yes, he was positively wild with rage! I thought he would do me some violence!" said the graceful, doe-eyed Lady Teresa.

Serafina turned suddenly.

The women stopped.

"Whom are you gossiping about?" she demanded, staring haughtily at them. She knew from long experience that if she did not use her rank against them, they would use their greater numbers to try to intimidate her.

They glanced at one another.

"I asked you a question."

"No one, Your Highness."

She gave them a look of derision and turned back to the mirror.

". . . was alone with him for a few days, wasn't she?"

"You don't suppose . . . ?"

"Too scandalous!"

"We all know he is a very bad boy."

"Never," someone whispered. "He'd never risk angering the king."

Eyes ablaze, Serafina gritted her teeth and stared straight ahead.

"Don't worry, Teresa, here's what we'll do. You and I will go to him together tonight, like that one time during Carnivale—"

Serafina pivoted in fury, ignoring the seamstress's noise of distress.

The ladies stared at her like little girls caught passing notes by the school headmistress. She suddenly realized they were as fiercely curious to ask her about her sojourn in the country with Darius as she was to find out what they were saying about him.

Disparaging herself for sinking to their level, she decided to switch tactics.

"Is this gown really all right?" she asked prettily, pouting. "White makes me look fat."

"You're not fat," the buxom blond Lady Antonia said hatefully.

Fashion and insecurity they understood.

They clamored to assure her she looked ravishing.

"Ah, Your Highness . . ." Julia Calazzi began.

"Yes?" she asked innocently.

"How did you find your stay in the country?" Julia asked politely.

Serafina's heart wavered dangerously. If she let herself think of the tumbledown villa with its peeling yellow paint, she knew tears would rise in her eyes.

She shrugged. "Boring."

"Was Colonel Santiago civil to you?"

"Rude as ever," she replied.

They looked relieved.

She hated it that she couldn't gloat to them how devoted and warm he had been. After all, maybe it had all been a game to him. That was all she had intended to say on the matter, but then, because she couldn't resist, she added archly, "I did overhear him playing his guitar one night. The melody was very sweet."

"He plays the guitar?" Teresa exclaimed.

Julia's shrewd gaze flicked back to Serafina.

Serafina smiled back at her coolly and thought, *I hate your guts.*

"Of course he plays the guitar, Teresa," Julia said smoothly. "Everyone knows that. But I know something about him no one does."

"Oh, really?" Serafina retorted.

Julia held her silence with a smug smile.

"Well?" Antonia demanded.

"It is a great secret," Julia said gravely, relishing the moment.

Serafina rolled her eyes and let out a vexed exhalation.

"His real name," Julia announced grandly, "is *Count* Darius Santiago."

The women exclaimed in amazed protest. In the mirror, Serafina pinned Julia's reflection in her stare. Julia met her gaze with a veiled look of triumph.

"You don't know what you're talking about," Serafina remarked while the others fussed and cooed. "Why would you start a rumor like this? Just to cause trouble for Darius? Don't you *know* he is illegitimate, or do you simply not care how much the fact hurts him?"

"He is not illegitimate anymore, as he knows full well. Oh, my dear, did he not tell you? His father acknowledged him right before he died."

"Really?" Antonia exclaimed.

Julia nodded sagely. "When the old count learned how well Darius has done for himself, he was eager to claim him for his son. Lord knows, his other sons are wastrels."

"He has brothers?" the women cried eagerly.

"Half-brothers. Two of them, both older," Julia clipped out. "They were the count's legitimate sons."

Serafina could barely find her voice for shock. "Who told you this?" she demanded.

Julia sipped her tea. "Someone at the bank where Santiago stows his millions."

The others exclaimed anew. "Millions?"

Serafina arched a brow at the woman, taken aback. What game was she playing? "Have you been prying into all of his affairs, then, Lady Julia?"

"I know everything about him," she replied. "Everything."

Serafina folded her arms over her chest. "How, pray tell, would the banker know about Darius's father?"

"Simple, my dear Principessa, because of the drafts which Darius withdrew on his father's behalf."

Serafina stared at her. "You mean to say his father wanted money from him?"

"Naturally. The man was a penniless drunkard."

Amazed and a little infuriated that she should learn such intimate details of Darius's past from this source, Serafina turned back to face the mirror, utterly routed.

She was also appalled to think that the callous man who had not acted the smallest part of a father to Darius when he was a boy—a man who had not protected him or provided for him, but had left him to fend for himself—had had the nerve to come looking for a handout.

"Oh, Your Highness, I almost forgot to mention . . ." Julia's smile was as smooth as the flat of a razor, but a few words sufficed to flick the blade. "Did you hear the news? Your husband arrived just after breakfast."

She stared at her, turning pale. "He's not my husband yet."

Julia took another sip of tea, then smiled. "Goodness, how we'll miss you when you're gone."

Serafina was suddenly out of patience. "Enough!" she snapped at the seamstresses ringing her in. They scrambled out of the way as she stepped down off the stool before the mirror and marched toward the dressing room, ignoring Julia and the others giggling at her.

"I will make a fine countess, don't you think?" Julia was asking the others blithely as Serafina slammed the door.

A few minutes later, she was striding down the hallway with one burning purpose in mind: to find Darius Santiago and give him a piece of her mind about his petty secret-keeping. Omission of the truth amounted to the same as lies, and she was sick of his spy machinations—and sick as well of her own naïveté. She had thought they were as close as two people could be, but he had been playing her false all along.

What an accomplished liar he was! she thought, her hackles up for a fight. She knew exactly why he had not told her about his title. He had hidden behind his lowly, half-Gypsy status because he did not want her to gain any inkling of the fact that he was, in reality, a perfectly eligible bachelor.

She had never cared what his birth was or what he owned. She had only ever loved him for himself. Why did that terrify him so much?

No doubt he would give a great sigh of relief when she was finally married to Anatole and could no longer plague him with her tedious, adolescent infatuation! But he had not found her breasts tedious, had he? she thought in a perfect fury, for if she didn't stay angry, she was going to start crying, and if she started, she was never going to stop.

"Where is he?" she muttered under her breath. The pair of footmen posted at the end of the hallway glanced at her in alarm as she passed. She strode out of the block that housed the royal living quarters and into the main corridor, where the courtiers and ladies lurked. She passed the open doors of the blue salon, where she saw, and was seen by, half a dozen of her devotees.

Young, clean-shaven faces lit up. She rolled her eyes and marched past the doors, continuing on her way, curls flouncing angrily down her back.

"Princess Cricket!"

"Principessa! Wait!"

She clenched her jaw, ignoring them as they ran out of the salon after her.

"May we walk with you?"

"This place has been a mausoleum without you!"

"What about the ball tonight? Is Prince Tyurinov going to let us dance with you?"

"I don't know. I don't even want to go," she grumbled.

"He'd better! The man's too jealous by half. You must save a dance for me—"

"And me!"

"All of us! Where are you going in such a huff, my lady fair?"

"Come play billiards with us!"

"You should have seen the joke we played on Roberto while you were gone—"

In truth, she adored her silly friends—it was, in part, for their sakes that she was marrying Tyurinov to prevent a war, for she could not imagine any of these pampered dandies surviving a battlefield. At the moment, however, she was in no mood for them.

Full of high spirits, giving her compliments, telling her jokes and exchanging boasts, they chattered rapidly as they followed her in a pack down the main hall. She paid them little mind, glancing in every gallery down the main hall. No trace of Santiago anywhere.

Maybe he was in bed with a new lover already, she thought in despair, someone he would have no qualms about giving himself to completely, as he had denied her the consummation she had all but begged for.

As she crossed the sprawling marble entrance hall, from which five hallways led to the various wings of the palace, one of the boys grabbed an orange lily from the huge bouquet on the center table and swept down on one knee in front of her.

"For our goddess," he said in playful gallantry, his eyes teasing her as he held out the flower.

She threw up her hands. "Leave me alone!"

"Do as she says."

They all looked over at the sound of a cold, accented voice.

For a moment, Serafina froze, the color draining from her face.

At once she backed away from the boy with the flower, her hands curling into fists at her sides as her betrothed held her in his frigid stare.

Framed by the hallway stood Prince Anatole Tyurinov, a massive man with a copper-gold mane, which he wore, vainly, spilling down upon his gigantic shoulders. He was clad in a dark blue uniform with shiny gold buttons down his broad chest. His eyes were the light azure blue of a bright January afternoon, sunny but pitilessly cold.

"Anatole," she forced out, dropping her gaze. She sketched a slight curtsy, her heart pounding.

"I am glad you remember me," he said in polite reproach, offering her a slight, mechanical bow. Still politely bent, he glanced up and shot her a knowing smile. She felt the crushing wave of his innate brutality rushing toward her.

The lily fell from the boy's hand as he murmured an apology and backed away.

When Anatole lifted his square chin, surveying the room as if he owned it, the boys shrank away like dogs before an approaching lion.

Serafina was left standing in the wide entrance hall alone with him. He was several yards away, but she felt cornered.

He began slowly striding toward her. She swallowed hard but held her ground, inwardly switching over to the regal manner she had been trained to execute from an early age.

With her hand, she swept a slight, graceful gesture toward the entrance hall. "Welcome to Ascencion and our home." She had to tilt her head back to look up at him as he neared.

His face cracked into a smile.

"Goddess, eh?" he murmured as he stepped squarely onto the fallen lily. "I hate to think I am wrecking their religion. Who was he?"

"That boy?" she stalled.

"That boy," he said indulgently.

"No one of any consequence, Your Highness." She forced one of her most winning smiles. "How was your journey?"

"Anatole," he whispered.

She quaked inwardly. "How was your journey, Anatole?"

He smiled and gently tucked a lock of her hair behind her ear. She fought not to flinch when he touched her.

"Have you been a good girl, my bride?"

For a second, she thought she would slap him. Delicately, she slipped away from him and took a few steps across the wide, empty hall, heart pounding. She went to the center table and made a show of smelling the flowers, turning her back on him, but then she could feel his eyes on her body. Nonchalantly, she rounded the center table so she could hide herself from his leer behind the bouquet.

Slowly, he trailed her. She kept the table and the giant flower arrangement between them.

"Were you long on the ship?" she asked with forced brightness.

"The voyage dragged, for my eagerness to see you." His voice was like a rusty plow being dragged over gravel.

She plucked a withered leaf from a peachy rose. Her smile remained fixed but her hand shook. "And when did you arrive?"

"Two hours ago. I've been having a drink with your most excellent father."

His compliment to her father did not go unnoticed. Her tension eased a degree or two. She looked up at him. "I hope Papa did not go sentimental on you. He is having trouble with my leaving. He is very protective."

"Yes, I know," he mused, "which is why I found it strange. . . ." He paused, rubbing his chin in thought.

"Found what strange, sir?"

"That he sent you unchaperoned into the country with a man over whom you once made a fool of yourself."

Staring up at him, she turned utterly white.

He cracked another terrifying smile. "Do you think this Santiago is the only one who can learn another's secrets, my bride?"

She parted her lips to speak. No sound came out.

"Of course, your father has no inkling of your fascination with this man."

"I was quite young," she forced out.

"Did he lay a hand on you?"

"No."

"Did he?" he demanded.

"No!" Her heart was beating like it would explode, her knees shaking.

"Your father trusts him."

"He has no reason not to. Santiago's conduct is impeccable. As for my prior infatuation with him, I will not deny it. The man took a bullet for my father."

"Does this impress you so? It is a common event on the battlefield for a man to give his life for his friends."

"I was twelve, Anatole, a mere child. I was standing right there. I had his *blood* on me."

Merely saying it sent odd reverberations down into her being.

He gave her a sour look, but he looked a trifle mollified. "You're telling me, then, that you were merely starstruck by this hero of yours."

"As a child I was, but that was years ago. Santiago and I have little more than a passing acquaintance now." She held his gaze matter-of-factly, hating herself for these bold-faced lies that seemed to cheapen the sweetness, tenderness, and beauty of what she and Darius had shared. She could only pray she was convincing.

Rounding the table toward her, Anatole gave her a sideward smile that probably beguiled other women. "I hope you are not lying to me, my sweet island rose." He reached to stroke her arm. She jerked away, cheeks flushing in a riot of color. "For I *will* find out the truth on our wedding night, won't I?" he added.

She gasped and pivoted, striding away from him on legs that shook beneath her. She heard his laughter behind her.

He followed. "Serafina—"

"Sir, you are too familiar," she said coldly as she walked swiftly ahead of him.

"Your Highness, I was only testing you."

She whirled around. "*Testing* me?"

"Aren't you glad you passed?"

Staring up at him, amazed by his effrontery, she found

herself slowly being backed toward the wall. She folded her arms tightly over her chest, shielding herself instinctively, glaring up at him in defiance as he loomed over her. He had sought to intimidate her like this last time they met, she recalled, the time he'd told her he must tame her.

Supremely sure of himself, he tilted his head, gazing down at her, the blond locks flowing over the front of his shoulder. "A little bird told me that three years ago, at your debut ball, when you flung yourself at this poor fellow, he fled. This says to me he is a man of honor, as you claim, and that he understands his place. I approve."

"You approve. I see."

He held up his hand to silence her, a long-suffering expression on his rough-hewn face. "Your father should be glad for such a man; such loyalty is rare. My only question is whether or not you sought to tempt poor Colonel Santiago again during this . . . cozy little sojourn in the country. A woman like you cannot abide a man who refuses to succumb to her charms, and a man can only be pushed so far."

"A woman like me?" She stared up at him in disbelief. "You obviously know nothing about me. Excuse me, Your Highness. I answered your question three times already." She turned to moved past him.

He stopped her, pinning her against the wall with one fingertip jabbed none too gently into the front of her shoulder. With so little effort, he held her in place. It was humiliating.

"Don't go. Pray, indulge me, my bride," he said, smiling.

At that moment, the front door banged back and in walked Santiago.

Oh, God. Her stomach plummeted.

There was a split second before he saw them. Anatole barely troubled himself to glance over his shoulder to see who had come in. Head down, the forelock veiling his eyes, Darius took a couple of slow, weary steps into the entrance hall, then he lifted his head, saw them, and froze.

His stare homed in on her, then locked on Anatole, and his eyes turned to blackest fire.

The air of weariness around him fell away. Without hesitation, he strode swiftly across the room, threw Anatole back, and punched him—a shattering blow across the face.

CHAPTER
⊰ THIRTEEN ⊱

Serafina gasped as Anatole tripped back a step. Darius pursued, driving him back to slam his spine hard against the far wall.

"You know who she is? You put your hands on her?" Darius roared at him.

Anatole grabbed Darius by the throat. Darius turned nimbly and drove his elbow into Anatole's abdomen. Anatole doubled over slightly for a moment with a curse. Darius looked down his nose at him in pure contempt and snarled something at him in Russian that brought pure savagery leaping into Anatole's blue eyes.

Anatole charged him.

The fight ensued. Serafina had never seen anything like it in her life. She could only stand there in shock, eyes wide, both hands pressed over her mouth, as her fiancé and her lover clashed like two powerful wild animals battling for supremacy. Tyurinov had the size and brute strength of an enraged bull, Darius the speed and finesse of an attacking panther. She knew she could not possibly separate them, but she could not seem to move to go for help, afraid that if she so much as looked away, they would kill each other.

She was aware of footmen who had come running. There were shouts. A servant ran off to get help, but no one dared go near them. Serafina was frozen where she was.

Scarcely breathing, she looked on in bewildered terror, flattening herself back against the wall as they crashed to the floor by her feet, rolling like embattled wolves. Darius wound up on top as Tyurinov and he tried to strangle each other.

He punched Tyurinov across the face again, causing the other man's grip on his throat to slip. In that instant, she saw Darius's hand go smoothly for his dagger. Horror filled her.

"Darius, no!"

He looked over at her, chest heaving, and she saw the beast in his eyes—the ferocious creature who had saved her that terrifying night in the maze. But as his gaze fixed on her, the savagery cleared.

In that second, Anatole recovered and dealt Darius a reeling blow under the chin.

The guards came flooding into the hall then and pulled the two men apart. It took several men to hold them back, and all the while Darius and Tyurinov screamed at each other in Russian.

"What are they saying?" she cried.

None of the guards knew.

She could not believe Darius had attacked Anatole so rashly. Of all the times he had been insulted by the courtiers who loved to bait him, he had never allowed himself to be drawn into a brawl under her father's roof.

Darius roughly shrugged off the men and turned away from them, raking a hand through his hair. Anatole's fury, too, began to simmer down to bristling edginess, but each man was still ringed by guards.

Anatole's mouth was bleeding at the corner, and she could see the crimson stain on Darius's shoulder where his stitches must have torn open again with his exertion.

Serafina dropped her face in both hands. She didn't know which of them to go to.

At that moment, she hated them both.

She lifted her head, cheeks burning with shame, and looked at Darius. Hair tousled, chest heaving, his fiery stare was fixed on her. His coal-black eyes glowed with stormy, anguished passion. In that moment, he was as beautiful as an avenging angel, and she had the strangest premonition that she was never going to see him again.

Seated at her writing desk in the privacy of her rooms, scratching out another flaming diatribe to a creditor who would not stop hounding her, Julia Calazzi was still stewing over the fact that, stupidly, she had showed her hand, revealing Darius's title. It was unlike her to act on emotion, but she had been simply unable to stomach Princess Perfect's gloating, lording it over everyone because she had had Santiago all to herself for nearly a week.

Julia really didn't wish to face the question of whether or not anything had happened between them while they were gone, but clearly Serafina was more in love with Darius than ever.

Anatole's arrival should bring her back down to earth, she thought in smug satisfaction.

Just then, Teresa burst in on her and swiftly related the news of the fight between Santiago and Tyurinov. Teresa gushed with the details as if this were some delicious scandal, but Julia's blood ran cold. The others did not know Anatole as she did.

When Teresa was through, Julia forced a cool smile. "Well, darling, you'd best run along. He may need some nursing."

"My thoughts exactly!" Teresa laughed gaily and hurried out of the room.

Julia's gaze traveled absently over her desk while her heart pounded. She refused to let herself panic. Instead, she rose, went to the mirror, and touched up her makeup as she considered her strategy.

She gave Anatole one hour to cool down, then left her rooms and walked slowly to his suite, chin high. At his door, she closed her eyes for a moment, gathering herself, then she knocked.

His valet admitted her. She walked into a room crowded with the towering Russian officers and nobles of Tyurinov's entourage. She could not understand their words, but the tension in the air made her certain this gathering was something of a war council. She knew who the enemy was.

She had come to plead for Santiago's life.

Oddly, she felt small and weak among them, but they parted before her so she could follow the valet, who beckoned her into the adjoining bedroom.

She stepped inside and found two men in whispered consultation with the prince. Anatole sat in an armchair as though it were a throne. He was bare-chested, golden hair flowing over his magnificent shoulders, his cold stare fixed straight ahead with a sullen look.

When his sapphire stare flicked to her, piercing her, he lowered the muslin-wrapped ice from his jaw and dismissed the two men. They brushed past her. The valet closed the door, and she was alone with him.

She thought of asking him if he was all right, but hesitated. No, that would only insult him.

"Quite a welcome," he remarked. "Don't you think?"

She crooked her mouth into a cool smile. "I've come to welcome you properly." She walked over to him and leaned down, gently kissing his bruised, sullen mouth. At once, he shoved his hand between her legs, cupping her mound. Julia hid her annoyance and straightened up, taking a step back.

"Not yet," she chided with a coy smile.

Smiling at her, he trailed his fingers lightly under his nose.

"What happened?" she asked as she went to lean with seeming idleness against the footboard of his bed.

"An insane Spaniard attacked me. For this, he is a dead man, of course."

"He is very close to the king," she pointed out. "What do you intend, a duel?"

"I haven't decided yet. Come sit on my lap," he invited her.

She arched a brow, smiling in smooth patience. "Not yet."

"It was a long voyage without women."

"Ah." She trailed her hand over the curve of the footboard. "Anatole? Is it really a good idea for you to rid the world of

Santiago? You realize the man has been her guardian all her life. She is like a little sister to him. How is he supposed to react when he sees you threatening her?"

"You should know better than to ask me to feel mercy, Julia."

He was right, she thought, staring at him. She wasn't going to get anywhere unless she appealed to his self-interest.

"And I doubt his feelings are brotherly," he added in a rumbling growl.

"These people are very clannish, Anatole. In fact . . ." She folded her arms under her breasts and decided to go out on a limb. "It is sometimes whispered that Darius Santiago is actually the king's byblow."

"Oh, really?"

"I don't know if that is true or not," she lied, "but I do know as a boy he was a ward of the king. If he is Lazar's son, you can well see it would be unwise to kill him. Besides, it is commonly known that if Santiago favors any one woman around here, it's me."

He propped his blunt, square chin on his fist and considered her words. "Brother and sister . . . ?"

"If you had a sister and perceived a threat to her, what would you do?"

He gave her a sullen look and glanced away, shifting in his chair.

"Anatole, really. I know everything about everyone in this palace, and Her Highness is not in love with him. How could you possibly doubt yourself?" She began walking slowly toward him, rolling her hips with each step. He watched, his eyes agleam.

She rounded the back of his chair and reached down to caress his chest slowly with both hands. "No woman could prefer any man to you," she whispered.

He lay back against the chair, soaking up her touch. When he closed his terrible, piercing eyes, she was glad.

"What if an accident befell him?" he murmured.

"They would see through it. Darling, I'd hate to see this minor incident prove a stumbling block in your marvelous career. So many people are counting on you, Anatole. Let him go. He's not worth it. He's nothing."

"He is nothing," he agreed as she continued stroking his smooth, ironlike body.

"Come, grant me this favor, Anatole," she wheedled softly. "There will be no more trouble. I'll keep him away from your bride for you."

The sapphire eyes swept open. His gaze locked on her face in cool amusement. "What's in it for you, Julia?"

"Well, if you must know ... money." She lowered her lashes. "His money. I mean to marry him."

He began laughing. It was the coldest sound she had ever heard.

"I am in rather dire straits," she protested, a bit rattled by the sound. "If you kill him, I don't know what I shall do."

Still chuckling, he closed his eyes again. "Having you for a wife is perhaps punishment enough in itself."

"God knows, I don't want to be anybody's wife, but I must have some security," she said indignantly.

"Do you promise to cuckold him until he is a laughingstock?"

"That *is* my way," she conceded.

"Give me a massage," he rumbled.

She obeyed, squeezing his glorious shoulders. He was unaccustomed to the Italian climate, his skin covered in a fine sweat.

He was silent for a long moment, sprawled in the chair while, out the window, the sun began to set over the distant hills.

"You are considering it?" she probed.

"Perhaps I could be persuaded." His steely fingers clasped around her wrist as he pulled her hand down to his groin.

He was fully erect, and in spite of herself, she was impressed.

"Persuade me, Julia," he whispered, eyes closed. "You know what to do."

Bare-chested, Darius sat alone in his suite at his dressing table, using the mirror as he tried to repair the damage to the stitches he had pulled. Serafina's careful handiwork had held him together until he had begun to heal, but now he was bleeding again.

His door barricaded against the harpies pleading to be let in, Darius glanced over when he heard a familiar male voice join in their midst.

"Why, here is camped the fairest army ever seen! Ladies, my loves, if you attack me for a change, unlike certain Spaniards, I swear I will surrender."

Darius rolled his eyes. Prince Charming was at it again. He could just picture the tanned, handsome youth swaggering into their midst. He heard peals of feminine laughter and barely dared imagine what the young Romeo was doing with the women out there.

"Run along, ladies, go put on your ball gowns, for I expect each and every one of you to dance with me tonight."

They whined at Prince Rafael to order Darius to open his door and let them in, but he deflected them with his irresistible, inborn charm. "Now, now, clear out, my lovelies. I must have a private word with our prizefighter, man to man."

An alarming thought struck Darius. What if Rafe had deduced the truth of his affair with Serafina? Good Lord, what if the little coxcomb had come to call him out? Dueling was the boy's new hobby.

His knock fell on the door. "Hey-ho, Santiago. Lemme in."

Warily, Darius rose and unlocked the door, admitting the crown prince. Leaving the door open, he walked away. The young man sauntered into the suite, shutting the door behind him.

"What are you doing, sitting here in the dark? Lord, Santiago, sometimes I swear you are part gargoyle." Rafael had a large scroll tucked under one arm. He threw it on the desk and picked up the single candle there which Darius had lit. He carried it around the room lighting the wall sconces. "I hate to be the bringer of bad news, Santiago, but I'm afraid you are disinvited to Tyurinov's welcome ball tonight."

Darius laughed wearily. "A reprieve."

"How novel, too, to find Father grumbling about you, and myself in his good graces. He wants to see you."

Darius sighed and rubbed his forehead. "Yes, I imagine he does." Elbow propped on the dressing table, he rested his head in his hand and stared gloomily at the floor.

A moment later, he saw Rafe's boots as the lad returned to stand before him, hands on hips. The prince's excellent black boots and tan breeches were flecked with mud, he noticed. "Where have you been, playing in a pigsty?" Darius asked, looking up at him.

Rafe flashed a rakish grin, revealing the dashing cleft in his chin. "Working on my maps. For Father's birthday," he added by way of explanation.

Darius nodded, recalling what Serafina had said about her brother mapping the underground tunnels. "An ambitious project."

Rafe drifted across the room and flung himself down into a brocaded armchair. "Not as ambitious as smashing Tyurinov a facer." He began laughing as he slipped an elegant hunting flask out of his waistcoat. "What on earth did you do that for?"

Darius heaved a sigh, raking his hand through his hair in distress. "I don't know. I cannot think what came over me."

The boy took a swig and wiped his mouth with the back of his hand. "Can't you?" he said matter-of-factly. For a moment, his penetrating gaze reminded Darius exactly of Lazar's, though Rafael had more his mother's coloring. Darius returned his gaze dully.

"He was bullying my sister, was he not?"

"So it appeared to me. God knows it was the last thing I expected to walk in and find."

Darius had already had a full day by the moment he had walked into the hall to find Tyurinov playing his intimidation games on Serafina. He had spent the morning interviewing a small, elite group of officers, seeking a replacement for Orsini to the post of captain of the Royal Guard, then he had overseen matters as young Cara was deported, sending her off to seek asylum with the French government.

This done, he had gone into town to send off his lengthy report to Czar Alexander, putting in place the last cogs and wheels of his subtle design, then visited his solicitor for the purpose of setting his final affairs in order, including a change to his will.

For sheer, wretched sentimentality, he had purchased the yellow villa from the government and had left it in his will to Serafina. He wanted to give it to her so she would always have a peaceful retreat where she could get away from the shallow, parasitical people of the court, and to remember him and the few, precious days they had shared there.

"She doesn't want him, you know," the youth said flatly, bringing him back to the present. "She's hiding it from Father and everyone. It's a disgrace! Why should one poor girl be forced to protect the lot of us? What of honor? We are men, aren't we?" He suddenly jumped up and began pacing.

"What do you suggest?"

Rafe clenched a fist. "I say we fight! If Napoleon thinks he can take us, let him try! She's my sister, I'll protect her! You'll help!"

"Ah, youth," Darius muttered cynically, turning away.

"You think it can't be done?" he demanded.

"We are sorely outnumbered, and besides, my fine hothead, we wouldn't even know where they would attack, which shore to defend," he said heavily. "Don't worry. Everything is going to be fine."

"That only means you already have something up your sleeve. Well, I damned well hope you do." Rafael gave a well-bred snort, pacing back and forth across the room. "Sometimes

I think the only reason Father is so bent on avoiding a war at all costs is because he's afraid I'll set one foot on a battlefield and instantly be blown to smithereens. Maybe if I didn't have the great Santiago outshining me at every turn, he would see I am not an utter imbecile," he said with a rueful grin.

Darius winced. "Don't say that. You are his son. His heir."

"Well, you're his protégé. Mere mortals like me will never quite measure up in his eyes."

Darius dropped his chin, realizing this was probably the last time he would see the boy who had been like a baby brother to him. "I know he's hard on you, Raffaele, but it is because he cares for you."

"Do you think he'll *ever* listen to me and trust my judgment the way he trusts yours?"

Darius lifted his shoulders, at a loss. "I merely have more experience than you."

"Well, I'm never going to *get* any experience to prove myself, because I'm never allowed to *do* anything. All he does is criticize me. Nothing I do is good enough, so you know what? I give up. The hell with it. There's no pleasing the man. Until he turns up his toes and it's my turn to rule, I'm just going to have my fun."

Darius stared at him, appalled.

Rafe glanced at him, blanching guiltily at his shocked, accusing gaze. "What?" he muttered.

"How can you say that? That man thinks the sun shines for you," he said angrily. "You think he's hard on you? You should have known my father. You wouldn't have lasted a day."

"Easy, Santiago, Jesus," the youth said with an uneasy laugh as he leaned against the windowsill and looked out at the view of the distant sea. "You'll be punching my face in next."

Just then, the door clicked and Darius tensed again, looking over. Julia Calazzi peeked into the room. *"Hellooo?"*

Darius shot a scowl at the prince. "You forgot to lock the door."

Julia sent him a flushed, almost girlish smile and slipped into the room. She shut the door behind her and came toward him with her sinuous, hip-swinging walk.

Rafe watched her pass, his gold-green eyes traveling slowly over her figure. He let out a low, admiring whistle. "There she is, the lady of my dreams."

"Go away, I want to talk to Santiago," she said to him as she smoothed her upswept hair.

"Why don't you ever visit me? I tell her daily that I am in love with her, but she won't listen, Santiago. Any advice?"

"Watch your back," Darius said prosaically.

Julia gave him a haughty, pointed look. "Indeed?"

Rafe shoved away from the windowsill, sneaked up behind her, and captured her by the waist. Darius looked on in mild amusement as the lad hauled her against him with a cubbish growl. "Come on, Jules, give me a go. What do you say?"

Julia gave him a dirty look over her shoulder. "I'm too old for you. Go find a girl your own age."

He grinned at Darius from over her shoulder and gave her a squeeze. "Be a sport, Jules. I'll show you the time of your life."

"You're a royal pest, you are!"

Darius smirked at her rare discomfiture.

Julia elbowed him harmlessly in the chest. "Go away! I came here to talk to Santiago!"

The prince whispered something probably lewd into her ear. She stamped her foot. "Santiago! Tell him to stop!"

"Stop," Darius said dryly.

"Well! I dare not tangle with the prizefighter. Your virtue is safe, my lovely. For now," the prince added, eyes laughing. "But when you need a *young* man with some stamina, you know where to find me."

Julia squeaked when Rafael pinched her backside, drifting casually by her. He went to the door, picking up his scrolled map off the desk as he passed. *"Ciao,"* he said. "Don't do anything I wouldn't do." He closed the door behind him.

Darius wished he had not gone.

Julia turned to him, looking almost flustered. "He is an abhorrent youth."

Darius reached for his shirt, draped over a nearby chair. He slipped it on. "You loved every minute of it."

"Well," she conceded, glancing toward the door, "the notion of educating him holds a certain appeal. After all, he will be king one day."

He gave her a stern look as he tucked his shirt in.

"Don't worry, I've obeyed your standing order. I will not corrupt him. He is safe." She slid Darius a look askance. "I've got bigger game to hunt."

He folded his arms over his chest and regarded her skeptically.

Julia sighed, gazing up at the ceiling. "I could have told you about Orsini. It upsets me to know you were in a dangerous situation when I could have forewarned you." She hesitated. "I acted badly the other night. I shouldn't have struck you."

He said nothing and waited for her to go away.

"Shortly after I left you that night," she continued, "I realized who it was you had in the room with you."

His gaze homed in on her with sudden fierceness.

"I recognized her voice."

He stared at her, bristling.

"I realize I overreacted," she went on in awkward contrition. "Obviously, you would never fool with the king's daughter. I know she has always had a mad crush on you and of course she's stunning," she said acidly, "but as you've told me a hundred times, she is like a little sister to you."

"Could you get to the point?"

She turned to face him, palms upward. "I'm trying to apologize. With all these spies you've uncovered, and what with the Russians' arrival, I understand now that you were in the middle of matters involving your work—"

"What do you want, Julia?"

At his curt interruption, she lowered her head and folded her hands behind her back. "You are angry."

"No, I am merely sick of games."

"So am I," she said emphatically. "That's what I'm trying to tell you. Santiago . . . Darius," she corrected herself more softly. "I want you to think about the future—and me."

He refrained from rolling his eyes. "You were widowed less than six months ago."

"Do you think I have any reputation left to lose if I don't observe the proper mourning period?" she said with deep, world-weary bitterness.

"Julia," he began gently, "it would never work. Put it out of your mind."

"I know this comes as a surprise," she protested. "You need time to think it over—"

"No, I don't," he said softly. "I'm sorry."

As she assessed him for a moment, he couldn't fail to see the vulnerability and creeping onset of despair in her carefully made-up eyes. In them, he read her fear of the future when her beauty had faded. Perhaps she had begun to see that one day she would be left alone with the bitter fruit of all the foolish choices she had made.

"We were good together. I think you and I could learn to love each other, Santiago."

"Julia, Julia," he sighed as he took her by both shoulders and pressed a brotherly kiss to her forehead.

She lifted a gaze full of bottomless need to his. "Try with me," she whispered. "I think I could make you happy."

"Face the truth," he said, staring steadily down at her. "You used me and I used you. That's all it ever was. That is all we were capable of together. Look at us, two hardened, battered souls. You'll find someone, Julia."

"I already have," she replied.

He merely shook his head and released her. "I think it would be best if you go now." He started toward the door to open it for her and see her out.

But she did not follow. To his perplexity, Julia began laughing.

"You arrogant fool," she spat in a tone of pure poison. "Do you think I don't see what's going on?"

He looked over his shoulder, one brow arched in surprise. "I beg your pardon?"

She folded her arms tightly over her chest, tears in her eyes. "Tell me, did you give it to her nice and slow when you were out in the country, *rusticating*?"

Darius froze. He pivoted and walked back to her, heart pounding. "How dare you?"

The tears had vanished. She tapped her lip thoughtfully. "Hmm, I wonder what the king would have to say if he knew."

"Knew what?" he snarled.

She considered for a moment, her eyes calculating. Smoothly, she switched tactics. "I heard what happened last night with Teresa."

"Nothing happened."

"Precisely. When I heard you wouldn't let Teresa stay with you last night, it confirmed what I've suspected all along. You poor, pathetic fool," she added bitterly. "Don't try to deny it. I know you've been panting after that girl since she was barely sixteen."

He paused for a long moment, trying to decide how to dodge this. It didn't appear that he could. "If you slander her, Julia," he said abruptly, "I will finish you. No jest."

"You can never have her, you know," she flung out. "She will never understand you as I do. She couldn't begin to handle the hate you've got inside you!"

He ignored her words. "What are you going to do?"

She laughed, gloating. "Excuse me, but this is just so amusing. I have finally discovered your weakness. I always knew you had one somewhere, hidden away but the king's daughter? Ah, well, you always had a taste for the forbidden. It seems I have you right where I want you, doesn't it?"

He glared at her, trembling with anger. "What do you want?"

"You, darling," she replied. "I want you. You say I don't

know what love is? I do. I've wanted you for years. Now, finally, I am free, and if I can't have you," she said coolly, "I'm going to destroy you."

He felt as though he had been punched very hard in the stomach. "How?"

"I'm going to tell the king that you seduced daddy's little precious."

"But she is pure," he cried. "You have no proof."

"Don't need it. I know you, Santiago. You won't lie to the king's face. Your eyes give you away."

"What is it, the money you're after?" he asked in fury. "The title?"

"They do add to your appeal. But it's you I want."

"Why would you want me when I don't want you? I'm never going to love you."

She merely smiled at his ire, but he felt her rage beneath her cool facade. "Let's just say it comforts me to know you're as thorough a slut as I am."

He stared at her, hurt by her words and bewildered.

"I'm giving you three days. At that time, you will either get down on your knees and propose to me, or prepare to be exposed for the fraud you are."

She lifted up on tiptoe, trying to kiss his cheek. He recoiled from her. She stepped back with a smirk, then prowled to the door.

"Think it over," she advised him. "You need me more than you know."

She left.

Darius raked a hand through his hair, cursing under his breath as he struggled for calm.

Nothing could come of Julia's threats, he assured himself, for he would be dead in a few days. The thought was hardly comforting. It filled him suddenly with the desperate need to see Serafina's artless smile and innocent, violet eyes. His whole body hurt with missing her, as if a part of himself had been torn away from him.

Standing alone in his room, he quivered in pain. He closed his eyes tightly and drove the heels of his hands into them, his mind filled with the memory of kissing the curve of her back, the taste of her silken skin under his lips. He felt his whole world hanging by a thread over some vast abyss, and thought, no, he could not go to her now. One look into her eyes would make it impossible for him to leave and to do what he must.

Forcing the pain from him as though throwing off an enemy, he went to his bed and dragged out the long, black case stowed underneath it. He collected his other weapons, took out a leather satchel, and began packing.

After a facial mud-mask, a bath in five gallons of milk, followed by one in tepid water which had been carefully perfumed, Serafina lounged on the divan in her sitting room while her lady's maid briskly filed and buffed her nails and her hairdresser trimmed the dried ends off her hair.

She felt like an elaborate entrée being prepared for a ravenous giant.

Her maid finished with her nails while the hairdresser brought over the diamond tiara Serafina was to wear tonight and placed it carefully on her head. Snapping orders at another maid to hold a mirror for them, the hairdresser explained several options of what they might do with her coiffure, piling her hair this way and that, coiling here, plaiting there.

"I shall wear my hair down," she said.

"Down? At a ball?" said Madame, aghast. "They will think you a wild savage!"

Serafina gave her a quelling stare in the mirror. "Down, please." Darius liked her hair down.

"But the neckline of your gown—it cries out for an upswept arrangement!"

"Then I'll wear a different gown."

"But no one will be able to see your neck! You have a perfect neck, like a swan! If I had such a neck, I would cut my hair up to my ears, like a man!"

Serafina gave a long-suffering sigh. She only tolerated the hairdresser's fits of passion because the woman was the best in the kingdom at what she did. At that moment, there was a knock at the door. Serafina gestured to the young maid holding the mirror. The girl went to the door and opened it.

"For Her Highness," a liveried footman said with a bow.

"Thank you," the maid murmured with a curtsy. She shut the door and came back to Serafina, offering a small velvet box.

She accepted it and opened the box with interest, but her heart sank when she peered inside. On the tiny bed of velvet sat her monstrous diamond engagement ring. It had been flawlessly repaired. Without expression, without flinching, she took Tyurinov's ring from its bed of velvet and put it back on.

"More wine, Your Highness?" the young maid asked, stepping forward to offer a fresh glass on a tray.

"Yes, please," she murmured, and when the girl brought the glass, Serafina lifted it to her lips and drank deeply.

At precisely eight o'clock, she gave herself one final survey in the full-length mirror.

Was that little confection in pink really her? she wondered. She felt jaded and lost inside, but the girl in the mirror looked like a princess from a fairy tale, innocent and fresh. Her mink-black curls were pulled back from her pale, heart-shaped face with a diamond tiara, while the mass of her hair spilled down her back. Her silk gown was a simple sheath with a strawberry sash. The dress was almost white, tinged ever so faintly with seashell pink. The sleeves were small puffs, her hands and arms concealed by high, white gloves.

What a joke, she thought, wallowing in hidden misery. But the pretty package was what Anatole had paid for.

She took a final, long draught of wine, turned from the mirror, and left her apartments with Els and a few other of her ladies a step behind.

By the time the powdered, liveried, and bewigged palace steward banged his gilded baton on the marble floor, announcing her entrance in his nasal voice to the thousand guests in the vast, gilded ballroom, she was feeling quite pleasant—drunk enough not to care what became of her, but not to the point where it showed. To the fanfare of trumpets, she proceeded down the long, curving, white staircase on the arm of her ever-cheerful father.

The dull roar of the crowd and the lilting melody of the orchestra's divertimento surrounded her as Papa led her proudly under the pendulous chandeliers to the dais where Mama sat. Anatole was already there and had risen at her entrance.

He waited for her now, standing like a sentry on duty, hands clasped behind his back, as if to say, *None shall pass!*

The savior of Ascencion was in full dress uniform. His black-belted, dark blue coat was heavily decorated with medals of all shapes and sizes, and a gold sash ran across his chest on a diagonal. The gold epaulets on his enormous shoulders and the dress sword at his side gleamed by the light of chandeliers. He had pulled his long, golden hair back in a queue.

The guests watched as Papa led her up the few steps to the dais. She faced her betrothed at the top. They met each other's gaze with mutual animosity, cold desire leaping in Anatole's eyes, hatred snapping in her own.

She saw he had a light bruise on his left cheek, a faint swelling there, evidence of his fight with Darius. He noticed her gaze on it; his sapphire eyes flickered in reproach. She suppressed a derisive smirk.

Before the glittering sea of guests, she gave Anatole a sweeping, picture perfect curtsy as he bowed to her and offered his right arm, the left tucked formally behind his back. She turned away from her father, rested her hand on the conqueror's forearm, and allowed him to lead her to her chair, beside his own.

He treated her with excruciating correctness the entire night because her parents were there. Indeed, he was the soul of charm, wooing the prime minister, the queen, and swapping war stories with the head generals of Ascencion. Gallantly, he even took the blame for the fight with Darius.

A misunderstanding, he magnanimously told them, deftly casting Darius by virtue of his own, breezy noblesse oblige as a volatile, unstable man. Anatole must have realized that if he expressed indignation against Darius, he would alienate Papa.

There were moments she wanted to scream and topple every fragrant, perfect bouquet on the dais, but she sat still as a china doll, hands folded in her lap, the slight smile carved into her face, dimples aching.

This was the destiny she had been born for, she told herself. No matter the cost, she would protect her father and Rafael from the loss of the throne; she would protect her people from war. Anatole's poor Russian conscripts would die in place of the kingdom's citizens. Was that fair?

She could merely watch the young war hero with a jaundiced eye. No one suspected what he was really like, she thought. Insulated from her fear of him by the presence of so many people, she laughed at his falseness outright from time to time, but most of the night she scanned the crowd for Darius.

She struggled to feel his presence as she had the night in the maze and again that day in the field when he had come looking for her astride his hell-horse. The first day they had kissed.

The memory of it throbbed through her body.

She knew then that he was not here tonight. She could not feel him anywhere near, and it was as if the world had been abandoned by its guardian angel. Yet she was acutely aware of the bond between them, alive, powerful.

The bond of blood.

And she realized: They could never truly be parted, not by any man or distance or the passage of time.

Be it heaven or hell, they were one.

Hands in pockets, his face expressionless, Darius stood at the rails as the captain of the small, hired barkentine sailed the vessel into the harbor at Genoa through the warm predawn mist, guided by the light of the port's famous Lanterna, the sixteenth century lighthouse. Its eerie glow flicked over the grim hulk of the Molo Vecchio, the city's hanging hill at the harbor.

At length, the bell clanged as the boat bumped gently into a slip. While the lightening day coaxed the city walls and cathedral spires out of darkness, Darius gathered his leather satchel and the guitar case concealing his weapons, and disembarked.

The sun had not yet risen as he stepped off the hired boat and onto the quay, feeling strangely detached and cool. Numb, he supposed.

The quayside was notoriously seedy, lined with taverns and brothels. One hand at the ready to reach for his dagger in so rough a part of town, the other holding the handle of his guitar case, he went into the largest inn, ignoring the whores eyeing him.

There he was shown to the stables and, after inspecting the animal's legs and wind, bought a dapple-gray stallion too fine for its ramshackle surroundings, obviously stolen.

As the bells of San Lorenzo tolled for the early Mass, he galloped down the road skirting the city walls, beginning the four-day trek to his inland destination at Milan. Every stride of the leggy gray bore him farther away from all he loved, but he carried the bond with Serafina deep inside him now, in the very marrow of his bones. He was serene.

He had loved her purely and well, and what he had experienced with her, though brief, was worlds beyond anything he had ever dreamed.

It would be a good death. Serafina would be free, and at last he would be one with his ideals.

CHAPTER
❧ FOURTEEN ❧

"My God, Pauline Bonaparte has had a nude statue made of herself!" cried Els, looking up from the scandal sheet.

Seated at the vanity as Madame worked on her coiffure, Serafina glanced dully at Els's reflection behind her in the mirror.

The morning was bright and clear, but the day did not match her mood. She had a bit of a sore head from the wine last night. She had waited all night for Darius to make an appearance in the ballroom, but he never did. Then, here in her bedroom, she had waited for him come to her by the secret door, but of course he didn't do that, either.

She took a sip of coffee, picked despondently at her breakfast tray, then fed her pet monkey another bit of melon.

"Did you hear what I said?" Els cried. "A naked statue!"

"Why do I care what Pauline Bonaparte does?"

"That tramp," Madame muttered under her breath.

Serafina had never met Napoleon's youngest sister. She had only seen a miniature of her once and heard, as did the rest of the world, the shocking tales of the famous beauty's countless conquests. Pauline collected men the way her brother collected countries.

Unfortunately, the beautiful twenty-five-year-old had also declared unofficial war on Serafina ever since some of the newspapers had begun making a contest of which of the two princesses was more beautiful, Serafina or herself.

"But Cricket, it's too delicious! You have to hear this," Els protested.

"Well, go on," she sighed in dejection.

Nearby, Els lay on her belly on Serafina's canopy bed, reading to them from the scandal sheets, for she had despaired of drawing Serafina into conversation. "It says here *Princess*— ahem—Pauline—"

"Princess!" Madame snorted.

"*Princess* Pauline has posed for a new statue by Canova— *Venus Victrix*—practically nude!" Els laughed as she followed the story. "Poor Prince Camillo, her husband, is so obsessed with jealousy, he keeps the statue locked in an empty room in the Villa Borghese!"

"If he was smart, he would lock *her* up there with it," Madame declared. "Such a fine young man, and he lets her make a pathetic cuckold of him before the whole world!"

Madame slanted a glance at Serafina. "You should have told him yes. And why not?" Madame went on as Serafina rolled her eyes. "He's from an excellent family. He's Italian, handsome, rich."

But he's not Darius, she thought, tears suddenly flooding her eyes. Abruptly, she shoved off Madame's fussing, pulling fingers and dropped her face in both hands. Resting her elbows on the vanity, she held her throbbing head in both hands, raking her fingers into her half-coiffed hair. She could feel both women staring at her. The room was filled with a tense silence until Els murmured a dismissal to Madame. Serafina heard the door click, then Els was standing beside her, leaning down to peer into her face in gentle concern.

"Cricket, what on earth? Pauline Bonaparte is not worth this. What is going on? You haven't been yourself since the night you left for the country."

She did not know how to answer. The need inside of her to see Darius felt something akin to panic. "Els," she said slowly, not opening her eyes, "please fetch Colonel Santiago for me."

She could feel her friend gazing at her in bewilderment. "Why?"

"Don't question me! I am the Princess Royal—just do it!"

Els folded her arms over her chest. "What is going on?" she demanded. "Are you Santiago's lover? Did he hurt you? Oh, God. Serafina . . . are you pregnant?"

"No, I am not pregnant." She almost wished she was. She just sat there for a long moment, slumped in silence. "Oh, Els," she whispered at last, "I love him so much. I need to see him. I just need to see him," she whispered in despair.

Els promptly sat down on the stool next to hers. "Tell me everything. Now. If you don't, I am going for your mother and you can talk to her."

"No!" She shot Els an aghast look. "If Mama knew the things I did with Darius, she would fall into a dead swoon."

Els snorted. "How do you think she came to be with child, dear?"

Serafina winced in disgust at that thought and massaged her throbbing temples.

"You know nothing you can say can shock me. Now, my dear," Els said as she poured her some more coffee, "begin at the beginning."

Els listened with compassion while Serafina related what had happened between them at the yellow villa, how deeply she had fallen in love, how he had given her the cut direct upon returning to the palace, only to defend her yesterday from Anatole. Teary-eyed, she told of the secrets Julia Calazzi had known about him which he had never confided in her.

"I did not realize at the time," she whispered with a pensive, downward stare, "but I think that I gave more of myself to him than I could safely part with. I could not help myself. He needs me. I know he does." She turned her brimming eyes to her friend. "If I could just see him one more time . . ." Her voice trailed off.

"Very well." Els patted her arm comfortingly. "I will go find him and bring him here to you."

Serafina turned to her, painful hope in her eyes. "Do you think he'll come?"

"I will make sure that he does," Els said stoutly. "No man

gets away with treating the Princess Royal this way, not even the great Santiago."

But half an hour later, Els returned alone.

"Where is he? Is he coming? Did you give him my message?"

Her expression was grim. "There was no answer when I knocked at his suite, so I went looking for Alec to find out where he might be. Alec suggested Darius had gone on the morning gallop with His Majesty, but I found one of the courtiers, and he told me, no, Tyurinov was there, but no Darius. Then I ran into your brother." She hesitated.

"Els! What?"

"Rafe said he left Santiago's suite last night when Julia Calazzi arrived to pay a call on him."

Serafina gasped. "No!"

"Your brother seemed sure Darius would not be available till well after breakfast, if you take my meaning."

"Julia Calazzi!" she wailed. "He wouldn't, Els, surely! She slapped him across the face last time they met! Did you check if he is practicing at swords in the *gymnasio*, or exercising his horse?"

"He's not."

"Maybe he went into the city or had errands to run," Serafina said helplessly, but she could not ignore the feeling of terrible foreboding that promptly settled in the pit of her stomach.

Everything in Darius's past pointed to the worst possible conclusion. Julia Calazzi!

"I don't know where he is, dearest. I'm so sorry. The one thing I *do* know is that I'm *not* going to permit either of us to sit around here moping over that man and waiting for him to show his face. I know exactly how to keep you preoccupied for the day." Els grasped her hand and pulled her toward the door. "I'm taking you shopping!"

The northward route followed the valley of the Scrivia River, flanked on both sides by the soaring peaks of the Italian

Alps. The road wound through woods of pine and chest-nut trees, and past medieval villages built spiral fashion around hilltops with terraced fields planted with fruit trees and vineyards.

Darius saved the horse's strength, content to take the wind-ing, hilly, and well-trod road at a brisk walk with an occa-sional canter to break the monotony. All there was to do was think.

He stopped now and then to let the horse drink while he gazed at the jagged outline of the soaring mountains sur-rounding him, their snowcapped peaks dreamy white against the blue sky. He sampled the river's rushing alpine water, breathed the crisp, thin freshness of the air.

By his estimate, he passed over the border from Liguria into the Piedmont at about sunset. Already the mountains had dwindled to rolling, vineyard-clad hills. He would only cut through the southeastern tip of this region once ruled by the Savoy kings, now the territory of Napoleon. Tomorrow he would gain Lombardy and the flat expanses of the rich Po Delta.

When the centuries-old way-station town of Busalla came in sight, he stopped, gazing down at the little handful of buildings scattered in the green vale in the shadow of the mountains.

What a lonely, country place, he thought.

But he dismounted, stiff after the full day's ride. He led the weary gray down the hill and took lodgings.

After a fruitful day of shopping, Els and Serafina returned, half-buried under packages in the open landau. As their car-riage rolled up the long, landscaped drive to the palace, they heard the flare and booming pound of drums. An impressive military demonstration was in progress on the parade ground between the two broad, ramrod-straight avenues leading up to the palace.

Smartly uniformed soldiers marched the intricate geometry of configurations from the manual of arms, parade rifles gleaming in the setting sun as they twirled them and slammed them against first one shoulder, then the other. Serafina spied Anatole standing at the side of the field before the small crowd of onlookers. Chin high, hands clasped behind his back, critically he watched his colonels drilling the troops.

"The newspapers told the truth. He does have an army of giants," Els said in quiet awe, staring at the tall, powerfully built Russian soldiers.

"He is flexing his might for us," Serafina murmured in foreboding.

When Anatole spotted her from far across the parade ground, he swept off his bicorne and sent her a bow of acknowledgment. A wave of cold seemed to wash over her but she lifted her hand in greeting, lowering it slowly.

"Drive on," she commanded.

A few minutes later, Els and she strode into the palace. She had bided her time and been patient all day; she had tried not to think or talk about him too much, but now the need to see and touch and be with Darius was paramount. She went over to the palace steward and inquired after his whereabouts, but Falconi knew nothing.

Serafina turned dazedly to Els. "Where can he be? We must find Alec. He'll know."

Els bit her lip. "I don't want to say this, but . . . perhaps he left, Cricket. If his feelings for you are as deep as he led you to believe, you have to admit it would be hard for him to stand by and watch you marry another man."

"He wouldn't leave me—not yet! Not when he knows how much I need him to be there during the wedding. Oh, God, Els." She gripped Els's arm as her face drained. "What if Tyurinov has done something terrible to him? They had that awful fight yesterday. You saw all those giant soldiers Anatole has—"

"Calm down." Els laid a hand on her arm. "We'll find him. Don't jump to any conclusions until we know more. It is very like Santiago to disappear without warning."

She pressed both hands to her stomach. "Oh, God, I shall be sick."

"Perhaps your father sent him on some mysterious new errand."

Serafina gasped. "Oh! Els, you're brilliant! Yes, that must be it!" She gripped her hand and began marching swiftly down the main corridor. "Come on. Papa will know where he is."

Els hurried to keep up with her. Serafina's heart pounded with every step. She clutched at the glimmer of hope, unwilling to heed her darkest fears.

"It's so like Papa to push him too hard. Why doesn't he give another man the dirty work for a change? His poor shoulder isn't even healed enough for the stitches to be removed yet!" she rattled on nervously. Perhaps if she could keep herself talking, she could ignore the terrible lump—the knowing—deep in the pit of her stomach.

At last, she flung the door to her father's office wide, bursting in on him, ready for a fight.

"Papa, where have you sent—" She stopped abruptly.

Everything inside her went cold and deadly.

Alec was standing between the two leather chairs before her father's desk. He turned at her entrance, his face greenish pale as he twisted his hat in his hands. He looked like he wanted to puke.

Staring out the window, her father didn't even turn to her.

Els crept up close behind her, nervous at being in the king's council chambers.

"What's going on?" Serafina forced out in a choked voice. "Papa, where's Darius?"

Her father didn't answer, didn't turn around, didn't move from staring out the window.

She took another step into the office. "Papa?" Behind her, Els closed the door quietly. Serafina's chest began heaving with fright. She swallowed hard. "Alec?" she demanded.

The young lieutenant glanced at the king's impassive figure

uncertainly. He looked at Serafina again. "I'm sorry, Your Highness."

"Where is he?" she forced out. "Where is Darius?"

At last, the king turned around, his weathered face pale, his jaw taut. "Alec suspects . . . We have pieced it together just moments ago. What I will tell you must not leave this room."

"Yes, Papa. What is it?" she asked in dread.

"Darius has gone," he said heavily, "to assassinate Napoleon."

She stared at him, lifting both hands over her mouth in horror.

"Jesus, Mary, and Joseph," Els breathed.

Serafina's mind flew to his purpose in such a mad scheme. *No Napoleon—no war—no need for Tyurinov.*

He could come back to her. Marry her. They could be together forever.

"Can he succeed?" Serafina choked out.

"Perhaps he can kill him," her father said, "but he'll never make it out alive."

She stared. "But—he's Darius, Papa. Of course he can. He can do anything."

"Your Highness," Alec said gently, shaking his head, "do not hope falsely. If the colonel is captured, it is customary . . . that is, there is a common practice . . ." Alec stopped, closing his eyes briefly, as though he could not bear to say it.

"Tell me!" she cried in dread.

"He will not allow the French to take him alive. He will not allow himself to be used as a pawn. He cannot possibly escape," her father ground out angrily. "If Darius sees that capture is imminent, he will swallow arsenic."

After caring for the dapple gray after the long day's ride, Darius refilled his canteens for tomorrow at the pump and went back to the grubby inn, where the innkeeper offered him dinner.

Returning to his dark, tiny cubicle, he washed his hands, splashed his face and neck, then examined his rifle once more. He glanced over the rest of his equipment, checked the arsenic powder folded into a tiny envelope, then lay down and tried to sleep, fully dressed, his dagger under his pillow.

Sleep was elusive.

It was earlier than he was accustomed to going to bed and he was aware with every inch of his body that he was alone tonight, but he intended to be on his way at first light. The sense of his own death, like a second presence in the room, made him uneasy about closing his eyes. He fought his resistance; it was a struggle to embrace death, as he must. Hope would only distract him now. His mission required a perfectly clear mind, one uncluttered with dreams and futile wishes.

He willed himself to pull together that same, numb resignation he had felt on the way back from Russia, before he had seen Serafina again on the night of the maze. It was slow in coming.

It had been easy then to welcome death, for it had meant only an end to his suffering: His had been the courage of despair. Now he had seen a side of life he had never known existed, a side worth holding on to. It left him battling his own survival instincts, great, powerful forces inside him, tearing him apart, love and hate, death and life.

He strove to blank his mind.

He didn't want to sleep, but he knew if he got an early enough start, he could make it all the way to Pavia by tomorrow night. The flatter terrain would allow a swifter pace.

Darius folded his arms under his head, idly crossed his heels, and shut his eyes with a faint smile. *I wonder what my Serafina is doing right now.*

She stood there for a long moment, utterly frozen with horror. Then something inside of her snapped.

"No!"

With an anguished cry, she swept everything off her father's desk in a blind rage, smashing the half-hull model of the royal flagship. She threw the broken pieces at her father when he tried to come near her. She punched him when he tried to comfort her.

"This is your fault! How could you do this? How could you do this?" she screamed at him, at no one, at Darius, at herself. "This is all your fault!"

"That's enough!" her father roared at her at last, gripping her by the shoulders. "Get control of yourself!"

He stared down wretchedly at her.

"He can't die. Papa, he can't, he can't. You've got to save him. Send men to stop him."

"Oh, Cricket, he's got too far a lead. He planned it all to a tee." When tears rushed into his eyes, she crumbled into his arms and wept.

She realized Darius had known all along what he was going to do. Too many of the seemingly innocent things he had said to her at the villa made perfect sense now, though she had not realized at the time that his meaning was dual.

What if I can't always be there to protect you? You've got to be able to survive without me.

"That bastard, he knew all along." Sobbing, she clung weakly to her father while he held her in his arms. "He didn't even give me a chance to stop him! How could he do this to me?" she said over and over.

At some point, her father passed her over to Els.

"I'll see what I can do," he said gruffly.

Both of them crying, Els led Serafina back to her rooms, for she could barely walk under her own power. Insensate, she didn't even hear what Els was saying to her. Only one thing pierced the totality of her outrage and her grief.

When she walked into her bedroom, she found Darius's guitar resting on her bed.

Through its strings was woven the stem of a white daisy and a folded letter.

With shaking hands, she pulled out the folded sheet of fine linen paper and unfolded it, trying to make out the words in his careful, late-taught script through her blinding tears.

My Love,
  Accept my gift, for it is freely given. A thousand kisses everywhere. My butterfly, be free. I will be watching over you always.

                                        Yours,
                                        Darius

CHAPTER
⚜ FIFTEEN ⚜

The people below looked like ants from where he sat, idly smoking what he supposed might well be his last cheroot. Behind three rows of troops guarding the route Napoleon would take through the city, the spectators lined the streets and thronged the piazza below.

Darius had been ensconced for nearly twenty-four hours on the roof of Milan's mighty Duomo. It had been nine in the morning when the tiny people began dropping to their knees in a wave that came closer as the pope's gilded coach drew near.

Peering through his compact folding telescope, Darius had seen the frail white hand emerge from the curtained coach, blessing the people. In the hours that followed, six carriages of cardinals, bishops, and priests came next, while all the church bells in the city began tolling.

He watched and waited with the patience of a cat stalking its prey as the coaches of state arrived next, each pulled by six horses with golden plumes. Everything was gilded, even the harnesses and reins, his telescope showed him. As time dragged, he watched the coaches disgorge velvet-clad ministers, diplomats, local nobility.

He shook his head wryly to see the Bonaparte so-called princesses emerge, two blushing, one preening. That would be Pauline, he supposed, the one who was always making catty remarks about Serafina.

Bitch.

231

Napoleon's sisters were followed by their maids of honor and the grenadiers of the guard.

Each group of new arrivals was assisted out of the carriages and escorted slowly through the huge iron doors of the cathedral. Darius knew his window of opportunity to get a clear shot at Napoleon would last only seconds.

He did not check his gun again. Everything was in order.

Yesterday he had discovered the roof of the Duomo as the ideal perch for the assassination. Knowing he would be faced with the problem of getting past the heavy security and into the walled city, Darius had discovered a group of monks from Pavia on the way to the coronation. It was just the solution he needed. He stabled the horse at a local livery and disguised himself as a friar, concealing his weapons under a baggy brown robe, then he joined the group of monks on the road.

Listening to the chatter of the holy men, he was unsurprised to find they were more excited about seeing Pope Pius VII than their new emperor. Once they reached their lodgings in Milan, the group was invited to tour the gigantic Duomo, the largest gothic cathedral in the world, according to the deacon who had so proudly offered them an unauthorized tour. Brother Santiago had tagged along through a city that was bursting with pride and excitement.

While preparations for the coronation were in full swing, workers adorning the altar and the nave with mounds of flowers, the deacon showed the group of monks the baptistry, where Saint Augustine himself had been baptized, then the deacon whispered to the group that, though it really wasn't allowed, he would show them the roof. He promised fine views of the city. On clear days, he said, one could even see the Maritime Alps.

Darius could see them right now.

The monks had moved on, but Darius had silently slipped away, left alone in the forest of well over a hundred spires, hordes of gargoyles, countless statues on the Duomo's roof. He had known it was the perfect place for his mission the moment he looked up at the central spire and saw the statue crowning it—the gilded Virgin gazing out serenely over the city.

Now, in the shadow of the Virgin, he shifted himself more securely between the sweeping curlicues of carved marble, squinting against the sun. The breeze was high, the day fine, and unsurprisingly, Napoleon was late.

Just when he checked his fob watch and read the time, three o'clock, amid the deafening clamor of the city's church bells, suddenly celebratory cannon fire boomed, vibrating in his chest.

Darius narrowed his eyes, put his fob away, took a last pull from the cheroot, then crushed it out. Calmly, he reached for the loaded flintlock rifle.

He wet his lips, chapped slightly by the constant breeze so far above the ground. Bringing the rifle up, he rested the muzzle on a convenient bit of tracery to secure his shot.

He might only get one shot, he realized, but as long as Napoleon was in the open, he planned to fire as many times as possible before they realized his location.

His objectives were very simple.

Kill Napoleon.

Don't be taken alive.

Next to his guitar case on the ground lay the brown robe of a friar. With the robe's cowl to hide his face and the sheer number of clergy in the city, he believed he might be able to escape the roof and blend in somewhere below in the church.

If that proved impossible, he had the arsenic.

In total concentration, Darius coolly watched the shimmering imperial coach, which was covered in mirrors and gilded honeybees. The afternoon sun glinted off the gaudy vehicle, momentarily dazzling him. He squinted.

Drawn by eight bay horses with golden plumes on their heads, the immense coach rolled majestically into the square below.

He felt increasingly aware of everything, the sun's warmth

on his skin, the sprawling crowd's unenthusiastic welcome below; in the corner of his eye, the fluttering of some pigeons.

With one hand, he snapped the tiny spyglass into place on the rifle. Staring through it, his finger on the trigger, all his focus homed in on the shimmering golden coach below.

Everything seemed to move very slowly.

First Joseph Bonaparte, then the younger one, Lucien, stepped out of the coach onto the ground. Both clad in white satin, together they waited at the coach door as the weak-chinned Empress Josephine emerged, dressed also in white, her imperial diadem on her head, her neck laden with jewels.

Darius watched her place her hands gracefully, one in each of her brothers-in-law's hands, and she stepped down.

He licked his lips. His fingertip caressed the trigger.

Napoleon Bonaparte appeared in the open door of the coach. Darius aimed.

He fired just as the sun glinted off the mirrored carriage into his eyes, blinding him.

He stared in shock—utter disbelief.

I missed.

He cursed, loaded again relentlessly, saw that there was only confusion among those standing nearest the emperor. With all the church bells and cannon fire, it had been too loud to hear his shot. He didn't know who or what he had hit, he only knew he had missed Napoleon. As he brought up the rifle again swiftly, he saw through the telescope that the dragoon who had been standing next to Lucien was on the ground. Napoleon had stepped down from the coach.

He fired again but he was shaken by his miss and the shot merely shattered one of the mirrors of the coach behind Napoleon, just over his shoulder. Then it was too late.

Below, the dragoons piled around Napoleon and the other three Bonapartes, rushing them into the cathedral.

Darius cast off the rifle. Moving swiftly and methodically, while his heart pounded as if it would burst, he jumped down from his stone perch and threw on the brown robe of his disguise. He was wearing a six-pistol chest holster, a sword, and his ebony-handled dagger. Drawing two of the six pistols, he ran for the roof's exit, the brown robe trailing out behind him, billowing in the high wind, catching on his sword.

Shouldn't have taken that second shot. Wasted time, he thought, too late, for even now the first guard appeared in the doorway of the roof's only exit.

He knew troops had been stationed inside the cathedral. They came up quickly. Following the first man, a squadron swarmed through the door to the roof. Darius stopped just long enough to consider trying to fight his way past them.

"Over there!" a man shouted, pointing at him.

Darius ran through the forest of spires shooting up out of the roof.

If he could elude them and double back around them to the door . . . But more kept coming, twenty men holding their post at the exit. He shrugged off the brown cloak and dodged behind a pair of large, fanged gargoyles.

"There he is!"

He whirled around the statue and fired the pistols, one then the other. Two men dropped.

"After him!"

He bolted, heart pounding. Again he ensconced himself behind a statue but he was not much nearer the door. He could feel them creeping closer. He drew two more of his guns.

"Come out with your hands up!" they shouted.

He stepped out and dropped two more of them, then threw the empty pistols. With two shots left, his sword and dagger remained.

More French soldiers piled up onto the roof.

"Give yourself up!" they screamed at him.

Gunshots careened off the stone, shattering one of the gargoyle's pointed ears. Darius ducked his head away from the flying, dusty fragments of stone.

"Hold your fire! Hold your fire!" some of the Frenchmen shouted at the others.

Shaken up, boys? he thought insolently. Chest heaving, he looked to the right and the left, trying to decide which way to run. He was beginning to think it didn't matter. He knew he could only play hide-and-seek with them for so long. There were too many. The sweeping glance he stole from behind the maimed gargoyle numbered at least thirty soldiers hunting him.

No problem, he told himself, dry-mouthed.

The exit was to his left but there had to be a dozen men blocking it. He ran for it, firing his last two guns, dodging a wave of bullets as he dove behind some saint's statue. Cursing under his breath, he jumped to his feet and unsheathed his dagger and his sword.

What bloody good's a sword going to do? They're going to make Swiss cheese of me.

Missing Napoleon once had been back luck—missing twice unthinkable—this sudden, ferocious hope, this will to live had not been part of his plan.

He stole a glance around the stone saint's shoulder and ducked back as gunfire roared.

The exit was too heavily guarded even to try.

Oh, God, he thought. Arsenic.

Pressing his eyes closed for a second, he reached into his waistcoat and pulled out the tiny, folded envelope. He blessed himself rapidly with the sign of the cross, then tore the paper and poured the arsenic powder into his hand. Chest heaving, he struggled to raise it to his mouth.

Oh, God, oh, God, I don't want to die, he thought, raising his pleading stare to the blue sky.

He saw her then—the golden Virgin above him. Her expression was so sweet, so sure, the only mother he had ever known. He gazed helplessly at her and then, as if she had blown the air from her lips herself, the wind scattered the little white mound of arsenic right out of his hand.

Darius gasped, clutching uselessly as the powder slipped away.

He could hear the guards coming closer. French voices shouted at him.

"Give yourself up! In the name of the emperor, I command you to surrender!"

Heart hammering, his back pressed up against the stone saint's back, Darius stared straight ahead at the edge of the roof.

It was the only way.

Shoving away from the base of the spire with all his strength, he charged the edge. *He would scream Serafina's name when he leaped.*

Half a dozen paces from the edge, the guardsmen tackled him to the ground.

He fought like a madman, cursed at them like a demoniac, willing one of them to kill him so his death might protect Lazar. There were ten men piled on him, kicking him, punching him. They wrested his sword away and whenever he struck one with his ebony-handled dagger, another soldier merely took his place.

They nearly broke his wrist to make him let go of the dagger. How many he wounded or killed, he did not know. He didn't feel their blows—he was too enraged. Fury poured and seethed from him, possessing him. It was as though some terrible door inside him had been opened. He was someone he didn't know, tasting his own blood in his mouth. He was frenzied, screaming threats at them even as they threw him down on his face and manacled his hands behind his back.

He was shoved and dragged down the many stairs, and thrown into a waiting carriage under heavy guard. He heard them say they were taking him to the ancient Castello Sforzesco, which served as the French troops' barracks.

It was a swift ride, for the ancient fortress was situated only several blocks north.

While in the cathedral Napoleon grasped the Iron Crown of Charlemagne and placed it upon his own head, Darius was thrown into the dungeons beneath the castle.

Panting, bruised, he stared through the rusty bars at the soldiers.

Their captain sauntered into their midst, the dim lanterns illumining his harsh, narrow face and gray hair. He reminded Darius of his father. The old man must be laughing at him from hell.

"You will tell us your name," the captain said.

"Come here and let me kill you," Darius spat at him.

The captain smiled, a cruel smile. Darius glared back at him, gripping the bars, then shoved himself back and began pacing, barely containing his frenzied ire. He watched them as he paced, chains clanking from arms and ankles. He listened to them discussing him quietly. Apparently he had killed seven and wounded three.

He could hardly congratulate himself at the news when he had missed the one man he had come to kill. *Failed. Worthless.*

A few minutes later, the captain ordered the warden to open his cell. With a large, beefy corporal in tow, the captain entered. He nodded from the corporal to Darius.

"Search him."

With a cold sneer, Darius endured as the corporal slammed him up against the clammy wall. They removed his cravat to stop him from hanging himself, his spurs to keep him from slashing his wrists. They cut his waistcoat away, leaving him in his torn shirt. When this was done, the corporal jerked him around to face the captain again.

Darius looked down his nose at him masterfully.

The captain narrowed his eyes. "Bravado won't save your life, my friend. What's this?" The captain's gaze fell to his chest. He stepped forward and lifted the medal of the Virgin in his hand.

Darius saw the captain's fist tighten on the medal, felt the chain go taut against his skin.

"Take it and I swear to God I'll rip your throat out," he said softly through clenched teeth.

Debating with himself, the captain held his stare for a long moment, then smirked at him and stepped back, dropping the medal against his chest. "A worthless trinket." The captain pivoted and left the cell.

The big corporal followed, sliding the rusty metal door shut and locking it securely.

Darius could only wonder how much worse he had just made things for himself.

Lying in bed on her side, staring at nothing, Serafina expected at any hour to hear news of Darius's fate. She had waited for two days, and now, again, night was closing in. She had to wonder if she was going a little mad, for in some bizarre way she was convinced she could keep him alive by an unflinching, inward focus on her love for him.

She had her father's solemn oath that he would send for her the moment he heard anything. The sound of her mother's sobs upon learning the news, as well as the prime minister's injunction to them all, still rang in her ears. *We must not give the Russians any cause for suspicion. Life must appear to go on as normal. Word will come soon. Until then, we can do nothing but wait.*

She, too, could do nothing but wait. She couldn't understand why she was the only one who believed that Darius could indeed succeed in killing Napoleon. Maybe she was mad, like him.

She held his carefully penned little note to her heart. Her gaze traveled over her tokens of him with which she had surrounded herself on the bed—his guitar and the Chinese kites and the countless other gifts he had given her over the years. There were treasures from all over the world to delight the little girl in her, satin dancing slippers from Constantinople with toes that curled upward, a headdress made of delicate chains hung with strange coins, a tiny piece of an ancient temple from Greece, a perfect ball of violet quartz from an African mine. But these exotic baubles were nothing compared to what

Darius had given of himself—the tenderness and safety he had shown her.

Now he had given his life for her.

No. She refused to believe he was dead. The Blessed Mother was taking care of him, just as she always had. If she concentrated very hard, deep down in the core of her being, she felt the bond between them, sure and alive, like a resplendent flame in the darkness. She closed her eyes.

My unicorn, my champion, my wolf. How I miss you.

Her blood ran cold as a knock sounded at the outer door.

It's time.

She had thought herself ready for this moment, but now that it had come, she did not know how to face it.

A moment later, Pia appeared in the doorway to her bedroom. The maid's timid voice brimmed with sorrow and worry. "Your Highness, His Majesty sends for you."

As if outside herself, Serafina watched herself calmly get up from her bed. She watched herself smooth her hair and walk out of her apartments, hands steady at her sides.

She was a royal princess with a proud lineage seven hundred years old, she told herself with every step. In her veins was the blood of kings. She would bear the fatal blow with her chin high.

At her father's office, she took a deep breath, then opened the door, at once taken aback to find that Anatole was already with him. The atmosphere was fraught with tension. At her entrance, both men looked over.

"Good, you're here," her father said sternly.

Anatole jolted with a half-remembered bow. He offered her one of the chairs in front of Papa's desk. Warily, she glanced from one tense man to the other, then walked over and sat, folding her hands in her lap.

Her father sat down heavily at his desk and searched her face. Her hands twisted in her lap. "No news, Papa?"

"No news."

Thank God. He could still be alive.

"Cricket, the reason I've called you here is because, in light of Darius's actions, Anatole feels it would behoove us to move the wedding up to tomorrow."

She glanced quickly at Anatole. "Tomorrow! But that is impossible!"

"Why wait, Your Highness?" he asked curtly, his sapphire eyes glinting with anger as he knowingly held her gaze. "Pardon me for speaking frankly, but I was disturbed from the outset to learn that this information was kept hidden from me. With all due respect, sir," he said to her father, "your Santiago will never succeed. Since the great conspiracy involving the Duc d'Enghien last year, Napoleon is extremely careful about his public appearances. Security at the coronation will be impossible to penetrate."

"You don't know Santiago," she said.

He cocked his head toward her. "Can he make himself invisible? Is he immune to bullets?"

"Sometimes."

"Even if he gets in, he won't get out. He will be captured, and when the link between him and Ascencion is discovered, France will turn on this island with a vengeance. He cannot possibly succeed, and by failing, he has endangered you all, and made war all but inevitable. The certainty of my protection is your only hope. Our alliance must be sealed before news reaches the world that a man of Your Majesty's inner circle tried to assassinate Napoleon. Sire, you will be instantly implicated."

"What if Darius succeeds?" she broke in softly.

"He can't succeed! You are missing the whole point, Your Highness," he lashed out at her. "Don't you care what happens to your father? To your people? Is this Spaniard's miserable life all you care about?"

"Watch your tone, sir," her father growled at Anatole in warning.

He looked over and the iron mask of his charm clanged back into place.

"Forgive me." He went down on one knee in front of her and took her hand, putting on a pretty show for Papa. "After my first wife, Margaret, died, Serafina, I was so broken, I said I would never remarry. But when I met you and heard of Ascencion's plight, I knew I must offer myself as the solution."

"And we are grateful for your generosity, my lord," her father said in a brooding tone, "but let us remind you that our daughter could win the heart of any man on the planet."

"Papa." She shot him a quick glance over Anatole's golden head. He only used the royal "we" when his anger was stirred. Perhaps he was beginning to see through Anatole's polished mask at last.

"Indeed she could, sir," Anatole agreed softly.

Serafina gazed at Anatole, wondering if there was one shred of sincerity behind his sudden show of solicitude. She didn't think so. All she knew was that she had to buy time until news came of whether or not Darius had killed Napoleon and survived. If he had failed, she would still need to marry Anatole, in which case it would be suicide to anger him.

She must manage him.

"Anatole," she said, her voice at its softest and most feminine as she carefully laid her hand over his. "You know I am fond of you and honored to become your wife, but I see no need to rush things. Mama has taken such pains to make everything perfect for the day. I daresay she has taxed herself overmuch with all her work, and in her delicate condition. The food, the church, the choirs, the fireworks. Of course, you understand these matters better than I, but please, can't we let the date stand?" She tucked her chin and offered him a shy smile, gazing at him.

Anatole stared at her, looking quite thoroughly enchanted.

She was aware, from the corner of her eye, of her father staring at her in astonishment.

"Please, Anatole?" she said cajolingly.

He stammered. "I—I—"

Just then, there was a knock at the door.

"Come," her father ordered.

She heard veiled mirth in his deep voice. When Anatole looked over at the door to see who had come, Papa shot her a knowing wink.

Anatole stayed where he was, crouched down before her, holding her hand as if it were made of delicate china.

The palace steward opened the door, bowed, and brought the king a note. "Urgent, Sire," he murmured.

Realizing that even here and now might be news of Darius's fate, Serafina watched, her heart hammering, while Papa opened it. His eyes widened as he read it. Abruptly he shoved up out of the chair with a look of mixed joy and dread.

"Cricket, your mother's in labor!"

"Good Lord!" she cried, jumping out of her chair past Anatole.

Papa was already striding across the room. "Anatole, we'll have to finish this later. Forgive my indelicacy, but the babe was not expected for another three weeks. My wife is strong, but she is not a girl anymore. I must go to her!"

He swept to his feet. "By all means, Sire."

"Me, too!" Serafina hurried after him, but Anatole grabbed her arm as she stepped over the threshold.

"A word with you, please, Your Highness."

She was in the doorway, but her father was already halfway down the hall.

"Papa, wait!" she called in distress, loath to be left alone with Anatole.

"You two work it out for yourselves," her father called with a wave of his hand. "Consider it a premarital lesson in compromise. But don't forget I warned you, Anatole," he added in a jaunty tone. "My girl always gets her way."

Oh, damn, she thought as her father disappeared around the corner. After that little display of her wiles in his office, Papa had no doubt concluded that she held Anatole in the palm of her hand, as she did so many others. In truth, she was not sure if the Russian's fleeting, smitten expression had been real or false. She looked up to find him studying her face.

"Let us finish this business, my bride."

She regarded him warily, saying nothing. Her chin was high as she leaned her back against the doorframe and folded her arms over her chest.

"Why do you want to delay our marriage?" he asked.

"Why do you want to move it up?"

He tilted his head, looming over her. He braced his hands on the door above her. "I'll tell you why. Because I think you are scheming to discard me."

"I am not."

"You'd better not be. We are pledged to each other, you and I. I am not a man to be trifled with. You insult me, you insult Russia, for without my armies, the czar is nothing. You insult Russia, and Ascencion will lose the friendship of *all* the allies of the Third Coalition. No one will give this island the slightest relief when Napoleon comes. Not even England."

"How do you know?"

He ticked them off on his fingers. "Naples is helpless. Sweden is too far away to care. Austria's strength is wasted. England will only give gold. But Russia's population is vast: We are the soldiers. We are the cannon fodder."

She winced and looked away.

"That's right, my sweet island rose. Human lives. That is the currency with which I've bought you."

She refused to heed him. *My Darius can do it!* she thought in rebellion. *He will kill Napoleon and come back to me. I know he will escape. He has to.*

She had to get out of here. Mama was in labor. Suddenly she seized upon a solution.

"We cannot move the wedding up because I will not get married without my mother present. She will need time to recover from the birthing. Anatole, you must respect that."

He stared at her for a long moment assessingly. "A baby is always born when someone in a family dies."

She looked up at him in agony. What a cruel and horrible thing to say.

He cracked a half-smile. "Don't imagine I will dote on you the way your father dotes on the queen."

"I would not so deceive myself, Your Highness."

He traced the curve of her face with one fingertip. "Anatole," he whispered.

She closed her eyes, clawing for strength, for she was still knocked off guard by his cruel remark. "Anatole," she repeated in a humiliating show of obedience.

Again she felt trapped by him and this time, Darius wasn't coming to her rescue. Where did Anatole get his talent for intimidating her? She had always been headstrong, never easily bullied.

Had he intimidated his first wife this way?

She opened her eyes and they studied each other in hostility.

"You have never spoken of Princess Margaret before."

"You knew of her."

"I knew of her, but you never spoke of her. Were you in love with her?"

"Very much. As I am in love with you."

She lifted a brow in astonishment, her jaw dropping open slightly.

"Are you so surprised?" he asked with a laugh. He touched her hair. "I am very attracted to you, Serafina."

That is not love, she almost said, but instead she thrust home for her opportunity. "Then indulge me, Anatole, and let the wedding date sit as planned." She gave him one of her most deliberately dazzling smiles.

He smiled back at her, eyes bright and cold.

"Well," he said softly, "persuade me, Serafina."

She flattened herself uneasily against the doorframe, inching back as he drew closer. "What do you mean?"

"Ask me nicely. I think you know what I mean."

She scowled up at him, barely biting back her opinion of him. "Will you let the date stand or won't you?"

"If you let me kiss you," he murmured.

Startled by his unforeseen request, she blushed and lowered her head, gooseflesh creeping down her arms. Fine, she thought, if it would buy her time for Darius.

"A-all right."

He stepped closer and touched her face, tipping her mouth upward, one hand firmly securing her chin. She was very tense as she leaned against the doorframe, her hands behind her. She tried not to grimace or wince as he lowered his head and pressed his hard, cold lips to hers.

His kiss bruised her lips against her teeth but she forced herself not to pull away. He gripped her hair hard, painfully, resting his other hand on her shoulder, where it squeezed and pawed her flesh.

She inched back, longing for him to have his fill of her and be done, but he became carried away by his own ardor, laying siege to her. She fought disgust, refusing to open her mouth in spite of all his efforts. Her jaw was clamped, and she hated every stroke of his tongue upon her lips, but when she felt the jut of his erection pressing against her stomach, she froze, frightened now and seized by waves of sheer repugnance.

"That is quite enough, sir!" she gasped out, pushing past him.

She heard his low, rough laughter behind her as she fled, wiping her mouth on her arm in trembling revulsion.

"You've got a lot to learn, child," he called after her. "But I'll teach you to like it."

Sometimes he told them to go to hell in Russian, sometimes in Spanish, English, Arabic, Italian, just to keep them guessing. Stoically, he had thwarted his captors' every attempt to make him talk, answering their questions with nothing but a slight, cold, mocking smile.

They had been gentle. So far, he had only a black eye, a

swollen jaw, and a few bruised ribs. Later, Darius knew, things would get rougher. For now, they were saving him for his audience tonight before the emperor.

His arrogance was in place like a shield. Behind it, he was calculating a second chance at killing Napoleon somehow when he was brought before him.

At the appointed hour, the big, apelike corporal with the reeking breath quit pummeling Darius's abdomen. He was pulled to his feet, dragged from his cell, and herded outside. He stole a glance at the moon and thought of Serafina dancing in her garden.

He smiled to himself, disconnected from everything, then they shoved his head down, throwing him into another carriage.

I'll get him this time. Just put me in the same room with the little bastard.

After about an hour's drive, they pushed him out of the carriage amid his guards, before a vast Baroque palace somewhere in the countryside. Uneasily, he scanned the landscape, taking stock of his surroundings.

Chin high, he was herded and prodded through the halls past gawking courtiers and ladies, driven ahead like a wild animal captured for some rich man's menagerie. He swaggered and smiled coolly at the women just to irk his captors.

At the end of the gleaming hall, huge doors were opened before him and he was shoved into a glittering great hall. He caught his balance, chains rattling, then swaggered in slowly, shoulders squared, chin high. Straight ahead of him at a long banquet table sat the man he'd tried and failed to kill. Failed.

Worthless, worthless.

He stared insolently at Napoleon and Napoleon stared insolently at him, looking rather bemused.

Darius was ordered to halt in the center of the room. They were eating dinner. Silver tableware, he noted in the back of his mind. Somewhere up there had to be a usable knife.

Contemptuously, he glanced askance at his guards, then surveyed the others in the room.

La Beauharnais sat between her husband and her son, Eugène, former contender for Serafina's hand. The empress and Eugène gazed at him in trepidation, but Napoleon's brothers looked at him with a purely Corsican thirst for revenge in their eyes. He cast them a sneering smile, then, for the sake of insolence, let his gaze wander freely over the three Bonaparte sisters.

When his stare wandered to Princess Pauline, he found her avidly inspecting him. He arched one brow as her gaze slowly traveled down his half-bared chest.

"Hey, sweetheart, why don't you come over here and get on your knees for me?" he called softly, giving her a look.

She gasped. Sounds of outrage filled the hall.

Darius smiled. Someone bludgeoned him in the backs of his knees and he fell. He was struck repeatedly. *Ah, childhood memories,* he thought. As he waited for the beating to end, he mused to himself that anyone who judged that underfed Corsican hussy in the same league with his Princesa had obviously never seen Serafina and did not know what a real princess was.

Darius heard young Eugène clear his throat. "That's really quite enough, isn't it? There are ladies present."

"I don't see any," Darius muttered from the floor.

Another swift kick in the ribs. He snarled, his whole body tensed, but they were done beating him for now so he climbed wearily to his feet and faced his captors with a bruised smirk.

Napoleon appeared amused, lounging on the arm of his chair, one hand thrust into his waistcoat as he stroked his stomach thoughtfully. "Closer, mystery man. Let us have a look at you."

Gladly, Darius walked forward, aware out of the corner of his eye of each gleaming knife on the banquet table.

"That's far enough," the captain muttered, holding him back a good eight feet from the emperor.

"I would be interested to hear what you have to say for yourself before I sentence you."

Darius considered. "Only that you make a very small target, General."

This remark got him rather severely beaten again.

"This is getting tedious," he growled as the soldiers pummeled him and finally backed off again.

"Who are you?" Napoleon asked pleasantly.

Darius dragged himself up off his knees and forced himself to stand, eyes blazing. He wove slightly on his feet, willed himself to stand tall and be steady. "No one of any consequence," he replied.

"Why did you try to kill me?"

He shrugged. "Don't like you."

Napoleon stared at him for a few seconds with an expression of intense thought, then abruptly laughed. "You may well be the cockiest bastard I have ever met in my life. Take him away. By morning, I want to know every secret he has to hide."

"What, no hasty execution?" Darius drawled. "If a quick death was good enough for the Duc d'Enghien, it's certainly good enough for me."

Napoleon's eyes narrowed and his face instantly grew flushed. "In due time," he promised through gritted teeth. He sent his men a violent, simmering nod to take him away.

As they stepped toward him to lay hold of him again, Darius lunged forward, running for the table and the nearest knife. Women screamed. The apelike corporal and a few others tackled him, tripping him in a tangle of chains, then there was more unpleasantness.

Napoleon was on his feet, throwing down his napkin. "Kill him! Now!"

Darius looked up from the floor under a pile of men and glared at Napoleon. The emperor moved nearer his wife protectively.

When they finally let Darius get to his feet, he kept his chin high, his stride a lazy saunter in a show of fearlessness, but he really was not looking forward to the next half hour. Glancing over his shoulder one last time, he saw Princess Pauline still staring at him.

The guards shoved him toward the huge doors.

"Wait!" a high-pitched voice called behind them.

"What is it, Paulina?" Napoleon snapped.

"My lady-in-waiting knows who he is," Princess Pauline said.

His back to them, Darius froze.

His mind was transported back to that morning several days ago when he had ushered Cara, Serafina's traitorous friend, into banishment.

"Turn around, you," the captain ordered him.

Suddenly he had a sick, cold lump in the pit of his stomach. Mentally cursing, Darius reluctantly obeyed. Sure enough, he saw the petite, blue-eyed blond standing behind Pauline, her viperous stare fixed on him. She had promised revenge on him and he had laughed it off.

"He is Count Darius Santiago," Cara spoke up, malicious triumph in her alpine-blue eyes. "King Lazar's adopted son and Princess Serafina's favorite. Ascencion will pay any price to have him back alive."

Napoleon began to laugh softly, tilting his head back.

"It won't work," Darius started. "Lazar will never bargain with the likes of you—"

"No? I recall the story a few years ago of how you saved your king's life—nearly in exchange for your own—and I know that in spite of all his liberal policies, Lazar is an Italian of the old school. Loyalty comes before everything."

"It won't work," Darius said again, heart pounding. "I'm not that valuable."

"We'll see."

"We should have known he was no common criminal." Pauline's glance flicked over his body.

Darius looked at her, feeling as though he might be sick.

Cara went on staring at him, gloating, her arms folded over her chest.

Napoleon chuckled. "Take him away, make him comfortable. I have to thank you, Santiago. You have made things so much easier for me. Why fight a war when I can just hand you over in exchange for the navy? And then there is that gorgeous bird, the princess. If we act quickly, we can snatch her right out of Tyurinov's hands and put her in yours instead, eh?" he said, elbowing his stepson. "On the other hand . . ." Napoleon turned to Josephine and gave her painted cheek a teasing pinch. "Maybe I'll get rid of you, old girl, and marry the chit myself."

CHAPTER
⚜ SIXTEEN ⚜

His self-disgust was deepening by the minute, but Darius kept up his show of nonchalance as a dozen guards ushered him into a rich, windowless chamber in a distant wing of the palazzo. A doctor was sent to look him over for broken bones and lacerations, then his right hand was unchained so he could eat the small portion of food and water that were brought to him.

He was so jittery, his stomach in knots, that he didn't want the food. But old ways were coming back to him. He ate voraciously, forcing the food down, eyeing the soldiers. No one spoke. They waited for him to finish the meal, then manacled his hands again before him. Finally, they locked him in, a few men posted outside the room's only door.

With a disgusted sigh, he lay back on the thick mattress, still barely able to comprehend how he had come to this. Why wasn't he dead? Not even his finest insolence had managed to get him killed. He'd thought for certain his lewd remark to Napoleon's sister would do the trick.

He cast his forearm over his brow and tried to still his mind, but countless times, lying there, he relived the moment he had fired the first shot at Napoleon, trying to understand what had gone wrong. He was still in shock that he had missed. As the immediate danger ebbed for now, humiliation set in.

Worthless. You failed at everything.

He had made a good show of arrogance, but here, in the silence, his pride was crushed and he felt not the slightest bit sorry for himself. He was supposed to be a trained, top-level agent and assassin, yet he had made an amateur's mistake, firing prematurely. Then, when the moment came to eat the arsenic, he had shown his true colors. That little, unwanted Gypsy pickpocket he had been so many years ago had emerged without warning, thwarting all his plans, saying, hell, no, would he ever kill himself off. He had survived too much to throw it all away. That was the part that shamed him most.

After all these years of striving to become something better, in the crucial moment he had proved himself the same as when the king and queen first found him. In the moment of truth, he had chosen survival over honor.

And why should his choice come as a surprise? he thought angrily. Honor! He was so bloody sick and tired of honor. Look where it had gotten him.

He got up and paced to burn off some of his restlessness, chains clanking like a ghost in a castle. Just then, he heard men arguing in hushed voices outside the door.

He listened intently, his senses leaping to the alert. *Lord, what now?*

"Are you mad? You'll get us all court-martialed!"

"Just do it," another snapped. "You're getting paid, aren't you?"

All of a sudden, four soldiers burst in and strode over to him. "Oh, so you're awake, eh, cocky? Come on."

He stared at them and his blood ran cold, for he knew all in a flash as they dragged him out of the chamber that Napoleon had changed his mind.

It was time.

He began to sweat as he realized he was going to be executed before the firing squad, just like they'd done to the young Bourbon duke, d'Enghien.

He fought for calm while they tied a black blindfold over his eyes. Eyes covered, wrists bound before him, he hadn't felt the full panic of helplessness since childhood.

He thought of Serafina and steadied himself, lifting his chin.

He had failed at everything and they'd take his life, but they would never take his pride. Heart pounding, he could not resist one sly attempt to learn his fate.

"Ah, so you've finally found the balls to shoot me," he said coolly as they led him out of the room.

He heard laughter. "Getting a little nervous, are you, pretty boy?"

"Fuck yourself."

Someone shoved him. He caught his balance and walked carefully, unable to see where he was going.

"Stairs. Up," a man nearby grumbled.

They climbed a long staircase. Up? he thought. Shouldn't they be going down to the yard, where the firing squad could shoot him against the wall?

"Here." The guard did not sound at all happy when they stopped. "In."

He heard a door being opened. Someone pushed him from behind. He stumbled forward and nearly fell with a low curse.

"He's all yours," the guard grumbled, then the door slammed behind him.

Darius listened for all he was worth, but the room was utterly silent. He felt a presence. Napoleon? he wondered, bracing himself for the blow, expecting a hard boot in the face or in the ribs.

But there was only silence. He had too much pride to ask who was there.

He jumped slightly when soft hands alighted on his arm. He smelled a woman's perfume. Understanding flooded his mind. *Oh, Jesus,* he thought. *Here we go.*

"Let me help you up," said a soft voice with a Parisian accent carefully crafted to disguise a Corsican one. "Don't be afraid. You are safe now."

"The hell I am," he muttered under his breath.

He shook her hands violently off his arm and climbed to his feet, his whole body tense. The blindfold slid away from his face and he found himself in a candlelit boudoir, Pauline Bonaparte standing before him clad in a rather transparent, gold-tinted peignoir.

Unsurprised, he stared at her without a word.

She gave him a coy little smile. "Hello."

He glowered at her.

"Do you know who I am?"

He rather sneered at her, saying nothing.

She gestured to a cozy settle. "Sit. We shall have a little visit, my lord. Would you care for a drink?"

His only reply was a flat stare.

"Very well. Sit, please," she said in amusement.

When she turned away, he glanced about swiftly at his surroundings for any means of escape. She might prove a very useful instrument, he thought. He had to be extremely careful, however, for he could hear the guards posted outside the door. Warily, he sauntered to the settle and sat.

The dark-haired woman came back with a glass of wine and sat down beside him. "We'll share," she said, smiling. She took a sip, then held the glass up to his lips. "Go on, have some."

Watching her as he drank, he decided he had never met a woman he trusted less. She was very difficult to read.

Smiling, she lowered the glass from his lips and raised it to her own. Then she folded her slim legs under her, one slender arm draped over the back of the settle. She sat there studying him. He kept his head down, but from under his forelock his gaze scanned the dim room.

Her fingertips began toying with the back of his hair. He clenched his jaw. She touched his chin, gently turning his face to her. He met her stare guardedly.

"They gave you a bit of a black eye. That wasn't very nice of them."

He said nothing.

Staring at him, she smiled again with a look of calculation, brushing his cheek with her knuckles. "Poor, brave Condé," she murmured. Her fingers trailed down his shoulder and his arm. "Perhaps I can ease your pain a little."

He pulled away, shooting her a simmering look. "What do you think I am?"

"You know, Condé, I paid well for a little of your time. Aren't you glad to be out of your dungeon? You never know how I might be able to help you. You could be civil."

"Forgive me, it's been a rough day," he said through gritted teeth.

She laughed gaily. "So," she said, linking her fingers over her crossed knee, "you are a friend of the splendid Princess Serafina. How good a friend?"

He looked at her suspiciously.

"Are you her lover?"

He narrowed his eyes at her. "Her Highness is unmarried and pure."

Pauline bristled. "My lady-in-waiting, Cara, who used to attend Serafina, says the princess has been in love with you all her life. Is this true?"

"How should I know?" he replied. "I would never presume to know such a thing about a member of the royal family."

"You do not care for her?" She leaned forward with a little, calculating flare in her dark eyes.

Not in a thousand years would he discuss Serafina with this malicious cat.

"Cara betrayed her. That is all I know," he said.

For a long moment, they sat in silence. Furtively, he eyed up the window, knowing it was too high to jump. He could hear the guards outside the door chuckling to each other over the way she had had him brought to her like a stud horse, a male whore.

He could play the part. He knew it well: It was a role he had been perfecting since he was thirteen and had discovered this particular way of avenging himself on the female race.

Only, after Serafina, any other woman's touch sickened him.

Again, she reached out and touched under his chin, turning

his face to her. "What's wrong, Condé? You weren't shy before." She rested her hand on his thigh and began caressing him.

God, I have to get out of here.

Just then, his gaze caught on a gold glint in her dark hair. A hairpin.

He went stock-still as his heart began to pound. He flicked his gaze away smoothly from the hairpin as Pauline moved closer, caressing his chest. Suddenly she leaned toward him, kissing his cheek near his mouth.

"I desired you from the first moment I saw you. You are possibly," she murmured, "the most beautiful man I have ever seen in my life."

All he could think about was getting his hands on that hairpin.

Her breathing deepened as she stroked higher up his thigh. "Beautiful stranger, I won't let them hurt you. Was it lonely in your cell?"

He closed his eyes so she wouldn't see his building fury as she slipped her warm, soft hands inside his torn shirt, caressing his chest, his sides, his belly. He knew exactly what she was doing, using him to strike at Serafina's very heart.

Somehow he forced himself to sit still, but he decided on the spot that he despised this woman more than all the others put together.

He flinched when she laid her hand on his groin, stroking him through his breeches. "My goodness, no wonder you are so arrogant," she purred. She slipped under his arm and into the circle formed by his bound wrists.

She sat on his lap, straddling him, and she slid herself against him, kissing his neck.

He swallowed hard.

"Don't you want me?" She teased his earlobe roughly and whispered obscene invitations.

He had to get the hairpin.

Kissing his neck, she paused when she felt his hands slide

over the curves of her backside, an exploratory caress through the thin silk of her peignoir.

"Ahh," she whispered in smug triumph. "I knew you'd change your mind with a little persuasion."

He ran his chained hands slowly up her back. "Pauline, Pauline," he crooned softly, "how could I resist? Your beauty is legendary."

She moaned for him, trailing her hands over her stomach and up to her breasts, touching herself. He kept talking to distract her as he ran his fingers up the back of her neck and through her hair until he reached the hairpin. "Maybe others can't satisfy you," he whispered, "but I'm going to give it to you like you've never had it, hard and fast and very deep. Would you like that?"

While she moaned and writhed with eagerness, he slid the jeweled hairpin out of her hair and maneuvered it between his fingers. He wiggled it around until he felt the pin's tip strike into the hole.

"What's your pleasure, my lady? Do you want me on top of you? Do you want to ride me? Shall I tie you down?" It was a familiar speech, one he had given many times, but tonight he laid it on thick, amused at how wild it drove her. "Maybe I should put my prick here," he whispered, caressing the cleft of her backside through the thin silk. "Would you like me to sodomize you, Pauline, hmm?"

"Oh, you are wicked," she breathed, all over him.

"Very," he murmured. Behind her back, he felt the mechanism of the first lock spring free with a tiny click. He endured her kiss as he picked the second lock and pulled the manacles off his wrists. He pulled back from her, clamped his left hand on the back of her neck and his right over her mouth.

She froze, her eyes wide, staring at him in shock.

"Hold still and don't make a sound, or I'm afraid I shall have to break your neck."

She choked on a gasp.

"Agreed?"

She nodded, the blush of lust draining from her face. For a moment, he listened for the guards outside the door, but they were quiet.

"Give me your right hand."

She obeyed. He slipped one of the manacles on her wrist.

"Get off of my lap. Slowly. We're going over to the bed."

Her eyes flared.

"Not for that," he scoffed.

She slid carefully off his lap, never taking her eyes off him. He reached for the discarded blindfold and replaced his hand swiftly with it, using the length of black silk to gag her. He edged her across the room. Reaching her well-trafficked bed, he secured the chain around a bedpost, then clamped the other manacle to her wrist.

"Now, then." He loomed over her, one hand wrapped lightly around her throat in warning. "How do I get out of here? When I lower the gag, you will answer. Do not attempt to lie to me. If you scream, I squeeze. Clear?"

Eyes round, she nodded.

Slowly, he lowered the gag, staring fiercely at her face.

"Through that door," she gasped, nodding toward a small door. "My maid's room. It connects to the service corridors, but I am not familiar with them."

He pulled the gag up over her mouth again, satisfied. He was unarmed, but if he could evade the legions of guards and escape the grounds of the Mombello Palace, he could remedy that soon enough. He could take the first carriage he met on the road, race back to Pavia, and ride the dapple gray all the way back to the coast.

"Good enough." He searched the room for anything he could use as a weapon. A hefty pewter candlestick was the best he could find. Holding it like a bludgeon, he crossed to her maid's door and paused, glancing back at her. "Oh, by the way, since I know you're dying to ask, Serafina *is* more beautiful than you—a thousand times more beautiful, more desirable, and infinitely more kind. She is a true royal princess." He looked her over in contempt. "You're just a cheap slut with a tinsel crown. And yes, I am her lover."

She kicked at him, cursing at him through the gag. He cast her a cold smile over his shoulder, then slipped out.

As he stole silently into the service corridor, it flashed through his mind that he could try one more time to locate and kill Napoleon.

Are you mad? Forget the damned heroics and get the hell out of here.

One hand trailing along the warm, smooth wall, he slipped down the hallway, moving soundlessly. He ducked into a broom closet as two maids came down the hall, absorbed in conversation. When they had passed, he crept out, heart pounding, and went on his way, jogging lightly down a flight of stairs at the end of the hallway. He knew that it would be difficult but possible to jump from the lower-story window if he could not find a door that led outside.

At the bottom of the steps, he found a door and inched it open. He glanced out, his grip white-knuckled on the pewter candlestick. The only person in the hall was a liveried footman, dozing at his post at the door to a salon.

Darius opened the door wider. *"Psst."*

The footman roused himself and looked over. Darius beckoned to him.

Moments later, Darius emerged from the service hall in light blue livery and powdered wig, a tray on his shoulder complete with a few empty silver-lidded plates. He walked out slowly, his stride stately, his face tucked slightly against the tray while he furtively watched for any means of escape. He felt ridiculous, but as he passed courtiers and ladies laughing together, no one paid him any mind.

Turning a corner, he came into another long corridor with no exit in sight. A chambermaid came out of a room ahead and hurried down the hall. She looked at the covered plates on his tray then gave him a disapproving glance.

"What took you so long? Kitchens slow tonight?"

Startled, he nodded.

"Well, you'd best hurry it. They've been working up an appetite in there planning their little war, and are none too pleasant, I can tell you," she muttered.

"Merci," he said.

She walked on. Darius looked ahead to the open doorway, his heart pounding, the hairs on his nape bristling under the hot, itchy wig, at his sixth sense's whispered proddings. Whatever was in that room, he had a feeling it concerned Ascencion, his king, and him.

At that moment, he heard shouts in the hall behind him, running footsteps. In the flash of an instant, he was sure he was caught. But before he could even steal a covert glance, three soldiers stampeded past him.

"Get out of the way, lackey!" They flung into the room. "Emperor, the prisoner has escaped!"

"What?"

There was a scouring blast of French curses. All Darius could do was stand aside, his head ducked behind his tray, as France's highest-level generals rushed out of the room with Napoleon marching in their midst. They stampeded by and disappeared around the corner of the hall. Darius was so frozen he wondered if his heart had stopped beating.

"You're late," the last one in their group said to him. The squat, ugly commander waddled angrily over to him. "What's under the lids?"

Darius kept his head ducked as he lowered the tray from his shoulder on one hand. He reached for one of the silver lids.

"Just . . . this." He smashed the lid in the fat commander's face, felling him.

Quickly, he dragged the unconscious man into the now-empty room and locked the doors. Whipping off the irritating wig, he strode to the room's vast center table and found himself staring down at a huge map of Europe, adorned with colored pins.

Red pins stuck out of the tiny shape of Ascencion near the boot of Italy. Darius stared.

Of course. The west shore! That is where they will strike.

Rapidly, he scanned the loose pages of notes, memorizing every detail. Numbers, armaments, supply lines. He studied the last page he found most closely.

In order to land the troops on Ascencion, France needed the ships of her newest ally, Spain. However, Spain's navy was not what it once was. The full attack could not be launched until Admiral Villeneuve was through with Horatio Nelson.

Destroying Nelson was Bonaparte's first priority, he read, for even with Ascencion's fleet added to the combined Franco-Spanish navy, no invasion of England could succeed so long as England's fearless admiral roamed the seas.

Just then, Darius heard more shouts in the hall. He put everything back where he'd found it so they would not know their battle plans had been discovered. Rather than going back out into the hall, he went through a pair of tall white doors and found himself in a dark music room. He exited the far end of it and came out in another hallway. Crossing into a sumptuous salon, he locked the doors behind him and heard more shouting, too close for comfort.

He strode across the room and opened the window, glancing down at the fifteen-foot drop. He climbed onto the ledge, braced himself, and plummeted. Landing with a curse, he rolled in a flower bed, sprang up, and ran for the gates, his heart beating like it would burst. The Mombello Palace was surrounded by sprawling grounds. He sprinted across open lawns, glad for the cover of darkness, but acutely aware that he was unarmed.

Panting, his lungs burning so much he vowed he would give up his cheroots if he ever got out of this alive, he came tearing up to the gates, where three of the sentries accosted him. He had no patience for them. He attacked the first one who blocked his path, sent him reeling with one square blow to the chin, and stole his sword.

He turned on the others, fighting furiously, pressing his skills to the limit as two more joined the fray. He dropped two of them with a wide, sweeping arc of the blade, but the third man tackled him from behind and tried to choke him. Fighting for air, finally Darius flipped the man over his shoulder and let out an angry cry of exertion as he killed him with the sword.

Sweat ran down his forehead, stinging his eyes. Quickly, Darius wiped his brow with his forearm, realizing he was still wearing the ridiculous powder-blue velvet livery. Circling with the last man standing, they engaged, blades clanging, just as the sentries' mounted captain came galloping onto the scene astride a white horse.

Darius dodged the blow as the captain swung his sword at him. As he turned, vulnerable for an instant, the man on the ground lunged at him. Darius whirled to parry and struck his opponent with a riposte. He thrust the sword in deeper with a cold look of ferocity as the soldier fell to his knees.

He turned to fight the captain on the horse. In short order, he left him bleeding with his men. Pulse throbbing, Darius opened the great iron gates, caught the horse with a few soft words, and swung up into the saddle.

A moment later, he galloped through the gates astride the white horse to freedom.

Despair.

Serafina sat for hours in the picture gallery, staring at the portrait of Darius, the life-sized original from which the miniature copy on her mantel had been made.

He seemed to dominate the long, echoey hall, daring all challengers with his fierce onyx stare. Against the canvas's dark background, his white coat and silver sword glowed with the light of his innate nobility, the knightly purity within himself that only Darius had never been able to see.

Six days and they had heard nothing.

She let out a long, careful sigh. When she finally had the strength to drag herself away, she got up, moving brittlely. She crossed the floor, skirts whispering like a ghost. She paused at the foot of the painting, kissed her fingers, and pressed them to the corner of his portrait. Her limbs were so heavy it was an effort to lift her arm. She then exited the gallery at the far end.

Continuing down the hall in a slow, trancelike walk, she heard the muffled shouting of many male voices coming from one of the rooms ahead. When she turned the corner, she saw that a large crowd of young men had gathered in the billiard room. The room must have been jammed full, for dozens of them were standing in the hallway outside the room. Repeatedly, they applauded and whistled, letting out cheers and almost angry shouts of agreement.

Suddenly Serafina paled at the sound of her brother's angry, grief-stricken voice above the rest. "Santiago is an inspiration for us all! Are we cowards? This policy of peace at any cost is a disgrace to our manhood! You see what is happening—my sister is being sold to buy us protection from a bully! Are we going to stand for it?"

She listened in dawning horror.

"The Russians mock us as cowards, and well they should if we are unwilling to fight our own battles!" he went on. *"This marriage is against her will!"*

Heart hammering, she ran to the billiard room, shoving her way through the pack of males. They turned to her in surprise.

"Principessa!"

"Let me through, you fools!" She pushed angrily through their midst and stalked into the billiard hall. She could barely believe what she saw.

About two hundred young lords and officers were crammed into the room, rallying around her brother. Their collective mood of hair-trigger excitement was palpable in the air. Eyes were bright, faces flushed. They seemed on the verge of riot, one more eager than the next to prove his manly prowess, and she, Serafina realized to her dread, was the banner around which they had been rallied.

They surged to their feet in wild cheering at her entrance,

yelling outrageous compliments, stamping their feet, whistling. She looked around her, frightened.

"Stop it!" she cried, but there was too much noise for them to hear her.

They ignored her.

She saw her brother standing on the table in the center of the huge room, several of his closest friends seated around him. Lieutenant Alec was there, too. She walked toward them. The young men cleared a path before her in their midst.

Their spontaneous cheers for her went on and on. She stared at the crown prince beseechingly but he paid no attention, flushed with the heady thrill of leading this volatile mob, relishing his first taste of power.

"Stop it!" she finally shouted at the top of her lungs, her face reddened with anger.

"We will fight for you, Principessa!" a young man cried near her right.

"No, that's not what I want!" she cried, but her blood ran cold as the others took up his vow. Stricken, she looked around at them. As her gaze moved over the young, unsuspecting faces, some handsome, some plain, her stare came to rest on her brother.

He was beckoning her over, his dimple flashing, his grin so like Papa's.

He will be killed. He has no concept of what he is doing. He is starting a war here.

Cold with dread, she walked to the billiard table.

There, two grinning members of the Royal Guard went down on one knee, offering their bent thighs for her to use as a stepping ladder. Rafael offered his hand from the table. She took it and carefully stepped up on the officers, then onto the billiard table. While the men around the two officers congratulated them and slapped them on the back like fools, she turned to Rafe.

"Rafael, disperse this crowd immediately. Don't you see you are stirring them to rise up against Papa?"

"Father is not always right," he said angrily, then he checked his temper and took her hand affectionately between both of his. He gave her a condescending smile. "Sister, this is men's business. You don't have to marry Tyurinov, and we will get revenge on the French for killing Darius!"

She flinched at the words. "Rafe, you have no business in this. Papa makes the policies—"

"He's gone soft, Cricket! He should never have agreed to sell you! *We will fight!*" he shouted to the fire-eating crowd.

They roared back at him, drowning out her protest.

"But I was the one who agreed!"

It was useless. She jumped down off the billiard table and fled, ignoring the cheers and adulation as they cleared back to let her pass, all exaggerated gallantry.

"You fools! You're all hotheaded, swaggering fools, and I won't let you die for me!" She ran, heedless of everything, fleeing to her garden. Outside, it was dark, the warmth of the night perforated by needling rain. As she stood there in despair, the rain cleared her head.

Yes. There was only one solution. She switched direction.

She began to run. The grass was slippery and wet under her satin slippers. She didn't stop running until she reached the stables. She shouted to have her mare saddled, but the grooms only stared at her, as if sensing her intention.

As she went to Diamante's stall, one of the older stable boys stepped in front of her. "It's late for a ride, Your Highness, and the weather is foul."

She gritted her teeth. "I love the rain. Get out of my way."

"Principessa, shouldn't you at least have a footman with you?" another asked gingerly.

"Stop trying to protect me! I'm sick of it!" With a wordless cry of impatience, she marched past them to Jihad's stall. She took the stallion's bridle down off the peg beside the stall. Jihad was as restless as she and accepted the bit more easily than she would have thought.

The worried boys came to the edge of the stall.

"Your Highness does not intend to ride that beast, surely!"

"He's dangerous!"

"You can't stop me!" she flung at them.

She hauled the stall door open, threw Jihad's reins over his midnight neck, then by sheer willpower climbed up onto the stallion's back, riding astride. She gathered the reins and urged the horse out of the stall.

"Get out of the way or be trampled," she ordered the boys.

They fell back. She ducked her head leaving the stall. Jihad tossed his head in excitement.

"Your Highness, where are you going?" the eldest boy demanded.

She urged Jihad crashing out of the stall, then they were galloping out into the night, heading for the promontory over the sea.

She would be with Darius forever.

Jihad's gallop was like the wind. Her head reeled with speed and recklessness.

Bareheaded and dripping with rain, she stood at the edge of the promontory, the night wind whipping her ruined dress around her, jagged rocks and the endless sea two hundred feet below her.

She had waited here for countless hours in the past, searching the horizons for his ship, always waiting for him to return to her.

But this time he wasn't coming back.

She dropped to her knees.

If she died, no one could fight a war over her.

If she died, she could be with Darius forever.

And if she took her life, his sacrifice would have been all in vain.

He had died to save her; her willful death would be a betrayal of everything he had stood for. He had abandoned her, cursed her with the burden of a life that would never know joy or love again.

"You heartless Gypsy thief," she whispered at the sea.

She crumpled down onto the rocky ledge and wept until there were no tears left in her.

The three Genoese fishermen were terrified of him. Darius shot them brooding, intimidating glances now and then to send them back to work and to dispel their curiosity about him—the wild-eyed madman who had commandeered their small boat and threatened to slit their throats if they didn't sail him immediately to Ascencion.

He sat against the bulkhead on deck, drowning in humiliation, his knees drawn up, arms wrapped around them. It was only hours now before he would see his Serafina. Knowing that helped him manage his fear and his terrible craving for her.

He had a lot to think about to pass the time. His experience in Milan had changed him, knocked the illusory ideals of honor right out of him, dissolved all those air castles and lies he had fed from for so many years. He was no knight; he could no longer pretend that he was. No, he was ruined again, a creature of instinct and survival, as he had once been on the streets of Sevilla, and he knew what he needed.

He didn't care anymore if it was wrong.

He was going to take her for himself. Just take her. No one else could have her, he thought, the edge of instinct bristling inside him. She was his.

Even though he had failed and would never deserve her. Even though Lazar was going to disown him. Even though he did not know how to be anybody's husband and was terrified he would be like his father, possessive of her, controlling. She was his and nothing else mattered.

His.

CHAPTER
⊰ SEVENTEEN ⊱

On the eve of her wedding, Serafina was an empty shell of her former self.

There was no point in hoping anymore. If Napoleon were dead, the whole world would have heard about it by now. If Darius were alive, he'd have sent some kind of news.

She was to marry Anatole in the morning. None of it felt real. Had Darius died alone? Had he suffered much? Had his last thoughts been of her? The questions had no answers. Not knowing what had become of him was worse than just hearing the awful truth once and for all.

She sought an opiate in slumber. Little hothouse flower who could not stand her pain, with contempt she watched herself progressing, as the days passed, from wine to whiskey to laudanum. Her doctor prescribed it.

The stable boys had told the head groom what she had done, taking Jihad out for a gallop in the rain. That excellent servant had, in turn, felt compelled to warn her parents of her dangerous behavior. They had come to try to have a talk with her. The sight of them made her sick, so in love. In the tragedy of Darius's self-sacrifice, they had turned to each other. Her loss, her devastation was the same event that somehow brought the two of them closer together—as had their new baby, to whom Serafina was coldly indifferent.

It was a boy and they were calling him Lorenzo. She didn't care. Why should her mother be the one giving birth to what was obviously a love child, unplanned, an accident? It was scandalous. The woman was nearly forty. For two decades, her mother had had the devotion of one of the two best men in the whole world. Would *she* never get her chance at happiness? Embittered by life at the age of twenty, she had turned away from her parents' attempt to reach out to her and include her in their perfect little world. She observed herself acting just like Darius, evading all their concerned questions by saying merely that she was not feeling herself. They had despaired of cracking her open and had sent the physician to examine her.

She had not stood for his prying, either. She could have given him her diagnosis in three words: *Darius is dead.* She was dead inside, comatose. But laudanum was her angel of mercy.

Sweet dreams brought Darius back to her, the feel of his honey-gold skin, the sound of his scoffing laughter, his bitter-sweet, molasses smile—and then he would vanish again.

Cruel, she thought. Cruel.

She lay now in her canopied bed. Two candles had burned down to stumps on the twin night tables, the wax pooled and sculpted into bizarre shapes.

She had not meant to fall asleep so early again tonight. It had been barely nine-thirty when she crawled into bed. She had meant to read for a while, but she couldn't concentrate and the book weighed too much to hold up. Her arms were too weak, her body so heavy, her eyelids almost too weighty to lift. Laudanum made her so tired, though the dose was mild. If she gave in to the urge to sleep, perhaps she could conjure him again to come to her in her dreams, her demon lover.

Her last thought before drifting off had been that she could sleep her life away under the white, pristine snowfalls of Anatole's homeland.

Oblivion. Blackness. No pain.

Hours passed.

The soft click at the wall did not altogether pierce her sleep. Very distantly, she was aware of her pet monkey chirruping to himself, but that was not unusual. She dreamed she was at the bottom of a great, black crypt, sleeping, with a mile of earth between her and the light.

Princesa.

Ah, she understood what this blackness was. She was in Darius's tomb with him. Her dreaming brain wound the thread of a story for her. She followed it like Ariadne, the princess in the Minotaur's labyrinth. He was here somewhere in the dark, if only she could find him. He was lost in this maze and she had to save him. He was waiting.

She called to him in her dream and the three musical syllables of his name echoed down the long black corridor like a singsong whisper, a sigh, *Daaariusss.*

He answered her call in his soft, lulling voice. *"Princesa, awake. I am here."*

No, I do not want to wake, she thought in anguish, for she could feel that she was getting closer to him. She had to glimpse his face one last time, even if it was horrible, even if he were the Minotaur in the maze and would kill her when she found him.

Soft notes rose around her as a hand brushed guitar strings, like a breeze over a moonlit lake. She opened her eyes and saw a tall, shadowy silhouette through the gauzy white netting of her bed.

She stared, not sure if she was awake or dreaming. She didn't dare breathe for fear that the beloved apparition would vanish.

As if the netting formed a magic circle into which he could not cross, he walked around the foot of her bed, lean and graceful, never taking his luminous eyes off her.

"You are so beautiful, I ache," he whispered, "here." He laid his hand on his heart, staring at her as he slowly glided nearer.

She clutched the sheets, pulling them higher over her chest, her eyes round as she stared at the ghostly revenant. From the netherworld, he had come to take her with him. They would be together for all eternity. She need only give him her soul. As if he did not already possess it.

"Don't be afraid."

"Are you real?" she breathed, her heart pounding.

Sauntering around to her right, he came to stand at the head of her wide bed. She stared in amazement as his sun-browned hand parted the mosquito netting.

When he placed his knee on the bed, the mattress bowed under his quite solid weight.

"You tell me," he breathed, and leaning down, he kissed her mouth, a satin caress, his warm, living breath blowing gently against her lips.

She gave a strangled cry and threw her arms around his neck. He pulled her to him in a crushing embrace as he stood beside the bed. His arms were hard and real and warm around her, the chafe of his dark, scruffy day-beard rough against her neck. Shaking uncontrollably, she barely knew what she was saying, squeezing his arms, clutching at his flesh, willing him not to disappear.

"Oh, God, Darius, Darius, tell me you're real, my God, tell me you're alive!"

He stroked her hair, his hands trembling. "Shh, angel, I'm here. I'm real."

"Oh, tell me you are alive!" she cried, still only half able to believe it. She was laughing, crying, sobbing all at once. "Are you hurt? Let me see you."

Hands shaking, she pushed back and grasped his shoulders, holding him at arm's length, her gaze traveling swiftly over him. He was bruised, a little gaunt, and his clothes were in tatters.

"Serafina, I'm back. I'm all right," he said forcefully.

She looked into his eyes, holding his gaze for a moment as the reality of it sank in. Her eyes filled with tears. Without a word, she flung her arms around him and held him with all her strength, squeezing her eyes shut.

She breathed him, filling her nostrils with the musky, male scent of him; the feel of him in her arms was ecstasy, so warm and strong and sure. Alive. Miraculously alive.

Over and over she breathed her thanks to heaven, running her hands all over Darius to assure herself he was not an illusion. She clung to him.

He wound his arms around her waist, soothing her. She clung to him as he rocked her gently. "Shh, it's all right now, angel. I'm here."

She hugged him tighter with tears of sweet relief streaming down her face, too overcome with emotion to speak.

He had come back to her, just as he always had in the past. Battered but unbowed, he had fought his way back from the grave. He was alive . . . *and that could only mean that Napoleon was dead.*

By God, he had done it.

He had put the tyrant of the age in his grave, and walked out of the lion's den unscathed.

The great Santiago had performed the impossible.

Again.

"Oh, you blackheart!" Rearing back to stare fiercely into his midnight eyes, she shoved at his chest. Before she gave him any part of a hero's welcome, she would bloody well give him a piece of her mind. "How could you *do* that to me?" she cried. "How could you lie to me all that time, then go out to get yourself killed? I thought you were *dead*. You have put me through hell. Pure hell!"

He just stared at her, looking lost, and gave a tiny shrug. "I'm sorry. I had to protect you."

"You had to protect me," she echoed. She threw up her hands. "How am I to stay angry at you when you give me an answer like that?"

"Don't be angry. Please. Not tonight. I've just been to hell and back. I've been beaten up, shot at, rode a horse until it didn't get up anymore, then I walked about sixty miles, and I swear it was all for you, Serafina." He held her gaze from under his forelock. "You're all that matters to me."

"Oh, Darius." She shook her head at him, petting his hair out of his eyes. "My beautiful madman, I am never letting you out of my sight again." She pulled him tenderly into her embrace.

He slid his arms around her waist, laid his head on her shoulder, and pressed his face into the crook of her neck, leaning on her. She tightened her protective embrace and cupped his head against her shoulder.

"What will we do now, darling?" she whispered.

He shook his head. "I am utterly out of plans."

"What of Tyurinov? I must know that much. My wedding is in . . ." She glanced over her shoulder and squinted against the dim illumination in the room at the mantel clock, then she turned back to him with a sniffle. "Nine hours."

"No, it isn't! You're not marrying him, ever!" He pulled back with a scowl. "You were *never* going to marry him! You're not a chess piece, Serafina, and I would never let you be used for one. I longed to tell you before to ease your worries, but I couldn't risk it. If you had known what I intended— admit it—you would have done anything to stop me. You would have gone to your Papa to get your way, but it was your father's overhasty agreement to the match that caused all of this. Anatole Tyurinov is more of a brute than you or your father yet realize, but tomorrow, I tell you, the truth will come out. Now, kiss me, damn it."

She obeyed gladly. "I love you, you brilliant, fearless . . . lunatic," she murmured, hugging him hard. "I owe you my life."

"You don't owe me anything," he said, then he snuggled against the crook of her neck and let out a soft, wistful sigh. "Just let me stay here."

She kissed his hair. "You're not going anywhere," she whispered. "Lie down with me and rest. You are exhausted. I'll call for food and drink—"

"All I want is you."

His sweet, simple statement pierced right through her heart. She pulled back and took his face gently between both her hands. "Oh, my poor baby," she said softly. "Look at you.

What have they done to you? You're a mess. You have a black eye. Your jaw is swollen."

"Mm-hmm," he murmured. He had begun kissing her neck, running his hands down her sides to hold her by the hips. "Kiss it for me?"

She did, cupping his face carefully. "I can't believe you're here. Oh, God, I wanted to die without you. Darius, say we will never be parted again. Say you won't scare me again. . . ."

He dipped his head and wove a necklace of kisses for her from one ear all the way across her throat to the other. "I love you, Serafina. That's the reason I went there. I have never loved another but you."

Surely she was dreaming, but she never wanted to wake. She tilted her head back in ecstasy as her eyes brimmed. "I love you, too. So much." Her hand slid down from his face to his chest. She began stroking the V of smooth, honey-gold skin where his shirt was torn.

His embrace tightened and her caress moved lower, savoring each taut ridge and plane of his flat, sculpted stomach. A tremor moved through him as she stroked him. She closed her eyes. She felt her skin heating under his caresses, her breathing deepening.

"God, I missed you," he whispered as he slid his hand under her breast, cupping its weight. He lowered his head, gazing at the sight of her breast in his hand through her thin muslin night rail. His downcast stare was so pensive she kissed his forehead.

He lifted his head and stared straight into her eyes. Neither she nor he moved. Desire leaped between them like lightning in the silence. He murmured her name. Then he took her face between his hands, tilted his head slightly, and kissed her mouth.

He tilted his head the other way and kissed her again. She felt his need rise up from deep in the core of him in one massive wave. It was stronger than she had ever felt it before.

He began slowly easing her down onto her bed. He kissed

her with exquisite gentleness as he laid her on her back and covered her with his hard, powerful body.

Resting on his elbows, he cradled her head in both hands and covered her face in soft, tender kisses, her eyelids, her brow, cheeks, and chin. He gave her a long, very sweet kiss, then lifted his head and stared down into her eyes, his beautiful lips moist and swollen with kissing.

She saw fire in his eyes, agonized need, and a question. In answer, she cupped her hand around the nape of his neck and pulled him down hungrily to her, opening her mouth wide for his kiss.

He moaned softly and took her mouth in hard, claiming possession. He rose up onto his hands over her, still kissing her. Slowly, he drove his body against hers. He swept his torn, gunpowder-stained shirt off over his head, muscles rippling all down his belly. She bit her lip as her gaze skipped down to the enormous bulge in the front of his breeches. He gave her a shadow of his arrogant half-smile as he cast the shirt away with a flick of his wrist.

Her heart tripped as he moved over her again. He bent to kiss her breast through her night rail. His breath was hot through the white muslin, his hair like silk, his bronzed skin like velvet under her caress.

He gathered her night rail in both his hands, pulling it higher up over her legs. Kissing her, he nipped at her lower lip, coaxing her mouth open wider still for his deepest kiss. She molded her hands over his muscular arms, caressing him, marveling at his sinewy power, but there was a little shivery thrill of fear mixed in with the admiration. She would never really tame this man.

No one would.

He moved back a small space and gently lifted her night rail off over her head. She was struck with an unprecedented bout of shyness. Lying naked before him, her hair fanned out over the pillow, she felt her face heat with a deep blush. Inexplicably, she wanted to cover herself with her hands. She didn't know why—she had never been shy in front of him before. But this time was different, and they both knew it.

Darius paused and sat up, tilting his head as he gazed at her with a half-smile, tender warmth in his eyes. He ran his hand down her leg, his touch sure and smooth. "You're ready for this," he murmured in assurance.

"Yes, I think so. I know I love you. Yes," she said again decisively.

"Relax." He smiled softly, then leaned down and kissed her belly, holding her gaze. His long lashes swept closed and he kissed her hip, then each of her thighs.

The light kisses roused her blood to liquid fire. The night was warm but the air felt cool moving over her heating skin. He nuzzled his way lower down her belly.

"W-what are you doing?"

"Loving you, Princesa."

Her eyes were wide, her heart racing, as she watched him bend his head and press a reverent kiss to her mound. His warm breath seeped down to meld with her surging wetness. He lingered there, not moving. She closed her eyes, waiting, enticed, a little bewildered.

He stroked her, a slow, light, two-fingered caress upward. She moaned.

The mattress shifted as he crept between her thighs and kissed her there once more. He kissed again, then again, more delicately. Then he explored her, touching her with his thumb. He roused breathless notes from her throat as skillfully as he played his guitar. Her embarrassment flared when he touched his tongue to her, but soon she was candy dissolving in his sulky, sculpted mouth, and she became his creature utterly, his mindless thrall. He licked deeply with his long, clever tongue, penetrating her, drinking her. She squirmed, bucked, writhed, but he held her hips still, forcing her to take the pleasure even when she knew her mind would break with it.

Abruptly, he crawled over her on all fours, his face wet as he took her mouth, ravishing her with his kiss. Caressing his shoulders, she could feel him shaking as he reached down and unfastened his breeches. Eagerly, she helped him slide them down his lean hips as he freed himself.

Ah, she had waited so long for this, she thought in hungry anguish, glancing up to find him looking into her eyes. She could see by his gaze that his thoughts were the same.

The tiny medal of the Virgin fell between her breasts as his hard chest eased down atop her, his flat belly to hers, the large, throbbing hardness of his potency sliding between her slicked folds of flesh. Her chest heaved against his with her deep, frenzied breathing and unbearable anticipation. Her body ached with a burning emptiness that only he could fill.

He wrapped his arms around her and kissed her cheek near her mouth. "Never leave me, Serafina. Never leave me." His voice was husky.

He held her in a stormy, aching gaze as he filled her slowly, inching ever so gently into her, merging them by love into one creature, born of love. He closed his eyes, pausing at the delicate barrier shielding her innocence. She swept her eyes open in tremulous wonder and saw silver tears under his lashes.

Her heart overflowing, she drew him down to kiss her. She felt him pulse inside of her. He gently pressed her lower back upward with one hand, lifting her very slightly. He brushed his cheek against hers, his body shaking.

"I will love you all my life," he whispered, and then he thrust once, deeply.

She gasped, her eyes flying open wide. Her chin on his shoulder, she stared at the canopy above as she slowly absorbed the shock of the pain.

Darius was whispering heartfelt apologies and stroking her hair. He glanced down at her anxiously. His eyes widened when he saw the tears sliding down her face, falling to the pillow.

"Did I hurt you so much?" he asked in distress, starting at once to pull back.

"No, no." She reached up and caressed his face with both

hands. Amid the pain was joy, for she knew now the circle was complete. "Now I have marked *you* with *my* blood."

He gave her a look of utter devotion and kissed her.

Slowly, his kisses and soft caresses gradually diffused the pain, and for his gentleness, her body opened like a flower. He waited for her unfolding, kissing her shoulders, caressing her face and hair. She ran her hands down his smooth, strong back and the sleek, hard curves of his backside, his lean hips. She could feel his taut control in every muscled inch of him as he enfolded her in his arms.

He quivered as she caressed his heated, gleaming skin. "I love your touch," he breathed. "It heals me." Eyes closed, he nestled his face against her hand as she caressed his cheek, then ran her fingers through his hair. "If I lost your love, I wouldn't want to live."

"You will never lose my love, Darius."

He shuddered. "I always knew I could come to you when I was ready, and that you would love me," he whispered. "The knowledge kept me alive." He held her more tightly and began to move deeply, slowly, inside of her. "God, Serafina, I want to give myself to you completely."

"Yes, Darius," she breathed.

"I'm afraid."

She stroked his back. "I will never hurt you."

His fevered lips alighted on her brow, his voice a shaken whisper. "All I ever wanted was to be good enough for you."

In answer, she took his angular face between both hands and kissed him, with her whole soul in it. *"You are, Darius.* You always were."

A sound of anguish registered from him. "You won't want me."

"I'll always want you. Give yourself to me, Darius," she whispered. "I won't hurt you. I love you."

He pressed her hands to his skin, his chest and his sides, as if he could not get enough of her touch.

"I love you," she said again, and again. He was trembling.

She caressed him everywhere. "Give in to my love, Darius. Surrender. No more secrets. You are safe here. I will protect you and keep you and give you everything you need."

When he looked down at her, his eyes blazed with fierce tears under his long, velvet lashes. She held his gaze, then closed her eyes and tilted her head back, yielding in perfect trust. She felt a single burning tear drop onto her throat, then he was kissing her throat and making love to her, taking from her what he so desperately craved.

The pleasure was laced with poignancy. She experienced the strangest sense of fullness, abundance. Perhaps it was the laudanum, but as he loved her, she felt as though she were a beautiful tree laden with fruit and it was her joy to know she fed this starved, thirsty man, nourished him, brought him delight. Then the strange sensation ebbed, and their union became an initiation by fire.

His gentleness frayed to reckless desperation. His body broke out in a sweat. This was no smooth Don Juan out to dazzle another conquest. This was a lost, lonely man reaching at last for what he most deeply needed. His greed for her astounded her, but she met him measure for measure, giving all she had for him. He rocked her and she moved with him as one, her legs wrapped around his thighs, her heels hooked behind his muscled calves. She clutched him to her, reveling in his penetration. She savored every sensation of his long, vigorous strokes. To give like this was ecstasy.

He moved faster.

He tangled his fingers in her hair, and when she dragged her eyes open to look up at him, she saw his eyes were closed, his fine-chiseled face transfigured with savage rapture. One glance told her his control was dissolving. She stroked his sides, his hair, eager to see how it would be when he abandoned all restraint.

The wait wasn't long.

He groaned again and again, his voice breathy and hoarse. "Oh, come for me, angel. I could explode."

When he lowered his head, his kiss drove her over the edge, her tongue thrusting wildly into his hot, wet, beautiful mouth.

She was his and he was hers.

His tortured moan cut the final cord of her control. She fell into a chasm of mindless bliss, gasping and groaning with anguished release as her body convulsed around him. With a rough cry, he thrust again and clutched her shoulder. She felt the brilliant infusion of his essence as he surrendered to his need with a deep cry of release.

They clung to each other in shuddering exhaustion, both of them panting, covered in a dewy sweat.

After a long moment, when she could be sure her sanity had not shattered, she let out a shaky sigh and dropped her arms from around his neck onto the bed, exhausted. Darius nestled against her. She looked at him and smiled in serene joy. He kissed her cheek, closed his long-lashed eyes, and laid his head on her shoulder, his stern, aquiline nose in the crook of her neck.

They lay like that for a long while, holding and touching in weary contentment. She didn't want to move an inch of her leaden, tingling body.

Somehow, she found the strength after a while to lift her head and check the time. The clock read three.

She knew that her mother, the hairdresser, and heaven knew how many other women would be arriving in her apartments early to begin fussing over her, the bride who was not getting married. At least not to Anatole, she thought. She let her gaze wander with a delicious sense of pleasure and possessiveness over Darius's long, lax body, and it was then that the first stirrings of an extraordinarily naughty idea began to form in her mind.

She stared at the guttering candle, in the grip of reckless inspiration.

Darius snuggled against her, wove his fingers through her hair, and sighed, closing his eyes. "You were wonderful," he murmured. His lean, muscular body was heavy with peace and contentment atop her.

She smiled absently as she pressed a kiss to his forehead. "I had a good teacher."

He chuckled, then sighed, then dozed.

Though his weight made it a little hard to breathe, she wouldn't have let him leave her embrace for the world. With a brief glance downward, she inspected his stitches, then wrapped her arms more snugly around his wide shoulders. His breathing deepened and softened. He was already asleep, but she remained wide-awake, her brain ticking with the idea.

No, you must not! Don't even think about it.

But honestly, she argued with herself, hadn't only good resulted from her pulling rank on him weeks ago, when she had commandeered him for her guard?

Now she had just given him her virginity; didn't she have a right to expect him to do the honorable thing? He had made an emphatic point of telling her she was not marrying Anatole, but he had said nothing of his own intentions toward her. What if he still didn't ask her to marry him? Was she to just sit passively by and wait and wait and wait for him? Really, didn't Darius regularly take matters into his own hands when necessary, acting on what he deemed her best interest? She felt she knew full well what was in *his* best interest, namely, herself. He should settle down, cease his dangerous work. He needed someone to take care of him, and she was the woman for the job.

Still, beneath all her rationalization was one basic fear. *I cannot let him leave me again. I cannot survive it.*

Inwardly, she wrestled with herself, though she held him with all the gentleness she possessed. He slept so trustfully upon her. He would hate her if she did this underhanded, Santiago-like thing. He had boasted to her weeks ago that no woman would ever tie him down. He loved his freedom.

Freedom, pah! she thought impatiently. His almighty freedom was nothing but his jealously guarded right to run away and hide from her whenever things got dangerous between them.

What if he had put a child in her womb even now? The thought sent a tremor of joyous arousal through the core of her.

Yes, he should have many children, she decided, swept away with her fantasy. He was so good with children. His children would teach him how to play. And who better to be mother to his babies than she?

Julia Calazzi? She scoffed at the thought. The woman didn't merit the care of a cat. Julia could never tap the reservoirs of sweetness in his heart, nor touch the fire of his soul's knightly purity. With a trace of anger, she recalled again the secrets Julia had revealed about Darius, and with that, her mind was made up.

She loved Darius and he loved her. He needed her. She knew that he did. She could no longer permit him to put his fears between them. It was rash, it was reckless, but it was for his own good.

Moving by delicate degrees, she extricated herself from beneath his warm weight without waking him. She rolled to the edge of her bed and silently rose, brushing the mosquito netting aside. She winced at the soreness and glanced down at the traces of her own dried blood on her thighs.

She glanced back at Darius, sleeping soundly. *So beautiful.* They were one now.

She didn't care how many lovers he had joined his body with in the past. The two of them shared a mystical union of soul and mind, each wholly unto the other. She had marked him with her blood and he was hers.

Now that she had won him and he had resolved her country's danger, she would pay any price to keep him.

She slipped her royal blue dressing gown on over her nude body and walked to her peach-and-gilt sitting room. She lit a candle, then knocked at her maid's door.

"Pia?" she called in a whisper. She opened the door a crack. "Pia, wake up, I need your help!"

* * *

Several minutes later, she returned to her bedroom, her heart pounding at her own recklessness. Darius still slept peacefully, and her ears still rang with Pia's useless protests.

Tiptoeing back to bed, she was tempted to leave her blue dressing gown on for modesty's sake, but the surprise must appear authentic. She pulled the robe off and dropped it on the floor, then climbed back into the bed. Darius slept on his stomach.

Gingerly lifting his heavy arm, she slipped back partly under him, the way she had been before. Peeking under the sheet, she saw with relief that he still had his breeches on, though loosened. As a final measure, she moved the top sheet away so the small, scarlet stain of her virgin blood on the flat sheet beneath would show. Her heart was pounding as she gathered Darius into her arms, placing his head on her chest.

She petted his hair, then kissed it. He stirred a bit and glanced up at her with a drowsy smile.

"Did you go somewhere?" he murmured, still half-asleep.

"The necessary."

"What time is it?" He lifted his head from her chest, looking around the room for the clock.

"Early. Hush," she whispered.

"Mm," he sighed, resting on her bosom again, all the coiled muscles of his shoulders and back loose and relaxed.

She kissed his forehead tenderly, caressing him as he dozed on her, peaceful and completely unsuspecting. She closed her eyes for a moment, wrestling with self-doubt.

Please don't hate me for this. I can't lose you again. If you won't fight for our love, I will.

She glanced out the wide windows and saw that dawn was shimmering along the horizon in gold and violet, like a secret promise.

The stage was set.

She waited.

CHAPTER
⚜ EIGHTEEN ⚜

The scandal struck at five A.M.

Hair tousled, heavy-eyed, Darius lifted his head from her chest and narrowed his eyes.

Serafina watched him, her mouth dry, her heart racing. "What is it, love?"

He looked drowsily over his shoulder. "I hear something."

Damn the man. She had forgotten he had six senses, like a blasted cat.

At that moment, she heard the crash of the outer door to her apartments banging open and a deep, familiar voice bellowing her names. Simultaneously, Darius swore in a language she didn't know. He was in motion, rolling off her, tangling himself in the sheet, frantically buttoning his breeches.

"Shit, shit, shit," he was saying under his breath.

She was frozen, staring at the door.

"Serafina!" her father shouted, panic in his voice. "Open the door! Honey, open the door!"

She could hear the key thrusting about in the lock and still she could not move. Wide-eyed, she turned and looked at Darius. He stared at her, trapped, his face ashen.

There was no time to react. The bedroom door burst open, banging back against the wall, and there stood the king, towering in the doorway.

"Sera—" he began, then stopped.

Oh, God, she thought, squeezing her eyes shut tight in the momentary silence that dropped like a wall of lead. Darius and she held perfectly still, the sheet draped over their waists.

Mama came a step behind Papa. Serafina winced at the wild panic in her mother's voice.

"Serafina! Lazar, is she all right? Is she all right?"

"Oh, I'd say so," her father said very, very coldly.

Her mother stopped behind him, looking under his arm. Darius swallowed.

Papa's stare of gathering rage moved from her to him.

"Good heavens!" her mother breathed.

Serafina saw Papa clenching and unclenching his fists. His voice was quiet. *"You son of a bitch."*

She screamed as her father charged the bed, tore the mosquito netting down, and reached for Darius. He hauled Darius out of her bed.

"Papa!"

"You son of a bitch!" he bellowed, throwing Darius up against the wall.

"Lazar, stop it!" her mother shouted.

"My daughter!" he roared at Darius, bringing up one powerful fist and drawing it back.

Darius didn't flinch and made no move to defend himself. He merely stared at the king, his expression perfectly blank, but for a trace of masterful insolence.

"I trusted you," Papa snarled. " 'Don't send chaperons,' you said. I didn't even question it. You lying, lecherous son of a bitch!"

"Don't hit him, Papa, it's not his fault!"

The blow didn't fall. Her father looked over his shoulder at her, his dark eyes blazing with fury.

"You little hussy," he said through gritted teeth. "You're damned right you'll take your half of the blame. Your mother and I taught you better than this! Where did you learn how to act like a tramp?"

She stared at him for a second in shock, then burst out in tears. "Papa! I am not a tramp! I love him!"

She sent a pleading look to her mother, but the queen had sunk down on a nearby chair, covering her face in both hands.

Serafina wanted to crawl under the bed and hide. Darius remained silent, chin high, arrogantly so, but his gaze was down.

"You've got a lot of explaining to do, *magnifico*," her father said coldly to Darius. "I want to see you in my office, then you can tell me everything else you've been lying about." He released him roughly with a look of disgust, shot her a look of contempt, and stalked toward the door.

"Papa?" Serafina asked tremulously, watching him pass. "Papa, please."

He turned pointing at her. "As for you . . ." He was so angry that he trembled. "Jesus, I thought you'd hurt yourself! Your maid came to us in a fit of terror saying she heard noises and feared you would take your own life! You strike death in our hearts, and this is what I find!" He paused, as though struggling to contain himself. "Reckless, headstrong, impetuous girl! I see this is all my fault *for spoiling you*!" he thundered, then he turned on Darius. "And don't think for an instant you're getting out of this, sir. You're marrying her. She's your headache now."

"I'm not a headache," she said miserably, and just when she thought she had never been more humiliated in her life, Anatole stepped into her doorway, his rugged face hardened with rage, his sapphire eyes bright and angry as the sun glinting off ice.

"What the hell are you doing here?" the king demanded.

Anatole ignored him, staring at Serafina. "So, it's true."

"This is a family matter, sir, begone!" Papa reiterated, stepping toward him in indignation.

"Anatole, please, leave us," the queen said in forced calm.

"This concerns me, does it not?" he flung back at them.

Then Anatole pinned her in his brutish stare, frankly taking in the wanton sight of her flushed skin and tousled bed with a look of derision and angry lust. From the shadows by the wall, she could feel Darius's killer instinct taking shape, homing in on him.

"I have had a servant watching your door at nights, my lady, for I knew you were too rich a beauty to be pure," he said coldly. "The only question was who your lovers were and how many were their number. You've proved me right. What a boon, that I did not marry you." He spoke a name at her in Russian that needed no translation.

Darius's reaction was immediate, but Papa intercepted him and slammed him against the wall again, less roughly. Darius winced, giving the king a rather dirty sideward glance.

Anatole stared at Darius like he wanted to maul him. "You, sir, are a dead man."

"Ah, get in line," Darius growled.

Anatole looked at the king. "I spit on this island. I will toast Napoleon when he crushes the lot of you."

"Napoleon is dead!" Serafina shouted at him triumphantly through her tears. She pointed to her champion. "Darius shot him!"

Everyone looked at Darius in shock.

For a moment, there was utter silence. He lifted his gaze and nonchalantly blew his forelock out of his eyes.

"Actually," he said, "I missed."

One could have heard the specks of dust drifting through the air, such a silence descended.

Nearly choking on her shock, Serafina turned and gaped at him, not sure she had heard him correctly. "Pardon me?"

The king snorted in contempt, shook his head, and stamped out of the room, shoving past Anatole. The Russian followed him out a moment later, chuckling coldly to himself.

Again, silence.

Head down, Darius stood leaning against the wall where her father had shoved him.

Serafina sat back in shock against the headboard, the sheets clutched to her chest.

Her mother rose, pushing up from the arms of the chair. She

smoothed her skirts and walked, head high, to the door. Serafina watched her, her heart pounding.

For a moment, the queen stood in the doorway, one hand on the doorknob.

"Darius," she said with quiet composure.

"Yes, ma'am."

"I am shocked and disappointed in you."

"Yes, ma'am."

"Mama!" Serafina cried, knowing the soft-spoken indictment from her mother would hurt him worst of all.

"And you," she said sharply, turning to Serafina, "I cannot think what to say to you. Once more you care for nothing but getting your way. You've made a fool of your father and Prince Tyurinov, as well. Now what will Ascencion do? We must go to war. If anything happens to Rafael . . ." She seemed unable to finish the thought.

"Is he all you care about?" she cried, as her mother folded her hands under her bosom and lifted her chin. "What about me? What about Darius? Don't you care what he has been through?"

"If you wanted each other, this was not the way to go about it. You both at least could have been a bit more discreet." The queen looked from Darius to Serafina, then picked up her skirts and left.

"Oh, God!" Serafina wrenched out. She dropped her face into both hands, then looked over anxiously at Darius.

He was still standing in exactly the same place where Papa had left him. He was slumped against the wall, head back, eyes closed.

She stared at him.

"You *missed*?" she shouted all of a sudden, pushing up onto her knees on the bed, clutching the sheet to her bosom. He looked over at her. She pointed at him furiously, jabbing the air. "You didn't mention that little detail, Santiago!"

"Oops," he said lightly, his scarred lips curving in a half-smile of razor sarcasm. "Still love me, darling?"

Incredulous, she stared at him, trying to comprehend. No apology? No explanation? No excuses?

"You tricked me!" she wailed. "You lied to me *again*!"

"I didn't lie. You didn't ask. It's not my fault you assumed what you wanted to assume."

"Not your fault?" she gasped. "You—you took my virginity under false pretenses, and now the blood of my people will be on my hands!"

"You wanted it. We both wanted it."

She gaped in utter astonishment. "You have no remorse."

"Are you so innocent?"

She eyed him warily. "What do you mean?"

"Come on, Serafina. Do you think I'm stupid? That was an awfully convenient interruption."

Her grip tightened on the sheets as she clutched them to her body. Her heart began to pound anew.

With a cold, mocking half-smile, he shook his head at her slowly. "That's my Princesa. She always gets her way."

"What are you accusing me of?" she cried, but she already knew she was guilty.

"Wouldn't you rather just admit it?"

"I admit nothing!"

The crescent-moon scar on his mouth became a twist of contempt. "You left the bed twenty minutes ago, angel."

"Darius," she whispered as her mouth went dry.

"Nice maneuver, Serafina. The minute I let my guard down, you make your move. I *have* taught you well, haven't I? You've ruined me," he said.

"Ruined you? I have not!" she forced out, eyes wide.

"In the span of a few minutes, you've just destroyed everything I've worked for and built for twenty years."

"What have I destroyed, your lies? Oh, how shall you live without your lies?" she shouted. "The truth is all that's come out here! You made this necessary, Darius, because the only way to get you to be honest is to force you into it! You'll lie about anything if you can get away with it! You have to be caught in the act!"

"So you would trap me?" he shouted furiously. "Play God with my life? And how dare you mistrust me? If I lie, I've got damned good reasons. How dare you assume I would seduce you and walk out on you?"

She crossed her arms over her chest. "Oh, you've never done that to a woman before!"

"That's not who I am with you."

"Who are you, Darius? Because I'd really like to know."

"You didn't even give me a chance to do the right thing!"

"Give you the chance? *I gave you three years!* You continually dodged me and evaded me and pushed me away, so why should I have expected this time to be any different? I didn't want to lose you again!"

"Well, guess what?" His taut smile was ice as he picked up his shirt. "You just have. Wife," he added in searing insolence.

He slung his shirt over his shoulder, strode across her room, and walked out the regular door instead of the secret one, and he slammed it behind him.

Surrender. I won't hurt you, he thought bitterly, echoing her words in his mind.

Darius strode down the hall, simmering, nay, bleeding inwardly. How many years had he devoted to protecting that damned, devious, infuriating little Queen of Sheba? How many mad risks had he taken, how many pints of blood had he shed?

He could not recall ever having been so hurt in all his adult life, for the truth was clear. It was not the fact that she had just trapped him in marriage. That scared the hell out of him, but it wasn't the part that hurt. The hurt came from knowing that an ordinary mortal capable of missing a shot was not good enough for her. The moment he admitted to failure, she had turned on him in repulsion. For all her talk of surrender and trust, the truth was clear: His Princesa had only wanted a champion.

He should have known. *Worthless. Worthless.*

What the hell was he going to do with a wife? he thought in disgust. But what other possibility had he been thinking of, taking her maidenhead?

All he had known was that he had to have her. The very thought of it made him want her again, in the midst of disaster. Irritated at his sheer, mindless appetite for her, he went into his suite, where he washed and dressed in fresh clothing after his extended misadventure. Finally, opening the hidden safe behind a landscape painting, he retrieved the report he'd written for Lazar in Moscow. He locked the safe again and crossed to the door.

One hand on the doorknob, he glanced back at the room, wondering if he'd ever be back. Without ceremony, he pulled the door shut behind him.

As he neared the main corridor, he felt the presence of dozens of people in the salons and galleries ahead. His stomach in knots, he braced himself, certain the scandal was already afoot.

It was a moment of destiny, he knew. There he was: the scapegoat in black, walking alone down the hall, past whispering clusters of ladies in pastel silks and dandies in loud-colored satin waistcoats who snickered as he passed. He heard what they were saying, and it cut him to the bone, but he kept his chin high on his walk of shame, staring straight ahead.

"Always knew he'd do something like this . . ."

"Bet he's been planning it for years."

"They should've realized. You can take the boy off the streets, but you can't take the streets out of the boy."

"How could he do this after all Their Majesties have done for him?"

"Poor, reckless child. She's thrown herself away!"

And then, the most vicious cut of all: *"Heavens, you sleep with Santiago, but you don't marry him."*

At the far end of this tunnel of malice, a voluptuous figure emerged.

Darius's heart sank lower, but relentlessly he kept going as Julia Calazzi tried to block his path.

He stopped when she stood directly in front of him. She stared up at him for a long moment with a look of pure hatred.

Suddenly her jeweled hand flashed as she slapped him, hard. He was vaguely aware of laughter and applause in the salon and along the hall.

Slowly, he turned his face to her, his cheek red and stinging, murder in his eyes.

"I will never forgive you for this," she hissed. "You will be sorry. And that, my love, is a promise."

She brushed past him and quickly walked away, high heels clicking on the marble.

Darius checked a tooth with his tongue, rubbed his cheek, then heaved a quiet sigh and forced himself onward.

To his relief, he went the rest of the way to the king's office without encountering the crown prince. If that young hothead called him out for seducing his sister, he did not know what he would do. One hand on the door to Lazar's office, he paused and steeled himself. He opened the door and went in as he had ten thousand times before.

Lazar stood at the window, his back to him, his arms folded over his chest.

"It's on the desk," he said in a deep, flat tone.

Darius watched him warily and stepped closer. Just as he'd expected, the king and the archbishop had already signed a special license and had it waiting for him. He picked it up.

"Now get out." His voice was curt like a whip. "I've decided I don't want to hear more of your lies today."

Darius clenched his jaw and looked at the ceiling. "Sir, there is more to this than you presently know."

"I'm sure there is. And you probably have a very good reason for keeping me in the dark like a damned old fool. But at the moment all I can think is that I trusted you and you betrayed me."

"Sir!"

The king held up one hand, still facing out the window. "I don't want to hear it, Santiago. What you've done, dishonoring my daughter, is inexcusable. I know you do not care for her as I would want a husband to love her and cherish her. I know that all you have for women is a bitter mix of lust and control and contempt. But that headstrong little hellion chose you, and now she's just going to have to live with her choice. So, get out, and take her with you. I will call for you when and if I ever feel prepared to hear you out."

Lazar's words pierced him mortally, but as Darius bowed his head, anger followed in the wake of pain.

"How dare you?" he heard himself utter. His heart was pounding.

Lazar turned around, one eyebrow arched high. "I beg your pardon?" he said with cold, regal condescension.

"How dare you?" he forced out, trembling now.

Lazar narrowed his eyes on him. "You forget yourself, my boy."

"No, it is you who forget me, Lazar. You forget everything I've done for you. I've dedicated my whole life to this kingdom and to your family. Have I ever asked for one thing for myself? Sometimes I am hard-pressed to wonder if I hold any significance to you other than the ways in which I can be useful—and don't tell me I don't love her!" he burst out, trembling as he fought to contain his outrage. "Was it you they tortured in Milan for her, you they humiliated? No, sir, you were here in your soft life, being wooed by that—that Russian animal!"

Lazar stared at him, seemingly stunned by his rare display of emotion.

Darius quickly regained his composure and tossed the leatherbound document on the massive mahogany desk. "I suggest you read this, Your Majesty," he said crisply. "It is the report I wrote in Moscow, on your orders. The one I had risked my life for, gathering information. The one you ignored. Take a look and find out exactly what kind of model husband you elected for your daughter." He pivoted and began walking toward the door, then paused. "By the way," he said, turning in aloof nonchalance, "the attack will come on the west shore. The French are waiting for Villeneuve to finish with Nelson. Then they'll strike."

"So you say. How do I know that is not a lie, too?" Lazar challenged.

Amazed and hurt, Darius shook his head. "The hell with you, Lazar. When you need someone to win your war for you, don't come knocking on my door. I quit."

He pivoted on his heel and began walking away in disgust.

"You think I can't manage without you, you arrogant little prick? God knows what all you've done behind my back! I've been fighting battles since before you were born!" the king bellowed after him.

Darius flicked a dismissive wave over his shoulder like an obscene gesture as he stalked out, not bothering even to close the door behind him.

CHAPTER
❧ NINETEEN ❧

In the guest wing of the palace, the outraged Anatole screamed his fury at the ambassador while he moved about his suite, preparing to kick the dust of Ascencion off his shoes.

In other parts of Belfort, his huge entourage of Russian nobles were angrily packing their things, their servants and the parade troops loading countless traveling trunks onto wagons to be brought to the docks. Their ship would soon set sail for Russia.

Inside the cathedral on the main city square, the flowers wilted on the altar, the orchestras' musicians put their instruments away, and the children's choirs were returned to their schools in their angel costumes, wings drooping.

Throughout the city, the invited guests gasped to hear the news of the Great Cancellation, while the poor feasted on the lavish dishes that had been prepared for the highest nobility of the land. Crews of workers began the tedious job of taking down the decorations for the royal wedding that was not to be.

Somewhere, Serafina was sure, Napoleon was rubbing his hands like a greedy villain.

Els seemed to be the only person who was not appalled at Serafina. As they said their goodbyes, the redhead offered to attend her, but as much as Serafina would have liked her friend's solace, it was going to be blasted uneasy in their home for a while, and she did not wish to place Els in the exceedingly uncomfortable position of arbitrator between warring husband and wife.

With the guilt-stricken Pia to attend her, Serafina climbed into the carriage with the shades pulled down to hide her face from the jeering crowd outside the palace gates. Darius rode Jihad and barked orders now and then at Alec and at the other Royal Guardsmen, who, out of loyalty to Darius, had insisted upon providing protection for them, in light of Tyurinov's death threat.

She clutched her reticule tightly in her lap, twisting the ribbons nervously as, once more, the cavalcade rolled away from the gleaming palace and through the great gates. She could not imagine what her fate held now, and she wasn't sure she wanted to try.

Julia Calazzi felt her whole world spiraling downward in a sickening spin of rage and hate and fear. Walking quickly down the hall toward the guest wing, however, she struggled to thrust her emotions aside, for she needed to focus all her wits on the task ahead.

As if losing Santiago to the princess were not a shattering enough blow, her midday meal had been interrupted when she was served with papers notifying her that she was being sued. Her largest creditor had forwarded an account of her delinquency to the civil courts.

She knew she had to act immediately, before the others followed suit.

Her financial crisis loomed. Word of the scandal was spreading like wildfire. When the shop owners in town and the rest of her creditors heard about it, they would realize at once that Santiago's money was not forthcoming to satisfy her debts. With the illusory promise that she would soon be his wife, she had strung them along for months on the strength of his name and occasional, meager payments to keep them from her door.

Now she knew she was doomed. She had feared the future before, but only now the very real possibility dawned of spending the rest of her dwindling youth in debtor's prison.

Her final hope was attaching herself to Anatole and leaving town with him.

She felt confident he would welcome her as his mistress. God knew they shared more than just a common enemy. His ego was probably bruised worse than hers, she thought, encouraged, for she knew just how to make him feel like a man again.

High heels clicking, she hurried down the guest hall to his suite, passing the steady stream of Russian lackeys who were carrying away Anatole's possessions in preparation for his swift departure. She braced herself as she neared the open door, for she could hear him bellowing in that frightening, guttural language of his all the way down the hall.

When she stepped into the doorway, he was giving orders to a few men, all of whom seemed dwarfed by him. His broad back was to her, his long, golden hair spilling down on his shoulders. She smoothed her upswept hair with a twinge of nervousness, licked her dry, painted lips, and glanced about the room.

Having received their orders, the three men bowed to their prince and left him. Anatole remained where he was, staring down at the floor, seemingly deep in thought. Julia moved aside as the three men brushed past her. Only a couple of servants remained, closing up the final traveling trunks.

"Anatole."

He stiffened visibly at her soft call. He turned his head like some strange, mechanical automaton, his blue eyes glinting. Her feminine senses instantly sent up warnings like smoke signals to her, but she could not afford to heed them.

She pushed away from the doorframe and walked languidly toward him.

"Anatole, darling, what a farce this day has been. I can't believe what they have done to you."

"What do you want?" he rumbled.

She slid her hands up his brawny biceps, savoring his musculature through the dark blue broadcloth of his coat. His face hard and forbidding, he stared down at her.

"Well?"

"I was thinking you could do with a friend right now," she murmured with a winning little smile. Hiding her fear, she reached up and gently tucked a lock of his long, blond hair behind his ear, then she trailed her fingers down his chest. "But there is something else, Anatole." She paused, lowering her lashes.

"Yes?" he asked in impatience.

She lifted her gaze to his intensely. "Take me with you."

"Why should I?" he asked with a sullen look.

"Anatole," she chided with a knowing little laugh. "That ought to be obvious by now."

He closed his eyes, tilting his head back slightly. "Julia, Julia. You understand nothing."

She knitted her brow and started to reply.

Before she knew what hit her, he grabbed her by the shoulders in a crushing grip and nearly lifted her off the ground. "You lied to me!" he roared in her face.

"No, I didn't!" she cried automatically, petrified. His sapphire eyes were wild, his grip bone-crushing. He looked like a madman, a berserk warrior.

"Put me down!" she gasped.

He thrust her from him.

She reeled back, barely catching her balance. She froze like a deer before the hunter, her breathing quick and shallow. He remained where he was, his hair rolling over his shoulders, his chest lifting and falling.

"You, Julia," he spat. He took a step toward her.

Her gaze darted in silent, terrified plea to the serfs on the other end of the room, behind him. They were both white-faced, staring.

Anatole pointed to the floor, his blinding, blue stare fixed on her. "You came here and lied to me to save Santiago, and by yielding to you, I allowed you to wreck my future for me." He took another slow, broad pace toward her, and another. Opulence and command and pure menace radiated from him. She was mesmerized and quite certain she was going to die. "Brother and sister, you said. Why did I listen to you?"

"I was only trying to help you," she whispered, her heart pounding. She took a step backward, but there was nowhere to hide.

When he stepped up in front of her, looming like a mountain before her, her response was impulsive, unpremeditated, instinctual.

She dropped to her knees and lowered her head, taking his large hand in both of hers, throwing herself on his mercy. "Please, Your Highness, take me with you. I'll do whatever you ask, I will take no lover but you. I am in desperate straits. Anatole, I am frightened. I swear I will never cause trouble for you again. Help me." She kissed his hand, her voice dwindling to a pathetic whisper. "Help me. Help me."

When at last she dared to lift her gaze, she caught only a glimpse of his blue eyes gleaming with cold satisfaction, then he pulled his hand out of hers, raised it, and struck her across the face with a mighty backhand.

She went sprawling, stars bursting across her eyes. She couldn't catch her breath. She lay on the gleaming floor, round-eyed. For a moment, she couldn't hear anything. She saw his huge boots at her eye level as he casually pivoted and walked away without another word.

She caught her breath with a gasp and slowly dragged herself up to a sitting position. The two servants were still standing there, frozen, staring at her, looking shocked and yet somehow essentially unsurprised. When she lifted her trembling hand to her mouth and touched the trickle of blood there, the two serfs turned away quickly and went back to their work.

In a state of complete shock, Julia climbed unsteadily to her feet and left Anatole's suite. Walking down the hall, her hand pressed to the trickle of blood, her stricken stare was straight ahead.

She scarcely knew where she was, walking as one in a trance. She passed countless rooms with people in them whom she knew. Some called out greetings to her, but she couldn't respond, completely inside of her dazed, empty self.

He hit me. He hit me. She couldn't seem to make herself believe it. At the end of the main corridor, she stopped, not knowing where to go or what to do.

She started shaking.

A wave of unbearable pain rose up from within her. She gulped it down, feeling clobbered, and walked numbly into the nearest empty room, a small salon. She closed the door behind her and walked to a chair, but instead of sitting, she crumpled slowly to the floor and stared at nothing. Then the first long, quiet sobs came, and she was weeping as she had not since she was a small child.

As the afternoon shadows lengthened, then bled into dusk, her sobs quieted to streaming tears, the salt of her tears stinging as it mingled with the cut on the corner of her mouth. Anatole had split her lip against her teeth. In the darkening room, she cupped her swollen cheek, wondering if he had blackened her eye, as well. What did it matter?

Just then, the door opened, the small salon flooded with light, and into the room swaggered half a dozen of the young bucks and the crown prince, all making stupid male jokes to each other.

She cringed in utter, shaking humiliation, seconds before anyone noticed her there. Sitting on the floor by the chair, she drew her knees up and clasped her hands around them, burying her face against her arm.

"By Jove, look who's here!"

"We've stumbled on hidden treasure, boys! It's our lucky night."

"La Divine Julia!"

"What are you doing alone here in the dark, my love?"

She turned away as they neared, covering her face. "Go away," she said, her voice muffled by her arm.

"Julia?" She recognized Prince Rafael's voice.

"Leave me alone." Like a trapped rabbit, she did not move. In her downcast field of vision, all she could see was shiny black boots all around her. She shivered with the frightening, irrational sensation that any moment now all these males were going to start kicking and tramping her.

She could feel the prince looking down at her curiously.

"Leave us," he said suddenly to his mates.

At once, she heard the usual sly remarks, laughter. "Ah, ha, ha, shall we leave you two alone?"

She wanted to cry again for sheer rage that this was what was always assumed.

"Go!" Rafael ordered, cutting them off in a tone of curt authority.

In moments, his cronies were gone.

She heard the door close and felt a few degrees of relief, but he was still there, intruding on her humiliation. She smelled the clean scent of his carelessly expensive cologne as he crouched down before her. She refused to look at him.

"What's wrong?" he demanded quietly.

"Nothing."

"What's wrong?"

"Nothing."

"Julia. Look at me. I want to help you."

I'll bet you do, she thought bitterly.

The boy had the audacity to touch her face—the uninjured side—for the hurt side she kept tightly tucked against her arm. When he touched her, she was not expecting it, however, and she jerked, and he saw. He swore.

"Julia, look at me."

She swallowed hard and lifted her head, meeting his angry, assessing stare. He was only a boy, someone she barely knew, and yet she felt as though one wrong word from him could make her crumble.

No one saw her in this state. No one.

Yet, for all her brains and wit and sophistication, she couldn't speak a word. She was too lost to hide.

"Who has done this to you?" he whispered fiercely, his eyes filling with youth's holy fire as he tenderly touched her face.

She winced in irritation and pulled away. "No one. I ran into the door."

"Who, Julia? I command you to tell me."

She turned to him, world-weary, her voice laced with bitterness. "What are you going to do about it?"

"Kill him," he replied.

She looked away. Shaking her head, she began laughing as fresh tears rose in her eyes. "Dueling is against the law, Your Highness."

"Tell me his name."

"What are you going to do, protect me?" she said dully. "Defend my honor?"

"Yes."

At last, she looked at him, studying him for a long moment. Maybe he was more of a man than she had thought.

Prince Rafael Giancarlo Ettore di Fiore had sun-kissed, tawny hair streaked with gold, and thoughtful, gold-green eyes with gold-tipped lashes. He was comely and well formed, his elegantly athletic body suntanned from hours at play, sailing his yacht around the Aeolian islands and Sicily. He was known as a hellion, but his antics were looked upon with smiles and winks; he was the unquestioned darling of the kingdom, the apple of the queen's eye, the king's pride and joy.

They kept a close eye on their golden boy. He could probably count on one hand the number of times he'd had a woman, she thought. And, God, he was rich.

Moving slowly, she reached out and caressed his face, a motherly gesture. His cheek was like velvet. His innocence pained her somehow. When she spoke, her voice was softer than she'd ever heard it. "You'll get yourself killed, loverboy."

"The hell I will," he said evenly. "Who was he? Because he's not going to get away with this."

Dangerously moved, she dropped her head, debating, debating. He was the heir apparent, just a boy, and she did not want him getting hurt, yet, oh, how she longed in some tiny, vulnerable corner of her heart for somebody, just once, to protect *her*.

"Name him, Julia."

She took a deep, shaky breath. "Tyurinov."

"Fine," the prince said smoothly, a flicker of wrath in his eyes. "I will call on you when it is done." He rose and headed for the door, shoulders squared.

She looked up, stricken. *What have I done?* Frightened, she tried to call him back. She forced lightness into her tone. "You don't need to risk your life to sleep with me, darling. Everybody knows that."

He stopped, came back, and bent down toward her. He cupped her face in strange tenderness. "Sad, pretty Julia." He gazed gently at her. "Perhaps you have forgotten, but I'm aware that there is more to you than that. Stay here. I will send the physician to care for you."

He kissed her forehead and left.

At six that evening, the cavalcade arrived before a quiet country church three miles west of the yellow villa.

The axles squeaked as the carriage halted. Pia looked at her uncertainly. Serafina said nothing, withdrawn, her arms folded over her bosom. The carriage door suddenly yanked back and there he stood.

"Out," Darius ordered, gesturing her maid away.

Pia fled him. When she was gone, he stepped up into the coach.

He tossed a black velvet box into her lap and sat on the seat opposite her, folding his arms, mirroring her pose, his face cool, sharp, and rude.

"What is this?"

He flicked an insolent gesture of impatience with one black-gloved hand.

She opened the box and found three beautiful rings: one with a single, heart-cut ruby; the second a rich cluster of amethysts and diamonds; the third a plain gold band.

"Pick one."

She lifted her gaze to his tense, angular face. "Why do you have all these rings?"

"I just do."

"Ah," she said coolly, stung. "Top secret. I guess I should get used to it."

"That's right. Pick one and let's get on with it."

Remembering the monstrous diamond Anatole had given her, she promptly chose the plain gold band. She slipped it on her finger and furrowed her brow to discover the ring fit perfectly. She slid him a suspicious look.

"It fits. Good," he clipped out. "Then let's get this over with." He jumped down from the carriage, not waiting to help her down. As he walked toward the church, he tossed the velvet box to her maid. "Catch."

"What's this, sir?" Pia asked in bewilderment.

"Something to put away for your retirement. Loyalty, Pia," he chided. "Some of us do know how to reward it." He jogged up the steps and strode into the church.

Serafina gritted her teeth and followed him and they were wed.

Alec and Pia were witnesses. The only guests were the guardsmen and a few other servants, plus one pious old widow who happened to be visiting her dead husband in the church graveyard. Serafina's emotions were in an uproar. At the altar, she held on to Darius's arm because now he was all she had.

Even as she sought his strength, she chafed under the knowledge that now he was her guardian in earnest, her lord and master, too. He'd better not even try pulling rank on her, she thought.

As the plain ceremony progressed, she watched the priest's lips moving but could not quite absorb any of it. She had gotten her way, but it sure didn't feel like it.

When the moment came for Darius to slip the gold band on her finger, he glanced at her for a second, meeting her eyes. She thought of making love with him last night, the way they had stared at each other then, when they had been one with each other. Heat, longing rushed through her body. She saw in his eyes a flicker of some raw, fiery turmoil, but he veiled his expression and turned away, tall and gorgeous, ever unattainable, his profile perfect and emotionless. The man of her dreams—hers forever now—and he hated her.

"I now pronounce you man and wife. Well, go on, kiss her," said the kindly old priest.

Santiago jolted a bit as if he'd been dozing on his feet through the whole thing. She clenched her teeth, knowing he was deliberately baiting her.

Her new husband leaned down and gave her a perfunctory kiss on each cheek. The gesture was so smooth and meaningless, she felt as though she had been slapped, not kissed. Tears of hurt and anger sprang into her eyes, but she was determined to be as coolly unemotional and in control as he. She took his arm when he politely offered it and led her from the church, his mask of aloof correctness firmly in place, neither of them smiling.

Back into the carriage again, and she was beginning to hate herself for ever thinking he would let her get away with this vile deed—trapping him like a common country wench out to snare the squire's son.

She tempered the guilt with reminding herself of his lies. Surely what she had done was no worse than his many falsehoods. She stared out the window while the coach rolled on toward the yellow villa.

Earlier, Darius had snarled at her that he had bought it from the crown before leaving for Milan. Why a man who had thought he was going to die needed a house, she did not know, but what was the point in asking when she knew he would only lie?

Morbidly, she found herself dwelling on horrible images of

the war to come. Blood on her hands. Their demon-love was cursed, like her cursed face.

When they arrived, her husband of half an hour ignored her to deal with his men, his horses, anyone but her. She walked slowly up the wide, shallow steps to the villa, glancing morosely at the misshapen, overgrown topiaries and the peeling yellow paint. She stopped inside the foyer, remembering the way it had looked when she had last seen it—smoke-filled, blood-spattered, chaotic. Wounded and dying men strewn over the floor, it had been a battleground.

Her gaze wandered over the walls, where curling streaks left by soap remained from the cleanup job afterward, but there was no blood or ashes left to see, thank God. She went heavily up the stairs to the pink bedroom.

Standing in the doorway, gazing at this room, she suddenly wanted to cry, wanted that beautiful, blackhearted liar to hold her. She walked over to the bed and sat down on it. Last time she'd slept here, she had been a virgin.

In misery, her gaze fell to the floor and wandered across the tapestry rug of the pastoral idyll, the celebration of youths and maidens dancing around the maypole. She remembered the hiding place beneath it. Nothing in her world was what it appeared, she thought. Nothing.

A lump of sorrow rose in her throat. Who were they fooling? This marriage was never going to succeed.

Why hadn't she seen the obvious before she undertook so rash a feat? Last night, blind love must have had her intoxicated, relief and desperation must have muddled her wits. Just because he was her husband now did not mean he couldn't leave. It only meant he'd have to make up some unassailable excuse before he could walk away without compunction, then he would be free to go. God knew he was resourceful at making up excuses. She supposed she had better start bracing herself somehow for his exit. She would have to be strong, because his last vanishing act had nearly destroyed her, and she could not, would not go through that devastation again.

Hearing his voice in the courtyard below as he impatiently ordered his troops about, she walked numbly to the window and spied on him around the curtain.

He sat astride his magnificent and mean-spirited black stallion. The setting sun rippled through the horse's black mane and tail, and through Darius's jet-black hair. It warmed his skin to burnished amber.

He looked like a god, her husband, she thought coldly. Oh, she could not resist that man. It was one more excellent reason to despise him. He had used those gorgeous looks of his against her, and his soft, irresistible voice to lull her lax morals into a trance, and his delicious mouth—

All of a sudden, Darius glanced up, as though he'd felt her stare. He saw her at the window. When their eyes met from across the cobbled yard, she felt his flash of hostility. He gave her a harsh look and wheeled the horse away with smooth, Spanish mastery, the reins in one hand, his spurred ankles flexed.

Arrogant, insolent heathen! she thought angrily. Why was he acting like the one who had been wronged? How dare he?

She pivoted and marched away from the window, eyes blazing. She was the Princess Royal and, by God, she was not budging from this room until that insolent Spaniard came to grovel at her feet. How she chose to handle this conflict would set a precedent for the rest of their marriage. She did not intend to live the rest of her life being the dupe of his lies.

If he must be free, let him leave, but if he intended to stay, he was going to have to meet her halfway.

She called to Pia to help her change out of her traveling clothes into a simple country dress, for they had work to do. The villa needed much repair if it was to serve as more than a temporary residence. For her part, she was claiming the pink bedroom for her own territory. Where that Spaniard would make camp, she neither knew nor cared—or so she told herself. The stable would be a fitting choice, she thought. He was certainly not sharing a bed with her.

*   *   *

Julia thought she had forgotten how to pray, but from the moment Rafael was out of sight she pleaded with God. *Let Anatole be gone—let him be on the ship. Don't kill this child.*

True to the prince's word, the physician came quickly to aid her. The kindly man walked her back to her rooms, avoiding the crowds.

After a nerve-racking wait, she found that, indeed, God heard the prayers of Jezebel, or perhaps it was merely that a larger destiny awaited the young future king.

Rafael stopped by her door about two hours later and regretfully informed her he had been too late to demand justice of Tyurinov. He had galloped hard all the way to the port, only to find the Russians' ship had just set sail. He was apologetic.

She put her arms around him and held him as hard as she could, her eyes squeezed tight.

The boy didn't ask questions, didn't try to get in her door. He simply hugged her in silence for as long as she wanted him to, then he murmured goodnight and said that he would check on her tomorrow.

As he walked off down the hall, she leaned in the doorway, watching him, her arms folded over her chest. As if he could feel her stare, he turned, saw her, and sent her a little farewell wave with a secret smile. She held up her hand in a slow, answering wave, and knew then that she had to have him.

CHAPTER
⊰ TWENTY ⊱

The walls that girded the yellow villa's acreage had once seemed to embrace him and Serafina, shielding their fantasy love from the harsh outer world, but a week into their disastrous marriage, those same walls marked the boundaries of his cage. He was trapped.

I've got to get out of here.

Darius cantered his black stallion through the gray mists of dawn. Jihad's exercise comprised a brisk lap around the property's wide perimeter. The wall streamed past like a long, gray ribbon unraveling on Darius's right as the horse's strides ate up the soft, rolling ground.

The situation with his new wife remained much the same: They spoke little, and then with cold courtesy. In the past, it had been an advantage that they were so much alike, both obstinately proud and wily, but now it locked them at odds, each playing a waiting game to see who would be the first either to apologize or to walk out.

Beyond the villa's walls, things were almost as glum. France had declared war. A handful of ships from the Franco-Spanish navy had begun blockading Ascencion to weaken them for Villeneuve's as yet unknown date of arrival.

With the French ships riding at anchor just beyond the boundaries of Ascencion's territorial waters, a fighting line of the king's frigates was arrayed for the island's defense. So far, no shots had been fired. For now, it remained naught but a great naval staring contest not unlike his marriage, Darius thought.

The diplomats were working feverishly to arrive at a peaceful solution, but the whole island was battening down for a siege. Parliament had declared rations and a curfew in the towns. Rumor had it that the king itched to attack.

Darius could well imagine Lazar longed for a worthy adversary on whom to vent his wrath, the true sources of which were his daughter and his formerly most-trusted man.

The French were also demanding that Darius be handed over to face trial, but this Lazar staunchly refused. There was no proof but the word of one disgruntled young traitoress that the lone assassin in Milan had been Darius Santiago, respected diplomat for the court of Ascencion, and son-in-law to the king. Indeed, Lazar had played at outrage over the accusation, naming himself and twenty of Ascencion's leading nobles as Darius's alibis for the days in question—and who dared call King Lazar di Fiore a liar?

Darius knew Lazar still considered him a vile, amoral seducer of innocents. The king's defense of him was merely a political consideration, or perhaps to protect his baby girl, because if there was one thing Darius knew for certain, it was that he, along with the parrot, the cat, and the monkey, was Her Highness's kept pet.

Two days ago, however, he had received a temporary lift out of the morass of his emotions in the form of a letter from a British intelligence colleague and friend, Sir James Richards. On leave in Sicily, Richards had sent Darius warning that Prince Tyurinov might not have left the area. It seemed that the glorious Anatole had brought his ship to port at Malta, where he had somehow received warning that Czar Alexander had issued orders to seize him the moment he returned to Moscow. The Russian ship had remained there, but no one had seen Tyurinov himself for a couple of days.

Richards had also invited Darius to visit him in Sicily if he was interested in being part of what the Englishman termed "an intriguing undertaking."

Darius could not imagine what it was, but he longed to go— longed for any work to do.

Richards was an excellent agent and weapons expert, and no doubt had something ingenious up his sleeve. Darius mulled the intriguing undertaking constantly, as now. He slowed the stallion to a trot, then tugged on the reins, halting as they came to the ridge overlooking the field and the lake where Serafina and he had picnicked, what seemed eons ago.

His gaze traveled over his lost paradise, shrouded in mist. The distant tree line in the background sprawled, irregular, against the paling sky.

He ought to join Richards's team, he reasoned, for what was the point in his being here? On those rare occasions when Serafina even looked at him, it was with bitterness, hurt, and angry reproach in her beautiful, violet eyes. He knew she despised him, but what could he do?

He felt paralyzed, helpless, and plain scared.

God, what had he done to his life? he thought heavily. He'd known from the day she was born that Serafina di Fiore would be his downfall. Once more, his prescient Gypsy senses had proved right. He was still reeling from the first time he had kissed her, yet somehow, suddenly, here he was, husband to the goddess of the age. He could exact his husbandly rights whenever he wanted, only he was terrified to go near her. Terrified of the accusations that would come hurling out at him if he gave her the chance to speak. He didn't want to hear how useless and false and what a failure he was. Not from her. Any day now, his rare, gorgeous butterfly was going to lift her wings and fly away from him. He was just waiting for it. That's what a female did when you needed her.

With his full iron will, he was determined to master his need for her for once and for all, become invulnerable again, yet he knew it was his very silence that was driving her away.

If you don't talk to her, you are going to lose her for certain.

The thought made him impatient. What could he say to her now, when every word from his mouth she judged a lie?

He squeezed the horse's midnight sides with his calves and they sprinted the short distance to the lake. There, Darius flung down out of the saddle and tried to feel the way he had felt here before, when it was safe to tell her anything about himself because there were no consequences—it was temporary—he had thought he was going to die.

The feeling escaped him, just beyond his grasp.

He couldn't even apologize, because truly being sorry meant trying to change, he thought as he stared at the lake, and he had no intention of doing so. He respected her too much to give her a sham apology. Couldn't she see by now that maybe a liar was what he needed to be? That maybe the truth, the full truth about him, was too damned pitiful for him to share with anyone?

Didn't she see that sometimes a lie was all a man had?

While his horse sneaked a few mouthfuls of the long grass behind him, Darius raked both hands slowly through his hair and drew a long, steadying breath. He was trapped.

I'm going crazy. I am obsessed with her. I can't hide from her forever.

Tell her. Tell her everything, said his heart. *Trust her.*

The thought was too threatening. He got back on his horse again and rode and rode, circling endlessly within the confines of his cage.

Julia awoke with the boy curled around her and hazy, candlelit images in her mind of the night before.

Forever, she knew, the taste of chocolate-covered caramels would remind her of her loverboy. It had been a strange week.

She had closeted herself in her rooms, crying ill, in order to hide the humiliation of her bruised face from everyone. The only visitor she admitted was Rafael. It was no use trying to discourage the youth from coming to see her. He came every day, supposedly to cheer her up. She knew the inevitable outcome, but, to her amusement, he wanted to get to know her first. She had the dismal feeling he was on a quest to save her.

All week, their visits had been innocent as she waited for her bruises to heal and calculated what she might be able to get out of this. Every moment in his presence she counted as a blow struck against Darius Santiago. Each day, they sat in her tiny antechamber playing chess, the boy asking her endless questions about herself, most of which she evaded. He must have divined her financial plight, for he had given her an enormous amount of money, no questions asked, saying with simple good-heartedness that he was glad to help a friend in need.

Of course, the full sum she still owed was three times his generous gift, but she didn't tell him that. Instead, she began wishing desperately he would wise up and quit coming to see her.

Each day, her swollen face healed a little more, then, yesterday afternoon, Rafael had showed up at her door with a box of chocolates. They ate the chocolates as they played chess, then suddenly, out of the blue, he had leaned across the table and kissed her. One kiss, that was all, then he gave her a slow, secret smile that very nearly melted what once had been her heart.

That evening, she had put in an appearance in the drawing room, for she was now able to hide the bruise with light make-up. The prince swaggered in half an hour later, and somehow, around eleven, she wound up in Rafe's room with him.

His enthusiasm was boundless, his energy and sheer appetite astonishing, but his touch was nothing short of reverent when he caressed her and took her breast into his mouth. It was all so new to him, the feel of a woman's body. He was so different from any man she'd ever known. They made love sitting on the edge of his huge, carved bed, but she had soon found herself laughing softly and kissing away his embarrassment, for he came almost immediately the first time. The second time, she knelt astride him, gently making him hold back, teaching him control. He was an apt pupil.

Very apt, she mused, running a hand down his warm, velvety-smooth back, for the third time, he'd brought her to climax with a tenderness she had not experienced in years, if ever.

She did not like it.

The way he had held her afterward had been unsettling. This could not last, obviously. For God's sake, he was nineteen. She was twenty-seven. He would be king one day. She was a jaded soul. Countless men had lain with her, and yet only this boy, with his sun-kissed hair and reckless grin, had somehow gotten inside of her. She was not sure she could forgive him for that.

Sooner or later, the queen was bound to learn of their liaison. There could be no worse enemy than Allegra di Fiore when it came to her boy. Fortunately, Her Majesty was preoccupied for the moment with the new baby, her daughter's scandal, and the threat of war with the French, but she would find out in time, and then what was Julia going to do? She would be asked to leave, and where could she possibly go?

How stupid of her to let this infant beguile her, she mused. She could only attribute it to the fact that he had found her in her moment of utter weakness —her hopes crushed, her creditors closing in, her face bashed and bleeding.

Presently, mama's royal favorite slept like a worn-out puppy atop her, but he didn't stir in the slightest when Julia pushed against his muscled shoulder and rolled him off her.

She got up silently and surveyed her surroundings as she began putting on her garters and stockings. She noticed the clock—half-past eleven already. Well, they had stayed up late, she thought. Then the sight of Rafe's gigantic, cluttered desk caught her eye. With a shrewd expression, she glanced over her shoulder to make sure he was still sleeping, then walked over to the desk and silently began opening the drawers, one by one, and going through them.

What she'd find, who could say? Experience had taught her she could always unearth something useful. She doubted the boy had any real skeletons in his closet; it was mere force of habit that sent her riffling through his belongings.

But the gold she struck was sitting right out on his desk, practically begging for her discovery. Gingerly unrolling the large scroll, she sliced the prince a sideward glance to make sure he was still asleep. His brown, muscled body was still, sprawled on the sheets, his baby-face angelic in sleep.

She examined the parchment. At first she thought it was some schoolboyish project. Then she realized she was staring at highly classified maps of the legendary Fiori tunnels.

Staring, her heart began to pound.

There was a myth that King Bonifacio the Black, the founder of the royal house, had ordered subterranean tunnels built throughout the island for the royal family to use in case of invasion or other emergency. In seven hundred years, no one outside the royal family had ever been admitted into the secret—except perhaps that Spaniard whom she hated more than hell itself.

Her gaze traveled over the detailed drawings.

You stupid boy. How could you leave this where I would find it? Eyes burning, she looked over at him again, sleeping there, a young Adonis.

The French were harbored in the bay.

Put it back, Julia, whispered her feeble conscience. *You give this to the French, you take his whole future away from him. Maybe even his life.*

Such a betrayal would kill the very tenderness and simple kindness in him which had moved her so dangerously.

But the force of habit was too strong. She would be rich. She could go anywhere she wanted. Never again would she have to depend on that most shiftless of creatures, the human male. The boy would have to sink or swim. The world was a jungle, his soft life an illusion. She told herself this was the most valuable lesson she could teach him.

Let Santiago save him, she thought acidly. She finished dressing quickly, her hands shaking, then walked silently to the door, the scroll in her grasp. Stepping over the threshold, she paused and stole a final, long gaze at him.

Something inside of her cracked and broke permanently, at that moment. Bitterness was in her mouth, her whole body shaking.

Stupid boy, she thought. She turned and left, pulling the door closed silently behind her.

By midmorning, Darius arrived at the villa once more.

He left Jihad with a groom and strode into the house, dreading the empty, lonely day ahead. What was he going to do with his time? he wondered. He had already exhausted every shred of work he could think of to occupy himself.

Walking into the foyer, he passed the morning room where he saw his young wife, writing something at the table beside her breakfast. His stolen glance took in the morning sunlight twining through her silky, sable tresses and gleaming on her skin like powdered pearls. Her head bent over her work, she was twirling a curl around her finger, which meant she was deep in thought, so he hurried past and down the hall to his office without trying to say hello.

He took breakfast in the library down the hall. The food was like ashes in his mouth, knowing she was so near and yet this was how it was.

At length, he pushed the food away in disgust and merely drank his coffee, reading for the thousandth time the letter from Richards. *An intriguing enterprise . . .*

How good it would be to feel he was of use again and to have something else to do instead of sitting around here, mentally cataloguing all the ways in which he was not good enough.

Just then, there was a knock at the door and a moment later his too-beautiful, too-highborn wife came in. Her chin was high, her expression one of cool hauteur. Her regal poise terrified him.

He rose slightly and bowed. "Madam."

She sliced him a nod, her gaze fixed on the floor. "I have come to say I am going into town to hire artisans to effect some repairs around here. The grounds are atrocious. The roof needs attention. And obviously, we must have fresh paint. We must also have modern w.c.'s put in and I want new cabinets for the kitchens." She lifted an insolent look to him, as though waiting for him—no, daring him—to deny her.

He did not. "The repairs you mention are indeed in order," he warily replied.

She studied him archly. "These changes are only the beginning. Half of the furniture's falling apart. Most of the rooms are hopelessly outdated. We will be redecorating after we rebuild." Again, she waited smugly for his refusal.

He wasn't worried. His pockets were deep, else he'd never have let things between them get this far. Shopping was, after all, the delight of her life. "I trust you will bring us to the height of fashion," he said. "In fact, I know an excellent architect by the name of Signore Ambrosetti."

"Has he offices in town? I will go see him."

"Not so fast," he said gently but firmly, staying her with a gesture. "I will send for him and fetch him here, then you can show him yourself what needs to be done. Order him around to your heart's content, if you like, but I don't want you going into town."

She folded her arms under her breasts. He checked his stare.

"I am *going* into town."

"No. It is not safe."

"Why?" she demanded.

"Because I said so," he replied, declining to tell her about the possibility of Tyurinov's presence. Nothing had been confirmed. Why burden her with something that was his problem? He could handle it alone and certainly there was no point in scaring her on top of making her wretched. "Signore Ambrosetti will need to make a survey of the property anyway." He smoothed his coat and sat down again.

"Darius."

To emphasize the point that the conversation was closed, he forced himself to take a nonchalant bite of his breakfast. The omelet had gone cold and rubbery. Disgusting, he thought as he chewed. Bravado wasn't worth this.

"Darius!"

"No."

"Look at this." She suddenly flung some papers onto his desk and stepped back, hands on her hips. "I didn't want to show you this, but I daresay now you'll see why I must go into town."

"What's this?" he murmured as he took them. It appeared to be a collection of those lurid gossip newspapers she was always reading. He looked down at the top page and promptly choked on his mouthful of cold eggs.

"They are lampooning us everywhere," she declared.

He stopped his choking with a swallow of hot coffee, then stared at the newspaper. It was the issue printed the day their scandal broke.

The headline was three inches tall: IN FLAGRANTE DELICTO!

"Dear God!"

Below it was a heartless caricature. He was depicted bare-chested, a snarl on his lips, his sword drawn to fight off a crowd of outraged people around her bed, while Serafina, curls wild, was shown on her knees behind him, clinging fearfully about his waist.

She's mine! read the caption.

He stared at the sketch for a long moment and then, slowly, he began to laugh.

"You think it's funny?" she cried in outrage.

"Well," he said. "We can either laugh or cry."

"We can bloody well do more than that, Santiago! *Ugh,* you may suffer in silence as usual if you want, but I'm not going to take this. I'm going into town. They think we are hiding our faces in shame here, but I'll show them! I'm going to walk in there and hold my head up and—and show them *all* that I don't give a fig what they think."

"Ah-hmm," he said skeptically as he skimmed the article.

Meanwhile, she paced, full of angry, pent-up energy.

His heart sank when he looked at the final column on the front page. It had a smaller headline that asked, TROUBLE IN PARADISE? and went on to proclaim that their marriage was already in ruins.

How the hell did they know that? he thought angrily. Damned journalists must have been spying on them somehow.

From across the room, she turned to him, arms tightly folded. "Now, are you coming with me or not?"

"Serafina, for the eighth time, you're not going anywhere."

"Yes, I am!" With a sudden look of fury, she marched toward the desk and braced both hands on the edge, leaning toward him, curls flying, violet eyes blazing, her chest heaving with anger, magnificent in her ire. "I am going mad here! There is no one to talk to and nothing to do!"

He stared up at her, rather awed, then snapped out of her spell. "Nevertheless, here you shall remain."

"Why?" she demanded.

"Because I said so."

"I am not your prisoner!" she cried, slamming her fist down on his desk, right on Sir James Richards's letter.

Darius looked down at her clenched hand, then flicked his gaze up to her face. "Calm yourself," he said through gritted teeth.

"Oh, shall I be like you? Without emotions? I'm going into town and you can't stop me!"

He shot to his feet, but refused to lose his temper. "I am your husband and you will obey me. That *is* what you wanted, isn't it? That *is* what you ruined my life for?"

"Ruined your life?" she gasped. Before he could stop her, she picked up his full breakfast plate and threw it across the room. The plate broke on the floor, cold eggs all over the wall.

"There! Now I've ruined your breakfast, too." She pivoted on her heel and marched out, fists clenched, curls flouncing down her back.

For a moment, he was in shock. He hadn't seen that trick since her nursery days. Then, suddenly, he was incensed.

"You *brat!*" he thundered, marching after her. "Get back here and clean it up!"

He walked out into the foyer to find she was running up the stairs.

"How old are you, seven, eight, my child bride?" he called angrily after her.

"Get away from me! I hate you! I never want to see you again!"

He paused, taken aback. "You hate me?" She had never said such a thing to him before. Had she been pushed as far as she could go? "Serafina!"

"Just go, Darius! I know you are going to! Just go and get it over with." She looked down at him over the railing at the top of the steps, her curls falling forward over her shoulders, her creamy cheeks bright pink, tears rising in her eyes. "Maybe I *am* immature, but I'm not the only one! I see now you only wanted me because I was forbidden. It excited you to take what you thought you could not have. Now that you've got me, the thrill is gone and all you want is your freedom again. So, go! And forget the stupid architect. I doubt we will be living here much longer."

She shoved away from the railing and disappeared. He could hear her crying as she hurried away down the hall, then he heard the predictable slam of the pink bedroom's door.

"Oh, God," he said under his breath as he dropped his chin almost to his chest. He was very still, his eyes squeezed tightly shut.

I've lost her.

The thought moved quietly, matter-of-factly through his brain. His eyes flicked open. He stared at the floor, realizing, too late, that her venturing into his office had been her haughty effort to reach out to him. She had held out the olive branch and he had set the other end of it afire.

She was going to leave him now. He could feel it, had heard it in her voice.

Throat constricted, he lifted his burning eyes to the empty space at the top of the stairs.

Don't leave me.

Suddenly he was in motion, climbing the stairs, leaping them, two at a time.

CHAPTER
⊰ TWENTY-ONE ⊱

"Open the door," came her husband's voice through the wood.

Serafina glared at the locked door as she moved about the room, angrily packing her belongings into a few open traveling trunks. She was done crying over that heartless Gypsy bastard. She was going home.

"Let me in."

"You won, Darius. I don't want to see you! Just go away!" She was so sick of his power over her, sick of being in his thrall.

The doorknob jiggled.

"You're not leaving me, Serafina."

"I'm sure as hell not staying here by myself!" she shouted at the door.

"Nobody's leaving."

"Lie!" she flung at him through the door.

A moment of silence passed in which she could practically hear him simmering.

"Serafina, open the goddamned door," he said quietly. "I want to see you."

She merely shot the door another glaring look and pushed her clothes down into the second traveling trunk.

"Child's play," he said in sharp mockery from the other side of the door, then she heard his heavy footfalls retreating down the hallway.

So, he was gone. Walking away again, she thought bitterly. He gave up so easily.

She had always been the only one who had fought for their love. He didn't care. She loved him, yes, so much her body ached for him, but her feelings for her demigod were as unrequited now that she was his wife as they had been when she was a mere smitten sixteen-year-old. She was fed up with it. She was still brooding on this when, about three minutes later, the doorknob made a click.

Packing some underclothes into the trunk, she glanced over her shoulder at the door, then her eyes widened as the doorknob clicked again, then turned.

The door opened and Darius sauntered into the room, holding up a hairpin, twirling it nimbly end over end between his fingers with a little sleight of hand. A smug, mocking curve twisted the scarred side of his mouth.

"Tsk, tsk, tsk," he said softly, clucking his tongue at her.

She straightened up near the traveling trunk and turned warily to face him, smoothing a folded chemise over her arm like a shield.

He slammed the door behind him. She flinched a little as it banged. He paced slowly toward her.

"You are my wife," he said darkly as he drew near. "You will go nowhere without my permission, and you will not lock your door to me."

"You are my husband," she replied. "Act like it."

He gave her a taut, mocking smile, then his gaze slid to her half-packed traveling trunks. "Where do you think you're going?"

"I'm done crying over you, Darius Santiago," she said as she worked, avoiding his stare. "I know you're itching to run, so go. I'm sorry I ever meddled in your life."

"You're sorry?" he seemed to marvel, both brows raised.

She shot him a glaring look, not sure if he was asking in earnest or in sarcasm. "Yes. I'm sorry," she fairly spat. "It was spoiled and selfish of me to trap you in matrimony. I'm sorry. I believed I was doing the right thing. Obviously, I was wrong.

I thought I could help you, but there's no point trying to reach out to you. You won't give an inch."

His cheeks flushed. "I won't give? I risked my life for you!"

"I never wanted that!" She flung down her armful of stockings haphazardly into the trunk and whirled to face him. "Oh, to be sure, you've got your heroics to stand on, don't you? But admit it, Darius—I'm the one who has taken all the risks here—the real risks, the ones that count! I gave you everything, my very self. I'm far more serious about you than you are about me, and I don't know what else to give to make you stop being afraid."

He looked stunned.

She let out a sigh and lowered her chin, pressing her fingertips to her forehead. "I don't want to make you unhappy anymore. I know you're going mad here. I can't stand seeing you so unhappy and knowing I am the cause. All I want is to give you what you need. Clearly, all you can think about is your precious freedom, so go, Darius. You don't owe me anything. It's only your sense of honor that keeps you here, and I'm not going to take advantage of that. I'll survive without you." She turned away and gazed down into the half-packed trunk in utter desolation.

She could feel his tension and his stare, burning into her back. "I don't want you to go," he whispered hoarsely. But by the time she turned around in surprise, the vulnerability she had heard in his voice had vanished, as if he, too, had heard it and fought to hide it.

"You can't leave. You need me," he said in rude insolence. "What are you going to do without me? Where can you possibly go?"

"Back to my parents and the people who care about me, I suppose."

"Damn it, I care about you! Don't you see me standing here—why else would I be here? I love you," he said harshly.

Arms crossed over her chest, she turned cautiously to him. "Quite a declaration."

"I love you," he tried again, this time a growl.

She sighed at the way he forced himself to say it. "What you have toward me is not love, Darius. What you have toward me is a chess game in which you are the mastermind and I am the little pawn being moved about the board—"

"How can you say that?" he said, his chiseled face flushed with escalating anger, a trace of panic beginning to show in his eyes. "Why do you think I went to Milan—"

"Because you would rather die than take the chance of opening yourself to me. If you really cared about me, you would try telling me the truth once in a while."

"You want the truth? Is that what will make you happy?" he cried sarcastically. "Fine! Pull up a chair, Princess! I'll give you some truth, my dear. Just don't blame me for breaking your illusions."

She paused, hiding her amazement at his compliance.

"Have a seat," he flung out.

Calmly, she went over and sat down on the stool to the vanity. She folded her hands in her lap and waited. Darius paced. He kicked one of her traveling trunks out of his way to broaden his path.

"You want the truth? All right. What do I care? I've got nothing to lose," he muttered, then he leveled a glaring look at her and pointed at her. "First, you will leave off with this idiotic notion that any kind of war here is your fault or that the blood is on your hands. Absurd! It is Napoleon's fault, not yours, do you understand me? You are just a girl. He is the tyrant. He is the aggressor, but the one iota of good that came out of my gigantic failure in Milan is that I was able to unearth some vital information on their war plans. They cannot launch any kind of large-scale attack on us until Spain's top admiral, Villeneuve, destroys the British flagship. You may find your dragon-slayer in Horatio Nelson, Princesa, if not in me."

She absorbed this information, her gaze downward. "It is a relief to hear this," she said quietly. "I wish you had told me a week ago. I have been torturing myself."

"Oh, but I'm just getting started. As for the glorious Anatole, when he arrives in Russia, he is going to find himself a wanted man for treason and"—he hesitated—"the murder of his first wife."

Her eyes flew open wide. "Princess Margaret?"

Darius nodded. "He locked her out in the snow one night in the middle of the Russian winter—punishment for giving a few of the serfs a day off while he was away. He found out about it when he came home and gave her a thrashing for defying his authority, then threw her out. She died of exposure. All she had on was her night rail."

"How horrible," she breathed, barely able to find her voice. "How evil of him! Oh, Darius, how could he do that to her?"

"I'm sure he had his reasons," he said bitterly. "They always do."

"Why did you not tell me this before? It concerned me directly—"

"I couldn't. I just couldn't." His raven forelock veiled his eyes.

"Why?"

"I didn't want you to know there were such men in the world. It was too horrible."

"Worse than seeing you kill Philippe Saint-Laurent?"

"Yes, to me."

"Why?"

"Let's just say it's a matter with which I have had some early experience."

His words reminded her of another point. "What about the fact that you are a count? Care to comment, my lord?"

He looked over at her. "You know about that?"

"Julia Calazzi told me."

He shrugged. "The title is meaningless. The point is not that I have it, but that my half-brothers do not."

She studied him. "And what of your father?"

"He's dead."

"I understand he came to you looking for a handout."

He nodded with a bitter smile.

"And you gave it to him."

"Don't think for an instant that it was out of my great sense of charity. There's only one reason I gave him the money."

"To get rid of him as quickly as possible?"

He shook his head as the cold smile curved his scarred mouth again. "Revenge."

"I don't understand. You helped him. How is that revenge?"

"Control over his destiny, my dear," he said tautly, pacing again. "To have merely denied him the money would have been too merciful. I first put his mind at ease—let him think his woes were over. He was in my power—my dependent, utterly. So grateful, the bootlicker," he said in contempt. "And then . . ." He turned away. "Well, you know what they say. The Lord giveth and the Lord taketh away."

"What did you do to him?" she whispered.

"He never should have come looking to me for help."

She stared at him, her blood running cold. "Did you kill him, Darius?"

"No. I thought about it, but he wasn't worthy of my skill. Instead, I let him believe he could resume his former standard of living, then without warning I ceased paying his bills. He did it to himself, you see. He died of disease in debtor's prison, old, unwept, and alone. A fitting punishment. Anything else you want to know, wife?"

Shaken by this revelation of his terrible ruthlessness, she swallowed down her fear. "I—I don't know. Is there anything else you want to tell me?"

"Well, let me see . . . the truth. She wants the truth," he mused aloud, hands clasped behind his back as he paced, head down. He shot her a piercing sideward glance. "Well, I suppose I ought to tell you before someone else does, because then we'll be right back where we started."

"Tell me what?"

He ran his hand over his hair, took a deep breath, and stared directly at her. "When I was captured in Milan, Pauline Bonaparte had me brought from my cell to her boudoir, where she tried to seduce me. I used her to escape."

She shot up out of her seat, aghast.

He laughed cynically.

"Did you—" she started, but her voice broke off. She couldn't say it. Heartbreak rushed in on her.

"Did I what?" he asked in frank insolence.

She felt her world teetering. "Did—did you amuse yourself with her, Darius?" she asked in a small, scratchy whisper.

He gazed at her tenderly from across the room, and for a moment there was hope.

"No, sweetheart," he murmured. "My every thought was of you."

She swallowed hard. "Are you lying?"

"Goddamn it!" he nearly screamed as fury flooded into his face. He strode toward her, yanked her to him, and caught her up in a crushing embrace. "Do I love you? Am I lying? You tell me," he growled, and then he kissed her fiercely.

She sagged against his hard body in instant, explosive longing as he parted her lips and filled her mouth with a driving, angry kiss. He slid his hand under the mass of her hair, curling his fingers around her nape. He paused with hot, labored breath.

"Oh, woman," he breathed, "get out of my blood."

"Never," she whispered.

He drew her to him and kissed her savagely. She wound her wrists around his neck and launched her all-out, final effort to make a conquest of her husband. He moaned low in his throat at her hungry kiss, his heartbeat thundering against her body. She pressed herself against him, but mentally checked her body's craving for him. She could not afford to be swept away by his seduction. She had to keep a clear head, for she wanted him helpless with lust, begging for her.

She would use her beauty, her body, his male hungers, and any other weapon she possessed to enslave him. And then he would not want to go.

She tore herself away from the kiss and stared up at him, her eyes afire, her lips swollen.

"Get in my bed," she whispered.

He cocked a brow at her. "My goodness. The lady knows what she wants."

"Yes, she wants you. She wants this." She cupped her hand and caressed his hardness through his clothes.

He licked his delicious lips, but eyed her warily from under his forelock. He wanted her but he wasn't sure what was going on. She gloried in his uncertainty.

"What's wrong? Scared?" she challenged him softly as she pushed him one step back toward the bed. "Surely you're not scared of me, little Cricket, who worships the ground you walk on? What threat could I possibly be to *you*, the great Santiago? Come on, Darius. One last time before we part." She took his hand and led him toward her bed.

Holding her hand, he followed, but at the edge of the bed he moved up behind her and wrapped his arms around her waist. "You're not leaving me. Nobody's going anywhere," he murmured, still unable to cast off his bravado.

Sensing her advantage, she forged on with her bluff.

"I *am* leaving you," she repeated, her heart pounding.

He was very still. Then he changed his hold on her, his right hand creeping down the front of her body, caressing her as only he could. "No, because I'm leaving you first."

She refused to be daunted. She didn't believe him.

"Fine. Go," she said.

"You won't shatter me, Serafina. Nobody is going to break me."

"Fine."

"I don't need anybody."

"Good for you."

He tucked his fingers between her legs, stroking her through her clothes. She fought not to shudder with pleasure.

"I didn't want this marriage. You forced me into this."

"You mean to say that in taking my virginity, you acted in dishonor? You had no intention of marrying me?"

He bristled as he stewed over that, no doubt knowing he was caught.

"No," he growled.

She laughed at him. "Ah, Santiago, every word from your lips is a lie. You were able to refrain from making love to me even when we lay naked together in this bed, so I know full well you could have refrained that night, too, if you had wanted to. Go on, tell your lies. I know the truth—that you need me far more than I need you."

"I'll tell you what I'm going to do. I'm going to take you," he murmured, "and then I'm going to leave you."

"We'll see," she said.

He pressed her gently down onto her stomach on the bed before him, rubbing her back for a moment. Then he climbed on behind her. She could feel the power and grace in his lean, exquisitely honed body as he eased down, covering her, the hard wall of his chest pressed against her back.

She was wild with excitement. She could feel his fast heartbeat, as well as his towering erection straining through his clothes, throbbing against her backside. He swept her hair aside, exposing the nape of her neck. He kissed it, his hot breath flowing down beneath her earlobe. As he tangled his fingers softly in her hair, she felt his tongue stroke her nape.

She bit her lip, closing her eyes, fighting the languorous pleasure stealing into her limbs.

His hand slid between her breast and the mattress. He squeezed gently, rhythmically, as he savored the curve of her neck with a long, open-mouthed kiss. She felt his jaws widen, then he held her nape lightly between his teeth. A barbaric surge of instinct slammed through her, rising up out of her blood, as he went still, dominating her, possessing her.

She was panting uncontrollably when the primal gesture of dominance became a kiss once more. His lips were smooth on her fiery skin. She shuddered with a sudden wave of need so wanton it shamed her.

"You're mine," he whispered. "Never forget it."

"Ooh, I hate you," she breathed.

Suddenly he rolled her onto her back and straddled her. He swooped down over her, pinning her hands above her with his own. His lips slammed upon hers, needy, demanding. He invaded her mouth with his deep, ravenous kiss, barely letting her breathe. She opened her mouth hungrily, and still he took of her, in a frenzy, as if he could never be filled, so great was his emptiness, so terrifying. Her hands shaking with desire, she touched him all over, caressing his shoulders, arms, and strong back.

His kiss was harsh as he undressed her roughly, his hands hot and shaking. Quickly frustrated with her buttons, he pulled roughly and ripped her dress open to the waist.

She didn't even have time to gasp. His mouth clamped over hers again, his tongue ravishing her mouth while, lower, his hands shoved the torn ends aside and cupped her breasts. He groaned with pleasure. A moment later, he bent down and suckled her with a greedy purr of hunger in his throat.

She melted under the regular, insistent tug of his wet mouth at her breast. That quickly, she realized, he had almost won. Ah, but he was so much more experienced and ruthless than she was, she thought, her will dissolving in pleasure, half-enticed by his mastery. With the way he held her pinned down, she could not touch him where she wanted to, and there was little she could do to stop him. In truth, she didn't try very hard to get free.

She could only fight the pleasure, weakening to him, struggling to keep her wits, but as warm arousal uncoiled low in her belly and spiraled through the core of her, spreading outward to her limbs, her body arched under him with a will of its own. She stopped herself with a mental curse, fighting for control. Tormenting her with her own, inner battle, he pulled her skirts up to her hips, caressed her thighs, then stroked between her legs. Her cheeks burned with embarrassment as he discovered the truth of her response.

He let out a hearty sound of satisfaction as his fingers glided in her flowing wetness. She burned for his touch even as she clawed for the strength to resist. She forbade herself to surrender. She refused to give him the satisfaction. Let him get himself hot and bothered with touching her, soon she would turn the tables on him and take him under her command.

She clamped every muscle, forcing herself to be still. He gave a soft, wicked laugh as he nuzzled her ear, his warm breath stirring tendrils of her hair, tickling her. She jerked with a bolt of pleasure when his thumb alighted on her pebble-hard center.

"So, you want to make a contest of it, do you?" he murmured.

Gritting her teeth, she did not answer. Eyes closed, she was fully focused on the dangerous source of bliss as his thumb circled lightly, languidly. Flirting with her. Teasing her.

She strained with all her strength to lie motionless. Her chest lifted and fell in short, shallow breaths, but she was poised to hold her passion for this man in check.

"Very well, my lady," he whispered. "You force me to play dirty."

And then he pleasured her ruthlessly.

She did not know how many times he drove her to the edge of climax, only to deny her. She did not know how much time passed, but the room grew bright and hot with day as he drowned her in sensation. Every time she caught her breath, he dunked her under again in the sea of pleasure until her need became unbearable, agonized craving, and she begged for him in mindless, barbaric demand, tearing at his clothes and pulling him down upon her sweat-slicked body. She touched his bare skin everywhere, stroking him, putting him inside her, heedless of her shame.

His black eyes glittered with victory, watching her face as he penetrated her so deeply that his tip touched the rim of her womb. He pulled back a hairbreadth, gliding against her tight inner walls, as they gripped him wetly.

Filled with him at last, she barely recognized the whimper of relief that left her lips as her own voice. *"Oh, Darius."*

"That's right, Princesa," he said, his low voice roughened with desire. "You be good and I'll give it to you."

Arrogant—pagan! His power over her infuriated her. Her blood swore she would dominate him before she ever admitted defeat. He had shattered her control and now her only hope was to do the same to him.

She swept her eyes open and gazed at him through the thick, drugging haze of lust. His eyes were closed, his forelock falling over them. He bit his lip as he slowly thrust and withdrew in a deep, lush, slow grind, visibly savoring every nuance of pleasure. She moaned, unable to temper her response. She wrapped herself around him, undulating sinuously beneath him.

"Mmm, yes, baby, just like that."

"Uhn, Darius, I can't bear it."

"Don't fail me, angel. Not yet. Not until I say," he panted.

He plunged into her again and all thought dissolved.

It was a mighty battle. Time became meaningless. In the middle of the afternoon, Darius did things to her in body and spirit that she had not known were possible, made her feel things she had never felt, a soul-tearing mix of despair and ecstasy, domination and total surrender, a whisper and a groan. They were immortals, tangled together in the golden net, neither able to escape the other, locked in loving combat, torn between mutual need and mutual mistrust, both battling for dominion.

They rolled and tussled across the bed, twisting the covers and dampening the sheets with their sweat and steam. His fingers' grip bruised her pale flesh. Her nails flayed his bronzed hide. They bit each other, leaving marks. Yielding in order to conquer, she indulged his every whim, every contorting position he demanded, glorying in the feel of his skin everywhere against her, licking its salty velvet, her kiss drinking all the bitterness from his scarred mouth.

"Sweet, so sweet," he whispered, drowning her with kisses as his hard, trembling body smothered hers, and throbbed, gloved inside hers.

In the end, he was as out of control as she was, drunk on the excess of pleasure. Loving her so wildly had reduced him to barbarity, but she was barely conscious of her triumph, reduced to the mindless abandon of instinct. They were copulating animals, mating fiercely—fighting, tooth and nail, to hold on to each other.

At last, he reared up on his fists over her, taking her with long, vigorous thrusts, his face taut with savage ecstasy. Sunlight gleamed on his slicked skin. Shining beads of sweat jeweled every sculpted muscle of his abdomen and the hard swells of his chest. Shadow and sun contoured his angular face, fierce and taut with passion. She gripped his arms, holding on for dear life as his hips pumped her like a piston. The violent rhythm rocked her body, until at long last she planted her heels on the mattress, arching high as a near-scream of release tore from her lips. Climax slammed through her in intense, rigid shudders, ripping through her. Blinding light blazed along her nerve endings, exalting her to heights of such transcendence that she was sobbing, her hands stroking his velvety skin. She felt like she was dying in a blaze of light, a maiden sacrifice devoured by a god.

Darius followed her over the edge. She felt him come, lost and weak, groaning loudly in surrender, buried to the hilt inside her, his whole golden body rigid. His teeth clamped her shoulder, his hands clutched her hips, holding her hard in position as he shot his seed inside her in straining, magnificent pulses.

He collapsed on her and neither of them moved for she knew not how long, panting, thoroughly spent. They were both left empty, uncertain, and undone.

He is heavy, she thought after a very long time. *I am not going to be able to walk tomorrow.*

These mindless observations seemed all that remained of her powers of reason. He must have eaten her wits. He started laughing lazily for no apparent reason. Wryly, she looked over at him, the handsomest man in the world.

"Ahh, little Cricket," he chuckled ruefully, eyes closed as he passed his hand over her bent knee. "I think it's a draw."

She gave him a sheepish smile as she rolled onto her side, propping her cheek against her hand. She laid her other hand on his ridged stomach, petting him gently. His eyes were closed when she looked uncertainly at his finely chiseled face.

What do we do now?

His lashes swept open and he gazed at her tenderly, cupping her face. "Still going to leave me?" he murmured.

There was such gentleness and love in his eyes, her throat closed with emotion. She moved toward him and crawled into his arms. He welcomed her. She laid her head on his chest, shuddering with the reprieve. He stroked her hair, holding her in his strong, powerful arms.

Darius laid his cheek against her hair. The sweet intimacy of the moment was bliss. Safe in his arms, lulled by the slow, strong beat of his heart, she could scarcely believe how close they had come to losing each other.

Several moments later, he kissed her hair, took a deep breath, and broke the silence.

"You asked me once how I got this scar." He gestured toward the crescent-moon line on his lips. "I want to tell you now. I couldn't then." He paused.

She did not move, waiting.

"Oh, this is hard," he whispered, closing his eyes.

"Take your time, sweetheart," she murmured, caressing his chest.

He avoided her gaze and kept his voice carefully toneless. "I was eight years old," he said. "They were fighting again, like always. I—I tried to make him come after me so he would leave her alone. My father, I mean, and my so-called mother."

She held her breath, every particle of her attention on him. Never before had he spoken of his parents this way, as if he had sprung into the world of his own doing and his own will.

"I got between them. I don't know what I thought I was going to do against a grown man at the time." He lowered his head with a taut grimace of a smile. "He just swatted me aside. He . . . hit me in the face with a wine bottle."

She closed her eyes, feeling the blow.

"Luckily it didn't break. Just split my mouth open pretty badly," he murmured, touching his scarred lip with his knuckle, as if the wound were still tender. "I tried to help her. I don't know why I bothered." His voice dwindled to an agonized whisper. "She was just a stupid whore, and I hated her."

She winced. His vulnerability pulsed around her, as if he were not a man who knew a dozen ways to kill with his bare hands, but a wounded child holding on to her as though she were a beloved toy, his sole comfort and companion.

"She didn't— Oh, what am I doing?" He suddenly cut himself off in savage disgust. "You don't want to hear this!"

"Yes, I do. Talk to me."

He closed his eyes for a long moment, his voice strangled. "Can't."

She caressed his chest, trying to calm him. "Take your time. You're doing fine."

"It's not a matter of time! It's just . . . pathetic. Embarrassing. To be so weak. I was helpless."

She caught his chin between her fingers and thumb and turned his face. "Look at me," she whispered.

He stared bleakly at her.

She smoothed his hair out of his eyes. "I've come this far, haven't I?" Lightly, she brushed the elegant line of his high cheekbone with her knuckles. "Nothing can change my love for you."

His eyes filled with anguish. "You still love me?"

"I still love you," she whispered, unable to withhold her heart from him. "Always."

He lowered his gaze in silence with a tortured expression. She leaned toward him and gently kissed the scar, stroking his cheek as her lips moved softly over the crescent-moon shape of it. He whispered a moan as her lips lingered over his. She felt him responding to her soft touch.

As he turned, seeking her lips, he cupped her face between both his hands and gave her a deep, loving kiss, then ended it softly, his eyes closed. "I need to be sure of you," he whispered. "That you won't turn on me . . . or anything."

She felt her heart open utterly to him. "Darius, look into my eyes."

He did. She caressed his face, as he did hers.

"I have loved you all my life, only you. I know you're afraid. So am I."

He nodded as his gaze slid away from hers. After a moment, he took her hand and held it. She had no idea what he had to tell her, but whatever it was, he was ready.

At that moment, their tense, difficult silence shattered with a sudden clamor outside of men's shouts, clattering hoofbeats.

Before her eyes, Darius clicked onto full alert, turning his head toward the window, all traces of vulnerability and emotion vanishing, like a wolf scenting an enemy.

"Darius."

"Shh." He didn't breathe, listening, his eyes sharp, his arms holding her protectively.

She despaired. "Darius!"

"One minute." He released her and smoothly rose from the bed in silent, liquid grace.

Her gaze traveled over his nude, lean body. She stared, at a loss. He picked up his trousers on his way to the window, then glanced out discreetly from the side of the curtain.

"Come back, I'm sure it's nothing," she attempted.

He pulled on his tan-colored trousers, then narrowed his

eyes as he dipped the curtain back slightly with two fingers. "It's your brother."

Of all the blasted nuisances! She lifted her gaze to the ceiling, striving for patience. "Darius, come back to me. This is no time to be distracted by Rafe and his ridiculous friends."

"He's alone." His soft, cool tone sent gooseflesh tingling down her arms. He looked over at her, his ancient eyes full of death. "Something's wrong. I can feel it."

CHAPTER
⚜ TWENTY-TWO ⚜

"Colonel, the crown prince has come!"

"I'm right here, Alec," Darius said to his aide, coming down the stairs, feeling oddly cool and collected.

Close call, he thought with a cold shiver as he strode across the foyer to the open door. God, he had nearly just made the biggest mistake of his life. What a way to ruin things that would have been, spilling his guts after the incredible afternoon of sex had brought them back together.

He felt damned guilty for walking out on her in the middle of everything, but, thank God fate had intervened and given him the means for a graceful exit before he said anything more. Never again would he let himself weaken like that.

Out on the cobbled drive, Prince Rafael sawed at the reins, halting his lathered bay stallion in a clatter of hoofbeats as Darius strode out to meet him.

"What is it?"

The youth flung down off the horse and ran to him. "Inside," Rafe urged him, pulling him by the elbow toward the villa's open door.

They stepped into the morning room. Darius saw Rafael's hand shaking as he closed the tall, white door behind them.

"What's happened?"

The young prince turned around, his face ashen. His chest heaved with exertion and he looked like he wanted to retch. "My maps. Last night—Julia."

Darius drew in his breath.

"When I woke up, my maps were gone. Santiago, she's gone!" he cried. "No one has seen her, not even her maid! I think she has gone to the French in the harbor! All she would've had to do is bribe some fisherman to row her out there. She could name her price and the French would pay it."

"They won't need to wait for Villeneuve, that's for sure," Darius said, eyes narrowed in thought. "Did you send word of this to your father?"

"No! You know he'd kill me, Santiago! He already thinks I can do nothing right! Besides, he's been busy at the wall over the harbor—the first shots have been fired."

"The king is there himself?"

"Yes, the old fool! He's commanding the cannons person-ally. The French began some light shelling about two hours ago."

His thoughts whirled. If the French had the maps, the shelling was surely just a distraction to hold attention on the harbor while they moved their men into the tunnels.

Rafe was turning white as he began to realize the implica-tions. "The main tunnel in that quadrant leads out behind the wall. They'll attack from behind . . . oh, God, Father will be trapped."

"Let's go." Darius clapped him hard on the shoulder, but Rafael was frozen in place, staring at nothing, stricken.

"They're going to die."

"Not if we get to the mouth of that tunnel first. Come on!" He pulled the boy's arm hard, dragging him away from the wall. "Alec!" he bellowed, and immediately began giving orders. He marched outside, called for a wagon, and had six horses hitched to it. "Be quick about it!" he barked, then he stalked to the magazine and slid the doors open wide. He ordered his men to load the wagon with all eight barrels of the gunpowder he'd brought here weeks ago.

Rafe visibly steeled himself and immediately got to work helping the men.

His mind crisp and crystal clear, Darius felt like himself for the first time since his humiliating failure at Milan. He marched back toward the house, intent on arming himself with his usual arsenal of weapons, and praying to God he might now redeem himself.

Sergeant Tomas appeared at his heels as he jogged up the wide, shallow front steps.

"What's going on, Colonel?"

"Get your squad together and arm them well. We're riding out and we may run into some fighting."

"Yes, sir!"

"Leave five of your best men behind to guard my wife. The rest will come with us. You've got ten minutes."

"Yes, sir!" The seasoned officer hurried off.

Thinking of his weapons, which were stowed in his small, spartan room upstairs, Darius stepped over the threshold, glanced up at the top of the steps, and stopped in his tracks, beholding a vision.

Scantily clad in her blue satin dressing gown, Serafina stood on the top step of the staircase, gazing down at him.

He caught his breath and stared up at his wife.

She held her head high with a calm, cool poise that was pure princess, but her translucent skin glowed after his savage loving. Her wild, sable mane was in disarray, but her eyes promptly caught him in their spell of stormy innocence, eyes the color of lilacs and eternity.

"You are leaving?" she asked, her soft, scratchy voice reined in to a careful tone.

"There is a crisis," he whispered, an echo of an excuse he had tried to give her once, weeks ago. She hadn't bought it then, either.

"I see." She turned her face away to stare at her hand, lying limply on the banister.

Some men walked into the foyer behind him and asked him a question. Startled, he answered curtly and scowled at them. His blasted wife was in her dressing gown. They had no place here.

When they were gone, he turned back to her, raising his gaze. She had not moved. Her stillness terrified him.

"My darling, I have to go," he said softly.

"I believe you." She did not look at him, but gave a little shrug of defeat as she stared at her hand on the banister. "I'll be here."

He took a step toward her. "Serafina, I have to do this."

"I know. These things come up. I suppose it's part of being wife to the bravest knight in all the world." At last she looked at him and gave him a slight, brave smile. "Be careful."

"You're not angry?"

"I'm proud of you," she answered, tears filling her eyes. "But I do— I just—I think it's important that we talk about this. Otherwise I don't see that there is any hope for us."

He said nothing, staring up at her.

Just then, Sergeant Tomas shouted to him from outside that the wagon was loaded and the twenty men were almost ready to ride. Serafina's gaze flicked toward the door, then they looked at each other again. He was still rather marveling. *Proud of me?*

"Will we talk when you get back, Darius?" she asked point-blank.

He searched her eyes, his heart pounding like the drums of war. "All right," he lied smoothly, nodding. "I have to go now." He couldn't bear to see her a second longer—it was like looking at an angel whose face shone like the dazzling sun. He pivoted and began striding away.

"You're lying again!" she cried softly behind him.

He stopped, midstride, but he did not turn around.

"How could you look in my eyes and lie?"

Slowly, he turned back and lifted his gaze to where she still stood at the top of the stairs.

Her face had reddened, and hot, vulnerable tears welled in her beautiful eyes. He made himself cold inside.

"You're right. That was a lie," he said. "I'm glad I didn't tell you. You weakened me for a moment, but I will never tell you, and believe me, you don't want to know."

"Then we are finished." Her shoulders slumped as she lowered her head. "You don't love me. What a fool I am. A naive, gullible fool."

"I don't love you?"

"You don't. You didn't want this marriage. I forced you into it. I was a fool ever to think I could make you happy. You won't share yourself with me, you won't be honest with me. All you do is manipulate and lie. You're stronger than me, you're smarter than me, and every chance you get, you break my heart, so just go, do what you have to. You're never going to love me, Darius, I give up." She sat down on the step where she had been standing and buried her face in both hands.

He stared at her for a long moment, fighting the quickening of anger within him. "I don't love you?" he repeated quietly.

"You said once that you did, but it must have been a lie."

"No, you're the one who lied to me on that point, sweetheart," he said in cold, building anger.

She looked up again, tears in her eyes. His own words had surprised even him. He tried to stop himself, but he couldn't. The hurt was still balled inside him, yearning to strike out.

"What are you talking about?"

Anger swept up from inside him as he walked closer, glaring up at her. "The first night we made love. You said you loved me. *Me,* and I trusted you," he wrenched out, striking his chest with his fist like a penitent. He heard the catch of anguish in his voice, but he didn't care anymore. "But the truth came to light the minute you found out I failed in Milan, didn't it? That's right," he said with rich contempt in answer to her look of dawning dread. "You threw me out your door. You only gave yourself to me because you thought I was the big hero! You wanted a champion, the dragon-slayer, eh?" He held out his arms at his sides, presenting himself, then dropped them. "Well, I tried to be that man you wished for, but I missed the bloody shot. It was a hard shot. But that didn't matter to my

Princesa. I failed to fulfill your fantasy. You don't give a damn for *me,* Serafina. And how could you? I don't blame you. How could anyone? I know what I am."

"What are you?" she whispered, staring at him, her face pale.

"You want to know? You want to know about your knight, Serafina?" he asked in cold, bitter insolence. "Can you even comprehend? I don't think you can, my little sheltered Princesa." Searing pain seeped up from the deepest, blackest core of him.

"Tell me."

"You want to know? You want to know how it feels when your mother's been running out on you since you were two years old, and doesn't give a damn what happens to you or who hits you when she's gone, or how it feels when she doesn't come back anymore? Do you want to know how it is when your father won't let you have a new set of clothes for four years so that other children won't talk to you, only throw rocks at you and call you dirty and skinny, because he says you don't deserve to have any friends?" he snarled, the words slashing from him like a killer's knife, vile as poison on his tongue. He was going down in flames. "How about getting thrown out on the street when you're ten years old? I could tell you all about that. Are you sick yet? Are you ready to throw up yet? But I'm not done, no, Princess, that's when the fun only starts. Because then come the back-alley fights for survival and scavenging for food off garbage heaps. And you wind up sick enough to die from some half-rotten thing that you've eaten, so you swallow your pride and go to the almshouse for help, but you can't stay there because one of the monks won't stop putting his hands on you. And then eventually you figure, there's only one thing I'm good for, what the hell? Do you follow me, Serafina? Do you understand what I'm saying to you?"

She placed her hand over her mouth as she stared at the floor, crying, listening to his words that charged on like a maddened bull, barbed pennants flying from its black hide.

"You're thirteen years old and you've seen things to keep

you jaded for three lifetimes. You're hardened, and lying's a necessity, and you survive because you lie so very well. You don't care what you have to do or say. You don't let anything touch you. You don't dare need anyone and you don't trust anyone in a million years, not even the angel God sends to save you."

She sobbed, holding her head in both hands.

His chest heaved. "I am empty, Serafina. I am nothing and I have nothing to give you."

But for the sound of her crying, there was a terrible silence. "Well, now you know. Happy?"

She looked up, crying like her heart was broken. He could see her shaking.

"I don't expect you to be here when I get back. Wife," he added bitterly as he turned to go.

He barely heard her whispered plea. "Don't leave."

He turned around, glaring at her from under his forelock. He felt naked in front of her.

She stood up and began walking down the stairs, taking them one by one, like a child. She looked so unsteady he thought she might fall down them, so he went up to her. She sat down on the middle step and leaned against the spindled banister.

She eyed him as he wearily crouched down near her. He thought she looked frightened of him, but when he lowered himself to her eye level, she put her arms around him like she would never let him go. She clung to him and laid her head on his shoulder, still crying softly.

"Don't go away from me now," she whispered.

He closed his eyes. The feel of her arms was warm, wonderful. He inhaled the vanilla-citrusy perfume that clung in her hair, then he sighed.

"You're the only pure thing in my life, Serafina," he said, his voice soft but heavy. "All I ever wanted was to build a kind of wall around your little garden world and let you be safe there, and happy. A little paradise just for you."

She pulled back and stared at him, agony and heartbreak in her red-rimmed eyes, an anguished smile on her trembling lips, and he knew what he had to do. A match with this girl? This royal creature, this angel? What hubris had ever made him think himself worthy of her? His heart sank to subterranean depths, but it was the only solution.

"Protecting you, Serafina, is the one thing that I can look back on and take pride in," he forced out. "I've done my best by you. At least, I've tried to. But look at what's happening to you. Look at what I'm doing to you now. You should never cry, butterfly. You should never have loved me—"

She clutched at his shirt, protest swimming in her violet eyes.

"But that is your nature," he went on gently, stroking her hair again. "Pure love, joyous and giving. That's my angel. How lucky I have been to watch you grow and share your life." He shook his head, avoiding her gaze. "I never should have reached for you, knowing what I am, knowing I could only contaminate you. It was unforgivably selfish of me. But I needed you so."

"As I need you," she whispered, holding on to two fistfuls of his shirt, as if she could already sense what he intended.

He wiped a tear from her cheek with his thumb. "I must give you up now, my Serafina. You know it's time to say goodbye."

"No, Darius! You're wrong!" she whispered frantically. "I need you here."

"No, you still don't understand," he said, beginning to lose patience. "There is something . . . deeply wrong inside of me. I don't know what it is, I only know it can't be fixed and it can't be helped—"

"Yes, it can! Together we can—"

"No! Look at what I've done to you. Throwing your food against the wall like a bedlamite?"

She winced. "I only did that to get your attention."

"Drinking? Taking laudanum? I heard about that. You nearly destroyed yourself. I nearly destroyed you."

"But, Darius, I thought you were dead! You are my love, my best friend! I was distraught!"

"What about this afternoon?" he whispered angrily. "Rutting with you like the whore of Babylon?"

"I wanted you."

"Serafina! That's scarcely the point."

She caught his face between her hands and stared pleadingly at him. "Darius, stop this. I know you've suffered things I'll never fully understand, but I love you. Yourself. I don't want a champion, I want you, and I accept it—"

He jerked away, growing angry and bewildered. "I said no! Can't you hear? You can't still want me. What's wrong with you?"

"I'm not going to hurt you. Let me love you."

"I can't do that!" he cried as he stood up, poised to flee. "Don't you see? I can't! I don't know how!"

She didn't flinch, holding on to his hand. "You can. You're my Darius—you can do anything. You did it before. You're just afraid. Quit running. I'll never catch you unless you let me. Let my love heal you, Darius."

She caressed him and her gentle touch snapped the last of his control even as its softness slid down into the core of his being.

"Why are you trying to destroy me?" With a strangled cry, he grasped the silver medal of the Virgin and ripped it off his neck, chain and all, throwing it far over the banister. "I can't do this! I never wanted to marry you!" he ranted at her, his throat straining, his eyes wild with anguish. "Why are you so cruel to me? Why do you make me wretched for what I can't have and what I can't be? Why couldn't you leave me alone? Why couldn't you let me die in Milan like I wanted?"

"No, Darius!" she said in dread, then she tried to slip past him. "I'll get the medal. You put it back on—"

"I don't want it," he said in a voice out of hell, teeth clenched. He gripped her by the shoulders, shut his eyes, and pressed his blazing lips to her forehead.

"Darius," she whispered.

He moved his face against her smooth brow. "I love you, Serafina. And for that reason," he whispered, "I release you. I release you from this bond of blood. Go now, while I am strong enough to let you."

"Darius!" she cried as he wrenched out of her arms.

Moving lightly, he descended the stairs, then stalked to the door, bloodlust pounding in his veins, for he had such wrath to vent.

"Darius!"

He paused on the threshold but did not turn around. "Do not be here when I come back. Go home, the way you planned. If you don't leave first, I will."

She cried out as he lurched out the door and ran down the front steps, going blindly to the waiting wagon. He flung himself up to the driver's seat next to Rafael and cracked the whip over the horses' backs.

He was going to die today. His mind was made up on the matter. He only prayed that he could stave off his own disintegration long enough to save Lazar and his men from massacre.

CHAPTER
❧ TWENTY-THREE ❧

Powder kegs secured, the wagon careened over the rough roads, winding west. Darius drove the wagon with Rafe watching over the barrels. The men rode in formation behind them. After a breakneck race of nearly two hours, they arrived at the high, sparse pine woods that shielded the mouth of the tunnels' western branch.

Leaving the wagon on the road, for half an hour they searched the boulder-strewn thicket, unable to find the cave's entrance, it was so well concealed. At last, Rafe found it.

They tore away brambles and vines to reveal the cave's mouth. Darius lit the torch that was always left just inside every tunnel's entrance, because the subterranean passages were as black as tar.

This tunnel, he saw as the flame leaped to life, was wide enough that three men could climb abreast through it. By torchlight, they began the backbreaking labor of carrying the powder kegs through the woods, up the hill, picking their way around the boulders, and deep into the tunnel. The sweat on his skin turned clammy in the tunnel's cool depths.

Darius held his breath every time anyone passed the torches, gingerly carrying their payload of explosives. They stacked the barrels, pyramid-fashion, about three hundred yards into the cave. As the last barrel was unloaded from the wagon, Darius ordered Sergeant Tomas to take his men over the ridge farther up the road so they would be a safe distance from the explosion.

Again the men mounted their horses while Darius kicked the final barrel until the side of it cracked. Then he and Rafe carried it into the tunnel, the barrel leaking a sandy black trail of gunpowder.

Just as they set it in position, their arms straining, faces beaded with sweat, they suddenly fell silent, hearing dull, muffled echoes coming from deep inside the cave.

They both turned, staring into the eerie, echoing blackness. They could not yet see the light of torches, but they could hear voices and the scrape and shuffle of countless boots.

"Poor bastards," Darius breathed. He hoped the mountain crushed them before the fire consumed them, he thought. Burning was no way to die.

He didn't know exactly how far the fireball would roll in both directions when the barrels blew, any more than he knew how many hundreds of unsuspecting soldiers would die when the mountain collapsed on them.

"Come on." Rafe tugged his sleeve.

They ran. Darius grabbed the torch on the way out of the cave.

"Get out of here," Darius ordered the boy, shoving him toward the wagon with one hand, holding the torch in the other.

Rafe stopped him. "I shall do it. Go with your men."

Darius scoffed. "Don't be ridiculous. I'm expendable. You're the heir to the throne. Get the hell out of here. I'll catch up."

"I caused the problem. It's my responsibility," Rafe said in an odd, hard, crisp tone that did not sound at all like the royal rogue Darius knew.

He stared at him. "Raffaele! Don't be a fool. This is extremely dangerous—"

"I know it is. Now go. That's an order, Santiago."

"You're giving me orders?" he asked incredulously.

Rafael held his stare coolly. "That's right. Go—now. Wait for me with the others."

Resistant and rather angrily amazed, Darius surveyed the

ground, searching for cover, then glanced at his young brother-in-law with a newfound measure of respect. "There's a cluster of boulders over there." He pointed. "I suggest you run like hell for them."

Rafe merely jerked a nod for him to leave, his gold-green eyes hard as the wind tousled his gold-streaked hair. Darius realized this was something the young man had to do. Even so, he didn't like it. Darius climbed up onto the wagon, picked up the reins, and slapped them over the horses' back, but he looked over his shoulder as the carriage began pulling away.

Rafe stood in the middle of the dusty road. "Gonna kill a hundred, maybe a thousand men with one blow, Santiago," the royal rogue called after him with a grin. "That's even better than your average."

"Just don't blow yourself to smithereens," he muttered. Then he urged the horses into a gallop and drove the carriage over the ridge.

"Hit the ground, hit the ground!" he ordered his men.

Several minutes later, the massive explosion tore through the belly of the mountain. The horses screamed in terror, rearing in the harness. Darius covered his ears, feeling the blast of heat. The roar went on and on as the hill fell in on itself, but when the noise finally rumbled to a halt, he was already on his feet, running back over the ridge.

"Raffaele!"

"Your Highness!" the men called.

Some began running back down the road. Darius joined them, his heart pounding. As he approached the site, he saw the tunnel's mouth no longer existed. Also, fortunately, they had planted the explosives deep enough inside the cave that fire had not spread to the woods.

The dust was settling, the men running toward the boulders. Though some of the birds were still screeching in the trees, the place was otherwise shockingly serene, as if nothing had happened.

"Rafe!"

Squinting against the bright late afternoon sun, he looked down the road and saw a figure climbing out from under the small, flat den between the boulders. The boy came out coughing and covered in dust and ash, but he was unscathed.

Sergeant Tomas hastened to give him his canteen. Rafe took a long drink.

"Victory!" he croaked with a weak grin, but his face was pale beneath the grime. "Let's go check on my old man."

Amid the men's congratulations to the prince on his feat accomplished, they walked back to the wagon and were soon under way.

They could hear the cannon fire rumbling from miles away, but when they finally rolled up into the shadow of the towering defensive wall from which Ascencion's fine long-range guns were blasting the ships in the blue-green harbor below, the skirmish was already drawing to a close, judging by the sound of things.

Darius shaded his eyes, gazing up at the wall's battlements, swathed in clouds of smoke from the cannons. Through the floating smoke, he saw the powerful figure of the king stalking back and forth behind the gun crews.

"Damned hothead," Darius murmured, shaking his head. As king, Lazar had no right exposing himself under fire, but Darius knew he was venting his wrath as outraged papa on the enemy.

By the look of it, the meager exchange with the French had only whetted Lazar's appetite for battle. He was ordering his men to fire and fire again, though the enemy had stopped shooting.

Rafe and Darius exchanged a grim, knowing look.

"Let's get this over with," the prince grumbled.

"Right." Darius jumped down from the wagon.

As they strode toward the tower and up the stone stairs leading to the battlements, Darius felt that familiar clench of anger in his stomach, knowing he was about to face Lazar for the first time since their break. He felt rather like he used to as a boy, called before his father for some bewildering, tiny transgression.

Upon reaching the top of the steps, they walked onto the breezy battlements and looked out to sea. Darius ignored the stares aimed at him and considered the situation.

The French were retreating to their blockade positions, a wary distance beyond the guns' range. He surveyed the battle-ships' formation, but his thoughts were far distant, on Serafina.

Right now, he thought, the five guards he'd left to look after her were probably loading onto the coach those traveling trunks she had been packing. He dreaded facing the empty villa when he went home. Home. Whatever that was.

He was glad he had told Serafina his disgusting secrets, driven her off forcefully rather than waiting around for her to leave him, he thought as he searched the sky. At least now it was over, no more waiting for the blade to drop. One day she'd thank him for this. For him, there was nothing left to do but get on with his life. If Ascencion didn't want him anymore, he would go to Sicily and help Richards in his "intriguing enterprise."

He was still brooding on his loss when a deep, cold voice rose behind him.

"You."

Darius whirled around, his back to the low stone wall. Lazar stalked toward him like a grand, angry lion.

Darius lifted his hands calmingly. "I just came to help."

"Don't you try to play me, Santiago," he growled.

Darius dropped his gaze, incredulous at the man's sustained hostility. "Fine. I'm leaving. Excuse me."

"You're not going anywhere till I've had a piece of you!"

He very nearly laughed. "Sire." He edged away from the wall, for there was a very long drop to the sea on the other side of the wall, and one never knew what an outraged Italian papa might do. "I'm getting out of here, don't worry," he said. Turning his back, he started walking away calmly, coolly.

Lazar tackled him.

"Ouch," Darius grunted as he hit the ground, banging his knees, his hands thrown out to catch himself just in time.

The big royal clod didn't know his own strength. Darius rolled, dodging a blow.

"Leave me alone! I married her, didn't I?"

"Only because I caught you, you schemer!" The king took a swing at him.

Darius ducked and kept trying to back away. "That's not true! I would have married her anyway!"

He realized only after he'd said it that it was the truth.

"After all I've done for you, this is how you repay me—you seduce my innocent baby girl!"

Darius laughed. "Oh, I have news for you about your innocent baby, old man. You want to see her claw marks on my back?"

Lazar let out a wordless bellow of fury and cuffed him alongside the head with his fist.

Darius caught himself against the tower wall and whirled back to him, taunting him. "That's it, isn't it? You can't accept that your little girl has gone and grown up on you!"

"I trusted you with her! You think I'm deaf *and* blind, that I don't hear of your conquests? You've had every hot-blooded bitch in the kingdom, but you couldn't leave one innocent young girl alone! You seduced her just like your countless others!"

"No!" He stepped toward Lazar and shoved him. "Not like the others! You know nothing of it!"

"How dare you?" Lazar uttered, shoving him back.

"Why don't you stop putting your own blame on me? Can't you just admit you made a mistake, promising her to Tyurinov? You had no right signing that betrothal before you heard from me, but you were taken in by him! If it weren't for me, that mistake could have cost us her life. I'm the one who cared enough about her to learn the truth. You're the one who sold her for an easy way out!"

Lazar made a sound of fury and hurled himself at Darius again. They went scuffling across the flagstone.

"Why didn't you come to me at once when you learned about Tyurinov's first wife? I could charge you with treason for keeping it from me!" Lazar bellowed.

"Because you, Your Majesty, are a hothead. Look at you now. The situation called for subtlety. Damn it, leave me alone, I've had enough!" Darius shouted as he elbowed Lazar hard in the kidney, spun free, and caught him a in a choke hold from behind. Trusting he'd proved his point, Darius dropped him and walked a few paces away, raking a hand furiously through his hair.

As soon as he turned his back, he was tackled again.

This time, the bigger man got the best of him, pinning him in a headlock. "What about the chaperons?" he demanded.

Darius shoved uselessly at the stonelike choke hold around his neck. "I'm sorry, I lied! But it was what she wanted."

"She put you up to it? She told you to lie?"

"No," he growled. "But I know how those people just gnaw at her spirit. Nobody has ever known how to manage that girl but me, you know that. You never bloody could! You let her walk all over you and twist you around her finger! I just wanted to be with her. Is that so wrong? Damn it, Lazar, she was my only hope."

The king stared down at him for a minute.

"That I believe," he declared, slamming him onto his back on the flagstone. Fists on his waist, Lazar stood over him like a wrathful Jehovah, his foot planted on Darius's chest.

Darius didn't really feel like fighting anymore. The flagstones were almost comfortable, tired as he was.

"Answer me one question," Lazar said ominously.

"What?" he muttered, lifting his head.

"Do you love her?"

He dropped his head back against the sun-warmed stone, then winced at the bang, and just lay there, eyes closed in defeat.

"Do you love her?" he demanded.

"Why do you think I went to kill Napoleon, you clod? I only wanted her to be free."

"You knew there was no way you could come back alive."

"Yes."

"And yet you went there."

"Yes! I love her! What do you want to know? I love her more than I love my own life."

Her father folded his arms over his brawny chest and stroked his chin, glowering down at him. "You really piss me off, Santiago."

"Mutual, Sire."

"Santiago."

"What?" he growled.

"If you love my daughter so much you were willing to die for her, why the hell did you never come to me and ask me for her hand?"

"Because you would have said no," he said wearily.

"Is that so?"

"Maybe you would have said yes out of obligation, because of the bullet I took for you."

"I'm the king. I don't *have* to do anything."

Darius fixed him with a sullen, moody stare.

Lazar shook his head. "You're a proud, obstinate fool, *magnifico*. I would have said yes, and been damned glad of it." He removed his booted foot from Darius's chest and bent to offer a hand to help him up.

Darius watched him warily, too weary to move. "You would have said yes? To me?"

Lazar only chuckled softly, sadly, and shook his head, his hand outstretched. "Get up, son."

"You like to help me clean up, don't you? Yes, that's a good kitty," she murmured softly to her fluffy white cat, petting the crouched animal as it hungrily gobbled the scraps of Darius's breakfast, which she had splattered against the wall many hours ago.

The yellow villa was quiet under the gathering sunset.

While the cat feasted, Serafina stood, her expression mournful as she wiped down the soiled wall with a wet cloth. All she could think was how awful her temper tantrum must have made her look in front of Darius. He had known starvation, and here she was, throwing a perfectly good plate of food across the room so it was fit only for a cat.

Spoiled, rotten brat, she thought in self-contempt.

Many times she had marveled at his capacity for violence, but tonight she was awed, looking back on the gentleness he had always shown her, both as her lover and as her guardian when she was a child. He had endured a nightmarish existence, yet somehow he had always managed to keep the small, pure flame of his humanity alight in the darkness. That was the fire that burned, always, in his onyx eyes, and the poignant sweetness that spoke to her in his guitar's tender music.

She knew he did not want to face her again after the things he had revealed, but there was no way she was leaving him now—or ever. He would never have to be alone again, nor face the demons of his past alone. He had only told her his secrets as a means of driving her off, she realized, but it had sealed her devotion to him. At last, she understood so many of his actions and reactions which had bewildered her before. She loved him completely, both the shining knight in him and the lost little boy. At last, she was needed and wanted for herself. She had found her purpose in giving to him.

When she was done cleaning up the ruined breakfast with her cat's help, she went searching for the medal of the Holy Virgin, which he had torn from his neck.

She found it all the way over by the entrance to the morning room. Picking it up, she discovered the chain was broken beyond repair. She brought it to the pink bedroom where her jewelry box sat on the bureau. She poked around in the jewelry box, determined to find a suitable replacement for the relic.

Still sniffling, her nose stuffed up and head throbbing from so much crying, she carefully extracted a sturdy gold chain from the knot of tangled necklaces.

The gold chain was even finer than the original silver one. It did not match as well, but it was stronger. Carefully, she restrung the medal on the gold chain, then put the necklace in her pocket, savoring the thought of putting it on him anew.

Perhaps it was mere superstition, but she did not like knowing he was out there doing something dangerous without its protection.

Bored and a little lonesome, the necklace wrapped loosely around her hand in her pocket, she wandered from room to room, restless for his return.

Everywhere she turned, the yellow villa offered images for her to meditate, memories of moments that Darius and she had shared in this magical place, both the good and the bad.

She toured the library where she had teased him and tweaked his pride. She lay awhile on the shiny dining room table, gazing up at the fresco of Mars and Venus caught for all to see in Vulcan's golden net. At length, she decided to go back up to her room and try to make herself presentable for her husband's return, but upstairs, she took a moment to continue her exploration. Out of curiosity, she went to the one room she had never entered, a narrow door at the end of the hall.

Opening the door quietly, she found herself for the first time in his quarters.

Her gaze traveled over the small, spartan box of a room. The narrow bed, fit for a servant, was tautly made. The cover was brown and the sheet was white. Beside it, one serviceable taper sat on one humble, no-nonsense table. His reading spectacles were on the table, too, and the sight of them clenched her heart somehow, this token of his hidden vulnerabilities and lovable little human flaws.

On the left wall, his orderly clothes hung on pegs. All the same, all black. The canvas curtain was neatly drawn over the window. Not a painting hung on the walls, which were of a nondescript color. Her throat closed, gazing at this dismal space. It was the most depressing room she had ever seen.

This is not a life, Darius. This is a prison sentence. But I swear I'll get you out of here.

Just as she pulled the door closed with a sniffle, she heard hoofbeats outside, and the sound of her five guards suddenly hollering. It couldn't be Darius who had arrived, she thought, for the men's voices sounded hostile. Then her eyes flared.

She stood frozen at the sound of a guttural Russian accent.

Under a canvas pavilion not far from the scene of the battle, Darius took a heavy hero's supper with the king, the crown prince, and the top officers present. All congratulated him on his nuptials.

They were all suddenly so happy for him, Darius didn't know how to tell them he'd already fumbled the marriage. His failure in Milan was nothing compared to this one.

His mind wandered again and again back to his wife as the men talked of the battle and agreed that their defenses were better than expected. When Rafe began boasting of how they would hold off Villeneuve when he came, Lazar voiced the opinion that, knowing Horatio Nelson's cool nerves and expertise, Villeneuve might not come back from the West Indies at all.

Finally, Darius nudged the prince into confessing about Julia and the tunnels.

Lazar was still bellowing at the lad when Darius took leave of them, chuckling ruefully as father and son shouted at each other, Italian gestures flying. He left his men at the feast. They had earned a celebration and, for his part, he wanted to be alone with his grief when it came time to face the empty yellow villa.

The whole long ride back to the villa astride his borrowed horse, Darius's mood was empty and sad. He was tired from the day's exertions, sated from the heavy meal, and he rode the horse at a lazy, ambling walk, dreading the thought of facing his empty house.

He was beginning to wonder about the wisdom of ending it with Serafina. If Lazar thought him worthy of her, perhaps . . . perhaps he wasn't as bad as he thought.

He couldn't go on like this, hating himself. It was pointless, he thought. If he wasn't going to find a way to get himself killed, then he was going to have to learn to live in his own skin somehow, and he would need her help to learn how to do that. She was his strength, his truest friend. She was his reason for living . . . and he had driven her away.

The road was quiet. He saw no one the whole journey. He watched birds swoop between boughs. Far above, a hawk soared, circling on an airy spiral.

The hot day cooled to dusk. As he neared the yellow villa, he grew more anxious about whether or not he would find his wife there. He had ordered her to go, but one never knew when she would choose to obey or defy. In this case, he wasn't sure which he preferred.

Now that she knew all the truth about him, she wasn't going to want to stay, anyway.

He thought for a while on the things he loved best about her and would miss most—her mischief, her sparkle. Her pout and her haughty scowl, when she was in her Queen of Sheba mood. And the sweetness of her soft arms around him as he drifted off to sleep.

The prospect of returning to his old life without her was unbearably bleak, but all he could do now was keep his desperation concealed beneath the surface of stoic resolve. Whether she chose to stay or go, either way, he would face her decision with equanimity.

The sun's glow was fading in the western sky as dusk deepened to night. Wearily, he let himself in through the tall iron gates and led the horse to the stable. His heart sank, for not a soul was in sight. Not a candle burned in the window.

They were all gone.

He stopped on the cobbled yard, hands in his pockets as he gazed at the house he had bought. God, how could he bear to go in there?

No, he told himself. This was as it should be. He had never deserved her, not really. She was too highborn for him, too beautiful, too pure. She was better off without her Spanish madman.

Open yourself to me, she had said, as if it were the simplest thing in the world to do. He remembered her asking him once, *What would it take to make you trust me?*

He didn't know. A miracle, maybe. Some kind of miracle to turn back the years and give him a father who didn't bash him around, and a mother who didn't dote on him and abandon him by turns, as if he were not her child but a little stray alley cat she fed scraps to when the whim took her.

Darius clenched his jaw as he stood there, not wanting to think about it, but he knew it drove straight to the heart of his problem. What stood in the way of his present happiness was his ancient past.

Viewed rationally, he knew his mother had been just as abused as he and had been sensible to flee. But on a deep, visceral level, he hated her almost worse than he hated his father, even though he knew it wasn't fair. His father had abused him, but his beautiful, sparkling mama had torn his heart out, betrayed him. She had been his only ally until she had abandoned him there.

If only he had not been so small and helpless. If only he had been strong enough to protect her, he thought. But all he had been able to do was take care of her after his father left her broken and bruised.

He supposed she had finally found some other wealthy protector to take care of her, someone who had not been afraid of his father. She took her chance at escape without looking back. She hadn't even said goodbye.

Whore, he thought, his lips curling in a cold, faint sneer. *Whore, whore.*

Her treachery hurt him so much that he usually could not bear even to think of her. It was easier remembering his father's kicks and blows than to think of her dazzling smile ... and perhaps he had been punishing her in every woman he had met since, showing them all what whores they were. Showing them that *he* was the one in control, he was the one who could leave *them*.

He had but to crook his finger to be worshiped by beautiful women. He could bring them to their knees with a look, then walk away without a scratch.

Until now.

Until the purest creature on earth had floated down beside him and fed him from the milk of her very body.

Had he won this time? Could it be called a victory, his driving her off deliberately so he would not have to face her eventual abandonment?

The hell with it.

He'd survive.

Abruptly, he lurched into motion, forcing himself to face the empty house. He dragged himself up the shallow front steps and opened the door.

As he stepped over the threshold into the darkened foyer, he heard a wooden thud at the same time he felt a startling blast of agony in his skull. He saw scarlet stars, blurring, black.

He realized too late who had come to keep a promise.

He was struck again.

Thank God she left.

At last, he thought, someone with the competence to kill him. Then nothing.

CHAPTER
⊰ TWENTY-FOUR ⊱

There had been a brief opportunity to run out the back door and flee into the tunnels that would take her safely into hiding, but when Serafina heard the shots and brief screams that told her that her few remaining guards had been killed, she abandoned all thought of flight.

Darius would be coming home soon, and she knew it was him they wanted. Somebody had to warn him.

So she stayed.

She had fumbled her way into the coffinlike secret compartment built into the floor in the pink bedroom. It was cobwebbed and claustrophobic, and how she had remained silent when they searched her room, she did not know.

The Russians' heavy, booted footfalls trod practically on her back through the hardwood floor. She had counted two male voices conversing as they searched the room, then left, but there could be more.

She knew Anatole was somewhere in the house. She could feel his icy presence.

She prayed Darius would not come, but strove to think of a plan in case he did. She considered what weapons she had at her disposal and asked herself what her wily, ruthless husband would do in this scenario. She knew the answer: Whatever necessary.

If only he had made some noise when he had arrived.

Then she could have screamed to warn him, but she realized he had come only once the shouting started. They already had him.

Silently, silently, she crept out of her hiding place and readied herself as quickly as possible for her own brash suicide mission. Her heart raced. Her hands shook madly, and she prayed she didn't get both of them killed.

As she edged down the hall and picked her way silently down the stairs, she could hear Darius mocking them and taunting them as they did whatever it was they were doing to him.

Their voices were coming from the library. She couldn't understand a word of the argument, which was taking place all in Russian, but she knew that insolent tone. It told her that his back was to the wall.

I'm coming, she told him silently.

Darius.

His head throbbed, his jaw hurt, and the world had gone a bit dizzy, so maybe that explained the sweet, tickling whisper he could have sworn he heard in his head. Her voice.

My Darius, I am here with you.

The illusion was comforting as he scowled up at the two biggest Russians he had ever seen in his life, the general's handpicked blond giants. He was almost cocky enough to be insulted that Tyurinov had brought only two, except there was no avoiding the fact that he was the one tied to the chair.

Tyurinov was looming over him, his blue eyes locked frigidly on him. "So, Santiago, you thought I'd let you get away with making a fool of me before the entire world. And now I find out you have been writing to my cousin about me." The general merely jerked a nod toward him and stepped back.

One of the giants went to work again. Darius gritted his teeth against the urge to cry out. He assured himself the pain involved with breathing suddenly and the blood trickling from his nostril and the corner of his mouth were nothing serious. Waiting for this round to end, he glared straight ahead, past the giant's bulging thighs, ignoring the blows by dint of will, and it was then that his second beatific vision that day appeared in the doorway.

When he saw her, he ceased feeling pain. *Ahhh.* His whole body sank in the chair as in relief, as if she had come to put her arms around him softly and make these mean fellows go away. It was a good thing she was just a hallucination, born of a few bad blows to the head.

Angel.

He smiled at her a little, pleased and a trifle shocked at the form in which his goddess had chosen to manifest herself tonight for his private vision. If today on the stairs she had appeared to him as an innocent angel of light, this was the Serafina he had only dared imagine when he was very hot and bothered late at night.

She had on a gauzy and quite indecent peignoir of deep scarlet. It had long, flowing, ruffled sleeves and a very low neckline revealing her creamy white chest. Her wild, black, spiraling curls flowed about her shoulders and a wineglass dangled from her hand.

In all her erotic splendor, this luscious figment of his dirty mind was a siren, a wicked temptress—the tigress he had unleashed during their final, incredible encounter this afternoon.

He watched her lean her curvy body languidly in the doorway, striking a pose.

"Ahem," she said in a voice that was surprisingly real.

All three Russians turned.

"What are you doing in my house?" she asked coolly with a haughty little lift of her elegant black brows. Her fingertips began to play at her neckline, teasing along the lace.

"Oh, my God," Darius said.

One of the giants stuttered. Anatole's eyes widened.

Radiating pure bitchery, which he could only guess she had learned from a lifetime of studying the palace ladies, she glided into action before any of them, stupid males, could react.

She was lethal.

Her walk was honeyed treachery as she flowed toward him, red silk swirling dreamily around her long legs, her pale face fixed in a marble mask of cold beauty. "I see you've found my philandering husband."

Darius stared at her in horror as she effortlessly nudged the giants aside as easily as if they were big, stupid plowhorses. She held the medal of the Virgin up before his eyes and swung it back and forth like a little pendulum.

"Where did this come from, hmm? No, don't bother to explain. I am sick of your lies."

With a mocking curve of her lips, she slipped the chain over his head, her hand touching the back of his hair with a stolen caress to reassure him. When she moved back, he stared into her eyes in bewildered pleading. *Get out of here! Are you trying to kill yourself?*

Tyurinov slowly began to laugh.

He's not falling for this, Darius tried to tell her with his hopeless stare. But he saw that her game had barely begun.

The giants were staring mutely at his wife while she turned to Tyurinov, folding her arms under her breasts, brazenly plumping them for his avid inspection.

"What are you going to do with him?" she asked in a bored tone.

"What game are you playing, my dear?" the prince growled through his difficult accent, his eyes blazing with undisguised lust. He took a step toward her.

"Well, he has served his purpose for me, hasn't he?"

"Has he? You tell me."

She pouted. "Oh, you are still cross with me." She reached out and hooked a fingertip through the buttonhole on his blue coat's lapel. "Anatole, we parted so bitterly. I really think we ought to talk."

Darius turned white. "Serafina." He did not want her going off alone with this brute.

"Oh, shut up," she snapped at him, taking him aback.

"They're going to kill you, and as far as I'm concerned, you deserve it." She looked back up at Tyurinov again with cool, calculated charm. "Husbands can be so tedious. Widowhood will be much more my style."

"Married under a fortnight and already you are tired of him?" Tyurinov asked, searching her face closely.

"This vainglorious schemer?" She glanced at Darius, but she avoided his eyes, as if she could not bear to meet his gaze. "A lover, maybe. But a husband? He tricked me. I never wanted to marry him. I enticed him into attempting to kill Napoleon—which he failed to do," she said, rolling her eyes. "But he lied about having failed, you see, and claimed his reward under false pretenses."

"Why did you not wish to marry me?" he demanded.

"Anatole, Anatole, my dear." She petted his chest soothingly, tilting her head back to meet his stare. "It's not that I didn't want to marry you. It's that I didn't want to marry— period. I relish my freedom. Surely you know how it is to be worshiped by many. Was I really to choose just one? My reasoning, simply, was that if I *must* marry then I shall have a husband weak enough of character to be someone I could control. You did not strike me as such a man."

This seemed to mollify him slightly. "Indeed, I am not."

"Santiago, on the other hand"—she glanced over at him— "why, he'd put his hand in a fire if I asked him to."

"How long has he been your lover?"

"Oh, we've always shared a certain . . . physical attraction," she admitted, "but ever since he tricked me, I have refused to give him what he wants. So, do you know what he does?" she demanded prettily. "He goes off sulking, scurrying into the arms of other women, yet he has a fit if I take an interest in another man," she neatly lied. "I ask you, Anatole, do I look like someone who need tolerate a man who does not appreciate me?" She ran her hands down her sides, artfully putting her curves on display.

Tyurinov's stare followed the route of her hands. He couldn't take his eyes off her and Darius was growing very worried indeed. She was certainly playing her part to the hilt.

"Has he been leaving you alone at nights already?" the general rumbled, practically drooling.

"Too many nights," she purred.

"Well. That is inexcusable."

Darius wanted to kill him for the way he was looking at her, but he bit his tongue, terrified to say a word because he might only make things worse somehow. There was a sliver-thin chance that the devious chit knew what she was doing. God knew, she had *him* half-convinced. By the look of it, she could have been standing there telling the Russians the moon was made of green cheese and they would nod agreement, too busy gawking at her celebrated breasts.

He cast about in a fury of frustration trying to find some means to free himself, but as his wife sidled up close to Tyurinov and began toying with one of his gold epaulets, Darius decided, eyes blazing, that his wayward little Cricket was long, long overdue for a lecture.

When she spoke, he grew uneasy. This *was* a charade, wasn't it?

"Anatole," she said sweetly, "can't your men finish up with my husband? I want to talk to you. Alone."

"You are treacherous," he panted at her.

She gave him a cool, narrow smile. "Do I frighten you?"

He laughed softly, eyes sparkling at the challenge, and sliced a nod to his men. "Kill him."

"Wait." She swayed over to Darius and draped her arms loosely around his shoulders, thrusting her breasts just under his face.

Lord, but her gown was low-cut.

"I told you you'd get what's coming to you, you wicked rake."

He stared at her in disbelief and bewilderment. *You're leaving me here?* She leaned toward him and gave him a soft kiss on the side of his mouth that wasn't bleeding, then her slow, soft kisses moved toward his neck in teasing seduction. He was stunned when she actually got a shiver out of him, though his whole body hurt.

She let the men watch as she nudged closer between his spread legs and embraced him more tightly. Furiously, he glared at the men standing behind her, for their gazes were fixed on her rounded backside as she bent over.

Serafina went on kissing him a moment longer, running her hands down his arms, which were tied behind him to the chair. Her caress stopped when she came to the ropes binding his hands.

Suddenly he felt an odd little jerk of his wrists.

He nearly choked on her kiss when his hands dropped, suddenly freed. He reacted immediately, holding his arms in position behind him so the men would not realize what she had done.

Unseen by them, she pressed a smooth, small cylindrical object into his hand. He knew at once it was the hilt of a small knife. He realized she had concealed it under her gown's long sleeve. His fingers closed around the hilt.

He didn't move a muscle as she released him with a smug, haughty little smile, her eyes locked on his.

"Goodbye, husband," she said nonchalantly as sparks flew between their stares.

"You heartless hussy," he ground out, but it was all he could do to make his tone harsh, as joy and sheer devotion for the magnificent, brazen creature blasted up from the core of his being, filling him with a last reserve of strength.

It all came clear to him, the significance of her little performance. He stared at her, feeling as though a veil were lifting from before his very eyes.

He thought of a little girl a long time ago, kicking and screaming when they tried to pull her away from his bedside as he lay there fighting for his life.

Loyalty. Absolute loyalty.

For him.

That was love, and she had just spoken it loud and clear in a language he could understand.

"I'll think of you and your philandering when I spend your fortune."

"You do that," he drawled, eyeing her up.

She brushed by Tyurinov, whose sapphire stare followed her hotly. "Come along, Anatole."

But then Darius's blood ran cold.

Tyurinov's hand clamped down on her shoulder. He spun her around. Darius only caught a glimpse of her terrified face as Tyurinov shoved her toward the wall.

"Right here, you sweet, hot-blooded little thing," he said as he pinned her against the wall with his body. "Your husband will enjoy the show."

The two blond giants started laughing.

"Do you have a good view, Spaniard?" Tyurinov asked as he reached for the falls of his breeches. "Let me show you how it's done. When I and my men are done with her, there'll be nothing left for you."

Darius bit back a curse.

The two blond giants glanced at each other in amazement. The one on his right had been using only his fists, but the one on his left was wielding a club. Heart pounding, Darius flicked his fingers over the knife's hilt behind his back, readying himself to spring.

Serafina stared up at Anatole, terrified, as she reeled back against the wall. Her ex-fiancé held her by the shoulders. Without warning, his mouth slammed down on hers, cold and dry.

Wild-eyed, she punched him and shoved against the solid wall of his chest, but he only laughed and answered her blows with a cruel squeeze of her breast.

She tried to knee him in the groin but he knocked her off balance when she raised her leg, using the maneuver to drive her legs apart with his knee. She had to grab his waist to keep from falling.

He reached down with one hand, exposing himself with lightning speed, then tearing her gown upward over her thigh. She heard hysterical noises coming from her lips, but all her struggle was useless. He was gigantic and he had absolutely no shame, no feeling, no remorse. He bent his knees, lowering himself as he prepared to penetrate her. She clawed his face.

He slapped her. "Be still and take it."

Gasping in shock, she stared up at him, her face stinging. She couldn't believe he had hit her. Suddenly there was a bloodcurdling scream and an explosive shout behind him from the direction where Darius sat.

Eyes glazed with lust, Tyurinov turned, panting. With his movement, her hand bumped something hard strapped over his hip. Her searching fingers found leather, metal, and wood.

A gun.

Before she even knew what she was doing, she slid Tyurinov's pistol out of its holster and pressed the muzzle to his exposed throat.

He froze.

She felt his erection wilt against her.

"Step back," she said, her voice shaking, chest heaving with fright.

He obeyed.

"Put that away," she added in disgust.

As he hastily fastened his breeches again, she glanced over and saw Darius, locked in mortal combat with one of Anatole's men. The other was dead, his throat a torn red mass.

With one hand, the blond giant was trying to strangle Darius. With the other hand, he held Darius's right wrist. Darius's arm shook with his effort to bring his bloody knife up to the big Russian's throat.

Anatole took a step toward them.

"Don't move," she said in a steely tone, the gun outstretched in both her shaking hands.

He gave her a cold, cruel smile. "Lower the gun. You don't even know how to use it."

"I'll figure it out." Her finger came to rest on the trigger.

He took a tentative step backward.

She stepped forward, the gun steady in her double-handed grasp.

His gaze roamed over her as he laughed softly. "You're not going to shoot anyone."

She swallowed hard, wondering if he had called her bluff, for she did not think she could pull the trigger. She could not possibly kill someone, not even him.

But she wouldn't have to, she assured herself as sweat began to gather on her brow. Any second now, Darius would fight his way free and finish this.

She flicked a glance in his direction just as the Russian dealt him a shattering blow to the knee with his club. Darius cried out furiously but as the Russian lunged forward, Darius thrust the knife up into the man's belly. The Russian toppled partly on him with a high-pitched squeal that became a bellow, then lay there gasping with almost black blood pouring out of his lower abdomen.

Serafina swallowed hard in revulsion.

Anatole showed no reaction to his men's deaths.

The gun wobbling slightly in her tense grasp, her gaze darted from Anatole to Darius. Her husband was on the floor, his face ashen in a grimace of pain. He glared at Anatole from under his forelock.

Anatole turned his back on her and took a step toward him. When Darius did not get up, she realized he couldn't.

A chill raced down her spine. "Darius."

He said nothing. He shoved the now-unconscious Russian off him and crawled onto all fours, favoring his right leg. He knelt on his left knee and labored to rise.

Anatole bent and punched him in the face, sending him sprawling back over the dying man. Darius cursed and struggled to get up again.

Anatole laughed and took another step toward him, sneering down at him. "Get up again, pretty boy. I like knocking you down."

"Anatole," Serafina said. A bead of sweat rolled down her cheek. She aimed for his back. "If you touch him again, I will shoot you."

Rounding the body of the other dead man, Anatole glanced arrogantly at her over his shoulder, then came to stand across from her, towering over Darius. "No, you won't." Without warning, he drew back to kick Darius.

Darius curled his body to ward off the blow and she pulled the trigger.

Anatole gasped, jolting back a step as his blood spattered in an arc, dusting Darius and the dead body. Everything seemed to move slowly. She saw Darius turn away from the sprinkling of blood. Tyurinov dropped to his knees, clutching his chest. He looked down, then lifted his head and stared at her in shock. Blood flowed through his fingers, which were pressed to his chest.

She dropped the gun and stared, riveted, as blood surged up out of his mouth.

His eyes grew dim. He fell onto his face, crawled onto his side, and lay there, his blue eyes wide. Several times he gasped for air with a choking sound, then the choking stopped and he did not stir.

Darius and she stared at each other in silence.

CHAPTER
❧ TWENTY-FIVE ❧

"Help me," he croaked as she ran to him.

She crouched down beside him, her heart pounding.

"I think my knee is broken," he forced out.

"Can you stand?"

He nodded, his face very pale. She helped him to his feet with difficulty. He couldn't bend his right leg. She pulled his right arm over her shoulders and bade him lean on her. For once, he did not argue. Slowly, painfully, they crossed the room.

"Can you get up the stairs?"

He nodded grimly, his jaw taut, his lips white. Steadying himself between her and the banister, Darius pulled himself up each step, putting no weight on his right foot. She kept glancing anxiously at him, frightened by the sight of him in such pain. Sweat beaded his face. His breathing was shallow and he was shaking.

"Almost there," she coaxed him softly.

He said nothing, his fingers digging into her shoulder as he gripped her tightly.

It seemed like an hour had passed by the time they reached the top of the stairs and progressed slowly down the hall, hobbling into the pink bedroom. Finally, Darius sat down on the bed, his heavy arm sliding off her shoulders.

He clenched his jaw, bracing himself for the pain as he swung his right leg up onto the bed. Gingerly, she helped him.

Lying on his back at last, he was panting with pain and exertion. "Thanks."

She was already lighting a candle and pulling out the sewing basket in which she kept all her doctoring supplies. Every time the image of Anatole looking down at his wounded chest occurred to her, she thrust it away—far, far away.

The first thing she did was cut off his breeches above the knee, gingerly pulling back the broadcloth. She paled, looking down to find his knee swollen up to the size of a grapefruit. The blow had not burst the skin, but the entire area was red and discolored.

She looked at Darius and found him staring at her, his eyes large and anxious under his long lashes.

"Is it broken?"

"It could be, but let's hope it's just a bad contusion," she said. "We won't know for a couple days until the swelling goes down. Oh, how I wish we had some ice." She moved toward the head of the bed, adjusting the pillow behind him. She wet one of the washcloths and gently wiped the dried blood from his split lip.

"My poor baby, look at you," she murmured. He stared at her while she wiped his face with the cool, wet cloth. She caressed his hair and leaned down to kiss his clammy forehead, drawing strength and calm from the contact. He embraced her suddenly, pulling her to him. She hugged him with all her might. He buried his fingers in her hair.

"Are you all right?" he whispered. "God, that was the most awful thing I've ever seen. He hit your precious face—"

"I'm all right, Darius. He didn't hit me that hard. Besides, it helps to know he got what he deserved," she added grimly. "What about you? Are you all right?"

"I am now." His arms tightened around her. "Never leave me, Serafina. Never leave me."

"I never will. I was never going to." She squeezed tears from her eyes. "We're going to be all right, yes? We have the rest of our lives. Say we do."

He caressed her hair, desperation in his onyx eyes that mirrored her own. "Yes, yes, we have forever, please."

"Yes," She closed her eyes and kissed his cheek. "I love you, Darius. You *must* know by now that I do!"

"Yes," he whispered. "I know it, and I love you, too. God, I thought I'd lost you."

"Never." She pulled back and laid her hand on his cheek very gently. "Now I've got to go pump some cold water from the well." She was not looking forward to going downstairs near the dead bodies, but she could make herself do it for him. "We're going to put cold compresses on your knee, then wrap it with some good, firm bandages so it can't swell any further. You're going to be all right. I promise. Do you want some whiskey?"

He shook his head sternly, then apparently thought better of it. "Please," he said sheepishly. "This hurts like hell."

"See, now, was that so hard to admit?" she asked as she poured a shot for each of them.

They lifted their glasses to each other, then downed the shots. They glanced at each other, both wincing, eyes watering. He gave her back the small, empty glass with a look of disdain.

She smiled in spite of herself, shaking her head at him. "I adore you, Santiago."

He was staring at her strangely. "You are a wild woman, Serafina."

She shot him a demure smile. "Well, I have to be, with such a man for a husband, don't I?"

"Nice shooting for a hothouse flower."

She gave him a mock scowl. Just then, she heard distant hoofbeats and male laughter. Instantly she tensed, fearing that more of Tyurinov's men had come. She flew to the window and moved the curtain back slightly, peering out.

"It's Alec and the rest of your men!" she exclaimed. "Thank God!" She whirled from the window and sped toward the door. "You just lie still and try to relax, Darius. I'll go get the cold water and send Alec for the constable and the doctor to examine you. I'll take care of everything—"

"Serafina."

She stopped, her hand on the doorknob, and turned back to him in brisk inquiry.

His face was still pale, but he looked a bit more himself as he arched one brow at her. "Do not leave this room until you change that dress."

A grin spread over her face as she blushed bright red.

He suddenly smiled beautifully and held out his arms to her. "Come back here, you rascal."

Joyously, she ran to him.

He pulled her onto the bed, flipped her over his hip onto the mattress, and turned on his side, kissing her whole face. "I love you, I love you, I love you!" he said between kisses.

She laughed, basking breathlessly in his playfulness. When he stopped and went still, gazing down at her, she slid her arms around his neck and held his tender stare.

"I love you," she whispered. "There's no part of you I don't love. Remember that."

He nodded. "I will. I still can't believe you risked yourself like that for me."

"Why not? You do it for me all the time."

He looked mystified. "You stayed for me. You walked into that room for me when you could have—*should have*—looked after your own safety. I feel . . ." He shook his head.

"What do you feel?" she asked softly, gazing at him.

"Like my life has just begun." He closed his eyes for a moment. "I am done hiding from you, Serafina. I've been so scared and behaved like such a bastard. But you've been so patient with me."

"You're worth it, Darius."

He opened his eyes again, misted, and could say nothing more.

She leaned up and kissed his lips, lingering gently and breathing her warm breath over the crescent-moon scar on his mouth.

As she ended the kiss and rested her head back on the bed again, he gave her a shy, little-boy smile.

They were silent, savoring each other. She sifted his silky black hair through her fingers, then petted it back from his eyes and noticed he was studying her strangely. He tilted his head.

"Will you marry me?" he asked suddenly.

"What?" she cried, lifting both eyebrows in surprise.

"I never got to ask you," he murmured with a tiny, nonchalant shrug.

She feigned grave deliberation. "Well, heavens, Santiago, I don't know. It's a big step. Do you think you're ready?"

"I'm ready," he whispered, eyes shining under his long lashes.

She laughed and hugged him. "Finally!" she exclaimed. "I've been waiting for you to ask me since I was four years old!"

"Then it seems I have a lot of catching up to do."

"Mm-hmm," she said heartily. Laughing, she pulled him down to kiss her.

❧ EPILOGUE ❧

October 27, 1805

"Oh, Serafina, it's beautiful!" Els cried, following her through the first floor of the yellow villa. "No wonder we never see you at court anymore. You've made a little paradise here!"

Serafina grinned and brushed a curl behind her ear, beckoning her best friend into the dining room. "Look at the fresco." She pointed at the ceiling, where the rich colors of the Baroque painting had been carefully restored. Mars and Venus were caught in their golden net and looked not a whit sorry for it.

Els laughed, marveling. "Reminds me of a couple I know."

Serafina chuckled. "Come, I'll show you the morning room. It gets such wonderful light that I have half a citrus orchard growing in there."

The completion of the repairs and remodeling of the house had coincided with the end of the threat of war that had hung over the kingdom for five months. On this day, Serafina and Darius were playing host to the harvest party celebrating the occasion.

A week ago, as Ascencion was bringing in the year's grapes, Admiral Horatio Nelson had lost his life but defeated Villeneuve and crushed the Franco-Spanish navy at Trafalgar.

Now Napoleon no longer had the means to invade Ascencion, let alone England. His threat of invasion was permanently foiled.

Showing Els the library, Serafina's private, sickening memories of Tyurinov and his pair of brutes were finally beginning to fade.

The room looked very different now. It had been thoroughly remodeled, brightened with fresh, creamy paint. New, lighter-toned rugs had replaced those that had been ruined by bloodshed. In spite of the death of so prominent a man, the inquest into the events of that night had been cut short by the intervention of Czar Alexander.

Commending Serafina for her bravery, the young ruler had written to thank Darius for information that had led to the discovery in Moscow of evidence confirming Tyurinov's murder of his first wife. By Tyurinov's having met his end on Ascencion, it was easier for Czar Alexander to sweep the details of his crimes under the carpet.

When they received the czar's letter, Darius had explained to her what was written between the lines. Had Tyurinov lived, his criminal trial would have caused a terrific scandal for the czar personally, as his cousin. It also would have polarized Tyurinov's supporters in the army and among the conservative nobles against his administration.

As far as Princess Margaret's family was concerned, the czar wrote that he condoled with them personally and explained the true facts of her death. Now that Anatole was dead, they felt a small sense of justice knowing their daughter had been avenged.

Els brought her out of her thoughts. "I love the color." She smiled as she took a turn about the room.

As the redhead cooed over the Greek antiquities placed tastefully here and there, Serafina's gaze came to rest on the desk. Darius's spectacles sat atop the thick ledger for his ship-and-trade firm.

Though he still acted as special diplomatic counselor to the Office of Foreign Affairs, the role of the prosperous merchant prince was as dangerous a lifework as he cared to undertake these days. She thanked God for it. He had worked hard enough for his adopted country and able, new men were stepping forward for the dangerous assignments. She liked to tease him that the world had not come to an end without his managing it, after all.

The two women continued their tour up the stairs.

Els turned to her. "What do you think of Alec?"

Serafina hid her smile. "Oh, he's very sweet. Very dependable. A good man."

"Straitlaced, though, and he's awfully tame," Els replied cautiously, knitting her brow.

"Maybe he needs someone to spice up his life."

Els snorted but blushed. Serafina chuckled and showed her the various rooms, until at last they came to the pink bedroom.

"Ah, the love nest."

"Els!" Now it was Serafina's turn to blush.

Els sighed. "You're so lucky. Such a life. Such a husband. Such a house."

"I know it," she murmured, folding her arms under her bosom as Els walked over to the window to inspect the view.

Serafina looked down to find her bare toes on the edge of the tapestry rug. She gazed down at the softly faded colors depicting the youths and maidens dancing around the maypole, with the world brightly flowering around them.

"Your poor brother," Els sighed as she stood looking down on the gathering below. She shook her head as Serafina joined her. "Look at him. He is not the same anymore."

Under the crisp, azure sky, the sunlit fields rolled out in every direction as far as the eye could see. Nearer, the golden fall day embraced the villa and all her guests, seated variously around the pleasingly landscaped back garden. Mama was presiding at the center with her sleeping infant, Prince Lorenzo, in her arms. Pia was sitting next to her, ready to offer aid and beaming down at the baby. By the garden wall, Papa was bending down to examine the late-blooming red roses.

But Rafe sat apart from everyone, sprawled in a chair, his

handsome chin propped on his fist as he stared restlessly at the horizon.

Serafina shook her head in concern. She felt sorry for him. "We heard Julia Calazzi has been seen in Rome," she confided. "It appears she has attached herself to Pauline Bonaparte."

"No!" Els gasped.

She nodded, turning away from the window to go sit on the bed. "Birds of a feather, don't you think? Julia could be captured easily enough, but Rafael won't allow her to be prosecuted. He told Darius all he wants is to go to her and ask her why."

Els shook her head sadly and continued gazing at the prince.

The gleeful clamor of children's shouting voices suddenly floated to them from a distance. Serafina smiled knowingly to herself at the sound. *He's late*.

"That cannot be your husband . . . oh, my Lord," Els said, staring, "I don't believe my eyes."

Smiling, Serafina walked back toward her. "Ah, yes, the Pied Piper." She joined Els at the window and laughed with sheer happiness at what she saw.

Kite ribbons trailing, the great Santiago and his entourage came trudging back toward the house through the sunlit fields.

Els turned and gaped at her. "Your husband is covered in children!"

"They're the local peasant children. They come to see him nearly every day." Children swung from his arms, skipped around him, and craned their necks to gauge his every smile and glance, all talking at once. Darius did not look particularly annoyed. When they came nearer, he pointed to the table laden with food. En masse, they ran for it like a tribe of wild heathens, ignoring the royal personages present.

Els stared, openmouthed.

Darius set the kites on the grass at the edge of the garden, then went and shook hands with her father. The two tall, dark men stood there in conversation for a few minutes.

Having helped themselves to the food on the table, the children promptly ran back to Darius, popping cookies in their mouths, wielding chicken drumsticks like tiny clubs. They tackled him until he gave in, laughing, and let himself be thrown onto the grass, then they piled on him.

"I am in shock," Els said.

"He is spoiling every single one of them," Serafina replied archly. "He used the scraps of wood the carpenters left and built them a playhouse. He reads to them. Arbitrates their quarrels. Now he is talking of buying a pony so he can teach them all how to ride."

"You sound jealous," Els laughed.

"No," she said softly. "They are my accomplices. They are helping me drown him in love."

Below, the children had relented and let Darius sit up. Presently, they all watched, spellbound, as he used his Gypsy magic to pull a shiny gold coin out of one little boy's ear.

He brandished the coin and grinned. They screeched and piled on him again.

Els shook her head in astonishment. "I'd say you had better give that man a baby."

"Actually . . ." Serafina began to blush.

Els turned to her in question, staring at her, her green eyes flying open wide. "Cricket!"

Serafina smiled shyly, turning bright pink.

Els threw her arms around her. "Oh, I am so happy for you!"

Serafina returned her hug, laughing with tears in her eyes, then she drew back and held both her friend's hands, giving them a squeeze. "I just found out myself. I can't wait to tell him."

"He doesn't know yet?"

"I was going to wait till tonight after everyone had gone—"

"No, no! You must tell him now, then you can share your happiness with all the people who love you both," Els said, her voice choking up with emotion. She quickly banished the tear that rose in her eye.

"Hmm," Serafina mused. "Maybe you're right."

"Of course I am! Come, now. You go tell him your wonderful tidings. I'm going to get something to eat before those little heathens devour it all."

Arm in arm, they returned to the gathering below. Els shot her a look of encouragement, then drifted over to try and coax a smile out of Rafe. She saw her brother lift his gaze to Els, but Serafina walked past them toward the onyx-eyed magician ringed by children on the grass.

"Uh-oh, everyone, here comes the fairy queen," Darius said to his captivated audience, his gaze holding hers with the shadow of a mischievous smile. "You must be on your best behavior. If you're very good, she'll make your wish come true. She did mine."

"And if you're bad, I will turn you all into toads," she finished, standing over them, hands on hips, as they screeched and laughed uproariously at this threat.

"I want to be a toad!" one yelled.

Serafina spread her hands over them. "Abracadabra, abracadoo, you are all toads!"

"I'm a toad, I'm a toad!" they cried. They began playing leapfrog.

Darius glanced at the leapfrogging children, then arched a brow at her from under his forelock. "Not bad."

"It is the least of my powers." She smiled. "Come with me," she said softly, "I have something to tell you."

He jumped up off the grass and took her hand. They walked close together as she led him under the grape trellis a short distance away. In its green, leafy shadows, he drew her into his arms and gazed down at her, then lowered his head and kissed her softly.

She caressed his clean-shaven face, parting her lips to taste him.

Desire leaped between them. He pulled back from the kiss with a shivery little sigh that silently expressed his regret for the inconvenience of company present. He stroked her hair and they stood holding each other.

"What is it you wanted to tell me, beauty?" he murmured after a moment, nuzzling her cheek.

She felt a twinge of anxiety, but when she lifted her gaze and looked into his dark, velvety eyes, glowing with warmth and kindness, her fear dissolved.

"The first thing is that I love you, Darius."

"And I love you." His smile widened. "What's the second thing?"

"Well . . ." Sliding her arms around his neck, she pulled him down and whispered in his ear.

All the guests looked over, when, from under the grape trellis, came the sound of deep, rolling, wonderful laughter. The curious children crept in to investigate, and a few minutes later, the children herded them back out to the party, arm in arm, Serafina blushing, Darius beaming with a grin of exhilaration.

"What are you two scoundrels up to now?" Rafael drawled at them from his chair on the lawn.

Darius held out one arm, turning toward them all. "My family," he said, unable to contain his smile, "we have an announcement. . . ."

The celebration had just begun.

❧ HISTORICAL NOTE ☙

On July 31, 1798, Horatio Nelson burned the French fleet in the Bay of Abukir. As a consequence, Napoleon was never able to catch up to British sea power. The lack of a strong fleet posed a continual problem for Napoleon, marking a limit to how far he could extend his power, no matter how victorious his armies were on land.

It seemed an easy enough stretch to imagine for this story's purposes that Napoleon would seek to ally himself with any country that had a strong navy, especially a country neighboring his native Corsica. Those of you who have read *The Pirate Prince* may remember how King Lazar of Ascencion came into power with an excellent navy already under his command!

Another aspect of extrapolating this plot from historical facts was that Napoleon's life was constantly being threatened. My research revealed he even employed body doubles in order to confuse those who wanted him dead. The threat of assassination was an annoying problem for him, but it was the Great Conspiracy that made him really angry. A lone gunman here and there was one matter, but this handful of would-be assassins, he discovered, had been sponsored financially by the British government. Napoleon was so outraged, he vowed to invade England and bring it to its knees. However, his lack of a strong fleet continued to pose a problem. My sources revealed he even considered using hot-air balloons to transport his troops across the English Channel! Instead, he muscled

Spain into an alliance and took control of what remained of the once Great Armada. But before he dared launch his invasion, he needed to get rid of his old nemesis, the indomitable Nelson.

Meanwhile, William Pitt was orchestrating the Third Coalition, an alliance of countries uniting to stand against Napoleon, including England, Russia, Austria, and Naples.

Two other pertinent historical facts I used to tie into this story were the mysterious circumstances behind Czar Alexander's succession to the throne after his mad father's murder, and Napoleon's ambition to wed his siblings as well as his stepson to authentic royalty in order to legitimize his growing empire. Eugène Beauharnais, incidentally, ended up marrying a Bavarian princess in 1806. In fact, after Napoleon received the Iron Crown of Lombardy in Milan (there was no assassination attempt there, by the way—pure fiction) he returned to Paris, leaving Eugène in charge as viceroy, though he was barely twenty-five. Eugène is still remembered in Lombardy as an enlightened and benevolent ruler.

Perhaps I owe Princess Pauline Bonaparte Borghese a bit of an apology, but after studying her and learning how she relished her reputation as a femme fatale, I can't help but think she'd have gotten a kick out of her role as Darius's unwitting rescuer.

As for Ascencion itself, you won't find it on any map—it is strictly a kingdom of the imagination. However, I based its topography, climate, and many aspects of its folkways on a blend of those of Corsica and Sicily.

Finally, I learned from the letters of the poet Percy Shelley that the two favored suicide poisons of the day were prussic acid and essential oil of bitter almonds. However, both of these are liquids, and for plot purposes, I needed to equip Darius with a powder. Thus I used arsenic, though this compound did not really become the poison of choice until a decade or so later. I hope the reader will forgive this and other liberties I have taken with history, keeping in mind that in works of the imagination, all else is secondary to the story. At least that's my opinion!

Thank you for visiting the mythical kingdom of Ascencion with me. I hope you will return again when the royal rogue Prince Rafael, disowned by King Lazar for his rakehell ways, seizes one last chance to prove himself worthy of the crown in King Lazar's absence.

Naturally, the moment he comes to power, all hell breaks loose on Ascencion.

The power-mongering courtiers challenge him, the people still think him a rake and resist his authority, and a drought jeopardizes the island's crops. But when a mysterious Robin Hood figure begins leading raids on royal carriages, his head-aches have just begun. Because to the defiant and impover-ished young Lady Daniela Chiaramonte, Rafael di Fiore is anything but *Prince Charming*.

See you there!

Best wishes,

Gaelen

Gaelen

If you loved

PRINCESS
by Gaelen Foley

Turn the page for a sneak peek
of her next exciting historical romance!

PRINCE CHARMING

Coming in Spring 2000

CHAPTER
❧ ONE ❧

Ascencion, 1816

There was a stretch of the King's Road, up from the port, where the moonlight seemed to dim, where a coach's blazing lanterns seemed to shrink down to flickering rushlights in the swallowing gloom. Here, even veteran coachmen felt their knees turn to jelly and were wise to whip their teams faster and reach for their guns.

As the heavy-wheeled wagon rolled slowly toward that cursed bend, the grizzled old farmer slapped the reins halfheartedly over Ned's swayed back, but the old draft horse could go no faster, especially not uphill. The docile beast plodded along, his huge, long-feathered hoofs sinking deeply into the clouding, red dust.

The farmer glanced warily up at the high, wooded embankments, but it was too dark to see much. The silence was eerie. Scowling at his own flighty nerves, he reminded himself that the Masked Rider did not attack poor, simple folk like him. No, indeed, the Masked Rider preyed only on the rich, useless aristocrats and their wild, rakehell sons, the type who snapped their fine fingers at right and wrong and ran headlong into whatever wickedness took their fancy.

A man couldn't let his maiden daughter out of his sight these days, the old farmer thought gruffly. He looked up quickly at some noise overhead, but it was only the hot, dry breeze like a dragon's breath, rattling the parched leaves.

This damned drought. He thought of his shriveled crops and shook his head bitterly. Ever since Good King Lazar fell ill, 'twas as if a sickness lay over all the land. Yes, he thought, the world was unraveling.

As his wagon moved deeper into the wide curve, the farmer felt eyes upon him from the woods. By the Baptist's head, if the Masked Rider was real, he would catch a glimpse of the bold lad for himself. That would be something to brag about tomorrow at the *taverna*!

Bravely, he lifted his feeble lantern and peered into the woods. He held his breath at the sight of shadowy, black figures among the trees.

One mounted figure slowly lifted a black-clad arm in silent salute. Petrified, the farmer only nodded, his heart in his throat, but when his wagon came out safely on the other side, he laughed aloud in amazement, and the sparkling stars guided him home.

Two hours later, the next traveler on the King's Road wasn't so fortunate.

"Looks promising," Mateo whispered, even as the boy signalled the owl's call from the distance.

The Masked Rider nodded and gestured the others into position.

Through the moonlight streaked a team of six smart, matched bays, their galloping strides eating up the ground, pulling a well-sprung coach of gleaming black and mahogany.

Down on the road, the liveried coachman laid his whip over the team's backs and slid his pistol out of his coat, his face sweaty and pale under his top hat. *There's no such thing as the Masked Rider. No silly Robin Hood! It's just another peasant tale—yes, that's it.* The driver's gaze skimmed nervously over the embankments.

Perhaps he should have said something to his passenger, he thought, warned him of the possible danger. Only, the man in the coach scared him worse than the shadowy Masked Rider.

A bead of sweat ran down the driver's face as the coach continued hurtling up the road.

Dead ahead lay that cursed bend.

Inside the coach, the disgraced prince sat in granite stillness, arms folded over his massive chest. Only his immense silhouette was visible in the coach's gloom, but the aura of authority around him was palpable, eloquent in the expansive planes of his shoulders and his hard-lined jaw, edged with the faintest flicker of starlight. As he brooded in silence, the space of the coach seemed full to brimming with his leashed, long-nursed anger and cunning, implacable will.

On this, the greatest night of his life, Prince Rafael di Fiore was carefully biding his time. Deep in his thoughts, his harsh gaze fell dead ahead and in his stillness, he was as dangerous as a rogue lion in the shadows, idly flicking its tail, silent, keenly watching.

Just then, the coach hit a rut in the road and bounced violently on its springs. Rafael narrowed his eyes in pain, registering the jolt in his bruised ribs, still sore after the attempt on his life several nights ago in Venice.

He drew breath to yell an imperious rebuke at the driver to have a care, when suddenly he heard shouts outside. A horse whinnied frantically and the coach began to slow. A gunshot ripped through the night.

His gold-green eyes narrowed in the gloom. Instantly alert, he crept forward, smoothly reaching for his pistol. He stole a glance from behind the window's pulled shade and stared, rather amazed.

Highwaymen? On Ascencion? Fury flooded him as he stared, incredulous. *So, the reports were indeed true.* Corruption flourishing in the ranks of government, crime on the rise—all signs of the king's disability. Eyes glinting with anger, he cocked his gun, angry to think that every cutthroat, robber, schemer, scoundrel, and thief had crawled out of the woodwork to take advantage of his father's weakness.

Could there be any doubt, any better proof than this, that

Ascencion needed his strength and vigor, his leadership? he thought. He checked his fob-watch and saw that his soldiers would not be far behind. He had no doubt whatsoever that he could cut the thieves down one by one, but no. Better to take them alive and hang them publicly.

His people thought he did not care for justice, but ridding Ascencion of these outlaws would not only assure the citizens that in spite of his past, he had come to protect them. It would also send a message—striking fear in the hearts of all criminals on the island, high and low—that they should know and be warned that a new regime had come to power.

Yes, the prince thought darkly. *Make an example of these bastards.*

Meanwhile, on the road, the Masked Rider was shouting at the coachman.

"Halt! Halt!"

Astride a leggy gelding whose true color was obscured by the ashes rubbed into its coat, the Masked Rider urged the horse alongside the galloping team and reached out a black-gauntleted hand for the leader's traces. The coachman was waving a pistol, but the Masked Rider ignored him—such men never used their weapons.

The thought was barely through the Masked Rider's mind when the moving coach's door swung open, a large, male figure leaned out from the inside, and a thunderous crack rent the air with a flash of orange.

The Masked Rider gasped out a cry and jolted forward over the horse's neck.

"Dan!" Mateo shouted.

The gelding veered away from the coach's team with a scream, rearing at the smell of the blood spattered on his sooty coat.

"Turn back! Turn back!" Alvi was shouting at the other highwaymen.

"You're hurt! What should we do?" Mateo bellowed.

"Let's turn back!" Alvi cried.

"Don't you dare! Never mind me! Get the loot!" the Masked Rider roared back at him in boyish tones, fighting the horse.

Then the gelding bolted.

"Stop, whoa! You miserable nag!" A stream of oaths she had never learned in convent school followed from Lady Daniela Chiaramonte's lips as her horse careened through the brake.

All the while her shoulder and arm burned as though she were literally on fire. *He shot me!* she thought, her astonishment equal to her pain. She couldn't believe it. Certainly in all her adventures, she had never been shot before.

She felt hot blood streaming down her right arm as her panicked horse crashed up over the wooded embankment. Heart pounding, she brought the animal under control, reeling him around in small circles.

When at last the horse stood heaving for breath, she suppressed the angry urge to punch the animal for his skittishness, and peered down anxiously at her wounded right arm. It was bleeding and it hurt like hell. She felt light-headed at the horrible sight of her own torn flesh, but when she carefully probed her bleeding arm with her fingers, she concluded in relief that it was only a flesh wound.

"That blackguard shot me," she panted in lingering amazement. Then her gaze zipped back to the road and she saw that the Gabbiano brothers—her men, such as they were—had brought the coach to a standstill and extinguished the carriage lantern, working by moonlight.

The driver was sprawled on his arse on the ground, Alvi holding him at swordpoint.

She scowled indignantly at the coachman's pitiful display, babbling for mercy. Did the man think them common cutthroats? Everyone knew the Masked Rider and company never killed anybody. Oh, occasionally they left some popinjay in an embarrassing predicament, naked and tied to a tree, perhaps, but they rarely drew blood.

Better get down there before we have a sudden change of policy, she thought as she saw Mateo and Rocco closing in on the big, lean passenger who had shot her. True, even from a distance, he looked more than able to fend for himself. Still, Mateo was a fire-eater, while the giant Rocco didn't know his own strength, and both were extremely protective of her. She didn't want anyone getting seriously hurt.

Dani passed her forearm over her brow, then adjusted the black satin mask over her face and hair to make sure her identity was still neatly concealed after her horse's mad dash. Satisfied, she urged her horse about face and back down onto the road, highly curious to see which of the idle, citified peacocks she had snared this time and what it would profit her.

Hopefully, enough to pay the crippling new taxes on her estate and to feed her people, in spite of the drought.

She drew her light, quick rapier as she guided her horse toward the tense trio of men.

Mateo and Rocco stepped aside to admit her, and for a moment, Dani faltered. She was startled by her own hesitation. Her captive was gigantic, with the eyes of a hungry lion and the body of a god, yet he continued standing there tamely, a smirk on his hard, angry lips.

"You all right?" Mateo, her oldest childhood friend, muttered to her.

Distracted by his question, she shook off her momentary awe for the man and quickly found her bravado again, forcing herself forward in a show of fearlessness.

"I'm just ... dandy," she said slowly, urging her horse closer. She stopped when the tip of her rapier floated gracefully under her captive's squared jaw. "Well, what have we here?" she drawled, using the tip of her sword to force him to lift his chin.

It was too dark to see much, but the moonlight picked out silvery-gold threads in his hair, which appeared to be of a tawny shade, quite long, but pulled back in a queue off his broad, straight forehead. Head high, his narrowed eyes glittered, fixed on her, but it was too dark to make out their color.

Even by darkness, there was something instantly familiar about him.

Perhaps she had known him in her other life, before Papa's death, she thought briefly, when she had been that other person—that rich, shy, awkward heiress, always trying to fit in, always trying to conceal her wild, tomboyish ways.

"You shot me," she said in reproach, leaning toward him from the saddle. She knew she mustn't let him see her fear. "Lucky for you, you merely grazed my arm."

"If I had wanted you dead, then dead you would be," he purred in a soft, murderous tone that fell like silk on her skin.

"Ha! Some excuse! You are a poor marksman," she taunted him. "It doesn't even hurt."

"And you, boy, are a poor liar." His voice was deep and rang with an air of command.

Dani sat up straight again in the saddle, considering him. As her gaze traveled over the length of his tall, warriorlike physique, her simple, feminine admiration mingled with a growing sense of inner warning. Her captive appeared built of pure muscle, so why wasn't he putting up more of a fight? True, his pistol now lay in the dust, but there was a gleam of treachery in his eyes that made her wonder what he had up his sleeve. Her better sense whispered to her to clear out immediately, but she needed the money and frankly was too intrigued to abort the robbery, which was moving along efficiently.

Mateo had relieved his brother of the task of holding the coachman at swordpoint. The prisoner's gaze, hard and brilliant as a diamond, followed Alvi as the quick, wiry youth hopped into the coach with an empty sack.

While her captive coldly watched Alvi, Dani studied her handsome prisoner freely. He had the velvety-smooth looking skin and the lusty, strapping size of a corn-fed stallion. A very expensive and pure-blooded one, at that. She despised his type, haughty and carelessly elegant down to his gleaming black boots. His clothes alone probably cost as much as the past six months' taxes, she thought in derision. She glanced at his no-doubt excellently manicured hands.

"Your ring," she ordered. "Hand it over."

Amused, she watched his fist clench.

"No," he growled.

"Why not? Is it your wedding ring?" she asked sarcastically.

The way his eyes narrowed on her in the dark, she thought he would have happily torn her beating heart out of her body if he got the chance.

"You will regret your audacity, boy," he said, his voice soft and deep and dangerous. "You have no idea with whom you are dealing."

Oh, he was not taking this humbling well. Smiling behind her mask at his ire, Dani laid her rapier gently on his cheek. "Shut up, peacock."

"Your youth will not save you from the hangman."

"They'll have to catch me first."

"Fine boasts. Your father ought to thrash your hide."

"My father is dead."

"Then one day I will thrash you for him. That's a promise."

In reply, she traced her rapier ever so tenderly under his chin, forcing him to tilt his proud head higher or feel the prick of her swordpoint. His Lordship clenched his handsome jaw. "You don't seem to understand your position."

Holding her angry gaze, he actually smiled. The sight chilled her. "I will have you drawn and quartered," he said pleasantly.

Under her mask, Dani blanched in spite of herself. He was trying to shake her up! "I want your shiny ring, m'lord. Hand it over!"

"You will have to kill me for it, boy." The white gleam of his smile was defiant.

Standing there in blue moonlight and black shadow, he was huge, powerful, and not lifting a finger to stop them.

Maybe he didn't know how to fight. These rich fellows

never dirtied their hands, she thought uncertainly. But one summary glance over the lean, fierce length of him made her scoff at her own suggestion.

No, something was wrong.

"Not losing your courage, are you, boy?" he asked softly, tauntingly.

"Be quiet!" she ordered, faltering and feeling herself inexplicably losing control of the situation to her vexing prisoner. Rocco, her tame giant, looked over at her in worry.

"Get the ponies loaded," she ordered him, suddenly in a testy mood, scowling under her mask. Obviously, her prisoner had somehow called her bluff and sensed she wasn't going to kill him, though God knew he vastly deserved it. Her arm hurt like the blazes. She ducked her head to peer into the coach, wishing Alvi would hurry up. "How's it going in there?"

"He's rich!" Alvi hollered, tossing out one full sack. "Filthy rich! Give me another sack!"

As Mateo hurried to fetch another sack from his horse's saddlebag, Dani saw the prisoner cast an almost imperceptible glance down the road.

"Expecting someone?" she demanded.

Slowly, he shook his head, and she found herself gazing at his pretty mouth, where a slight, innocent smile tugged, one full of wicked charm. He was so familiar . . .

It was almost worth relighting the carriage lantern so she could have a better look at his face and satisfy the nagging sense that she knew him, but it was unsafe to do so.

Suddenly, a high-pitched voice pealed through the night, some distance down the road.

The youngest of the Gabbiano brothers, Gianni, age ten, was running toward them, arms churning. "Soldiers! Soldiers are coming! Run!"

Dani gasped, then stared at her prisoner, aghast.

He was smirking coolly at her, ever so pleased with himself.

"You bastard," she hissed. "You were stalling us here!"

"Move out, move out!" Mateo was yelling at the others.

Gianni kept on shouting. "Run! Soldiers! They'll be here any second!"

Dani's gaze snapped down the road again. She knew her horse was the fastest. Every womanly instinct in her blood screamed for her to go scoop the little boy up into the saddle with her before the soldiers were upon them. The child had no place here—it was her fault. A dozen times they had forbidden Gianni to follow them, but he never listened, until finally, she had given in and assigned him the relatively safe job of signaller.

"The hell with you, peacock," she muttered, abandoning her prisoner. She tugged on her gelding's reins, reeling the horse away, while Rocco lumbered up onto his slow draft horse and Alvi and Mateo each took one of the coin-laden bags and swung up onto their ponies' backs.

The little boy was running desperately toward them. But as she turned, out of the corner of her eye she saw the haughty prisoner dive in the dust for his pistol and roll onto his shoulder, taking aim at Mateo.

"Mateo!" She reeled her horse around, lurching him straight at the prisoner. The gun went off, shooting skyward.

The prisoner leaped deftly onto his feet and seized her, trying to pull her bodily off her horse. She punched and kicked at him. Mateo drove his pony toward them to help her.

She shot him a fiery glare. "I'll handle him! Just get your brother!"

Mateo hesitated.

The thunder of the soldiers' horses was growing louder.

"Go!" she roared at him as she kicked the prisoner in his broad chest. The big man fell back a step, holding his ribs protectively with a curse.

Mateo saw that she had fought the man off and nodded, whirling his pony to go fetch the little boy. But His Lordship charged her again the moment Mateo galloped away.

As she and the prisoner grappled in the road, her horse reared with a frightened whinny. She clung to the reins, fighting to keep her balance, but overpowering her with sheer physical strength, the prisoner pulled her down out of the saddle. Freed of its rider, her thankless gelding bolted at once.

She let out a wordless cry of fury and found herself standing in the road, clutched in her erstwhile prisoner's grasp. He towered over her. His eyes were like lanterns and he was grasping her hard by her arms. Strands of his hair had fallen from the queue; he looked ferocious and huge, barbaric in his elegant clothes.

"You little shit," he snarled in her face.

"Let me go!" She fought him. He gripped her harder, and she shouted in pain when he jerked her hurt arm. "Ow! Damn it!"

He gave her a shake. "You're caught! You understand?"

She hauled back and punched him across the face with all her strength, tore out of his arms, and fled up the embankment. He was but two steps behind her. Her heart beating wildly, she scrambled up through the dust and slippery dried leaves. With a frantic glance down the road, she saw Mateo lift Gianni into the saddle with him and ride up over the far embankment, riding hard towards home.

Her relief was short-lived, however, for then the prisoner tackled her at the top of the embankment, hooking rock-hard arms around her hips.

He smashed her under him onto the ground and fell on her back, snaking his forearm around her throat.

I hate men, she thought, closing her eyes in distress.

"Hold still," he growled, panting hard.

Dani rested for half a second, then did the opposite, kicking and squirming in the dust, thrashing and punching and scrabbling with her leather-gauntleted fingers. "Let me go!"

"Stop squirming! You're caught, damn it! Give in!" Dodging the boy's blows, Rafe held the slim body pinned beneath his own, but the boy bucked and thrashed, fighting him furiously. "Yield," he said through gritted teeth.

"Go to hell!" The pitch of the boy's voice climbed higher, shrill with fright.

Panting with exertion, Rafe drove his full, muscular weight more firmly down to still the little hellion's writhing. "Hold still!" He jerked a look over his shoulder toward the road and his approaching men. "Over here!"

At his movement, the bloodthirsty little outlaw somehow flopped over onto his back, still trapped by Rafe's arms.

"I told you you would hang," he growled.

"No, you said I would be drawn and quartered—"

Rafe caught a flying fist in his hand. "Be still, for God's sake!"

Suddenly the boy froze and drew in his breath, staring up at him. *"You . . ."* the boy croaked in a hoarse gasp.

Scowling toward his men, Rafael glanced down and found himself gazing into wide, very innocent aqua-blue eyes. He narrowed his eyes in satisfaction. "Aha, brat. Finally catching on, are you?"

The remarkable eyes never blinked, staring at him, looking horror-stricken.

Rafe's laugh was soft and smug, then suddenly the boy moved like a flash of lightning. Rafe supposed he should have seen it coming. The dusty, bleeding little hellion kneed him hard in the groin, a direct hit to the royal jewels. Rafe bellowed, gasping for breath in a momentary state of blind helplessness. The boy pushed against his shoulder, rolling him off onto his side, then scrambled clear of his feebly grasping hand, and tore off into the woods.

Dani didn't stop running even when she heard his deep roar echo through the woods behind her.

"After them!"

The thunder of hoofbeats from the soldiers on the road filled her ears. She could see them through the trees.

The shortcut, she thought, and raced deeper into the woods while the soldiers chased in the direction Mateo and the others had gone. She ran for her life down the little deer path, tearing through the sharp nets of briars and branches that tried to catch her, leaping fallen logs, her heart racing. She found her horse grazing in a cornfield halfway home.

Heart pounding with terror and dread, hands shaking, she swung up onto the gelding and rode at a hard gallop all the way to the rusted gates of home and up the dusty, overgrown drive.

Behind the stable, she had the precious half-bucket of water waiting to splash the soot off her horse's coat. Still no sign of her men. *Please, God. I know they're idiots but they're all I've got.* The Gabbianos had been like brothers to her since she was a child, when none of the other little girls wanted to play with her.

She put the horse away, hot but clean, and ran into the house. Maria, the stout old housekeeper, came hurrying to her.

"Get the hiding place ready—the boys will be right behind me!" Dani ordered. The hiding place was a false wall built into the corner of the wine cellar, beneath the ancient villa. "Oh, and fix something to eat—we'll soon have company." Experience had taught her that soldiers would believe whatever she told them if she put food in their bellies and ale in their mugs. The fact had saved her hide several times in the past.

As she pounded up the stairs toward her room to make the necessary transformation from outlaw back to genteel-poor lady of the manor, Maria gasped behind her.

"My lady! You are hurt!"

"Never mind that! Just do as I say! We have no time!" Dani hurried down the narrow corridor to her room. At once she closed the curtains against the night air, then pulled off the stifling black mask.

A cascade of wavy, chestnut-red hair tumbled down to her shoulders. With trembling hands, she stripped off her shirt and used more of the precious water to wash her wound. Thankfully, she saw it was no longer bleeding. The sight of her gunshot wound frightened her, but not as much as the terrible realization of whom she'd robbed—whom she'd *seen*!—as well as the knowledge of what would happen to her men if she allowed Prince Rafael's soldiers to find them.

With that thought, she stripped off her trousers and wiped the dust quickly from her skin, relishing the cool, wet cloth after her ordeal. She pulled on a chemise, a simple, dreary-beige work-dress, and worn kid slippers, then tied back her hair in a net. She hurried back downstairs and put on an apron, smoothing it as she met Maria in the hall.

"Are they here yet?"

Maria shook her head grimly.

They can't have gotten caught. "They'll be here any minute now. I'm sure they will. I'm going to check on Grandfather."

Willing calm, Dani folded her hands demurely over her stomach, though her heart was still pounding in fright for her friends. She drew a deep breath and walked to her grandfather's bedroom. He was sleeping, and Maria had left the taper burning, because if Grandfather woke up in the dark, he was wont to start screaming with night terrors.

He, the great Duke of Chiaramonte, who had once stood unflinchingly at the head of an army, now needed to be cared for like a small child. There were days he did not know who she was, yet she found his presence comforting still. He was her only living relative now, and when he died her estates would revert back to the Crown because there was no new male heir—nor would there be one, for she was never getting married.

Never, never would any man be her master.

Standing in the doorway, Dani's gaze skimmed over her grandfather's aristocratic profile, the jut of a hard, proud nose, a most distinguished moustache, a lofty, wrinkled forehead. Then she closed the door quietly, went over, and knelt down by his bed, taking his gnarled hand between both of hers.

She laid her head on his hand. Her shoulder hurt so badly. She tried to tell herself that that was the source of the odd pain rising up, twisting in her heart.

Rafael.

Why had he come back? How dare he show his face? she thought in useless, burning fury. What did he want?

An appalling thought struck her. Surely the king had not forgiven him!

She certainly hadn't.

Prince Charming, she thought in utter bitterness. She would never forgive him. Golden, magnificent Rafael. She would hate him forever and ever, until the day she died.

She had thought she would never see Prince Rafael di Fiore again, and she had never wanted to. She hated him with every fiber of her being. Three years ago, he had single-handedly ruined her life. With a wink and a dazzling smile, he had stepped on her tender heart and smashed it, then just kept on going, like a giant passing.

She wished she had thrust her swordpoint into his neck tonight—well, that would be murder, she amended with a sniffle, and murder was too good for the man who had practically left her standing at the altar.

A shout from outside suddenly broke into her thoughts.

Finally! Thank God they're all right. She swept away from her grandfather's bedside and dashed to the window, but then her blood ran cold.

She stared down at the dusty lawn, gripping the windowframe as her knuckles turned white. Mateo, Alvi, Rocco, and little Gianni had made it onto her property, but even now, before her eyes, the thundering pack of soldiers closed in on them, surrounded them, and pulled them down out of their saddles, brawling on her lawn.

One soldier brought the butt of his pistol down on the back of Alvi's head. Another shoved little Gianni to the ground. She knew the fire-eater, Mateo, would fight them with all he had and likely get himself killed.

Dani whirled away from the window and ran for the door, swearing to herself that Rafael would not take her friends, her brothers, away from her. Aside from Grandfather and Maria, they were all she had. Tearing down the stairway and toward the front door, her heart pounding, she swore to herself on her parents' graves that he would not have them. He had taken everything else she possessed. He could have even his filthy gold back, but she would not be left all alone in the world by that man again. Her large pride, her whole being, forbade it.

Enraged and reckless, she threw open the door and burst out into the night, eyes blazing, but when she saw them, in her heart of hearts, she knew it was already too late.

Mateo and the others were already being placed under arrest by Prince Rafael's soldiers.

She saw red. A duke's daughter, descended from a line as proud and old and nearly as royal as the prince's own, she stood clenching and unclenching her fists for a second, feeling the blood of generals and commanders surging, warlike, in her veins.

Rafael di Fiore, she thought, *this is war.*

Then she charged forth with a battle cry. *"Let them go!"*